PLAYING WITH FIRE

PLAYING WITH FIRE

THE WITCH OF TOPHET COUNTY BOOK 2

J. H. SCHILLER

Podium

PLAYING WITH FIRE

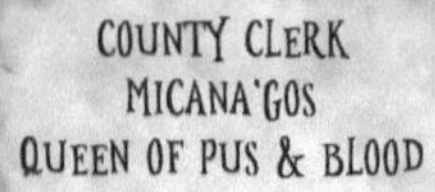

COUNTY CLERK
MICANA'GOS
QUEEN OF PUS & BLOOD

HUMAN MAYOR
HEATHER CHADWICK
#LADYBOSS

SHERIFF
LOMELZAR
DEVOURER OF HOPES & PEOPLE

HIGH LORD OF
RECREATION & CULTURE
ELLIE DAWSON
SHE WHO WON THE GOLD

HIGH LORD OF
PUBLIC SAFETY
ACHARTHO
THE WINGED HORROR

HIGH LORD OF
PUBLIC WORKS
YI'DANAG
THE UNSEEN CREEPING HORR

DREAD LIBRARIAN
CHLOGHA
KEEPER OF ARCANE KNOWLEDGE

CHIEF MEDICAL EXAMINER
XAY CHANTHAVONG

DREAD LORD
ANIMAL CONTR
MEG'ATHAT
MOTHER OF NIGHT

DREAD CULTURE CZAR
STHOTHUGUA
BANE OF THE UNCLEAN REALMS

DREAD LORD OF CORRECTIONS
ZSTHAOR
SPILLER OF THE LIFEBLOOD
OF THE ANCIENTS

DREAD LORD
SOLID WASTE MANA
YI'DANAG
THE UNSEEN CREEPIN

DREAD LORD OF
FIRE & RESCUE
E'STHACT
THE LIVING FLOOD

DREAD LORD
WATER & SEW
FRANCISCO SA

DREAD LORD
ENERGY & INFRASTR
TIFFANY CLAR

TOPHET COUNTY ORGANIZATION CHART

HIGH LORD OF
...MIC DEVELOPMENT
...Y'GGARLOS
...TRESS OF DESPAIR

HIGH LORD OF
HEALTH & HUMAN SERVICES
N'EITHAMIQUG
THE SPINNER OF SORROW

HIGH LORD OF
ADMINISTATION
NOMMAQUTH
BUBBLES

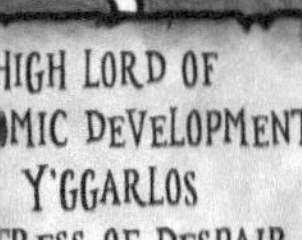

LIAISON TO
CATACHTHONIC UNIVERSITY
DR. CHRISTIAN CARCOSA

DIRECTOR
HEALTH DEPARTMENT
MH'ADRASH
THE JEWELED MONSTROSITY

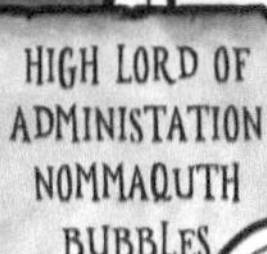

DREAD LORD OF
HUMAN RESOURCES
SATHACH
LOATHSOME OF LOATHSOMES

DREAD LORD OF ZONING
NAGHACTHOSHA
LORD OF FESTERING SORES

DREAD HEALTH INSPECTOR
MY'YGGDESS
THE ELDRITCH EARWORM

DREAD LORD OF
INFORMATION TECHNOLOGY
ICHAGNO
DOOM OF WORLDS

DIRECTOR
...MALL BUSINESS ADMINISTATION
PATRICIA JONES

DIRECTOR
MANAGEMENT & BUDGET
RONNIE COFFMAN

COUNTY WITCH
CONNIE LINGUS*
GODSFORSAKEN CHAOS GNOME

*PSEUDONYM

DREAD LORD OF
INTERNAL AFFAIRS
STAAR'LAT
SHE WHO LURKS IN DARKNESS

Ugly Truths

A crowd of toad-like beings gathered on the meteor-pocked surface of the alien corpse commonly known as the Moon. The moon-beasts' flesh was a slick, mottled gray, save for the squirming mass of pink tentacles that served as a snout. They stood in a ragged circle under a shallow dome of atmosphere, ringed around a moon-beast easily twice the size of the others. The massive hierophant raised its clawed hands, and the assembled faithful sank to their haunches.

In eerie unison, they lifted their bone flutes and played the soul-searing strains of an eldritch hymn to their fell lord. The flutes produced a chorus of plaintive yowls reminiscent of a cat in heat—if, that is, the Moon had cats. Or heat. Under the light of dying stars, the melody carried ardent messages of worship and praise.

All hail the Masked Messenger!
Bow before the Stalker among the Stars!
Praise be to the Dreamwalker, bringer of madness!

The largest moon-beast swayed with the rhythm. For the first time in ages, the hierophant allowed the fullness of its true power to course through its energetic meridians. It had forsaken its magic eons ago in a desperate act of self-preservation, but after a few cautious tests over the past week, it had grown bolder. Sheathed in a fluorescent purple-yellow-green glow, its bloated body rippled and swelled with strange protuberances, flickering through diverse forms worn in the distant past. It crooned to the music, the only spoken voice amidst the wailing din.

Unnoticed by the towering hierophant, one of the moon-beasts lowered its flute. Its eyeless gaze followed a jagged blue firebolt that zigged and zagged across the twinkling starscape. The spectacle snagged another beast's attention, and it, too, ceased playing. The blaze streaked from star to star, traveling thousands of light-years in a mere fraction of a second. Given the vast distance, the light of its passage would not be visible to human eyes for millennia, but the moon-beasts' astral vision easily followed the etheric trail.

One by one, their flutes fell silent.

The hierophant snapped out of its reverie, at last aware it had lost the reverent attention of its flock. A worshipper pointed at the ominous celestial object and played a shrill blast of alarm. The great moon-beast lifted its face to the stars and the color drained from its pink tentacles, leaving them the oily gray of a dead fish. Memories of an ancient betrayal flooded its mind with an ichor of bitterness. The moment the hierophant had feared since before humanity's earliest ancestor slimed forth from the primordial sludge had arrived—and with it, the realization that it had not been bold.

It had been reckless.

"Ka'met," whispered the hierophant.

The mere word struck terror in its general thoracic region.

As the firebolt caromed ever closer, the hierophant sensed the tenor of its auric field. Scalding rage. A lust for vengeance. And most of all, an overpowering drive to *feed*.

Millennia of safety—first, in the Dreamlands, and more recently, in the long-ago voided bowels of Luna—had relaxed the hierophant's vigilance. It had grown complacent. Perhaps it would pay with its life.

(Well, with *someone's* life. The specifics could be worked out later.)

"Ka'met!" the hierophant shouted.

The moon-beasts scattered, sounding the alarm on their loathsome flutes. *Ka'met! Ka'met!*

"To the Black Galley!"

Spurred on by the hierophant, the moon-beasts bounded toward an abyssal crater. Half their number leaped into the shadowed depths, while the others unwound lengths of heavy rope from iron spikes driven deep into the lunar surface. The hierophant kept its face fixed on the heavens, tracking the blue light that darted from star to star, moving ever closer with terrifying speed.

Heave! shrilled a flute.

Corded muscles bunched as dozens of moon-beasts planted their webbed feet in the dusty scree and pulled.

Heave!

Again, they strained at the ropes. The smallest beast slid to its knees. Its line went slack, and it cartwheeled into the crater's gaping maw.

Heave!

The ebony spike of a mainmast emerged from the crater.

Heave!

The foremast and mizzenmast followed, trailed by the draping mesh of shrouds woven from the silk of long-dead Leng spiders.

Heave!

The hierophant gibbered and howled, clawing the air as though it could rip the blue streak from the sky.

Heave!

The bowsprit appeared and, with another mighty tug, the sleek hull of the Black Galley breached the rim. The moon-beasts tugged it onto a wheeled raft concealed under drifts of sandy lunar soil. Working in eerie silence, the crew crawled over the ship like agitated ants, preparing it for their desperate flight.

A bolt of ice-blue lightning sizzled from the void between stars and struck a moon-beast as it spooled the discarded mooring lines. It stiffened, wrapped in the coils of a serpent formed of azure fire. Teeth like foot-long electric arcs sank into the base of the moon-beast's skull, impossibly leaving its hide intact. Hungry jaws worked as the ka'met fed. It consumed neither flesh nor blood, but something . . . different. Something intangible. Something that flowed in a silver river from the dying beast's skull into the ka'met's ravenous gullet. When the stream ran dry, the victim's body exploded into gouts of cerulean fire. If moon-beasts had eyes, the blaze would've been bright enough to blind them.

"Flee!" cried the hierophant.

It boarded the ship with one powerful leap. Its taloned fingers closed around an obsidian staff that jutted up from the deck at the base of the mainmast. At its touch, the Black Galley lifted from its raft.

"To the oars!"

Moon-beasts scrambled to fill the benches, but a third of their number had yet to board the galley. The hopping horde on Luna's surface surged toward the rising ship.

"Row!"

The first officer raised its flute. *The others?*

"Leave them!" The hierophant watched as the blue firebolt lanced from the ashy remains of the first victim to another moon-beast. "Row or die!"

The first officer's nimble fingers danced over the flute. *But we cannot abandon our brethren! We must—*

Its warbling protest cut off in a discordant squeak as the hierophant grabbed it and threw it over the edge. The galley lurched into flight.

"Screw those guys," the hierophant muttered. The mass of tentacles that was its face turned toward the sparsely populated benches. "Pull!"

The moon-beasts, whom Azathoth had gifted with a healthy sense of self-preservation, pulled. Though they had no eyes to see the massacre below, their astral vision bore witness to the savage destruction of their kin.

"Pull!"

The hierophant's bellow was barely audible over the psychic screams of panicking moon-beasts. Each oarsman suffered a hundred deaths, writhing in mental agony as the skin of their comrades bubbled and burned far below. Worse, the survivors felt the ka'met consume the very essence of their dying friends, down to the last memory. Only when every shimmering drop of life force was drained from the victim did the ka'met release them and move on to the next . . . and the next.

The hierophant keened a half-hearted mourning dirge, but its efforts at consolation fell upon deaf ears.

Er, deaf auditory organs.

The crew exchanged fluted ditties of outrage as they rowed. The hierophant had deserted its people. It had left them to the mercy of a hungry ka'met!

But as they left the Moon behind, as the monster's rampage ceased and screams faded into silence, their ragged band was forced to reckon with the ugly truth. (Ugly is, in fact, the only sort of truth moon-beasts recognize.) Their escape, purchased at a terrible price, had done nothing more than buy time.

The slaughter had ended for now, but the ka'met was still out there.

Watching.

Waiting.

Hungry.

CHAPTER ONE

Live, Laugh, Leave

The witch of Tophet County finished her last bite of funnel cake. It was almost as good as Dee's legendary sticky 'nuts. Almost as messy too. She snaked her arm around Chad's waist, surreptitiously wiping her powdered sugar–caked fingers on the back of his black T-shirt.

He heaved a mournful sigh. "I have napkins right here."

Looked like her surreption needed work.

"Hello, young lovers!" A barker in a round-brimmed hat and a striped vest waggled his eyebrows suggestively. "Care for an amorous adventure in the Tunnel of Love? Three tickets each buys you three minutes alone with your sweetheart."

"Sounds romantic," Chad said, tugging her to halt. "What do you think?"

The witch stared into the pulsating depths of the tunnel, which was lit with a reddish, uterine glow. A pair of coquettish eyes embedded in the flesh above the tunnel's lipsticked mouth favored her with a salacious wink.

Hard pass.

"I think if you're down to enter a love tunnel, we should go back to my place."

Chad blushed furiously. "Witch!" He flashed an awkward smile at the barker. "I guess that's a no."

She hadn't actually expected him to take her up on it, but that didn't mean she wasn't disappointed.

Chad had been clear about his intentions from the start. He wanted a . . . a *relationship*. (It'd taken the witch a few weeks before she could think the word without dry heaving, but she'd powered through.) Her romantic experience was limited to Tinder hookups, so she'd assumed step one was a thorough shagging, and step two was . . . maybe weirder shagging? But no. Chad had a pre-Poundtown prerequisite.

Feelings.

And talking about them.

Only after navigating that bit of rough water would he pole his raft through her tunnel of love.

She wasn't ready to talk, and he wasn't ready to bone. They had themselves a Kadathian standoff. The whole thing was beginning to take a toll on her ego (and, after months of operating in manual override, her carpal tunnel). As much as she loved Amish romance novels, she had no desire to dramatically reenact one—hence her unsubtle *Hexually Frustrated* tee.

As if reading her mind, Chad took her hand and gave her a very uncelibate kiss. Even now, after a few months of dating, it sparked a fluttering storm of butterflies in her stomach.

"So," he said when they came up for air, "what's next?"

"We haven't seen the sideshow."

His head jerked in a panicked shake. "Nope. Don't have the stomach for it."

The Odditorium's menagerie of exhibitionist Archonic performers *was* a little rough on the gastric system. She'd just eaten a pound of deep-fried dough. Watching a flesh-eating blob consume itself and defecate into a new incarnation was perhaps not the best choice.

"We could check out the fortune teller," he said. "Magnolia saw her last night and said she was great."

"Oh, I'm sure she is . . . great at taking your money."

Chad shrugged. "It's all in good fun," he said. "It's not like I'm asking for lottery numbers."

He did the thing with the blinky eyes and the pouty mouth.

"Fine."

Chad grinned and hooked her arm in his. They strolled along the midway, taking in the glittering spectacle. Despite her continuing journey through the no-booty desert, the witch was in a godsdamned good mood. The Midnight Carnival was her favorite Tophet County event, after the annual Whacking Day parade. She closed her eyes and inhaled. Sugary-sweet cotton candy. Road dust and hot machine oil. The sour tang of vomit outside the Odditorium. It all combined to form an alluring, if slightly nauseating, bouquet. It was the scent of wonder, of mystery, of *Things That Never Should Have Been Fried.*

The fortune teller's tent was a patchwork of vividly colored fabric. Royal blue velvet adorned with peeling silver stars. Plum-and-burnt-orange paisley. Crimson satin stained with water spots. Twinkling fairy lights climbed the tent poles, and a gauzy gray veil over the entrance billowed in the midsummer night's breeze. A hand-painted sign propped on a metal folding chair bore an image of a hand with an eye embedded in the palm. The text read:

Psychic readings, 10 tickets
Love ~ Luck ~ Lotto
All will be revealed!
NO REFUNDS.

Chad leaned down to read a blocky chunk of minuscule fine print at the bottom of the sign. "This looks kinda lame," he said. "Let's find something else."

Naturally, the witch went inside.

The first thing that hit her was the smell—a cloyingly sweet, fruity scent thick enough to coat her teeth. But what she saw pushed the olfactory assault right out of her mind.

If the deranged folks at Mattel had ever designed a fortune teller annex for the Barbie Dreamhouse, it might've looked something like this. (Not that the witch had ever possessed such a toy. Her playthings had been closer to *Blair Witch* twig dollies than molded plastic monuments to patriarcho-capitalism.) The interior walls were millennial pink. A square white table, topped with a rose quartz crystal ball, occupied the center of the small space. Baby-pink bookshelves held a bewildering array of glass and metal objects—among them, a rusting egg-beater, an umbrella stripped of its fabric, and a tall, thin glass cylinder filled with fluid and brightly colored orbs. On the top shelf, a wooden plaque on a small easel broadcast a chilling message: LIVE, LAUGH, LOVE!

The witch nearly broke out in a blood sweat. Desperate to escape before the denizen of this nightmare returned to Frappucino her immortal soul, she whirled and ran smack into Chad.

"Whoa," he breathed, wide-eyed. He pointed at the glass cylinder. "A Galileo thermometer! My dad has one of those. When the temperature changes, the density of the liquid—"

"You can nerd out later." She gripped his shoulders and turned him toward the exit. "We need to get the hex out of here."

But the gauzy veil parted, and a woman who could only be the tent's proprietress entered the chat.

In keeping with the Barbie aesthetic, she was tall, blond, and busty. She wore a flowing pink maxi dress and matching enamel hoops big enough to serve as bracelets. Her unlined face bore the faintly surprised expression of a woman who'd been Botoxed to plastic perfection. She clutched a wriggling ball of wiry fur close to her chest—a dog, the witch presumed, though it was mostly concealed by her platinum extensions.

"You are County Witch, no?" the woman said. In contrast to the saccharine tone the witch would've expected given the color scheme, she had a deep-throated voice and a thick Russian accent. "I am big fan of your . . . work."

Chad gasped and elbowed her. "She knows who you are," he said in an awed whisper. "Magnolia said she was the real thing."

The witch rolled her eyes. "Did the pointy black hat give it away?"

"Sure." The seer's perfectly glossed lips quirked in a sardonic smile. She gestured to the pair of tufted pink velvet chairs on the client side of the table. "Sit."

"Yeah, I think we're gonna jet," the witch said. "So much to see, so little—"

"For you, no charge."

"I don't think—"

"We're already here, Witch," Chad said. "It could be fun."

Translation: *I'm too nice to walk out on a chromatically challenged Witch fan.*

"Yes," the woman said, baring aggressively white teeth. "Fun."

The witch sighed and followed him to the chairs.

Metaphysical Barbie sat down and swept a curtain of faux hair over her shoulders. The creature clutched to her chest stretched and looked up at them. Chad squawked in alarm, and the witch damn near fell off her chair. It had a quivering, terrier-like body coated in disturbingly pubic fur. Its tail was long and hairless, its feet were pink and rodent-like, and it had the wizened face of a tiny old man. If a Chihuahua, a rat-thing, and an elderly terror-Muppet had the world's most accursed three-way, the resulting offspring would look something like this.

Its eyes glowed red, and it opened its mouth and hissed, revealing inch-long yellowed fangs. If murderous spite had an odor, this thing would reek. The woman patted its liver-spotted scalp and nestled it in her lap.

"What the screaming shit is *that?*"

"His name is Jenkin," the seer said, her voice softening for the first time. "My little *zaychik*." She scratched behind the beast's all-too-human ears. "He is sweetest boy, most adorable . . ." She seemed to feel the witch's horrified gaze and cleared her throat. "We have not been properly introduced. I am Sibyl."

"Cool." The witch stood, keeping a wary eye on Jenkin. "I am leaving."

"Wait." Sibyl reached under the table and removed a small (pink) drawstring bag, from which she pulled an item wrapped in black silk. She unfolded the cloth to reveal a deck of cards, and the air in the tent thickened with magic. "Stay."

The witch wanted to leave, but the last time she'd felt anything like this had been with Vera, and Vera was . . .

Complicated.

She sat down, averting her eyes from Jenkin's gimlet glare.

Sibyl tapped the deck three times with one French-manicured fingernail. The cards proceeded to shuffle themselves.

"Cut."

Though the witch wasn't one to follow commands, she eagerly reached for the cards. She *needed* to touch them. This deck was a magical artifact, created by witches before the Archons' Emergence. She'd seen plenty of artifacts—her broom foremost among them—but she'd never felt latent magic this strong. Her fingers tingled from the buzz of entropine. Discordia only knew what power these cards held.

The power to see the future.

The power to reveal arcane secrets.

The power to—

"Are those Garbage Pail Kids?" Chad asked, his voice bright with excitement. He peered at the back of the topmost card, which looked like a small certificate. *Most Unpopular Student Award.* What in the seven hells . . .

"They are!" Chad's face lit up in a broad grin. "A dude in IT collects them. Some of these go for, like, thousands on eBay."

"You're telling me they're . . ." The witch had no idea how to finish the sentence. "What *are* they?"

"Trading cards," Chad said. "For kids."

Sibyl lifted her chin. "I did not choose deck. Deck chose me. Now cut."

The witch cut the cards, then watched as Sibyl restacked them and dealt three face down.

"Shouldn't I ask a question first?"

"Deck does not care what you want to know, only what you need to know." She tapped the leftmost card, then flipped it. "Split Kit. Represents past."

The card showed a boy divided in two. His left half was a normal kid, but his right half looked like a member of a punk rock motorcycle gang.

"Deceiver with two faces," Sibyl said. "Traitor. Playing both sides."

"Both sides of what?"

Sibyl ignored her and turned up the card in the center, which depicted a girl in a yellow rain slicker screaming as lightning struck her forehead. "Present. Stormy Heather." Her eyebrows trembled in an effort to frown, but her paralyzed facial muscles held firm. "Sudden violence. Catastrophe."

The witch snorted. "I think you're reading it wrong. Everything's been going—"

"Last card is probable future. Represents most likely outcome if you take no action." Sibyl flipped the final card. Fryin' Ryan, a Godzilla-esque monster, breathed fire and stomped a town to rubble. Her peaches and cream complexion paled. "Very bad."

"The hell you say," the witch said. "Let me guess . . . for fifty bucks, you'll give me something to ward off evil." She reached for Chad's hand and stood. "Time for us to live, laugh, leave. I'd say it's been a pleasure, but—"

"Stay," Sibyl said. "We must learn more. Is up to *you* to stop this. I—"

The witch waved a hand to mute her. She tugged Chad to his feet and dragged him toward the door. The seer watched, dead-eyed and expressionless, stroking Jenkin's wrinkled pate.

Once they were safely outside the tent, the witch waggled her fingers to return Sibyl's voice. A stream of angry Russian followed them until they drifted out of earshot.

"Well, that was a total bust," Chad said. "You were right, Witch."

She barely heard him over the words *magical* and *artifact* beating a drum of dread in her mind, accompanied by the crashing cymbals of *traitor*, *violence*, and *catastrophe*. But who knew what the original purpose of those cards had been? Maybe they'd been designed to intimidate the rubes into forking over fistfuls of cash. In the so-called good old days, witching came with a high risk of being rotisseried before a cheering crowd. Witches were nothing if not resourceful.

She smothered her unease with a simpering smile. "Oooh, say that again, Chad."

He gave his best approximation of bedroom eyes, which left him looking mildly concussed. "You were right."

The witch moaned in mock pleasure.

"What next . . ." Chad looked up and down the midway. "Hey, what would you say to the Phæras Wheel?"

She eyed the towering attraction. Phæras was a world-renowned performer—an Archon who was essentially a sentient electromagnetic field. He spun torchlit gondolas in stately orbits around his metallic core. The experience was mesmerizing. Literally. Anyone who stared directly at the display for too long risked permanent hypnosis. Over the years, he'd accumulated quite a large crew of ensorcelled groupies who called themselves Phæries.

As a de facto Archon, the witch was immune. And she could put a vision-distorting bubble around their gondola—one that would both protect Chad from Phærification and provide a bit of privacy. Her tunnel of love might not get any action tonight, but she had other bits that wouldn't mind some attention.

"Let's do it."

When they reached the Phæras Wheel, Chad forked over a fistful of tickets to an androgynous person wearing a pair of bedraggled wings and a strip club worth of body glitter. The Phærie whispered a prayerful petition in the Ouranian-Barbaric tongue, and an empty gondola drifted down to the loading ramp. The witch slipped a twenty to the attendant and whispered a special instruction. Then she boarded and held out her hand to help a lightly entranced Chad inside. Once he was settled on the bench, she sheathed their gondola in a protective entropic field. His dazzled eyes cleared, and he snuggled closer to her.

As the gondola smoothly launched into motion, Chad's hand found its way to her knee. She wiggled around until she scooched it a few inches thighward. He grinned and nuzzled her neck.

"Hey there," he said, his breath hot in her ear.

"Hey yourself."

As she'd requested, their gondola rose above the rest of the drifting cars until it hung seventy-five feet above the sights and sounds of the midway, spinning slowly so they could take in the view. A gibbous moon shone above them in a carpet of stars.

It was, the witch shuddered to admit, pretty godsdamned romantic.

Chad's lips found hers, and she melted into a toe-curling kiss. When they came up for air, his deep brown eyes met hers.

"You know," he said, his hand inching even farther up her thigh, "I've been thinking . . ."

Liquid heat pooled in her belly. "Oh yeah?"

"Yeah." He traced a finger along the curve of her jaw. "We've been dating a few months now, and it's getting harder—"

"That's what she—"

He shut her up with another kiss.

"Witch, I think it's time we . . ." His gaze shifted from her face to the night sky.

"Time we what?"

He sat bolt upright. "Holy shit!"

She grabbed his chin and aimed his face in her direction. "You think it's time we . . ." She gestured for him to continue.

"Something just hit the Moon!"

"Screw the Moon. Never liked it anyway," she said. "Finish the freaking sentence, Chad! Time we *what?*"

He leaped to his feet, and their gondola lurched and swayed. "Something's on fire up there!"

"It can't be," the witch said, ducking under his outstretched arm. "There's no air." She looked up and saw a flickering blue dot on the Moon's surface. "Maybe the Roswell Grays came back?"

"Man, I wish I had binoculars."

"Wouldn't you need a telescope?"

"Not for the Moon," he said. "What you see through binoculars is as good as what Galileo saw."

The witch burned some entropine and borrowed two pairs from her favorite sporting goods retailer (Dick's, of course). "As you wish, buttercup."

She passed one pair to Chad, then peered through her own eyepiece. The Moon's cratered surface was marred by a cluster of guttering blue lights. As she watched, another tongue of flame bloomed.

"What in Ghroth's name . . ."

Chad tucked his binoculars under his arm, whipped out his BlackBerry, and started typing. "I'm texting Dr. Carcosa. His undergrad was in astronomy."

The witch gazed through the eyepiece at the spreading pox of blue fire. She sensed a malevolence there, a predatory hunger. Her growing discomfort roused Keyser Söze from his nap back at the apartment. He examined the Moon through her eyes and promptly shat in her papasan chair.

"Sent." Chad raised his binoculars and fiddled with the focus. "What's that black spot moving south?"

The witch located a small splotch drifting away from the constellation of blue dots, but the magnification wasn't strong enough to identify it. She flipped the binoculars around, fogged the lenses with her entropine-infused breath, and looked again. The blurry inkblot resolved into an easily recognizable shape—an old-fashioned ship, its hull even blacker than the void between stars. As she watched, tiny oars along each side raised and lowered, raised and lowered.

Each pull carried the ship further from the Moon.

Each pull brought it closer to Earth.

She wordlessly handed her binoculars to Chad, who swapped them for his.

He stared in stunned silence, then passed them back. "That can't be what I think it is."

As she'd expected, he recognized it too. The collected writings of one Howard Phillips Lovecraft had unsurprisingly exploded in popularity after the Emergence. Most modern humans had at least a passing familiarity with his work, but the witch had always tried to steer clear. Who needed to read that bigoted chucklefuck's purple prose about cosmic horrors, when said horrors ruled the world, dominated late-night TV, and ran thirst trap accounts on DikTok? But despite her vigorous objections, Mother Mayhem had forced her to read HPL's greatest hits when she was a kid.

According to the Cthulhu Mythos, what she saw slouching its way toward Earth was one of the moon-beasts' Black Galleys.

Which was impossible.

Moon-beasts were from the Dreamlands. The Swarm had assimilated that realm and used it to send *oneiric inspiration* to Dr. Carcosa last year, which meant no more moon-beasts—and, since her victory over the Great White, no more little white men . . .

. . . right?

Another trickle of entropine created a curved lens that hung in midair at the business end of her binoculars, and a finer level of detail emerged. The galley's oars were manned by squat gray toads with a face full of pink spaghetti. Canonically moon-beasty. A hulking specimen tall enough to be two small ones in a trench coat paced the elevated walkway between banks of rowing benches. Without apparent provocation, it froze midstep and aimed its tentacled face at the Earth.

Even at a distance of more than two hundred thousand miles, the jolt of connection nearly brought the witch to her knees.

That big bastard wasn't looking at the planet. It was looking at *her*. The moon-beast raised its clenched fists, which glowed with octarine netherlight—a neon blend of green, yellow, and purple.

Both middle fingers shot up, and the free-floating lens shattered in a rain of broken glass.

CHAPTER TWO

The Eldritch Salute

Lomelzar, Sheriff of Tophet County and Devourer of Hopes and People, issued his distinctive "aggrieved donkey" shriek, shattering the predawn quiet.

!!!THE EYE IN THE SKY REPORTS THE BLACK GALLEY IS ENTERING EARTH'S ATMOSPHERE!!!

With most nonverbal Archons—Bubbles, the Dread Lord of IT, the Unseen Creeping Horror—her "little sister" status produced a passive mental transliteration of their various modes of speech. The Sheriff's messages, on the other hand, sucker punched her in the third ear with all the subtlety of a televangelist's fundraising appeal. She glared daggers at him—a useless gesture, as his acid-filled glowing orbs promptly dissolved the blades.

"Please instruct her to seize the ship and bring it down," the County Clerk said with stiff formality.

The Clerk's interactions with Lomelzar were deliciously awkward these days. Their winter dalliance had fizzled when she realized he was only interested in one thing: spraying evildoers with acid and drinking their liquefied remains.

Males.

Lomelzar brayed a terse acknowledgment, lifted his twitching mouthparts skyward, and relayed the order to the Eye in the Sky. He practically tripped over his own tentacles rushing to get away from the Clerk.

Thirty miles overhead, a giant eyeball with noodly jellyfish appendages a dozen miles long blinked once for yes. All this excitement must be a nice change for the Eye. Goloth usually spent her days trolling the stratosphere for etheric plankton and keeping her eye peeled for alien incursions. (The Roswell Grays and the little green men were pretty chill—minus the anal probing—but who knew what horrors lurked in the wild black yonder of deep space?) Goloth hadn't seen this much action since she'd defeated and devoured Skynet's sentient satellites right after the Emergence.

"Why are we . . ." A jaw-cracking yawn stole the witch's voice. She glanced at her BlackBerry; it was 5:32. Gods below, she was exhausted. "Why are we bringing the ship down *here*?"

Her eyes roamed over the treacherous terrain of the Dunwich Park softball field. Entropic spillover from the Battle of the Threenagers had infused the turf with a heaping helping of high weirdness. The shrubs grew hallucinogenic fish-shaped crackers. (The witch pocketed a few for a rainy day.) A vicious patch of flesh-eating dandelions had claimed the western reaches of the outfield. And any normie who spent more than a half hour on the pitch grew tiny extra heads. She'd spent a solid week zapping them off the T-ball team before Parks & Rec shut the place down.

The Clerk's shroud rustled on the breeze of a gusty sigh, revealing a flash of bacon-print leggings. "I suppose this field is where we shall deal with *all* our existential threats," she trilled.

"You think the moon-beasts are a threat?"

Her six eyes exchanged a worried glance. "With the Dreamlands destroyed, they should not exist. In my experience, things that should not exist are generally . . . unpleasant."

One of the Clerk's black-robed servitors glided past holding the tether of an Olaf the Snowman Mylar balloon roughly the size of a parade float. The Chief Deputy Sheriff, who looked like a fetal Xenomorph suspended in a Jell-O of bad vibes, jiggled along behind him. The Clerk didn't give them a second glance. Her threshold for *things that should not exist* was pretty godsdamned high.

"You are certain you saw a moon-beast use magic, Witch?"

"I told you, that asshole flipped me a double bird and broke my telescope lens." She paused to replay the scene in her mind. "But actually . . . I'm not sure it was magic—at least, not *my* kind. Its hands glowed octarine, like—"

"Netherlight," the Clerk said. "Which would mean it used Archonic power. That is simply not—"

The Sheriff shrieked.

!!!EVACUATE THE LANDING ZONE! GOLOTH HAS CAPTURED THE BLACK GALLEY!!!

The witch winced and massaged her aching forehead. Lomelzar's squirming knot of razored tentacles and luminous orbs cartwheeled to the center of the field, flanked by Spectral Forces goons. Hank O'Brien, the one and only Deputy Eye Candy, caught the witch's gaze and flashed a grin that would drop panties like flies. She waved and followed the Clerk off the pitch until they were outside the staked-off area. The thick blanket of gray clouds that perpetually covered Tophet County's skies roiled ominously, but she saw no sign of the ship.

"Have you heard from Mr. Chadwick?" the Clerk asked.

Shit. She'd forgotten about Chad.

After the Phæras Wheel, he'd left to meet Dr. Carcosa at the Mountains of Madness Observatory, while the witch alerted County leadership. Speaking of which, the field was currently one human mayor short of a government.

"Where in Hades is Heather?"

"Mayor Chadwick? She is . . ." The Clerk's shifty eyes suddenly found somewhere else to look. "Well, as of yesterday afternoon, she has taken a brief leave of absence."

"What?" the witch asked. "Why? Are the, uh . . . the infants okay?"

"Oh, Sawyer and Skyler are fine," the Clerk said. "Sathach is just having a difficult time adjusting to . . ."

"Parenthood?"

"No, he is a wonderful parent, if a bit overprotective—"

Now, *that* was a lesson in the art of dramatic understatement. According to Magnolia, the Dread Lord of Human Resources had temporarily eaten the UPS guy on no fewer than three separate occasions.

"—but he has felt a bit . . . displaced since Mayor Chadwick hired Barclay."

The ludicrously named Barclay was their manny—a curse-breaker capable of neutralizing baby Skyler's witchly powers . . . or was Skyler the Archonic twin? She couldn't keep them straight. One female witchling, one male Archonet, two kids named after items from a predatory leggings line. They even looked alike, minus the suckers on the boy's otherwise-human limbs.

"So Heather just *left* him?"

"Not at all," the Clerk said. "She and Barclay are taking the twins to visit her parents for a week or two. It will give Sathach a chance to rediscover his love for human resources and disengage from his . . . other pursuits."

Other pursuits.

The Clerk had pronounced those words as if they tasted bad. What had Sathach been up to? Had he joined the vegans in the Seitanic Temple? Started a pickleball league? Launched an OnlyFans?

"What are you not saying?"

Whatever it was, the Clerk not-said it even louder.

The witch's BlackBerry vibrated. "Here's Chad now." She rubbed her grainy eyes and scrolled through a discouragingly dense wall of text. "Dr. Carcosa says the Black Galley didn't just sail in Earth's general direction. It adjusted its speed and heading to accommodate for . . . blah, blah, math words . . . blah, blah, orbital mechanics . . ." She scanned the rest of the message. "He says, 'Though the ship appears to have no navigational equipment, its carefully plotted course aligned it perfectly with Tophet County, almost as though . . .'"

Her voice trailed off as she read the rest of the sentence.

. . . almost as though homing in on a beacon.

The witch shuddered, remembering the jolt of connection she'd felt right before that overgrown toad gave her the ol' eldritch salute. She had a sinking feeling she knew exactly what—or *who*—that beacon might be.

"Uh, Clerk? I think—"

"There it is!" the Clerk warbled.

Lomelzar screeched, and a Spectral Forces goon aimed a spotlight at the sky. The flat keel of the Black Galley breached the rippling clouds, cradled in looping lengths of gelatinous tentacle. Its fuligin hull swallowed the spotlight like the Sheriff slurping up a repeat offender, and unmanned oars dangled from the sides, as limp as Lovecraft's loins. The only thing about the ship that wasn't the approximate shade of tar was a white signal flag emblazoned with an Ouranian-Barbaric rune. After spending thirteen years deciphering grimoires and Nomicons, the witch didn't need to consult her pocket dictionary of barbarous tongues to decipher it. The closest English could come to capturing the meaning was something like *Why aren't you shitting yourself in terror? For the love of Azathoth, we are well and truly FUCKED.*

Gods, they could've started with hello.

She watched as thousands of feet rapidly closed to hundreds, then dozens. Goloth's translucent tentacle deposited the ship on the field and stickily retracted into the clouds, trailing thinning strands of slime.

The Sheriff seized a nightstick in one razored tentacle and gave Hank a firm poke.

"Ow!" Hank rubbed his arm, taking care to avoid a rash of miniscule heads, and took a few halting steps toward the ship. "Hello? Is anyone there?"

No reply.

Hank glanced at the Sheriff, who growled and jabbed his nightstick at the galley. He walked a few steps closer. "It's okay," he called. "You can come out now!"

A chorus of muted yowls drifted from the bowels of the ship, then a vaguely amphibian creature hopped up onto the starboard rail.

No eyes. No ears. Face full of noodles. It was a moon-beast, no doubt about it.

One clawed hand jammed what looked like a child's femur into an orifice hidden beneath the nest of wriggling pink tentacles. The creature's oddly jointed fingers danced over the bone flute, producing a caterwauling din. A tentacle shot forth from the Sheriff's tangle of limbs, grabbed the beast, and yanked it into his largest mouth.

"Lomelzar," the Clerk said, an unmistakable note of warning in her voice.

"While I appreciate you putting an end to that godsawful racket, eating our visitors' emissary is a poor way to commence this . . . inquiry."

After a sulky pause, the Sheriff spit out the moon-beast. It lurched to its feet and hopped over to cower behind Hank. Its wide head hit at his waist, which made it about three and a half feet tall, and its skin was a shade of gray best described as "rotting eel." The trembling beast played another strain of discordant music.

The Clerk flinched and jammed tentacles into a trio of shrouded orifices that were presumably her ears. "Stop that! We cannot understand you."

The Sheriff thrashed and shrieked.

!!!IT IS NOT OUR JOB TO UNDERSTAND! IF THEY WANT TO TALK TO US, THEY CAN LEARN THE LANGUAGE OF THE LAND!!!

"*You* don't speak the language of the land," the witch said.

The Sheriff advanced on her, roaring. *!!!THAT IS DIFFERENT BECAUSE IT IS ME!!!*

She twitched her nose and magically scooped a hole in the ground beneath him. The effort of moving a ton of dirt while already criminally fatigued dropped her to her knees. Lomelzar surged out of the pit before he'd even hit the bottom, neon orbs pulsing as he prepared to douse her in acid.

"Enough!" shouted the Clerk.

Fluted whispers (whispered flutings?) emanated from the Black Galley. The witch struggled to her feet, gaping at the ship. Moon-beasts now lined the full length of the starboard rail, but she saw neither taint nor tentacle of the big bastard who'd shot her the finger.

Finger*s*.

"We can do nothing here until we find a way to communicate with these . . . creatures." The Clerk raised a limb and beckoned to the cowled figure lurking behind a squad of Spectral Forces goons. "Jeremy, if you please."

The servitor glided across the field, Olaf the Snowman bobbing above him, and dropped like a stone into the witch's hole. (At least one of her holes was getting some action.) The Clerk rolled all six eyes and snaked a tentacle into the pit to retrieve him. He brushed clods of dirt from his robe and solemnly handed her the balloon's tether.

"Please clear the area around the ship," the Clerk said.

A pouty Lomelzar instructed his troops to comply. Moon-beasts watched eyelessly as a circle emptied around the Black Galley. The Clerk twisted a valve at the bottom of the balloon, and a swirling vortex of glitter wheezed out of the deflating Mylar carcass. The Unseen Creeping Horror spread himself into a shimmering sphere around the ship. The bottom half penetrated at least thirty feet underground, sealing the moon-beasts inside.

"What's up with the cage?" the witch asked. "Those little dudes seem relatively harmless." Hell, unlike her signature amphibian rain, they didn't even have fangs.

"Until we know more, it's safest for everyone to keep them . . . contained." Three of the Clerk's eyes flicked to the Sheriff. "Besides, Yi'danag will also keep others *out*."

A moon-beast cocked its head, hopped to the sparkling border, and extended a long, triple-jointed finger toward the membrane.

The witch waved her arms. "Hey! Don't touch the—"

The beast recoiled and drew back a hand that was now one finger shy of the full octet.

She shook her head and turned to the Clerk. "So what now?"

"I shall consult the Dread Librarian and the Mindless Mother," the Clerk said. "Perhaps one of them can help us speak with the moon-beasts. Lomelzar's men will secure the field, and *you* will go home and get some rest."

The word *rest* summoned another yawn and a flash flood of fatigue. "I should probably stay," she said. "I don't trust the goons to—"

The witch's voice cut off in a strangled yelp as the Clerk shoved her through a portal. She landed on her bed next to not one but two indignant raccoons. Keyser Söze's lady friend hissed, pissed, and fled. The witch groaned. She should really get up and change the sheets, but now that she was horizontal, the lure of sleep was too strong to resist. Her eyes drifted closed, and the night's events flickered through her mind in a confused blur. As sleep claimed her, Doomsday Barbie's parting words echoed in her mind.

Is up to you *to stop this.*

CHAPTER THREE

Paranormal Phenomena

The witch pulled her pillow over her head, blocking out both the morning sun and the strident ring of her demonic BlackBerry. If it was Chad, he could leave a message and she'd curse him later. If it was anyone else, she gave not a single solitary shit what they had to say.

And she'd curse them later.

Finally, blessedly, the auditory assault ceased . . .

. . . and suddenly, sadistically, the mental klaxon of her Archonic contract commenced. Keyser Söze, who—as her familiar—was on the receiving end of the same summons, bit her earlobe hard enough to make her eyes water.

"Gods, *fine*," the witch snapped. "I'm awake."

A portal opened above a pile of dirty laundry, and the Clerk—unshrouded, because of freaking *course* she was—stepped through. The witch choked back a dry heave and fired off an intercessory prayer to Discordia.

Cartoon puppy ears appeared on all the Clerk's eyeballs. Not helpful.

The witch squinted to blunt the visual trauma. "I thought you wanted me to get some rest."

"It has been nearly three hours."

"That's not even half of a nap!"

A cloud of acrid steam formed as corrosive slime dissolved a pair of perfectly broken-in jeans. The Clerk waved a tentacle to disperse the fog. "I am convening an emergency General Session at ten o'clock."

Work? On a Saturday morning? Unless the tiny toad people had escaped the glitter-dome and overrun Asphodel, that was a wild overreaction.

"Since the Unseen Creeping Horror is . . . keeping watch over the Black Galley," the Clerk said, "we will meet on the softball field so he may participate."

After he'd been unwhitened last year, Yi'danag had returned to his dual posts as High Lord of Public Works and Dread Lord of Solid Waste Management. That asshole made sure everyone knew he was the hardest working cloud of flesh-eating vapor in Tophet County. Goddess forbid he miss a meeting and lose the chance to complain about it later.

Sadly, missing a meeting wasn't in the cards for the witch either. A few months ago, she could've sent Magnolia in her place, but that was no longer an option. Magnolia had left public service to take over as CEO of Boss Babe Enterprises, the umbrella company that ran Heather's many side hustles.

The witch groaned. "Can't it wait until Monday?"

"It cannot," the Clerk said. "We must appoint an acting human mayor and decide on a course of action regarding the moon-beasts."

"But I really need to . . ." Her voice trailed off as three bone-chilling words floated to the surface of her mind like turds in the proverbial punch bowl.

Acting. Human. Mayor.

The witch met the Clerk's unflinching sextuplicate gaze.

She wouldn't.

She *couldn't*.

"Oh, calm down," the Clerk said, puppy ears twitching in annoyance. "I plan to nominate Ellie Dawson."

The witch wheezed out a desperate sigh of relief. Too bad she'd quit smoking, because news that good deserved a celebratory cigarillo.

"Seconded. See you at the meeting."

"Indeed, you will—after you pick up Sathach." The Clerk's looping mass of tentacles writhed anxiously. "We need his mind-flaying skills to communicate with the moon-beasts. The Dread Librarian located a primer on their language in an appendix of *The Necronomicon*, but translation has proven difficult."

"Did you ask Za'gathoth?"

"As it turns out, the Mindless Mother is rather . . . closed-minded about Dreamlanders."

"Mom is problematic, eh?" the witch said. "That tracks. Look, can't you just pop over to Sathach's on your way? He loves meetings."

"I cannot *pop over*. After the babies were born, Sathach implemented the same protections I have in place in my office. No one can portal in."

"Then portal to the godsdamned front door and godsdamned knock!"

The frosty silence was broken only by the soft raspberry of a raccoon fart.

"That is your first strike, Witch," the Clerk said. "I would not recommend a second."

Whatever. The witch was an Archon now. What was the worst that could happen?

Her palace of memory replayed the Clerk's pre-coital clash with Lomelzar at the landfill, when the Clerk had *eaten* one of his glowy orbs.

Shit on a Shoggoth.

"I'm listening."

"I have called, texted, and emailed, and Sathach has not replied," the Clerk said. "I sent Deputy O'Brien to his home this morning, but . . ."

Oh, gods. She didn't like the sound of this.

"But what?"

"My deputy has not returned, and I cannot reach him."

Hank was good people—happy, helpful, and hotter than hell. In the unlikely event the witch ever needed rescuing, she knew in her bones Hank would ride at dawn. The least she could do was mosey out at a quarter till nine.

She held out her right hand and summoned her broom. It hurtled out of her open closet, whacked the Clerk's rightmost eyestalk, and smacked into her open palm.

"I'm on it."

"Last warning," the witch yelled after her thirteenth volley of knocks. "Open up, or I'll—"

The door flew open.

Hank grabbed her arm, pulled her into the pitch-black interior of the house, and slammed the door behind her. She heard the ratcheting click of no fewer than four locks.

The witch yanked her arm free. "I can't see a godsdamned thing." She conjured a light bulb over her head.

Hank peered at her through a pair of wire-rimmed sunglasses with cobalt-blue lenses. He grinned, dimpling adorably, and said, "Hi, Witch! I'm helping the Dread Lord conduct a paranormal investigation."

"You're *what?*"

"He's being haunted by a poltergeist," Hank said in a confidential whisper. "It started after he tried to contact his dead father."

When the Swarm assimilated the Archons' home universe eons ago, Sathach's father would've become one of them, so he hadn't exactly *died*. But then the witch sort of unmade the Swarm, so maybe he *had* died, but as a little white man. Either way, an afterlife presumably required something in the neighborhood of a soul—which, as far as she knew, neither Archons nor little white men possessed.

More importantly, poltergeists weren't real.

"Yep, a real poltergeist!" Hank held up a black device that looked a little bit like one of Vera's walkie-talkies. "This is a spirit box. If there's a ghost around, it can talk to us through the radio."

"Uh . . . Hank, I—"

"And these," he said, tapping the lenses of his sunglasses, "can see spirits and auras. Pretty cool, huh?" His salt-and-pepper eyebrows drew together as he examined her. "Your aura is blue."

"With those on, *everything* is blue."

A smattering of barely audible voices chimed in with less-than-helpful contributions. The witch sighed and zapped a dozen tiny heads off of Hank's nicely muscled forearm. Those threenagers had done one hell of a number on the softball field.

"Aw man," he said, gazing morosely at the smoking blotches. "I was just getting to know them."

She massaged her temples. "Where is the Dread Lord?"

"He's in the cellar," Hank said. "That's where he first saw the phenonenom . . . the phemonenomicon . . ."

The witch put her hand over his mouth. "Just take me to Sathach."

"Mmph, mmph!"

She withdrew her hand.

"Sure thing!" He slid a headlamp down over his forehead and turned on a lighthouse-grade bulb. "This way."

She followed him through rooms decorated in an aesthetic she'd describe as *high cringe*. Bad News Barbie would feel right at home. The erratic beam of Hank's headlamp gave the otherwise-innocuous surroundings a creepy "found footage" feel. The witch juiced up her shields. Poltergeists were bullshit, but an unbalanced Sathach with a witchly battle form was nothing to screw around with.

They descended a narrow, carpeted staircase in tense silence, save for the hiss of definitely not-paranormal static. Unlike the main floor, the cellar was in a witch-level state of filthy disarray. She followed Hank through a maze formed from boxes of unsold It Hurts!™ weight-loss wraps, mounds of surplus leggings, and utterly baffling product samples from Toys in Us, Heather's interspecies sex-toy emporium. The sheer number of orifices and protuberances implied by what she saw defied the limits of her imagination. (Thank Discordia for small mercies.)

Hank led the witch into an open area near the rear of the basement. He turned off his headlamp and gestured for her to extinguish her entropic bulb. The Dread Lord sat in an office chair facing away from them, haloed by the greenish glow from a wall of monitors. He leaned back and threw a slim projectile at the ceiling. It stuck, quivering, in a polystyrene tile that bristled with . . .

Huh, #2 pencils.

Sathach, who was either ignoring them or hadn't yet registered their presence, turned his attention back to the screens. Most of them displayed CCTV footage from home security cameras, but a few had shows playing. A "documentary" about cryptids. Shaky handheld footage of what looked like an abandoned asylum. The primary-colored hellscape of *Sesame Street*. Dirty dishes were stacked on the floor next to a small trash can that was overflowing with Monster energy drink cans and surrounded by a drift of sunflower seed hulls.

The Dread Lord wasn't even recycling. This was *bad*.

A stuttering burst of static spewed from the spirit box. Sathach leaped to his feet and turned to face them. He wore a vegan human suit from Sustainable Skyns, another of Heather's many business ventures. It was giving strong "department-store mannequin in a newscaster wig" vibes. In contrast to his previously over-stuffed human suits, the vegan version sagged, revealing just how much weight he'd lost since the babies were born.

"Hey there, Sathach," the witch said. "I've been meaning to stop by, but—"

"Take the thermal imager." He thrust what looked like a no-contact thermometer into her hands. "Keep an eye out for cold spots."

She glanced at the imager's small screen, which showed a heat map of the cellar. Naturally, Hank was the hottest object in the place. The Dread Lord picked up a stun gun–like device bedecked with flashing colored lights and paced the open area, muttering about fluctuating fields.

"Listen, we have a situation," the witch said. "The Clerk sent me to bring you to—"

"Can't," he said distractedly, watching the flickering lights. "I've got paranormal phenomena here."

"You *are* a paranormal phenomenon."

Static whooshed from the speaker.

"Aha!" the Dread Lord cried in triumph. "Something is trying to communicate!"

"*I* am trying to communicate," the witch said. "We need you to—"

"No time." The Dread Lord's Skyn squeaked as he gave his head a vehement shake. "I must cleanse this space before Heather and the babies get home."

"But the Clerk—"

"I tried to contact the other side." He aimed a steely gaze into a distant corner of the basement, which was occupied by a prototype of a sex swing with loops for four legs and dozens of tentacles. "Sometimes when you stare into the void," he said in a lisping, Batman-esque growl, "the void stares back."

The witch stalked to the wall and flipped on the lights. "Look around, Sathach. This is a perfectly normal basement. Well, except for"—she waved her hand at the bewildering menagerie of intimate appliances—"all *that*. But there are no ghosts. No paranormal beasties. No . . ."

Her voice trailed off. That wasn't quite true, was it?

Or at least it didn't have to be.

"If you want a real metaphysical mystery," the witch said, "a Black Galley full of moon-beasts just landed on the Dunwich Park softball field."

The Dread Lord's head swiveled toward her with a Tupperware-ish chirp. "Impossible. The Swarm took the Dreamlands. No moon-beasts could've survived."

"And yet . . ." She tapped her temples. "Take a peek. About three and a half hours ago."

The sticky tendrils of his etheric presence oozed into her mind as he rifled through her memories. He gasped and dropped the ghost Taser. His eyes grew so wide that one fell out of its socket and dangled on his cheek, suspended from a pinkie-width tentacle.

The witch very nearly tossed her cookies. When she was sure she wouldn't gag, she said, "See? Moon-beasts."

The eye retracted with a nauseatingly squelchy pop. "It's all connected. It *has* to be."

A pencil fell from the ceiling, hit the Dread Lord's head, and stuck point-first in his arm. He ignored it.

"The truth," he said in a hoarse whisper, "is out there."

CHAPTER FOUR

Public Excretion

NERD-ROMANCER: Could you please text me back? Getting worried.

The witch tucked her BlackBerry into her bra and kicked her broomstick into overdrive. She owed Chad two calls and at least five messages, but hurtling through the air at forty miles per hour wasn't the best time to reply.

Keyser Söze grumbled and gripped the staff with all three paws as they streaked over downtown Asphodel. After a brief stop at her apartment to pick him up, followed by a drive-by coffee raid on Dee's 'Nuts, she was running five minutes late for the Clerk's meeting. Hopefully, Hank and Sathach were already at Dunwich Park. She'd sent them over in Hank's Spectral Forces Hummer, but they'd insisted on bringing a full complement of utterly batshit paranormal investigation equipment. Gods only knew what mischief they'd get up to unsupervised.

The glittering dome of the Unseen Creeping Horror made the park look like a desert mirage. A ring of familiar eldritch flames now encircled the softball field. As she soared over the blistering barrier, she dropped her to-go cup into the conflagration. A jet of blue fire roared up and burned the bristles off of her broom. Keyser managed to leap free before they crashed, but the witch tumbled to the ground, skidded across the turf, and knocked Hank over like a well-built bowling pin. Before she'd even registered her injuries, the Archonic contract was force-feeding her entropine to heal one fractured wrist, two chipped teeth, and a constellation of gnarly contusions. (It didn't do a godsdamned thing for the tear in her *I Smell Children* T-shirt.)

"Hi, Witch!" Hank said, his voice muffled by her left thigh.

"You okay?"

"I think so." He wriggled underneath her in an inordinately distracting fashion. "Good news! I didn't land on the spirit box!"

"What a relief."

He craned his neck to peek up at her from between her legs. "Hey, while I've got you, is there anything you can do about getting heads?"

Too easy. And he probably wouldn't get it anyway.

She sighed and coated him in a film of anti-mutagenic magic. The witch disentangled herself, stood, and scanned the field for Keyser, whom she spotted humping the tentacle of a gently amused Lomelzar. (The Sheriff's attitude toward sentient beings was mildly murderous at best, but he was a total Disney Princess when it came to animals.) She breathed a sigh of relief—Keyser was fine, she was fine, Hank was *very* fine—but her fading concern quickly gave way to anger.

The witch stalked toward the Unquenchable Flame, City Hall's Archonic Head of Security, who surrounded the field in a crackling ring of fire. A petulant face appeared formed in the blaze and smirked at her as she approached.

"I've told you before," he said. "I'm an all-consuming inferno of eldritch fury—*not* a garbage fire."

"What you are is a raging asshole."

She considered conjuring a deluge to temporarily extinguish him, but an annoying prickle of guilt rained on her parade. This whole conscience thing was overrated. She settled for blowing out his facial flames with a blast of air before she headed off to find Sathach.

In the hours since the Clerk booted her, the Sheriff had hauled in three ball lightning cannons, which were triangulated on the Black Galley. The witch kept a wary eye on that trigger-happy danger squid as she searched the field for the Dread Lord. She located him pacing the circumference of the Unseen Creeping Horror's dome. He held his spectral stun gun out in front him, observing its display of colored lights. On the other side of the sparkly membrane, an inquisitive moon-beast hopped alongside him.

"So, um . . . whatcha doin'?" the witch asked, her voice carefully casual.

"Ahem. I'm using an EMF meter to assess the electromagnetic fields around the anomaly." He tapped an arc of tiny colored bulbs that ran from green to yellow to amber to orange to red. "If the light stays green, there's little to no paranormal activity."

"And if it's red?"

His crossed eyes unfocused to a million-mile stare. "Trust me, Witch," he said gravely. "You don't want to know."

One hundred percent accurate.

The Clerk oozed up behind him, her arrival heralded by the smell of melting grass. "Sathach, you're looking . . ." Her eyes raked over the baggy Skyn. "Are you well?"

"Well enough for now." He showed her the glowing display. "We're in the green."

"The green?" the Clerk repeated. "That sounds . . . good?"

"I'm not after good, Micana'gos." The Dread Lord stowed his EMF meter in a nylon holster on his belt. "I'm after the truth."

"I've made contact!" Hank hurried toward them clutching the spirit box. He tripped on a bit of uneven ground and attempted to cover it up by breaking into an impromptu jog. "Listen to this." He aimed the box at the Black Galley and fiddled with the buttons. "Spirit, can you hear me?"

The static continued its unremarkable hiss.

Hank furrowed his brow and shook the box. "Are you still there?"

The rushing whoosh rippled and stuttered, then a breathy voice broke through the white noise and said, "Piss off."

What the phantasmal fuck . . .

Sathach whooped a triumphant yell. "I knew it!"

The witch hadn't seen him this animated since he led an excruciating game of I Like Me Because at his last prebirth All Hands meeting. A psychic nudge dragged her attention away from the Dread Lord—the same jarring connection she'd felt when gazing through her lens at the Moon. She looked up at the deck of the Black Galley. There, at the prow of the ship, stood the big-ass moon-beast. It was looking (or the eyeless equivalent) not at *her*, but at Sathach.

She elbowed the Clerk's shroud. "There it is," she said under her breath. "The big one."

The Clerk twitched her eyestalks to peek around the witch. "The moon-beast who shattered your lens?"

"Yep." She waved a hand at the dome. "Tell the UCH to get lost so I can talk to it."

The Clerk's eyes flicked toward the Sheriff, who was digging a trench around the dome with his razored tentacles. Keyser sat perched on his—for lack of a better anatomical term—*shoulder* and supervised the excavation.

"Later," she said. "Lomelzar is not in a peaceable state of mind."

"I believe we have a quorum, Clerk," said a familiar voice.

The witch turned to see Ellie Dawson approaching in her wheelchair, accompanied by Chad. Behind them lurched Chlogha, the Dread Librarian—a nine-foot-tall amphibian Archon with a cyclopean eye, an insectile proboscis, and rainbow-slicked skin.

Chad handed the witch one of the two coffees he held and offered her a hesitant, somewhat-wounded smile.

Son of a Shantak. She'd forgotten to answer his godsdamned messages.

"Thanks, Chad," she said. "I've been meaning to—"

"Shall we convene?" Ellie asked. "I'm told we humans should limit our time on the field due to quantum mutagenesis."

Hank cocked his head in puppylike inquiry.

"The tiny heads, Deputy O'Brien," the Clerk said.

"Oh, don't worry about that." He aimed finger guns at the witch and fired. "The witch is great at heads!"

Chad sprayed a mouthful of coffee into the awkward silence.

"Thanks, Hank," the witch said, through gritted teeth. She sprinkled Chad and Ellie with entropic fairy dust. "That should keep you un-mutagenated."

The Clerk curled a dripping tentacle in a beckoning motion. "Follow me, if you please."

The witch tried to hang back and walk with Chad so she could explain and—*ugh*—apologize, but Sathach grabbed her elbow and dragged her into a tête-à-tête. A tentacle shot out of his shirt sleeve, snatched her coffee, and deposited it, cup and all, into his mouth.

"Something supernatural is onboard that ship," he lisped, steam pluming from his slightly melted lips. "You heard the spirit speak."

"I'm pretty sure the voice came from that monster moon-beast."

"Moon-beasts don't *have* voices," he said. "Besides, it isn't even dead!"

"Okay, well, I can think of at least three Archons, including *you*, who could pull off a trick like that," she said. "Besides, I thought your gadget cleared the Black Galley."

The Dread Lord unholstered the EMF meter and skewered it with a skeptical glare. "Sabotage." His eyes darted from side to side. "Trust no one."

The Clerk stopped under the canopy of the coaches' box, the northern end of which was under the Unseen Creeping Horror's dome. A wheeled aquarium containing the soapy bubbles of Nommaquth, the High Lord of Administration, sat at the end of a wooden bench. With him were Y'ggarlos, the winged octo-pussian High Lord of Economic Development (who was liberally smeared with Vaseline to prevent grievous desiccation); Achartho, the scorpion-like High Lord of Public Safety; and N'eithamiqug, Spinner of Sorrow—the monstrous terror-spider who served as the High Lord of Health and Human Services. Ellie Dawson and the Unseen Creeping Horror rounded out the complement of Tophet County executives.

And there was one more. *Her.*

Per their agreement last year, the Clerk had freed the witch from her unwanted role as High Lord of Public Works. But she'd executed a nifty double cross and reclassified the County Witch position as a High Lord equivalent. It was infuriating, but, well . . . game recognized game.

"This emergency General Session is now called to order," trilled the Clerk. "Our first order of business is to appoint an acting human mayor. Per my email, Mayor Chadwick is taking a brief leave of absence to attend to"—her eyes flicked to Sathach—"family matters."

"It's all my fault." Goopy yellow tears pooled in corners of the Dread Lord's eyes. "I summoned the dead and caused a paranormal infestation!"

Achartho broke into a buzzing chuckle, which ended in a choked gasp when he realized Sathach was serious. Since the Emergence had catastrophically increased the universe's baseline level of entropine, Earth spawned monsters like an RPG dungeon. Dimensional shamblers. Corner hounds. Influencers. With so much legit occult fuckery on offer, those deluded souls who believed in myths like poltergeists and zombies and a functional federal government were met with a mix of pity and scorn.

"That is . . . alarming," the Clerk said. "But let us focus on the matter at hand." She rubbed two tentacles together squelchily. "First, I nominate Ellie Dawson to become our acting human mayor. High Lord Dawson, do you accept the nomination?"

A ray of sun broke through the cloud cover and struck the Gold Award pin on Ellie's sash. She nodded solemnly and said, "I do."

Swirls of glitter spiraled through the Unseen Creeping Horror's fog. **Seconded**

One unanimous vote later, Tophet County had an acting human mayor.

Ellie began her reign by asking the witch to recount what she'd witnessed on the Phæras Wheel—which she did, minus the make-out session. After Chad shared Dr. Carcosa's findings and the Clerk filled in the remaining details, the floor opened for discussion.

"Based on the distress rune on the Black Galley's signal flag," the Clerk said, "it seems we are playing host to a ship of . . . refugees."

"Refugees?" Achartho buzzed. "From the *Moon*?"

"One of our many unanswered questions. We're working to overcome a significant language barrier." The Clerk aimed her wobbling eyestalks at the Dread Librarian. "Chlogha, if you please?"

The wickedly sharp pincers framing Chlogha's long proboscis flexed as she unwrapped a bundle of black velvet to reveal the mole-bedecked, human-skin-bound cover of *The Necronomicon*.

"Howard, turn to Appendix X: Races of the Dreamlands." The pages fluttered as the book flipped to a section near the very end. "The language of the moon-beasts is a transliteration of Ouranian-Barbaric into musical notation. Basically, specific combinations of notes correspond to certain phonemes."

"That sounds straightforward enough," Ellie said.

"In theory, it is," Chlogha said. "But in practice, we face significant challenges. First, the sound of the moon-beasts' language is extremely distasteful to the Archonic ear."

Y'ggarlos quivered in a wobbly, cephalopodic shudder. "I don't know how Yi'danag endures it."

The Unseen Creeping Horror's sparkles roiled in a blatant display of self-satisfaction. **Transcendental meditation**

"The second challenge," Chlogha said, "is that, even when we successfully translate their speech, we can't speak to *them*. Their flutes are made from the bones of Zoogs, which lived only in the Dreamlands. They have special acoustic properties we can't replicate."

The witch shrugged. "So borrow a freaking flute."

"Even if we had one, reproducing the tones requires eight triple-jointed fingers."

Gods, it was like the Archons were actively *looking* for reasons not to talk to the toad people.

"You guys are lousy with tentacles. Infinite joints. I'm sure you can figure it out."

"You may not have to," Chad said. "I'm working on a translation app. I already have a database of the Ouranian-Barbaric language, so all I need to do is add the corresponding musical elements. Once I've done that, I'll record samples of moon-beast speech to reproduce the flute's unique acoustics." His lips quirked. "I even have a name in mind for the app."

Uh-oh. The witch recognized that particular expression.

"Tootle Translate," he said with a hopeful dad-joke grin.

Silence.

"Like Google Translate."

Not even crickets.

Anxiety sweat beaded on Chad's brow, but he was in too deep to stop now. "You know, because people call playing an instrument *tootling*."

Literally no one called it that.

Hank raised his hand. "I don't get it."

"Thank you, Chad," Ellie said. "In the meantime, perhaps the Dread Lord of Human Resources can attempt to speak to them more directly."

The Dread Lord stared longingly at his spirit box, but he caved under the force of the Clerk's six-way warning glare. He approached a trio of moon-beasts standing just inside the dome. His crossed eyes locked on the smallest creature.

After a few moments of intense eyeballing, he said, "The language barrier obstructs even telepathic communication, but I should be able to view the beast's memories." Another pause. "How odd. I can't *see* anything at all. All I'm picking up are emotions. Terror . . . grief . . . confusion . . ."

The moon-beast twitched spasmodically and toppled over.

The Dread Lord gasped. "I have flayed it to death!"

But the beast was already stirring. It staggered to its feet and took a few dazed hops.

"Moon-beasts are eyeless, which most likely means they have no visual cortex," Ellie said. "It stands to reason that their memories would not consist of images."

Sathach gave a dejected shrug, producing a rubbery squeak.

"Dread Librarian," Ellie said, "your earlier comments implied you've had some success with translation. What have the moon-beasts said?"

"*Moon* and *fire* and . . . and *death*." Chlogha's proboscis twitched in apparent agitation. "One phrase keeps recurring, but I suspect we're translating it wrong."

"What's that?" the witch asked.

"Hungry comet."

"Comet," Chad repeated. "I saw something hit the Moon. I thought it might've been a meteor, but Dr. Carcosa said there's no impact site. That would rule out a comet, too."

The bubbles in Nommaquth's tank roiled, which translated to: *What are those weirdos doing?*

The witch turned to look. Three moon-beasts were using their long-fingered hands to dig a hole in the field. Two of them politely turned their backs as the third squatted over the hole.

"Stop that," Achartho shouted in a shrill buzz. "What kind of savages engage in public excretion?"

In a rewarding display of Discordian karma at work, retching sounds came from beneath the Clerk's dingy shroud.

"What do you expect them to do?" the witch asked. "Hold it?"

She scanned the field inside the dome. Some of the moon-beasts wandered aimlessly, pacing the confines of their sparkly cell. Some sat in the shade of the ship, listless and still. All of them looked miserable.

"We can't just leave them like this," she said. "Do they have food in there? Or water? It's midsummer, and they're out here baking in full sun." The witch crossed her arms and glared at the assembled Executives. "Which of you losers is in charge of . . . I don't know, helping people?"

N'eithamiqug pushed her cat's-eye glasses up her nose with one hairy spider leg. "Health and Human Services is not resourced to feed and house refugees." She sniffed and patted her beehive hairdo. "This feels like a public safety issue to me."

Achartho's scorpion tail stiffened in outrage. "You're not pushing this mess off on *my* department, Spinner!"

Not it, Nommaquth bubbled.

"You've got to be shitting me," the witch said. "Not one of you is willing to help the poor bastards?"

"They aren't citizens," the Clerk said. "They are . . . uninvited guests. Tophet County doesn't owe them anything."

"Unbe-freaking-lievable." The witch scowled at her chthonic colleagues. "You know, the Archons came here as refugees."

Y'ggarlos fluttered her wings to correct a startled bobble. "We certainly did not!"

"You escaped a genocide and fled to this universe with your tentacles tucked between your legs," the witch said. "What would *you* call it?"

"That was different." The Clerk tugged irritably at her shroud. "It was a long time ago, and . . . and it was *us*."

"You sound like Lomelzar."

"Take that back!"

"Order," Ellie called. "High Lord Innominanda is right."

The witch looked around for a moment before she remembered High Lord Innominanda was *her*. Sathach's choice for her new pseudonym—Magna Innominanda, the Great Not-to-be-Named—was undoubtedly an upgrade, but a part of her still missed Connie Lingus.

More than one part, actually.

"*Someone* needs to take the lead on coordinating our response," Ellie continued.

The meeting erupted into a cacophony of shouts, buzzes, and bubbles.

A flash of movement near the dome caught the witch's eye. She turned her back on the bickering executives and stepped away for a closer look. Keyser Söze waddled up to the wall of glittering etheric fog, watching one of the moon-beasts play its flute. The eyeless creature seemed to sense Keyser's attention and hopped to the edge of the enclosure, where it squatted on its haunches. Keyser stood on his hind legs and stared at the beast intently.

The witch crouched next to her familiar. "What is it, buddy?"

Keyser's black eyes met hers, then he hijacked her third eye and played a scene from his memory.

A growling coyote dragged a raccoon sow from her den in a hollow tree stump. She snarled and fought, slashing at the thing's face as it pulled her away from her whimpering kits. If the coyote had been alone, she might've been able to fend it off, but a second waited outside the den. It dove for the sow's exposed belly, gnawing and ripping. One by one, the coyotes yanked cowering kits from the stump, until only the smallest remained. Vicious fangs clamped on the runt's front paw and dragged him into the cold night air. He screamed in pain and terror. Then . . .

A brilliant blaze of light.

A flurry of panicked yips.

Gentle hands cradling his bloody body.

He gazed up at the face of his rescuer—a human face he wouldn't see again for seventeen years.

The image faded.

The witch had often wondered how Keyser was chosen to be her familiar. She had her answer. He'd been hand-picked by none other than Vera fucking Vásquez, an avatar of Discordia Herself.

But why was he showing her this now?

Keyser huffed in irritation. Once more, the injured raccoon kit loomed large in her astral sight, only this time, it had a face full of wriggling pink pasta-cles.

Like him, the moon-beasts had been attacked.

Like him, they'd lost their home, perhaps their families.

Gods dammit, he knew how to grab her by the frigging feels and squeeze. He also knew she had a soft spot for underdogs.

The witch picked her familiar up and carried him back to a meeting that had turned into an exceedingly violent game of hot potato. Then she shocked Tophet County's leadership into silence with three little words.

"I'll do it."

CHAPTER FIVE

The Moon-Beast Menace

N'eithamiqug retracted her dripping fangs from Achartho's thorax and gaped at the witch. The Clerk, who'd been trying to separate the two combatants, served up six eyeballs' worth of pure disbelief.

Sathach cocked his head and turned the volume down on his spirit box. "Ahem," he said. "What was that, Witch?"

"I said I'll do it. I'll take the lead on . . . uh . . ."

What the Flying Spaghetti Monster had she just signed herself up for?

"Coordinating Tophet County's response to the unfolding refugee crisis?" Ellie asked.

The witch pointed at her. "Yeah, I'll do that shit."

The Clerk disentangled herself from sixteen arachnid legs, two pincers, and a stinger-equipped tail and straightened her shroud. "You are . . . *volunteering*?"

Hives rippled up the witch's arms. She took a deep breath, fighting the instinct to run screaming in the other direction. Keyser nuzzled his fuzzy head into her neck.

She sighed. "Looks like I am."

Sathach nearly swooned. If not for Hank's lightning reflexes and pro-wrestler arms, he'd have gone down like a sack of crystal skulls.

"Thank you, High Lord Innominanda," Ellie said. "While I have full confidence in your abilities, I rather suspect this is bigger than a one-witch job."

Chad met the witch's eyes and raised a tentative hand. "I can help out."

"Perhaps after your translation app is up and running," Ellie said. "It's essential we establish communication with the moon-beasts."

"In fact, Mr. Chadwick," the Dread Librarian said, "I suggest we return to the library and get started." She peered up at the clearing sky. "*The Necronomicon* is already getting a sunburn."

Chad's face fell. "Oh. Sure, okay." He flashed a wan smile at the witch. "Talk to you later?"

She raised her hand, thumb and pinkie extended, in the universal (and woefully outdated, given the shape of modern cell phones) sign language for *I'll call you.*

And she would, gods dammit . . . just as soon as she got home.

After Chad and Chlogha left, Ellie surveyed the remaining bureaucrats. "Any other volunteers?"

The High Lords squirmed like guilty children, but none of them—not even the Clerk—would meet her eyes.

"I'll pitch in if it's all right with the boss." Hank grinned a perfect Colgate smile at the moon-beasts gathered on the other side of the dome. "They're cute little guys, aren't they?"

Two of the Clerk's eyes blinked at each other in surprise. "Cute," she repeated. "Indeed. You have my support, Deputy O'Brien. Sathach, please prepare the paperwork for his temporary assignment."

The Dread Lord spat a sunflower seed shell on the turf and sniffed. "Whatever."

Whatever?

He loved paperwork with a passion the witch reserved for Chicken Cock Kentucky bourbon and Amish romance novels. The Sathach she knew and formerly loathed would've jumped at the chance.

"We'll reconvene at our regular session on Tuesday," Ellie said. "Until then, this meeting is—"

Y'ggarlos, Achartho, and N'eithamiqug vanished in stuttering bursts of netherlight.

"—adjourned."

"Come, Deputy O'Brien," the Clerk said. "We must inform Lomelzar of your new duties."

Sathach wandered closer to the dome holding his thermal imager in one hand and his EMF meter in the other.

Ellie watched until they'd all drifted out of earshot, then wheeled her chair closer to the witch. "That was disappointing," she said in a low voice. "I've always known the Archons are soulless cosmic horrors, but they've displayed a remarkable civic-mindedness until now."

The witch shrugged. "People are assholes."

"Sometimes they are," Ellie said. "I appreciate you stepping up. So where do you plan to begin?"

Huh. Good question.

"Getting them out from under that flesh-devouring fog monster seems like as good a place as any." Keyser squirmed and nipped her chin. She put him down, and he trundled off—presumably in search of something to eat, screw, or emotionally blackmail into a charitable relief effort. "The moon-beasts are probably broiling out here in the sun. We need somewhere dark, cool, and—"

"Out of sight," said the Clerk, who glided toward them trailing Hank and Lomelzar in her wake.

"That was quick," the witch said.

"Lomelzar was already . . . observing our meeting."

Eavesdropping. How very on-brand.

The Sheriff bellowed and thrashed his tentacles. *!!!I WILL BUILD A WALL AROUND THE FIELD!!!*

"A wall?" Ellie repeated.

The Deep Ones' failed attempt to transform Ellie into one of their number had left her inexplicably fluent in bubbles, brays, and Ouranian-Barbaric. (It had left the rest of her Girl Scout troop with gills and a hard-core sushi habit.) Yet another reason the Archons had appointed her unofficial queen of the humans . . .

"Why a wall?" Hank asked.

Deputy Eye Candy's ability to understand Sheriff-speak was rooted in self-preservation. Working for an entity who could chug him like a cold beer on a hot day was, as it turned out, a more powerful linguistic tool than the Rosetta Stone.

!!!THE MOON-BEASTS ARE NOT FROM HERE! THEY ARE CRIMINALS!!!

Gods, not this shit again.

"*You're* not from here," the witch snapped, trying unsuccessfully to ignore her throbbing head.

The Sheriff ignored her and continued his least-favorite-uncle-on-Facebook tirade. *!!!MY WALL WILL CONTAIN THE MOON-BEAST MENACE! WE MUST PROTECT OUR WOMEN AND CHILDREN!!!*

The Clerk's eyes flashed dangerously. And literally. "Protect our *women*?"

Hank raised his hand. "Couldn't the moon-beasts jump over the wall?"

!!!IT WILL BE THE BIGGEST WALL! ALL WALLS WILL TREMBLE BEFORE THE MIGHT OF THIS WALL!!!

"They could tunnel under it," Hank said. "Did you see how fast they dug that latrine?"

!!!I WILL FILL THE EARTH WITH BOOBY TRAPS! AND LAND MINES! AND . . . AND WEASELS!!!

"They could make a ladder."

"Enough." With that single word, Ellie somehow gave the impression of a furious shout, though her voice was as calm and measured as ever. "There will be no wall."

"I bet they'd just fly out in their ship anyway," Hank added helpfully.

The Sheriff screeched in protest.

The Clerk tore her furious gaze away from Lomelzar. "Might I suggest we relocate the moon-beasts to the cavern Mayor Chadwick excavated near the Fathomless Abyss?"

!!!I WILL SHOVE THE ENTIRE BLACK GALLEY INTO THE ABYSS!!! the Sheriff shrieked. *!!!PROBLEM SOLVED!!!*

"First, *no*." Ellie regarded the Sheriff as though he were a potty-mouthed middle schooler instead of a homicidal croctopus. "Second, we cannot put anything into the Fathomless Abyss. After Maggie dropped the sphere in, the Abyss and its pocket dimension sort of . . . untethered from our universe."

"So what's down there now?" the witch asked.

"As far as we know, there *is* no 'down there.' Dr. Carcosa and I have conducted a number of experiments. Anything dropped into the Abyss remains suspended in the shaft until you retrieve it." Ellie regarded the Clerk with a considering glance. "The cavern is an excellent option."

"I haven't set foot in there since the solstice." The witch squinted against the sunlight at the far end of the field. The gleaming white garage door set into the hill behind second base still shimmered with her *keep-the-fuck* out spell. "Looks like no one has. We should make sure there's nothing dangerous lying around before we turn the little guys loose. Are you up for checking it out?"

"Sure," Ellie said.

!!!I AM THE SHERIFF! YOU WILL WATCH AS I CHECK IT OUT!!!

The Dread Lord of Human Resources perked up and said, "I shall come too." He held up his EMF meter. "I'd like to get some baseline readings of the cavern."

"I don't think so, Sathach," the Clerk said. "There's no need to—"

"Can't hurt." The witch arched her eyebrows at the Clerk.

"Right . . ." The Clerk's eyes darted from the witch to Sathach and back. "Yes, I suppose it couldn't hurt." She cast a baleful six-way glance at the Sheriff. "It seems you have things in hand here. I have . . . work to catch up on. In my office. Away from here." She vanished in a swirl of netherlight.

!!!DEPUTY O'BRIEN, YOU WILL SUPERVISE THE PRISONERS IN MY ABSENCE!!!

"They aren't prisoners, Sheriff," Ellie said.

. . . ARE SO . . .

Dr. Carcosa and his grad students had removed the salvageable pieces of the quantum tunneler shortly after the solstice. After that, the witch had sealed the door, and no one had come in or out since. All that remained now were the battery-powered industrial lights and a single office chair, which the witch's palace of memory populated with a gleefully spinning Vera Vásquez. A swirl of debris floated in the shaft of the Fathomless Abyss, confirming Ellie's earlier comments. Sathach made a beeline for it, detectors at the ready.

"What do you think?" Ellie asked.

"It'll do," the witch said, examining the rough-hewn stone walls. "It's chilly down here, and they can turn the lights off if they want it dark." She turned and gazed at the busted metal grate at the base of the inclined tunnel. "We can requisition a few goons to stand guard so no one messes with them."

!!!DO NOT CALL THEM GOONS!!! The Sheriff's donkey squeal was deafening in the enclosed space. *!!!I DEEM THIS AN ACCEPTABLE HOLDING CELL!!!*

He whipped out a Maglite and commenced an ostentatiously thorough examination of the cavern.

"What shall we do with the Black Galley?" Ellie wheeled her chair in a wide circle. She gazed up at the ceiling and shook her head. "It definitely won't fit in here. Even if we removed the masts, it would eat up too much living space."

"Maybe we could store it in a hangar at the airfield?"

"That could work," Ellie said. "What do we need to provide for the moon-beasts? Cots? Blankets?"

"Well, they'll definitely need porta-potties. Water, I'm sure. Beyond that, we might have to wait on Chad's app to find out the specifics."

"You mean Tootle Translate?" Ellie wore a deadpan expression, but a spark of mischief glinted in her eyes.

The witch grinned and opened her mouth to reply, but a whoop of triumph cut her short.

"Red!" Sathach sprinted across the cavern, his Skyn squeaking in rhythm with his steps. He held the EMF meter aloft like an Olympic torch. He stopped in front of them, panting. "Paranormal . . . activity . . ."

"Take a breath, Sathach," the witch said. "Tell me what happened."

He obediently took a breath. With the extra room inside the Skyn due to his weight loss, his exhalation raspberried out of all available orifices. Unperturbed, he wiped his brow with a tentacle protruding from gods knew where and said, "At first, all readings were normal. Thermal imaging showed a steady fifty-two degrees, and we were in the green." Another deep breath. Another chorus of raspberries. "Then the EMF meter pegged all the way red."

Ellie shot a dubious glance at the Dread Lord's ghost-hunting gear. "Dread Lord, you *do* realize what you're doing isn't remotely grounded in—"

A psychic shriek tore through the witch's mind. Sathach wailed and gripped his head, his rubbery face contorted in agony. Across the cavern, Lomelzar bellowed and flailed. He tore out of the cavern in a flurry of thrashing tentacles.

"What's happening?" Ellie asked.

"I . . ." The witch shook her head, trying to think past the tortured, bone-rattling scream. "I don't—"

"It's the Archonic contract," Sathach said. "One of us is . . . is . . ."

He gripped the witch's arm in one hand and Ellie's in the other. An octarine pinprick formed in midair. It grew into a glowing portal that engulfed the three of them in a tide of netherlight.

The witch stumbled out of the portal onto the softball field. Thank Discordia, the mental howl had ceased as she transited reality's underbelly.

Her relief was short-lived.

The shimmering dome of the Unseen Creeping Horror was now a wall of azure fire. Ellie and Sathach stared in stunned horror as Lomelzar cartwheeled erratically around the circumference, searching for a way in. He reached a tentacle toward the roaring flames and instantly withdrew it, blistered and scorched. The witch pulled a metric shit-ton of entropine and hauled a swimming pool's worth of Tehom Lake through the ether. She flooded the dome with lake water, extinguishing the blaze in thick clouds of steam. Black spots swam in her vision as the Archonic contract replenished her stores.

The Clerk apparated in front of her, unshrouded and clearly halfway through stripping her tentacles of bacon-print leggings. "What in Azathoth's name is—"

Her largest mouth gaped at the ragged circle of glittery dust around the smoldering remains of the Black Galley.

"Yi'danag?" the Clerk said in a hoarse whisper.

But he was gone.

Every Archon, including the witch, could feel it in their bones. Or carapaces. The Unseen Creeping Horror was not transmogrified. Not unconscious. Not spirited away to parts unknown.

He was *gone*.

Flashes of netherlight sparked at the edge of the field as Archon after Archon portaled in. A tentacled elephant that appeared to be made of tar landed on the third-base altar with a splintering crack. Sathach and Ellie exchanged a glance.

"That's the President of Gomorrah Township's Board of Commissioners," Ellie said. "This could get ugly."

That was putting it mildly.

Archons were fiercely territorial. Though they loved to trumpet the fact that they *ran the world's governments*, they didn't often intermingle with others outside their area of predation and/or governance. After the post-Emergence wars, they'd battled it out amongst themselves and claimed their turf. Functionally, an embarrassment of Archons—to use the proper collective noun—operated like an all-gender pride of lions. A designated group dwelt together in relative peace, but they didn't socialize with the pride next door.

Not peacefully, anyway.

The Clerk ripped off her remaining leggings and cast a pleading glance at Sathach. "I could use your help here."

His eyes glistened with grayish-yellow slime. "I just . . . I can't believe that Yi'danag—"

"Later." The Clerk wound a tentacle around his hand and led him toward Darth Dumbo.

Ellie watched for a moment, then she lifted her chin and followed them.

"What are you doing?"

"I'm the acting mayor," she said. "I'm going too."

A psychic nudge drew the witch's attention to a ball lightning cannon positioned in front of the concession stand. At the base of the weapon, Keyser stood on his hind legs next to a crumpled body.

Oh, *shit* . . .

Hank.

She tore across the field like a ghast out of hell. Hank lay sprawled on the grass, the spirit box on the ground beside him. She didn't see any burns or wounds, but he was so still. So lifeless.

"Hank?" She shook his shoulder, wrestling a growing panic. "Wake up!"

Nothing.

The witch leaned over his head, placing her cheek near his mouth. She felt the moist warmth of his breath and nearly cried from relief. Then he turned his head, and his lips brushed her neck.

"Witch . . ."

The low rumble of his voice so close to her ear raised goose bumps. She moved to sit up so she could get a better look at him, but he wrapped one strong arm around her shoulders and pulled her closer. She felt the heat of his skin through his uniform shirt, and her shock and fear drifted away on a wave of loin-melting lust.

Keyser bit her pinkie finger hard enough to draw blood, and the liquid warmth in her belly receded.

Gods below, what was *wrong* with her? The man was hurt, probably delirious, and she was ready to strip him naked and—

"Witch?"

She pulled free of Hank's arm and looked up. "Chad!"

Hank moaned in a way that was less *possible head injury* and more *let's get it on*. The witch scrambled away from him and stood up.

"The Dread Librarian said something awful happened. I asked her for a lift when she portaled over," Chad said. "I wanted to make sure you were okay."

"I'm good."

His eyes darted to Hank. "What about him? Is he—"

Hank rose to his feet in one fluid motion. For the briefest instant, his eyes seemed to shine a luminous blue. Then he shivered and smiled his usual puppy-dog smile.

"Hey, Chad!"

"Uh . . . hi, man. You feeling all right?"

"I feel . . ." Hank trailed off and licked his lips. "I feel *hot.*"

CHAPTER SIX

A Light Haze of Suspicion

The witch stared at the smoking husk of the Black Galley.

Those poor bastards . . .

The little toad-people had fled the Moon and made it all the way to Tophet County, but whatever they'd been running from had caught up with them—*and* the Unseen Creeping Horror. Given Keyser Söze's emotional appeal on the moon-beasts' behalf, she'd expected him to be broken up about their fiery demise. Instead, he took advantage of the commotion to steal every Payday bar in the concession stand. He was currently passed out in a stage IV sugar coma, and Dunwich Park was finally, blessedly quiet.

Quiet*ish*.

After the Clerk sent Darth Dumbo on his way, the Sheriff had ordered the softball field cleared of all personnel except Ellie Dawson, Hank, Sathach, and the witch. (And the Clerk. He knew better than to try moving so much as one of her tentacles.) The witch hadn't even gotten a chance to say goodbye to Chad. The Dread Librarian just scooped him up and portaled away.

Lomelzar then commenced an "investigation," which consisted of stamped-ing back and forth across the softball pitch while roaring at the top of his lungs and destroying any possible traces of physical evidence. His rampage continued until the Clerk tackled him and subdued him with the promise of interviewing the sole witness to the UCH's murder. Hank now sat in a dented metal folding chair in the parking lot, squinting into the fifteen-thousand-lumen glare of the Dread Lord's headlamp.

"Walk me through what happened, Deputy O'Brien," the Clerk said.

!!!THIS IS MY INTERVIEW! WALK ME THROUGH WHAT HAPPENED!!!

Hank grinned and flashed a thumbs-up. "Sure thing!"

Ellie flipped to a fresh page on her legal pad and nodded for Hank to begin. He rolled his shoulders and stretched, showcasing an impressive collection of taut muscles. Then his eyes met the witch's—had they always been *that* blue?— and he . . . he *smoldered* at her. Her cheeks heated in an honest-to-gods blush, and she looked away. But when she dared to look again, he wore his usual expression of dopey good cheer.

She must've overly repressed her inner horndog, that's all it was. Once Chad was ready to tickle her TARDIS, she'd be right as rain.

Right?

Right.

"After you guys went down to the cavern, I heard something by the concession stand and went to check it out," Hank said. "But it was just Keyser Söze trying to jimmy open the candy locker. I popped it open for him—"

The Sheriff brayed an admonishment, and Hank winced.

"Sorry!"

"And then?" the Clerk prompted.

"Then there was this bright flash, like lightning, and a . . . a zappy sound. I turned around, and I saw . . ." Hank's speckled eyebrows drew together as he searched for the right words. "I saw a giant blue fire-snake."

"A spectral manifestation," Sathach lisped.

A wave of confused blinks rippled over the Clerk's eyes. "A fire-snake?"

"Yeah, and it bit the Unseen Creeping Horror," Hank said. "I remember reaching for the ball lightning cannon. I . . . I *think* I fired it, but . . ." He shook his head. "The next thing I remember is the witch waking me up."

"Well, thank Azathoth you are unharmed!" The Clerk whirled to face the Sheriff, all six of her eyes flashing with rage. "Why did you leave only one officer on the field, Lomelzar?"

!!!I DIDN'T! THE UNQUENCHABLE FLAME WAS STANDING GUARD!!!

Gods, he was right. Monsieur Flambé *had* been here, encircling the softball field in a ring of . . .

Blue fire.

"Where in the seven hells *is* that flaming asshole?"

Hank stood, shaded his eyes, and gazed at the field. "He's not here."

"We know where he is *not*, Deputy," the Clerk said with exaggerated patience. "I would very much like to know where he *is*."

He shrugged. "Must be somewhere else."

"Blue. Flame-y. Fled the scene of a crime," the witch said. "Seems to me we've got ourselves a suspect."

Lomelzar reflexively shrieked in wordless excitement, but Sathach and the Clerk exchanged an incredulous look.

"It is staggeringly unlikely that the Unquenchable Flame would attack Yi'danag in such a way," the Clerk said. "When we . . . damage each other, we do it in combat, as befits our status as apex predators. In the countless eons of our existence, I have never heard of an attack such as this one." Her eyes exchanged a worried glance. "But the circumstances do cast a light haze of suspicion."

"I can personally vouch for Flame," the Dread Lord said. "He couldn't have done this. He's a dedicated member of my primal-scream-therapy circle. We have a shared commitment to mastering our anger."

The Dread Lord's poreless forehead wrinkled in a frown. "But . . ."

"But what?" the witch asked.

"Why was he here in the first place? He shouldn't even have been on duty today." Sathach pulled out his BlackBerry and scrolled through his messages. "Ah, there it is. Flame has been on leave for two weeks." He glanced up at the Clerk. "He's not due back at the office until Monday."

The witch stared down at her torn T-shirt. Fourteen days of R&R didn't seem to have cooled the Unquenchable Flame's temper by so much as a degree.

So much for primal-scream therapy.

"If he is not on the duty roster," the Clerk said, "why was he here?"

!!!I COMMANDED HIM TO REPORT TO THE FIELD!!!

"That is unacceptable, Lomelzar," Sathach said, sounding more like his old self than he had in weeks. "First of all, he doesn't report to you. And second, you cannot order employees to work during their planned time off."

!!!OBVIOUSLY, I CAN! BECAUSE I ALREADY DID IT!!!

"Deputy O'Brien," Ellie said, "did you see the Unquenchable Flame before the incident? Or perhaps during the attack?"

"I wasn't really paying attention."

"Outstanding police work," the Clerk muttered.

!!!DO NOT CHASTISE MY GOONS!!!

The witch smirked. "I'm told they don't like it when you call them goons."

A discordant chorus of yowls interrupted the Sheriff mid-shriek. The eerie cries emanated from the hulking ruin at the center of the softball field.

"Paranormal activity!" Sathach cried. "I *knew* it."

He stalked toward the Black Galley, holding a pseudo-scientific instrument in each hand. The witch gritted her teeth and followed him. If there were actual ghosts onboard that thing, she'd eat her pointy black hat.

They stopped about fifty feet from the ship. Its masts and sails had been burned to ash, along with the tentacled figurehead that once adorned the bow. The rowing benches were now charred hunks of wood, and the inferno had entirely consumed the rails along the ship's port and starboard sides. In fact, the only parts of the ship that were largely intact were the deck, the lower third of the hull, and the keel.

The Dread Lord raised his thermal imager, and his face fell. "No cold spots."

"It was just on *fire*," the witch said. "What did you—"

The haunted house squeal of rusty hinges stopped her in her tracks. A rectangle of decking at the base of what had once been a towering mast lifted, and a face full of squirming pink tentacles poked up through the hatch. The moon-beast jammed its flute into the wriggling nest. Its fingers danced over the length of drilled bone, producing what sounded very much like a question. Another head popped up, and another. Then the first beast was shoved up and out of the opening by a surging tide of amphibian bodies.

Though the witch couldn't understand their harsh fluted blasts, she got the general gist of it: *Let me OUT.*

The ruckus roused Keyser, who emerged from a drift of candy wrappers and trundled toward the Black Galley at top speed. Sathach flew past him at a dead run, his Skyn squeaking like a chew toy.

Beast after beast crawled out of the ship like it was a godsdamned clown car. Moon-beasts climbed over the hull and hopped away from the galley, gathering in a huddled mass. Lomelzar surged toward them with a furious bellow, but the Clerk tripped him with an outstretched tentacle. The witch left the former lovers to what was either foreplay or a fight to the death and jogged to the Dread Lord's side, followed closely by Ellie.

Sathach circled the moon-beasts with his EMF meter. "It doesn't make sense," he muttered, casting a skeptical glance at its display.

"What's that?"

"We're in the green," he said, showing her the glowing light, "but either the heat or the smoke should've killed them."

The witch swept a hand toward the very much alive moon-beasts. "And yet . . ."

"Dread Lord, please tell me you didn't think the creatures who just climbed out of that ship did so while dead," Ellie said, oozing skepticism like the Clerk oozed corrosive slime.

"I thought they might not be fully alive." He gave the thermal imager another try, then heaved an Eeyore-ish sigh. "Perfectly normal."

"I'm sure they're sorry to disappoint you with their continued existence," the witch said.

"That's not what I meant."

The witch cocked her head. "Isn't it, though?" She examined the cluster of cowering moon-beasts, who were eyelessly watching the Clerk beat the Sheriff like a drum. "We should get a head count."

She scanned the group. A few dozen creatures, more or less—all identical as far as she could tell. Same gray skin. Same pink tentacles. Same diminutive height.

"Where's the supersized one?"

Sathach circled the beasts. "It's not here."

"It *has* to be here," the witch said. "The UCH had that ship locked down tighter than a gnat's ass, then Hank's mystical fire-snake burned him to glitter. They had no way out."

Ellie gestured toward the beasts. "And yet . . ."

Touché.

"Maybe it perished in the blaze," Sathach said. "It was twice the size of the others. If it was standing on the deck when the ship caught fire . . ."

"We need to search the Black Galley," Ellie said, "and not just for survivors. Whatever the moon-beasts were running from, it found them. It found *us*." She gazed at the fuligin hull. "There could be something onboard that will shed light on what we're dealing with."

"Good call," the witch said. "I'll—"

"Dibs!" Sathach shouted.

He disappeared into a bubble of netherlight.

The Dread Lord emerged on the deck of the Black Galley in a shooter's stance, holding his EMF meter in front of him in a stiff-armed two-handed grip. He prowled across the deck like a Spectral Forces goon wading into a nest of nightgaunts.

The witch knelt and beckoned to Keyser Söze. He disentangled himself from the loving embrace of a moon-beast and waddled up to her. "Get Hank over here," she said. "You two keep an eye on the beasts, make sure none of them wander off."

Keyser answered with an enthusiastic eldritch salute, but he set off to retrieve Hank.

The witch glanced at Ellie. "Mind if I join Sathach?"

"Not at all."

She approached the ship and, with a wee entropic boost, leaped onboard to examine the scene.

Partially burned benches. The charred stumps of the galley's masts. A few abandoned oars. Other than that, the jet-black planks were bare.

Having completed a circuit of the deck, the Dread Lord knelt and poked his thousand-watt headlamp into the open hatch. He gripped the deck and swung himself down into the hole.

The witch frowned and considered the facts. The heat of the blaze would've been intense, but unless the moon-beasts were made of kindling, there should be at least *something* left of a body. A limb. A bone. Hell, even a toenail. But not only were there no remains, she saw no belongings. No personal possessions. No food stores. In short, the deck was an evidence-free zone.

The sandy-blond head of Sathach's Skyn popped up out of the hatch like a prairie dog.

"Anything?" Ellie called from the field.

"No sign of the missing moon-beast," he said, levering himself out of the hatch, "and no clues." He stood and ran a hand through his hair, dusting it with ash.

"I didn't find anything on the deck either," the witch said. She jumped down to the grass, followed by Sathach, who tucked, rolled, and sprang up in a crouch.

"The moon-beasts' leader must have burned up in the fire." His eyes widened. The eyeball on the left wobbled alarmingly, but he blinked it back into place. "The spirit box!"

"Must you?" Ellie's voice carried a tone somewhere between disapproval and disdain.

"Sathach," the witch said, "even if your toy really worked—"

"It's *not* a toy!"

"—how would you understand them? Did you miss the part where no one speaks moon-beast?"

"You heard the voice before," he said. "*Something* on that ship spoke English."

"Like I told you, someone's probably fucking with you. All of this"—she waved a hand at his supernatural equipment—"is imminently fuck-with-able. And even if it *was* a bilingual moon-ghost, which it very much was not, it said 'Piss off.' Not exactly an invitation to communicate."

He ignored her, opened a portal, and reached through to grab the box, which lay on the ground by the concession stand. He retrieved it and flipped a switch. White noise whispered from the speaker.

"Come on, say something . . ."

Over the rippling hush of static, a faint voice said, "Comet."

The pronunciation was odd, with the stress on the *met* instead of the *co*, but the word itself was crystal clear.

Ellie sucked in a surprised breath, and the Dread Lord's face lit with transcendent joy. The witch rolled her eyes.

"Acting Mayor Dawson," Sathach said, squaring his shoulders, "I volunteer to investigate this anomaly."

The witch threw up her hands. "It's not an anomaly! Some asshole hijacked your low-rent walkie-talkie and—"

"Actually," Ellie said, "this situation *is* anomalous. A space-faring wooden galley. Refugees from an interdimensional realm that should no longer exist. A homicidal flaming serpent. One Archon murdered, one missing. And . . ." Her eyes darted to the spirit box. "And *that*."

"Sure," the witch said, "but there's a logical explanation, just like with the Swarm. And I guaran-godsdamn-tee it will not involve a ghost."

Ellie propped her elbows on the padded arms of her wheelchair and steepled her fingers. Her ice-blue eyes flicked from the witch to Sathach and back.

"Both of you are viewing the facts through a lens of inherent bias. You," she said, focusing on Sathach, "are seeking confirmation of your paranormal phenomena hypothesis. And you"—her gaze shifted to the witch—"entirely refuse to consider explanations inconsistent with your preconceived worldview."

The witch crossed her arms. "With *reality*, you mean."

Ellie stared her into submission. She'd definitely earned her badass badge. "Perhaps you're correct about the voices, High Lord Innominanda," she said. "But can you explain why the Dread Lord's EMF meter detected a powerful burst of electromagnetic radiation at the precise moment the Unseen Creeping Horror was murdered?"

The witch opened her mouth, smart-ass retort at the ready, but Ellie's question burrowed into her mind like an eldritch earworm. "It could've been . . ." Her mind raced, frantically searching for possibilities. "A power surge," she said triumphantly. "That would do it."

"Sure." Ellie offered a small, cool smile. "But there's no wired electricity in the cavern. The equipment was run by a generator, which Dr. Carcosa took back to his lab, and the lights are powered by batteries."

Well, *shit.*

The ichor-spattered Clerk slithered into the sullen silence. "I hope I haven't overstepped, Mayor Dawson, but I asked Deputy O'Brien to escort the moonbeasts into the cavern," she said. "Lomelzar just summoned a Spectral Forces squad to stand watch over the tunnel. I've convinced him to direct his . . . protective energies toward containing the"—she made air quotes with two dripping tentacles—"'*moon-beast menace.*'"

Ellie nodded. "A prudent course of action."

The Clerk kept one pair of eyes trained on Ellie. She aimed a second pair at the witch and a third at Sathach, clearly sensing the tension. "What has happened?"

Ellie flashed a beatific smile.

"I'm reconvening the Witch's Task Force."

CHAPTER SEVEN

Netflix and Kill

But he's a Whovian!"

The witch blinked in confusion. She'd been midway through a blow-by-blow of all Chad had missed while he was off tootling with the Dread Librarian. Now she'd entirely lost the thread.

"Who's a what?"

"The Unquenchable Flame is on my trivia team," Chad said. "You know that—he's in all my best Whovian stories. His team name is Nardole, remember?"

The witch had tried to take an interest in his team, she really had. But she inevitably zoned out during his spirited reenactments of last-minute buzz-ins. As much as she cared about Chad, she couldn't make herself give a single solitary shit about trivia.

He scanned her face, clearly reading the truth in her eyes, and sighed. "Look, Flame's a good guy. He's just sensitive about his . . . appearance. If you'd chill with the whole garbage fire thing—"

"He was standing watch when the Unseen Creeping Horror was murdered."

"Okay, but—"

"And the murder weapon was blue fire."

"I *know* him, Witch," Chad said. "There's no way he was involved."

The Clerk and Sathach seemed inclined to agree with him. Plus, Flame's guilt would make things simple, and nothing in Tophet County was *ever* simple.

But he'd fled the scene—not the behavior of an innocent bystander.

"Then why did he run?"

"I . . ." He shook his head. "Maybe he was scared."

"Maybe he didn't want to get caught." Chad opened his mouth to reply, but she raised a hand to forestall him. "I'm not trying to be a dick, but we can't rule him out just because you know him. We've both seen people do shit we didn't think they were capable of."

Like Heather, Chad's ex, who'd once aligned herself with the Swarm.

Like Dr. Carcosa, who'd been possessed by a little white man and betrayed the witch's trust.

Like the witch herself, who'd kept secrets from her team.

They sat in strained silence at her kitchen table. Keyser Söze sprawled between their plates, snoring softly. She stroked his silky fur, and he stretched to expose more belly.

The witch had no idea what to say, no clue how to fix the wrecked vibe. She busied herself refilling their coffee mugs—his with red wine, hers with Chicken Cock.

"Well, I was really happy to get your text," Chad said.

She'd finally Ubered home from the park around 1:30. By the time she'd showered, fed Keyser, and changed her sheets, exhaustion was catching up to her, so she'd texted instead of returning Chad's calls.

Netflix & chill. My place, 7:00. I'll cook.

The witch had punctuated this terse masterpiece with what was shaping up to be an overly optimistic eggplant emoji, then face-planted on her bed for a few hours.

He grinned, and it felt like the sun coming out after a storm. "You know, I hadn't eaten a Hot Pocket since high school."

She eyed the half-eaten pastry shell on his plate. "Not your favorite?"

"Let's just say I'm not here for the ham and cheese."

The witch's stomach did a slow flip.

Her earlier reactions to Hank had left her feeling rattled and unsure. She needed a fun night with Chad, needed to connect with him—even if his eggplant didn't find its way to her Hot Pocket. Perhaps there was still hope for *Date Night: The Sequel.*

"Want to—"

"What else—"

Chad gestured for her to speak, but the witch said, "You first."

"What else happened after I left?"

Shit.

She'd been about to suggest they retire to the futon for the Netflix portion of the evening. The last thing she wanted was to talk about work.

"Sure you don't want to skip this for now and go watch a movie?"

He lifted one shoulder in a half shrug. "I guess I'm feeling a little out of the loop," he said with a small, self-conscious smile. "Whatever's going on in your life, I want to be part of it."

The witch took a deep breath and sighed it out. "Okay, where was I . . . the UCH is dead, and the Unquenchable Flame is missing. Oh, and then Sathach's ghost radio picks up a voice again, only this time it says 'comet.'"

Chad frowned at the odd pronunciation. "Comet?" he repeated. "Comet is one of the words the Dread Librarian was able to transfer from Lunatic."

"Lunatic?"

"The moon-beast language." He drummed his fingers on the table. "Comet. Comet. Man, I wish I knew what the beasts were trying to tell us."

"You and me both."

"Have you tried to do a reading on them?"

A reading. The word tugged at a thread of memory, something that needed to be at the forefront of her mind. If she could just—

Chad waved his hands as though signaling an airplane. "Earth to Witch."

"Yeah, sorry," she said. "The Clerk asked me to try before I left the park, but whatever interferes with Sathach's mind-flaying fucks with my readings too. I can trace the moon-beasts' location back to the Moon, even further back to the Dreamlands. But I can't *see* anything."

He sat up straighter, practically vibrating with urgency. "Can you track down Flame?"

"If I could, he'd be in an interrogation room having a little chat with Zsthaor."

The glow of hope in Chad's eyes dimmed. "You'd turn him over to the Dread Lord of Corrections? Even knowing how he and the Sheriff treat suspects?"

"If I could find him," she said. "But the Archons' master contract lets each individual control access to certain information. It's like how you can turn off location services on your phone. So I can't do a reading on . . ."

Her voice trailed off. There it was again. A *reading*. What was it about that word?

The answer hit her like a bolt of—

"Lightning!"

Chad recoiled at her shout. "Are you okay?"

"Violence! Catastrophe!"

"Witch, I don't . . ." He shook his head. "You're just yelling scary words."

"The reading we got at the Midnight Carnival," she said. "The pink psychic . . ." She groped for the woman's name. "Sibyl." The witch dipped into her palace of memory, scanned the cards turned up by the seer. "Stormy Heather. That was the card she drew for the present. It showed someone getting hit by lightning."

"And Hank told you he saw a flash of lightning right before the, uh . . . fire-snake attacked the Unseen Creeping Horror."

She nodded. "That deck was a magical artifact, Chad."

"I figured as much when it shuffled itself."

"I thought the cards might be spelled to shake down the rubes, but now . . ." The witch stood so suddenly she knocked over her chair, startling a grumble of protest from Keyser. "We have to go back."

"Back?" he repeated. "To the park?"

"To the Midnight Carnival."

In contrast to the witch's last visit, the bright colors and tilting calliope music felt eerie. Almost ominous.

The crowd was a little thinner, and it included far fewer tentacles—most likely due to the Unseen Creeping Horror's recent demise. The handful of Archons on the midway seemed tense and subdued, but she didn't think they were grieving. The ol' cosmic horrors weren't known for their sentimentality. They were practically immortal, but they could—and did—kill each other in combat on rare occasions. News of an Archonic death was generally received with matter-of-fact acceptance. But cold-ichored murder?

That was a different kettle of eels.

Tophet County's humans, on the other hand, were out in full force. No doubt, they'd heard rumors about the Black Galley. They might've even seen the UCH go up in flames. But how were they to know these events weren't just more of the usual eldritch shenanigans? Sharing the Earth with a menagerie of chthonic nightmares had resulted in a pretty godsdamned unflappable populace.

"So you and Hank will be, uh . . . working together on the moon-beast relief effort?" Chad asked.

"Not anymore," the witch said distractedly. She scanned the tents and booths lining the midway. Where was Sideshow Barbie's pink palace? "Ellie decided to make Achartho and N'eithamiqug take that on. She said it would do them good." She spotted the glistening membranes of the Tunnel of Love thirty-odd feet ahead. They were getting close. "Hank's still going to help out. The Clerk had him round up the moon-beasts and get them settled in the cavern. He was trying to teach them to play Irish drinking songs when I left."

Chad's face relaxed. "Then you're off the hook?"

"Unfortunately not." Keyser wriggled irritably in her arms. The witch put him down, and he tore off toward the food trucks to beg for treats. "I hadn't quite finished filling you in."

"Oh yeah? What—"

"Hello, young lovers!" called a familiar voice. The barker from last night. Same striped vest. Same suggestive eyebrow dance. "Can I interest you in a trip through the Tunnel of Love?"

She hit him with a temporary mute.

"I told you how Sathach's on a ghost-hunting kick, right?"

"Yeah," Chad said. "Poor guy seems pretty tightly wound these days."

"If the wind blows, he chalks it up to paranormal activity. Meanwhile, I'm more interested in, you know, reality."

"Sure."

"The thing is, Sathach's EMF meter *did* turn red just before the attack, and then Hank saw that freaking fire-snake, and something's been talking to us through the dumbass spirit box." The witch chewed her lower lip. "I know there's a logical explanation, but Ellie thinks the woo-woo shit is worth considering."

Chad shrugged. "Fair enough."

"So she's bringing back the WTF."

"Seriously?" His eyebrows tried to climb right into his locs. "To do what?"

"Investigate," the witch said. "The Black Galley, the moon-beasts, the UCH . . . all the spooky hits."

"That job seems solidly in Sheriff territory. Why wouldn't Ellie ask *him* to—"

"He already ate a moon-beast and destroyed any possible evidence."

"Good point," Chad said. "When's our first meeting?"

The witch winced. "I asked for you, but Ellie really wants you focused on . . ." She closed her eyes. He'd hate being left out. Surely, she could give him this one small thing. "Tootle Translate. Anyway, I'm hoping it'll all be sorted out by the time you're done with the app."

"But Magnolia's a civilian now," he said. "And Vera's . . . out of pocket. Is it just you and the Dread Lord of Human Resources?"

"For now." She spotted a flash of crimson up ahead—the seer's patchwork tent, if she wasn't mistaken—and picked up the pace. "Ellie said we can recruit people as we need them. Sathach had to run home for a video chat with Heather and the twins, so we're having our first meeting tomorrow at ten."

"Tomorrow's Sunday."

"I know. Working on the weekend is bullshit, but—"

Chad grabbed her elbow and tugged her to a halt. "We're supposed to have brunch with my parents in the morning."

The witch couldn't quite suppress a shudder of dread. The words *parents* and *brunch* and *morning* were bad enough on their own, but together? She hadn't exactly *forgotten* about their plans—more like she'd blocked them from her memory in an act of desperate self-preservation.

"We've already rescheduled twice," he said. "I'm starting to think you don't want to meet them."

"Of course I do!" And she did. Theoretically. But the prospect of actually *doing* it filled her with existential dread. "The UCH was murdered, Chad. I'm sure they'll understand."

His expression softened. "I guess you're right," he said. "Next weekend for sure, though?"

"For sure."

The witch grabbed his hand and pulled him toward the Tent of Doom.

Sibyl's sign had fallen off its folding chair and lay face up on the midway, its surface marked with shoe prints and tentacle trails. Chad retrieved it, brushed it off, and propped it up again, but the sign wasn't the only thing amiss. The fairy lights climbing the tent's poles were unlit, and the interior was dark behind the gauzy curtain.

"Maybe she's closed."

"On Saturday night of the Carnival's first weekend?" The witch shook her head. "I don't think so."

The sweet-and-savory smell of roasting meat filled her nose—not a surprise this close to the food carts. But the aroma carried an acrid, sulfuric tinge, and the air itself felt heavy. Charged. Her witchly spidey senses were on full alert. She didn't like this one bit.

The pallid drape of gray gauze rustled as they drew closer.

"Someone's already in there," Chad said. "We should probably—"

His voice ended in a panicked squeal as a creature burst through the curtain's flap, climbed him like a tree, and wrapped its stubby arms around his neck.

"Get it off, get it off!"

The witch peeled a quivering bundle of wiry hair away from Chad's neck to reveal the wizened, tear-streaked face of Sibyl's . . . pet, Jenkin. She deposited him on the folding chair and locked eyes with Chad.

"It's going to be bad in there," she said.

"I know."

He took her hand, and they stepped through the curtain.

The cooked meat smell was so thick and strong it nearly triggered the witch's sensitive gag reflex. Underneath it was the cloying fruity note she'd noticed last night, which added extra *ick* to the nauseating bouquet.

What in gods' names . . .

Then her eyes adjusted to the dim light, and she understood.

Sibyl's blackened corpse sat in her pink velvet chair. Her hair and clothes had been burned away, but the witch instantly recognized the pink enamel hoops still hanging from her ears. The fingertips of her charred right hand rested on the deck of Garbage Pail Kids cards, as though she'd been on the verge of flipping one over. Only the fact that the witch had barely nibbled her Hot Pocket saved her from hurling. Chad, on the other hand, squeezed her hand, gagged, and fled the tent. He started retching as soon as he made it outside.

The witch forced herself to scan the tent through a veil of shock-induced tears, comparing what she saw now to what she'd observed last night. Impossibly, the chair Sibyl sat in was totally intact, the cards were unharmed, and the white table bore not so much as a smudge of ash. The reading area was precisely as she remembered it. But the bookshelves . . . those were different. The *LIVE, LAUGH, LOVE!* sign still assaulted her eyes, but the rest of Sibyl's collection was gone. No eggbeater. No stripped umbrella. No eccentric glassware. The obvious conclusion was that whoever took the stuff was the killer, but who would want that junk? And why?

The curtain rustled behind her.

"Don't come in, Chad," she said without turning. "Just . . . just call Spectral Forces. We need to—"

"Sibyl . . ."

The voice was hollow and tinny, like someone talking into an aluminum can, and it most definitely didn't belong to Chad. The witch pivoted to face the doorway. A gleaming orb of quicksilver floated in the opening, spinning slowly. She recognized the Archon immediately—she'd seen him only last night.

"Phæras?"

The silver core drifted toward her.

"Witch, we need to talk."

CHAPTER EIGHT

Full Nutjob

Chad poked his head into the tent, squeezing his eyes shut to block out the horrific scene.

"Spectral Forces is en route," he said. "Do you . . ." His Adam's apple bobbed as he battled a surge of nausea. " . . . want me to come in?"

Phæras hung in the air less than a foot from Chad's nose. His shining orb twisted sharply from side to side, a clear request not to announce his presence.

The witch hesitated. After her colossal Carcosa cock-up last year, she wasn't too keen on hiding things, but Phæras's visit didn't have to *stay* hidden. She could hear him out and fill Chad in after she left the tent.

"I'm good, Chad," she said. "I'll be out in a few."

He nodded, relief evident on his face, and backed out into the comparatively fresh night air.

Phæras drifted a few feet closer to Sibyl's remains. "If only I'd gotten here faster," he said in a metallic whisper. "I should've portaled, but I was afraid the renegade would feel me coming."

"What renegade?" She gestured toward the blackened body. "Do you mean *her*?"

"You're leading the inquiry into Yi'danag's death," he said.

It wasn't a question.

The witch supposed she shouldn't be surprised that word had traveled so fast. Half of Tophet County's Archons had turned up at the scene of the Unseen Creeping Horror's murder. The squidwards' gossip hotline rivaled a middle school lunch table.

"Is that why we need to talk?"

Phæras bobbed in an approximation of a nod. "That . . ." He rotated slowly, his focus shifting from the charred corpse to the empty baby pink bookshelves. "And this."

"This?" She swept her gaze around the tent. "Phæras, *this* is a crime scene. Lomelzar's office will—"

As if summoned by speaking the Sheriff's name, the shrill ululation of a siren cut through the background noise of the Midnight Carnival. Lomelzar must've had goons near the fairgrounds.

Phæras's mirrored surface rippled in agitation. "I'll gladly talk to *you*, Witch," he said, "as an anonymous source. But you know as well as I do that I'll be spending the night in a windowless cell if I officially come forward."

That was actually the best-case scenario. The Sheriff's investigative strategy was *liquefy first, ask questions later.*

"My next break is at eleven." A flat disc of netherlight appeared beneath his hovering orb. "We can talk in my trailer."

"Hold up a second!"

"Bring the cards," he said. "They tried to warn her too."

"Can we just—"

But Phæras was already gone.

Her stomach clenched, and it wasn't just the sights and smells of the tent. She could feel old mistakes lining up, ready to be made anew. A secret source of information. A clandestine offer of assistance. An off-the-record conversation.

Well, to hell with that.

The witch would be the first to admit she was prone to screwups. But, whenever possible, she liked to screw up in new and interesting ways rather than repeating the same tired missteps. She'd talk to Phæras, but she'd ask Chad to come with her. And she'd bring the cards if she could, but she'd do it on the up-and-up—*after* the forensics folks did a sweep of the scene.

No more secrets. No more lies.

She turned to leave and nearly stepped into a growing octarine starburst.

Another portal. Maybe Phæras had reconsidered.

But it was the Dread Lord of Human Resources who stepped through the shimmering oval, accompanied by a symphony of rubbery squeaks.

The witch gaped at him. "How in Discordia's name did you—"

"I heard the call come in on my police scanner," Sathach said, staring down at his EMF meter. "The dispatcher said you were already on the scene." He jabbed a triumphant finger at the display as the colored lights shifted from orange to yellow. "Aha! A recent paranormal presence!"

Phæras's metallic core generated an electromagnetic field. Nothing paranormal about that.

Nothing *abnormally* paranormal.

She opened her mouth to explain, but his crossed eyes landed on Sibyl's body, and he gasped.

"Azathoth's tears," he lisped. "Spontaneous human combustion!"

"Assigned to *me*?" The witch glared at the stone-faced plainclothes detective, who clearly didn't like the situation any more than she did. "What do you mean, Mayor Dawson assigned this case to me?"

Sathach looked up from his thermal imager. "To *us*," he corrected.

"Since when does the mayor's office stick its snout into Lomelzar's domain?"

Detective Parker ran a hand through her short red hair. "Since now. She said the carny's death appears to be related to what went down at the park."

Two deaths by immolation in less than twelve hours . . .

Yeah, Ellie could be onto something.

"The body's en route to the morgue," Parker said. "The ME will send over autopsy results in a few days. We'll get you the crime scene investigation report too. The Fire Marshal didn't see any obvious signs of arson, but—"

"Because it was not arson." The Dread Lord slid the imager into its nylon holster. "It was spontaneous human combustion."

"Sathach," the witch snapped. "Could we *not*?"

"I'm getting awfully tired of your arbitrary skepticism."

The lead crime scene tech, an Archon who looked like a mop with a pelican's beak and way too many arms, chuckled and shook her head. "Spontaneous human combustion?" She snorted. "Nice one, Spooky Sathach."

Detective Parker arched an eyebrow at the witch. "On that note, I'll leave you to it." She held out a clear plastic evidence bag, pinching the edge between thumb and forefinger as though it contained recently scooped dog shit instead of a deck of cards. "As requested."

Lurid Garbage Pail Kids leered at her through the bag. "Don't you need to, like . . . dust them for prints or something?"

"We tried," Parker said. "The dust wouldn't stick, our swabs melted on contact, and the techs kept getting paper cuts. Anyway, I highly doubt they're germane to the case." She shook the bag at the witch, who took the hint and grabbed it. "Good riddance. I *hate* magic."

"Oh yeah?"

The detective didn't even flinch at the witch's best "fuck around and find out" smirk. "Yeah."

"What about all that stuff missing from the bookshelves?" she asked. "You'll let me know if any stolen shit turns up . . . like, on the black market?"

Detective Parker slid a notepad from her shirt pocket and opened it to the inventory the witch had provided based on a screenshot from her palace of memory.

"Let's see here," Parker said. "One kinetic ball sculpture, assorted glassware, a magnifying glass, a vintage eggbeater, a fluid-filled glass cylinder—"

"It's called a Galileo thermometer," the witch said.

Having a nerdy boyfriend came in handy sometimes.

Boyfriend.

She filed that away for future consideration.

"—a clockwork 'something,'" Parker continued.

"I couldn't tell what it was!"

"—a broken umbrella, 'a bunch of weird metal shit,' and a pink journal." She flipped the notebook closed and returned it to her pocket. "Sounds like black market gold to me."

"You don't have to be a dick about it."

"I don't *have* to." Parker looked over her shoulder and caught the lead tech's eye. "All packed up?" The Archon's beak dipped in acknowledgment. "All right, let's roll out."

"Roll out? Already?"

"The tent's a twelve-foot square and neat as a pin. Doesn't take long to process a space this size. Besides," Parker said, "it's *your* case."

"But what if you missed something?"

The detective shrugged. "Not my circus, not my nightgaunts."

Gods dammit, the Clerk was right. That was freaking *infuriating.*

In a matter of seconds, the tent was empty, save for the witch and Sathach.

"Can you believe it?" He rubbed his hands together, producing a flurry of plastic-y chirps. "Another anomaly!"

"I suspect it's more of the same one."

"Is not."

"What makes you so sure?"

"Observe, Witch." Sathach pointed at Sibyl's pristine chair. "Despite the fact that the vic's body was burned to a crisp, her chair remains intact." He bent and sniffed the tufted pink velvet. "Not so much as a whiff of smoke."

"Don't they make fire-retardant fabric?"

Granted, it would have to be *very* fire-retardant.

"And those atrocious cards," he said, "which are made of paper, I might add, weren't even singed by the blaze."

They *were* uncharacteristically flame-resistant, she had to give him that. But still…

What happened to the Unseen Creeping Horror had most definitely *not* been spontaneous combustion. It was an attack: murder by fire-snake. And it stood to reason that Sibyl's fiery death had come at the hands (or flaming tentacles, if Monsieur Flambé was the guilty party) of the same killer.

"This deck is magicked to hell and back, Sathach," she said. "I can feel it through the bag."

Which was a little strange, come to think of it. Most magical artifacts were incredibly difficult to detect when they weren't in active use.

The Dread Lord executed a reverse mind-flaying sneak attack, filling her third eye with an image of the post-conflagration Black Galley. "Where are the ship's masts?" he asked. "Where is the figurehead?"

"They . . ." Oh, Lordess. He might have an actual point. "They burned up in the fire."

"Exactly." Sathach directed a pointed gaze at the thoroughly unburnt crime scene. "I rest my—"

"Can we head out now, Witch?" Chad pushed through the curtain. Keyser Söze perched on his shoulder, clutching a handful of hair. "I'm totally wiped."

"You and me both," the witch said. "We just need to swing by Phæras's trailer." She'd told Chad and Sathach about her brief and bizarre exchange with Phæras while the forensics team went over the tent with a fine-toothed mandible. "He said his next break was at eleven, right? What time is it now?"

Chad fished his BlackBerry out of his pocket. "10:33. We've got plenty of time to—"

The buzz of an incoming text message cut him off mid-sentence. He frowned and tapped the screen.

"I shall accompany you," Sathach said. "We must rule out Phæras's involvement."

"But he got here *after* I found the body. He couldn't have been involved."

"Phæras is an Archon. He could've portaled out when he heard you and Chad arrive"—Sathach vanished in a flare of netherlight and waved to her from outside the tent—"and returned after you found the body." He reappeared at the witch's side.

"True, but—"

"Actually, Witch," Chad said, "I think I'll head back to my place."

She blinked in surprise. "Oh. Okay. Don't you want to hear what Phæras has to say?"

"I *do*, but . . ." Keyser squirmed on his shoulder, and Chad gently lowered him to the earthen floor. "I'm not technically part of the WTF yet, so Phæras might feel more comfortable if it's just you and the Dread Lord."

Huh. She hadn't thought about how he'd react to Chad's presence.

"Good point," she said. "I'll swing by on my way home and fill you in."

"No!" He winced at the sharpness of his own voice and held up a hand in apology. "I'm sorry, Witch. I'm tired and jumpy. This has all been a bit much." He stared fixedly at the ground between her Doc Martens. "I just need to crash. And I should probably wake up early and get a jump start on Tootle Translate."

The witch shoved aside what felt suspiciously like hurt feelings and forced a smile. "I get it. So . . . maybe I'll see you tomorrow?"

Chad flashed a quick smile, but his forehead was still creased with tension. "Yeah," he said. "Maybe."

With twenty-odd minutes to make a two-minute walk, the witch saw no reason to deny Keyser Söze's ardent-yet-unspoken plea for a snack. Sathach furtively scanned passers-by with his paranormal playthings while she stood in line at the Rat-Things-Onna-Stick cart. Once she returned with her purchases (black coffee for her, Junior Rat-Thing—hold the stick—for Keyser), she joined the Dread Lord on a bench painted to resemble a clown's gaping mouth. She propped herself up on the uvula, took a tongue-scalding gulp of coffee, and sighed.

"So how are the offspring?"

Sathach holstered his EMF meter and pulled out his phone. "Bigger every day," he said. "Barclay says our wee witchling is keeping him on his toes." He showed her a picture of two squishy faces surrounded by a mound of primary-colored plastic toys.

The witch barely managed to smother the *awwww* that bubbled up of its own accord. Instead, she went with a more dignified "Cute."

What was it about even a photo of those round little dumplings that made her want to talk in a high-pitched, singsong voice? Must be Sawyer's burgeoning witchly power . . . or was it Skyler's?

As they sat in semi-awkward silence, the witch realized she hadn't had a real conversation with Sathach in weeks. Now that they were alone, she had a perfect opportunity to do a little delicate digging, to figure out what sent him down this ghost-filled rabbit hole.

"So, uh . . . what made you go full nutjob?"

"That is offensive, Witch." He snatched his phone and sat up straighter. "Just because my worldview is not aligned with yours—"

"Or with, you know, the *world*."

"—is no reason for mockery. I could make the argument that you are injecting hostility into the workplace."

Well, you can take the tentacled monster out of HR, but you can't take HR out of the tentacled monster.

"I'm trying to inject reality."

He stiffened, outraged, but she reached out a tentative hand and rested it on his rubbery forearm.

"Seriously, Sathach. I know I suck at this, but I . . ."

I'm worried about you.

"Help me understand," she said.

His lower lip quivered. Yellow-gray goo began to pool in the corners of his eyes.

Oh, gods. Oh no. *Discordia, deliver me from—*

"I don't know how to be a good father," he wailed. "I watched a lot of daytime TV during my parental leave, and . . . and Dr. Bill always says the best dads learned from having a great dad themselves . . . only I never knew mine . . . and . . ."

"We don't have to talk about it." The witch's words flew out on a cresting tide of panic. "You do you. You want to chase ghosts? Sign up with Scoob and the gang. I'm totally on board with—"

"One of the twins is always awake, always hungry, or wet, or generally dissatisfied with the service. I can't shake the feeling that I'm doing this wrong, you know?" He wiped his eyes, and slimy strands stretched from his fingertips to his face. "I started watching this show called *Plum Island Medium*, and I thought, why not try to make contact with my father? What could it hurt? It made the people on the show feel so much better. I just . . . I wanted to feel better too."

"Mm-hmm. I get it."

The witch yearned to flee into the crowd, but she was trapped. Keyser Söze, that godsdamned traitor, finished his Junior Rat-Thing, cast a sidelong glance at Sathach, and disappeared behind the You Bring It, We'll Fry It truck.

"So I tried," he said. "I didn't even know his name—Mother has been *most* unhelpful—but I tried. I reached out with all my power. I mind-flayed the universe itself searching for any sign of my father."

"And there was nothing." The witch squeezed his arm, feeling the anxious writhing of tentacles beneath his Skyn. "That must've been—"

"No," he said. "Something took notice. I was immediately beset by paranormal phenomena. The lights flicked on and off. Drawers slammed open and shut in unoccupied rooms. And I started to hear whispers, just at the edge of my hearing."

"You've got a witchling in the house, Sathach," the witch said. "Until she can control her power—"

"It's not her. I know the feel of her magic as well as I know my own." He shook his head. "This is something else. Something sinister. And I cannot let it harm Sawyer and Skyler."

His left eye met hers. The right rolled restlessly in its socket.

"Witch, I must protect my children."

CHAPTER NINE

A Blowtorch and a Pair of Brass Balls

The witch pointed at a vintage Airstream tucked behind rows of empty Phæras Wheel gondolas. "That's it, right?"

"That's it." Sathach stared up at the constellation of cars sailing through the night sky. "We're a few minutes early. Shall we find a place to—"

A man's body flew out of the shadowed gap between the Phæras Wheel's ticket booth and the neighboring attraction, landing at the Dread Lord's feet with a muffled *oof.* The ground shook beneath the pounding footfalls of a towering Archon who looked like an inverted squid with goat's legs.

"If you want to peep," the Archon said in a husky female voice, "you have to pay."

The witch glanced up at the faded marquee over the tent's curtained entrance. *Sphinxter's Peep Show: A Salacious & Scintillating Archonic Revue!* Not her personal cup of Chicken Cock, but plenty of humans were keen to get down and dirty with a chthonic horror.

The man groaned and rolled onto his back, revealing an impressive physique, a chiseled jawline, and . . .

And a godsdamned dimpled chin.

"Hank?"

"Hi, Witch," he wheezed with a shade less chirpy enthusiasm than usual.

The Archonic bouncer jabbed a tentacle in Hank's direction. "Friend of yours?"

"Uh . . . yeah."

"Well, he owes me eight tickets." The bouncer clacked her chitinous beak in a not-so-veiled threat. "Or his eyes. Either will do."

A reflexive surge of entropine flooded the witch's bloodstream. She stepped forward, placing herself between Hank and the agitated Archon, but Sathach rested a hand on her shoulder and leaned in close to her ear.

"I'll smooth this over," he said in a low voice. "Help Deputy O'Brien up and send him on his way." He straightened his tie and pasted on a smile. "Greetings, burly friend!"

The witch offered Hank her hand and tugged him to his feet. "I know the Sheriff pays you enough to buy tickets," she said in a harsh whisper. "What's with the Peeping Tom bullshit?"

He smiled and shrugged. "I don't know!"

She waited for him to elaborate, but he just stood there grinning a faintly confused grin.

"What are you even doing here?" she asked. "I thought you were babysitting moon-beasts."

Hank's smooth forehead creased in a frown. "I was, but I was starving. Cooper and Woods said they'd keep an eye on the cavern, so I . . ." His eyes drifted to the peep show tent, and he sniffed the air. "Doesn't it smell delicious?"

Whatever eldritch aroma permeated the interior of that tent, the witch highly doubted it smelled *delicious*.

She grabbed his ears and tugged his head down to eye level, running a hand over his scalp to check for goose eggs. "Did you hit your head when you landed?"

"Nope!"

"Well, food's *that* way." She gripped his shoulders, aimed him toward the food trucks, and gave him a gentle push. "And take the rest of the night off. Witch's orders."

He stumbled down the midway, sniffing the air like a bloodhound.

The witch shook her head. That man needed a drink, a shag, or a vacation. Probably all three . . . and he wasn't the only one.

She turned and rejoined Sathach and the squid-goat, who were huddled around Sathach's phone cooing at a video of the twins blowing spit bubbles.

"So adorable!" squealed the bouncer.

"Thank you," he said. "Witch, this is Mh'imbra." He swept a courtly hand toward the witch. "Mh'imbra, meet Magna Innominanda, the witch of Tophet County."

"Just 'Witch' will do," she said, shaking the proffered tentacle. "So what happened here?"

Mh'imbra's smile faded. "He's not our first peeper. I circle the tent a few times a night, and I nab a perv maybe one time in ten. There's a certain type that gets as much titillation out of the peeping as they do from what they see." She stared at Hank's retreating back, shifting restlessly on her hircine hooves. "That one's an odd duck, though."

"How's that?"

"From where he was standing," Mh'imbra said, "all he could see was the audience."

"An unknown Archon?" The Dread Lord shook his head. "That's impossible."

"This is exactly why I wanted to talk to *you*, Witch." An annoyed wave of spiky protuberances rose from Phæras's smooth orb. Defying the absence of both lungs and mouth, he heaved a tinny sigh. "I knew no Archon would believe me."

"I believe that *you* believe it," Sathach said.

"What do you mean by unknown?" The witch leaned against the Airstream's bare metal wall, trying to ignore the discomfort of her bony backside digging into the corrugated floor. Phæras's invitation to *have a seat and make yourself comfortable* was proving to be a real challenge. "Unknown to *you?*"

"Unknown to anyone," Phæras said. "The individual in question is not party to our contract."

"That's preposterous." Sathach's lisp misted the orb with a fine spray of saliva. "All Archons are added to the master contract as juveniles, and the only cause for termination is collusion with the Swarm. Everyone knows that."

The witch arched an eyebrow at him. "Everyone *also* knows there's no such thing as ghosts."

One eye swiveled and glared at her, but Sathach pressed on. "The Swarm absorbed everyone left behind in our home universe," he said. "And Mother said the Morpheus Gate was sealed, so no one could've escaped to the Dreamlands. Even if they had, the Swarm took the Dreamlands sometime after the Emergence, so any Archon hiding there would've been assimilated."

"I don't know, Sathach . . ." The witch's inner sight replayed the arrival of the Black Galley. "We've got a boatful of moon-beasts that sure as hell came from *somewhere*."

"True." He chewed his lip so hard he bit right through it with the Skyn's Chiclet-esque veneers. "But moon-beasts are not Archons."

The witch gazed at her reflection in Phæras's silver sphere. "Can you walk us through the whole thing again?"

He floated around the small space in a lazy circle, giving the impression of pacing. "I was working the Wheel this morning when I felt a massive burst of electromagnetic energy."

"The unknown Archon?"

"No. The energy burst occurred right before Yi'danag . . ."

Phæras drifted to a halt, and his voice trailed off. The Unseen Creeping Horror's agonized shriek echoed through the halls of the witch's palace of memory. She shivered and shoved the recollection away.

"Okay, so you felt this burst of energy, then the UCH was attacked," she said. "Then what?"

"I detected an unknown portal signature leaving the park."

The witch turned questioning eyes to Sathach, who shrugged.

"What's a portal signature?" she asked.

"Because of my physiology, I can sense Archonic teleportation," Phæras said. "I usually don't pay much attention. It's just passive sensory input, like being at a dinner party and hearing the conversations around you without really listening."

The witch, who'd never been to a dinner party in her life, nodded. "Got it."

"Just as humans have distinct voices, every Archon has a unique etheric footprint," he said. "Immediately after the attack, I felt an Archon portal away from Dunwich Park—an Archon whose 'footprint' does not belong to anyone on the master contract."

The Dread Lord opened his mouth, but the witch blew an entropic kiss at him and it snapped shut again.

"Where did this mysterious Archon's portal lead?"

"I don't know," Phæras said. "The only reason I noticed the signature in the first place was that my attention was already focused on that location. To pick up the destination, I'd have had to be paying active attention to the point of egress, and it would need to be within the range of my abilities."

"And you're *sure* you couldn't have read the signature wrong?" the witch asked. "What happened to Yi'danag was pretty freaking traumatic for all of us."

"It was." Phæras's smooth spin stuttered in momentary agitation. "And I wondered the same thing, but then I detected the same etheric footprint again this evening."

A mental puzzle piece clicked into place.

"The renegade," she said. "When you came to Sibyl's tent, you said you should've portaled in, but you were afraid the renegade would know you were coming. You meant—"

"The unknown Archon," Phæras said. "I'd been keeping an eye on nearby portal activity all afternoon while I ran the Wheel. When I sensed that signature within the fairgrounds, I was so shocked I nearly dropped a gondola. I stopped the ride and got to the source as fast as I could, but . . . but I was too late."

"Ahem," the Dread Lord said. "I am very sorry for your loss."

The orb's mirrored surface rippled in acknowledgment, but Phæras made no spoken reply.

"Are you, uh . . . cool to keep talking?" the witch asked. He bobbed in affirmation. "Did anybody else portal out of the park when the UCH was attacked?"

"Many Archons portaled in afterward," Phæras said, a jagged note evident in his metallic voice. "But *out?*" He pivoted in a head-shaking motion. "No."

"That," the witch said, "is very godsdamned interesting."

"How so?"

"The Unquenchable Flame was standing watch when Yi'danag was murdered," she said. "We were on the scene within seconds, but he was gone by the time we got there."

"He could've fled on foot," the Dread Lord said.

The witch smirked. "He doesn't have feet."

"Then he couldn't have an etheric footprint either, could he?"

Nicely played, Sathach.

"Phæras, is there any way the Flame could've changed his portal-signature thing?" she asked.

"Can you change your fingerprints?"

"I'm the witch of Tophet County," she said. "If you want, I can make them say 'Eat a bag of dicks' in Ouranian-Barbaric."

In fact, she made a mental note to do just that—and then she'd find her way to that smart-ass detective's next crime scene.

Phæras gave an irritable spin. "Can a *normal human* change her fingerprints?"

"No, but if she had a blowtorch and a pair of brass balls, she could burn them off." The witch stood, unable to bear another second of the steel floor's gluteal torture. "Just because we don't know how to do it doesn't mean it can't be done."

Sathach rose to his feet and braced his hands on his hips. "Deputy O'Brien's account was quite clear, Witch. The attacker was a mystical serpent."

"Made of *blue fire.*"

The Dread Lord closed his eyes and took a deep breath, then released it in a multi-orifice exhalation. "Ahem. Phæras, this is perhaps an . . . indelicate question," he said, "but would you mind terribly if I took a look for myself?"

 The orb wobbled alarmingly. "You wish to flay my mind?"

"You *were* the first to arrive at a murder scene," the Dread Lord said, "and it seems—"

"I was the second," Phæras amended. "The witch preceded me."

"And Chad was with me, so he was actually the third."

"Not the point, Witch," Sathach said through gritted teeth. "I'm simply suggesting we confirm the details of Phæras's account."

"I have nothing to hide," he said. "Flay away."

The Dread Lord plunged his head into the gleaming orb, startling an undignified squeak from the witch. He withdrew mere seconds later and furrowed his Ken-doll brow.

"Phæras speaks the truth."

"Now we're getting somewhere," the witch said. "That means an unknown Archon was present at the scene of two murders."

Suspect . . . check.

A few more clues, and she could cancel the Sunday morning WTF meeting and have this shit wrapped up in time for brunch.

Or maybe just after brunch.

"Ahem, Witch," Sathach said, "is Keyser Söze in your backpack?"

She snorted and looked at her half-empty bag, which she'd dropped by the door on her way in. "Does it look like there's an overfed—"

The canvas twitched.

"What the shivering shit . . ."

She snatched the bag and unzipped it. All it contained was her wallet, her keys, a magically camouflaged copy of *Chaste Makes Waste*, and . . .

And Sibyl's cards, which were shuffling themselves inside the evidence bag. She yanked the plastic bag out of her backpack and dropped it on Phæras's coffee table—the sole piece of furniture in his trailer.

"Is that normal behavior for magical artifacts?" Sathach asked.

"Nope." She ripped open the tamper-proof seal and spilled the cards onto the table, where they began a skillful riffle. "Artifacts are kind of like batteries. They store up magic for a specific purpose. Witches made them out of mundane crap so they could fly under the radar back in the pre-Emergence days. They're supposed to lie around and look innocent until a witch or a wielder activates them."

She knelt next to the table, ignoring the metal ridges digging into her knee-caps, and glanced up at Phæras. "You asked me to bring these cards," she said. "Why?"

He descended toward the table. "Look."

Three familiar cards formed a row on the brushed metal surface: Split Kit, Stormy Heather, and Fryin' Ryan.

"Son of a star-spawn," the witch said. "These are the same cards Sibyl showed me last night."

"And the same ones she received for every reading she did after yours." The bright gleam of Phæras's orb seemed to dim. "The deck even dealt them out while she was sleeping. It really spooked her, and she said poor Jenkin was so upset he babbled all night."

The witch imagined the creature's wrinkly old man face gibbering in her ear while she tried to sleep. She shuddered. Sibyl must've *really* loved animals.

"From what I've read, it can be a real witch to figure out what an artifact's meant to do." She stared at the chubby-cheeked images. "But this deck certainly seems inclined to prognostication. An eyewitness saw a flash of lightning just before the UCH's murder—that's pretty godsdamned Stormy Heather-ish. As for the others . . ." The witch shook her head. "No freaking clue."

"The other artifacts?" Phæras asked.

"The deck's all one artifact."

"Ah," he said. "You meant the other two cards."

The witch frowned. "As opposed to?"

"As opposed to the rest of Sibyl's collection." In response to her blank stare, he added, "You know—the eggbeater, the umbrella, the thermometer . . ."

"All that stuff from her bookshelves?" she asked. "What about it?"

Phæras's orb tilted on its axis, telegraphing mild puzzlement. "I thought you knew."

"Apparently, I do not."

"Every one of those items is a magical artifact. When Sibyl told me, I advised her to keep her collection hidden, but she said one of the items provides passive concealment. It makes you think what you see is nothing but—"

"Worthless junk," the witch said.

Magical artifacts were practically priceless. Violent crime wasn't all that common given the immediate and permanent consequences of getting caught, but plenty of wielders would do some dirt to get their hands on even *one* of them.

Motive . . . *check.*

Sathach and the witch exchanged a glance. Nearly fourteen years as coworkers infused it with a conversation's worth of nonverbal communication. The witch gave a tight nod.

"Ahem, Phæras," the Dread Lord said, "are you perchance free tomorrow morning?"

CHAPTER TEN

The Aisle of R'lyeh

An unregistered Archon." The Clerk's six eyes exchanged a dubious glance. "I don't doubt your abilities, Phæras, but I cannot imagine how such a thing could be possible."

The guttering torches that lit Derleth Memorial Library's Read at Your Own Risk room produced flickering reflections in his mirrored orb.

"Nor can I," Phæras said, "but I know what I sensed."

Though the WTF technically had only three members—the witch, Sathach, and, as of last night, Phæras—the RAYOR room was stuffed to capacity. Ellie Dawson was in attendance to ensure she stayed mayorally abreast of the latest developments. The Clerk and Hank came to provide updates on moon-beast management and the search for the Unquenchable Flame. And since the Dread Librarian was already in the building, she was sitting in on the off chance of learning information that could help with . . .

The witch trembled with sympathetic mortification.

Tootle Translate.

She'd texted Chad to see if he wanted to join remotely, but his answer was unusually brusque.

NERD-ROMANCER: Can't. Busy.
WITCH: Right. Brunch. Any updates to share?
NERD-ROMANCER: Nothing yet.
WITCH: Want me to stop by & fill you in after?
NERD-ROMANCER: No thx.

It was an awkward exchange, but at least he'd responded. She'd texted him last night and sat up restrawing her whole-ass broom while she waited to hear back. Nada. The witch had a sneaking suspicion he'd picked up on her reluctance to meet his parents and was . . . pissed? Hurt? Offended? She'd never had parents to threaten a romantic partner with—or a romantic partner to threaten, for that matter. Odds were she'd stepped in social-graces shit. Again.

Which meant they'd probably have to *talk*.

About their *feelings*.

She shuddered and turned her attention back to the much less terrifying topic of a possible serial killer. She'd save the scary stuff for later.

Ellie unfolded a lap desk from the left arm of her wheelchair and jotted a few notes on a yellow legal pad. "Mr., ah, Wheel—"

"Please call me Phæras," he said. "All are welcome to use my given name."

The Clerk's shroud gave a huffy rustle, but she didn't protest.

"Thank you, Phæras," Ellie said. "You said the renegade couldn't alter their etheric footprint, but could they have disguised it? I'm thinking of a process analogous to encrypting a radio signal."

His direction of spin tilted off-center, giving the impression of a cocked head. "I'm not sure how one would accomplish it," he said, "but I suppose it's theoretically possible." Phæras pivoted and scanned the shelves. "Chlogha, would you mind pulling *The Cryptonomicon* and *The Quantumnomicon* for me? After we adjourn, I'd like to stay and do a little research."

"Happy to help."

The Dread Librarian hopped to the shelves. A grievously sunburned *Necronomicon* lay open page-side-down, its crimson hide liberally smeared with greenish aloe gel. Chlogha bypassed it, pulled two thick volumes, and thunked them down on the table. The books stirred up a cloud of the artificial dust scattered throughout the RAYOR room for atmosphere, prompting the witch to sneeze eight times in rapid succession.

"I'll stay too, if you don't mind." Ellie smiled up at her reflection in Phæras's gleaming orb. "Two heads are better than one."

Especially if one of those heads belonged to the Nobel-nominated supergenius who'd co-authored the Q.

The witch consulted the agenda she'd dashed off on a Post-it during the broom ride over. (Gods, she missed Magnolia. Her agendas were legendary—and she brought coffee and snacks.) Yep, all the information gathered by the WTF had been discussed ad infuriam.

"That's it for my list," she said. "The floor's open."

"High Lord Innominanda, you seem quite confident that both the Unseen Creeping Horror and . . ." Ellie turned apologetic eyes toward Phæras. "I'm so sorry, but I didn't catch your friend's name."

"Sibyl," he said, his tinny voice taut with emotion. "Sibyl Tiburtine."

Ellie repeated the name, allowing a moment of respectful silence before she locked eyes with the witch and spoke. "You seem certain both murders were committed by the same killer."

"Well, yeah." The witch shrugged. "It kind of beggars belief that we'd have two unrelated deaths by immolation within hours of each other. Plus, Phæras's renegade was there for both of them."

"Ahem. I'd like to point out that there are numerous differences between the two crime scenes."

"You already covered that, Sathach." The witch arched an eyebrow and glared at him. "Three times, if memory serves."

"Let's circle back to one of those dissimilarities." Ellie returned her laser-like focus to Phæras. "Do you have any theories to explain the burst of electromagnetic energy you sensed prior to the attack on the Unseen Creeping Horror?"

He rotated sharply from side to side. "I don't. All I can tell you is that it felt similar to lightning."

"Which brings us right back to Stormy Heather," the witch said. "Sibyl's cards aren't exactly the fortune-telling norm, but I'll try working with them this afternoon. Chad knows eighties pop culture. I can ask . . ."

. . . him for help.

Or at least she could if he was still speaking to her.

"An excellent idea," Ellie said, oblivious to the witch's angst. "The other detail I'm stuck on is the missing magical artifacts. I agree that theft would be a powerful motive in Sibyl's case, but I suspect the UCH's death is related to our recently arrived visitors." She shook her head. "If these murders are connected, I can't see how."

"That's because one of them wasn't a murder," the Dread Lord said. "Spontaneous human combustion is a paranormal—"

"Oh, for the love of Azathoth." The Clerk rolled all six eyes. "No wonder Lomelzar's team is calling you Spooky Sathach."

The witch bristled. She wasn't about to put up with some bird-brained crime scene tech talking trash about one of her best—

About the Dread Lord of Human Resources.

"Tell them I said to knock that shit off." She took a deep breath and cast a wary glance at Hank, on guard for any possible signs of smoldering. "How are the moon-beasts holding up?"

He grinned. "They've mostly learned 'The Widow and the Devil,' but they're having a little trouble with the bridge."

"Deputy O'Brien," the Clerk said, "I think the witch would like to hear about their general well-being."

"Oh. They seem okay," he said. "We put a few water coolers in the cavern, but they weren't interested. Then one of them stole all the ice cubes out of Cooper's Yeti mug. The Sheriff brought them an ice machine from Dante's Burgertory. Turns out they're *wild* for ice."

The Clerk's standard steely gaze softened. "Lomelzar did that?"

Oh, dear gods. If her on-again-off-again with the Sheriff switched on again one more time . . .

"What about food?" Ellie asked.

"We've tried all kinds of stuff." Hank ticked off options on his fingers. "Salads from Mile High Clubs, sticky 'nuts, rat-things—roasted *and* fresh . . . they won't eat any of it. I know they're starving, though. A few of them have been trying to eat rocks."

"Rocks?"

He nodded. "Yeah, but they just spit those out too."

"I wonder . . ." Ellie glanced at the Clerk. "Most of the rock found on the lunar surface is igneous."

"Bless you," Hank said.

"Igneous rock is formed from cooling lava," she continued. "We know nothing of moon-beast physiology. It could be a staple of their diet. I can't imagine there's much else they *could* eat on the Moon." Ellie wrote a note on her legal pad. "I'll call Dr. Carcosa. I'm sure he has contacts in the School of Earth Sciences at Catachthonic University. We'll get some samples and see if that tempts them."

"Any luck tracking down the Unquenchable Flame?" the witch asked.

The Clerk's shroud fluttered with a frustrated sigh. "I'm afraid not. His BlackBerry is off, and he hasn't returned to his residence. Wherever he is, he's staying off the grill."

"If we don't know where he *is*," the witch said, "maybe we should start with where he *was*. You said he just got back from two weeks of vacation, Sathach. Where'd he go?"

"It is not appropriate for me to discuss an employee's private affairs."

"I think an exception is warranted in this case, Dread Lord," Ellie said gently.

"I suppose I could share generalities." Sathach's Skyn squeaked as he shifted with obvious unease. "He was off on his annual . . . culinary adventure."

The witch frowned. "His what?"

"Flame only feeds once a year—"

"Once a *year*?" No wonder he was such a jerk. Hanger had that effect on her too.

"What does he eat?" Ellie asked.

"As I understand it, he eats . . ." The Dread Lord trailed off, drumming his fingers on the table.

"Spit it out, gods dammit!" the witch snapped.

"Ahem. Newborn stars."

"Newborn stars, you say?"

"Yes."

"And he eats them?"

"Indeed."

"Well, that's fucking weird."

"I'll thank you not to disparage another employee's dietary needs."

Chlogha cupped a hand around her wide mouth and leaned toward the witch. "But it *is* weird. And weak. I mean, what sort of Archon eats a vegan diet?"

"Come, now," the Clerk said. "The Unquenchable Flame cannot help being . . . different."

The witch felt an unexpected pang of something in the neighborhood of empathy. "Different how?"

"His name, for one thing." The Dread Librarian lowered her voice to a scandalized whisper. "He doesn't have one."

"What do you mean?" she asked. "He's the Unquenchable Flame."

"That is an . . . appellation," the Clerk said. "A sobriquet suitable for use by humans. But the rest of us have an Archonic name, a *true* name. Flame does not."

The witch, who'd spent the first thirteen years of her life thinking *she* didn't have a name either, bristled on his behalf. "Why didn't Za'gathoth name him? That's a dick move."

"Mother found his egg as she was fleeing from the Swarm. Archons are typically born—or hatched—knowing their own names, but Flame did not." The Clerk's tentacled form shifted in something like a shrug. "We don't know why."

"Huh. Well, keep me posted on the manhunt."

"Search," the Clerk said carefully. "My security team is calling it a search. We wouldn't want any vigilantes to encounter him and take . . . premature judiciary measures against an innocent Archon."

Innocent?

Just because Monsieur Flambé was a vegan with a tragic backstory didn't mean he wasn't also a killer.

"Fine. The *search*," the witch said. "So the Clerk's goons—"

Hank shook his head sadly.

"—will keep hunting for Flame, Phæras and Ellie will dig into the portal signature thing, and Chlogha and Chad are working on Tootle Translate. Once that's up and running, we'll see what the moon-beasts can tell us."

"And I," the Dread Lord said, "will research spontaneous human combustion."

The witch ignored him. "One last thing I want to say before we wrap up." She leaned back in her chair and crossed her arms. "Cards on the table, Archons."

Two of the Clerk's eyes exchanged a confused look. "What do you mean?"

"We're not doing the same bullshit we did with the Swarm. You guys knew what little white men were from the giddy-up."

"We thought they were a children's fairy tale!" Sathach said.

"I don't give a good godsdamn if you thought they were a frigging army of tooth fairies. You hid information."

"But—"

The witch held up a hand to silence him. "I get it. Tantrum of terror. But I need to know if you have any idea what we're dealing with, and I need to know *now*." She allowed a burst of entropine to lift her hair on swirling currents and turn her eyes a glowing red. Archons appreciated a show of power. "If you're holding out on me again, I will absolutely LOSE . . . MY . . . SHIT."

Her last three words rang in the air like thunderclaps.

"Ouch," Ellie muttered, massaging her ears.

"Are you finished?" the Clerk asked.

The witch conjured a light burst of fanged toads.

Sathach gasped. "How *could* you?"

"I understand your frustration, High Lord Innominanda," the Clerk said, "but I assure you, I haven't a clue who or what is behind these events."

Phæras's orb trembled in something like a shiver. "You could speak with Mother. We don't remember the old world, but *she* does."

"I need to talk to her anyway," Sathach said. "I'll stop by and—"

"Nope." The witch could only imagine the spin he'd put on the facts. "We'll go together."

He reached for one of the many nylon holsters at his belt and withdrew an instrument. "I'll text her now."

"That's an EMF meter," Hank said.

Sathach reholstered it, whipped out his BlackBerry, and started tapping out a text message.

"That's it for today, folks," the witch said. "If you learn anything new, hit me up. I'll be in touch when we have another meeting scheduled."

"I'm off to supervise Story Corner," Chlogha said. "Mr. Chadwick and I will let you know when Tootle Translate is ready." She lifted the massive femur-like bone securing the door and hopped out into the library proper.

The Clerk stood, stretched, and beckoned to Hank with a dripping tentacle. "Come, Deputy."

"Bye, Wit—"

A glimmering portal swallowed Hank whole before he could finish.

The witch followed Sathach out of the RAYOR room, leaving Phæras and Ellie huddled over *The Quantumnomicon*. "Let me know when you hear from—"

His BlackBerry vibrated. He tapped the screen and said, "Have you eaten?"

Her stomach growled at the thought of food. "Not yet. Wanna swing by Dee's, maybe grab a pair of 'nuts?"

"Mother says we can visit now," he said. "She has ordered brunch."

Gods dammit.

She'd survived the witch-pocalypse and evaded the Swarm, but apparently, there was no escaping brunch.

"Do you mind if we walk?" Sathach asked.

The witch stared up at the sky. It was overcast and ten degrees below average temperature with the promise of a storm in the air.

A perfect summer day.

"Fine by me." She magically nudged her broom, which was parked in a motorcycle spot outside the library, and sent it home on autopilot. "That fake dust in the RAYOR room plays merry hell with my allergies. Fresh air will do me good."

They walked a few blocks down Kingsport Street, careful to avoid the low-hanging bows of carnivorous trees. The Dread Lord usually filled any quiet moment with idle chatter, but he was uncharacteristically silent. The witch let him be. He'd talk when he was ready—or, if she was very lucky, not.

Sathach slowed when they approached the intersection of Kingsport and Miskatonic, where a massive big-box store hulked at the far side of a six-acre parking lot.

"Is it all right if I pop into The Aisle of R'lyeh to pick up something for Mother?"

The witch shrugged. "Knock yourself out."

The Aisle was a successor to the pre-Emergence Walmart, which the Archons had promptly shut down on the grounds that its predatory capitalism was a little too predatory. The store consisted of a single aisle stretching onward into infinity, simultaneously straight as an arrow and contorted in non-Euclidean doom spirals. It was a pain in the ass to navigate, but nowhere near as bad as the ginormous Ikea in Gomorrah Township. And they carried everything from occult supplies to produce to auto parts. As the ads said:

If you can't find it in The Aisle of R'lyeh, you don't need it!
(Or you're lost in the hypercube at the store's rotting heart, slowly succumbing to madness.)
20% discount for teachers!

The witch lounged on a bench by the entrance, nearly lulled to sleep by the panicked shrieks of lost shoppers. A mental pulse of alarm from Keyser Söze jarred her to nerve-jangling alertness and drew her psychic attention back to her apartment. She peeked through Keyser's eyes and nearly fell off the godsdamned bench. Sibyl's nightmare puppy, Jenkin, was staring at Keyser through the bedroom window.

Saints below, that thing was creepy . . .

"Shall we?"

She opened her eyes to see the Dread Lord standing before her, clutching a flat brown paper bag to his chest.

"Let's shall."

The witch pushed herself up with a groan—gods, she was *tired*—and followed him to the corner. They descended a heavily graffitied concrete staircase into the welcome gloom of the pedestrian tunnel that cut under Kingsport to the Cat U campus.

"Find what you needed?"

Sathach slid a magazine out of the bag. A neon-yellow WWE logo practically glowed on the top left corner of the cover, which featured two pro wrestlers standing face-to-face. The dude on the left was labeled *Seth Freakin' Rollins.* He had a beard, a mop of greased-back hair, and an apparent grudge against shirts. On the right was N'gotha, a man-sized slug with a trio of burning eyes . . . and also a mop of greased-back hair. It was a perfect ass-kissing gift for Za'gathoth, the multiverse's most rabid wrestling fan.

"Trying to get on her good side, eh?"

The Dread Lord grimaced. "Maybe this will be enough to get her talking about my father." He returned the magazine to the bag and slowed his pace. "Unless . . ."

"Unless what?"

"Well, I know you're sensitive about magical favors, but I was wondering . . ."

The witch sighed. "What do you want?"

"Could you do a spell to make me more persuasive?" He leaned toward her eagerly. "I was flipping through *The Hexonomicon* before the WTF meeting, and I saw a 'silver-tongue' spell that looked—"

"*Hell* no." The witch shook her head in violent negation. "That's metaphorical magic. Finicky as shit."

"But I'm sure you could—"

"The last time I screwed around with it, I created a literal green-eyed monster so gnarly even the Sheriff couldn't kill it," she said. "The godsdamned thing's still in the Tophet County Zoo. It'd be way too easy to aim for a silver tongue and wind up with a permanent mouthful of metal."

"Oh," Sathach said in a small, dejected voice.

"A word of advice . . ." The witch didn't know Za'gathoth all that well, but she knew the old bug was as stubborn as a threenager who wanted to do it herself. "Don't go at it head-on. You've gotta make her think it's *her* idea. If you push—"

She froze midstep, as though she were a movie and someone had pressed pause. She couldn't blink, she couldn't breathe, and her heart wasn't beating.

Unless she was dead, that meant *she* wasn't frozen. Time was.

Rhythmic metallic clicks echoed through the tunnel, accompanied by the distinctive footfalls of male dress shoes on concrete. A man in a dark business suit strode toward the witch, backlit by the cloudy morning light at the far end of the tunnel. He held something in his left hand, but the only detail she could make out was a glint of silver and a hint of motion.

The man stopped about twenty feet away and pulled something from his inner coat pocket. He pressed a short, slim rod to his lips and inhaled, then breathed out a peaches-and-cream cloud.

He was *vaping*.

Being magically outclassed was humiliating enough, but to be totally owned by a douche with a taste for fruity steam?

Intolerable.

"I'm sure you have questions," the man said as the metallic clicks began to slow. "I could give you the answers, but they'd fly in the face of everything you think you know. You aren't ready to believe."

Though she was immobilized, though she couldn't shift her eyes to see the Dread Lord, the witch could sense his unspoken *I believe*.

"So instead of answers"—he paused to hit the vape, filling the tunnel with sickly sweet vapor—"I'll give you a question."

Tick . . . tick . . . tick . . .

The witch strained to make out his features, but his face was a pool of shadows.

"How did Lovecraft know so much about the Archons?"

CHAPTER ELEVEN

The Vaping Douche

ick...
Tick...
Tick.

"Already?" the man said around his vape pen. "Seriously?" His voice carried a hint of panic.

The witch's limbs tingled as though they'd been asleep and normal circulation was being restored. Whatever magic he'd used to immobilize her was wearing off, and he obviously knew it. He fussed with the item he held in his left hand. A flurry of clicks and ticks echoed through the tunnel, but whatever he was trying to do wasn't working. She strained toward him, but she only succeeded in taking an awkward lunging step that left her on her knees in a puddle of rat-thing piss. The witch wriggled her fingers and toes, exulting in the tingle of her body's returning entropine.

When she could move again, she'd go full Ragnarok on this shit-gibbon.

The man shrugged out of a drawstring backpack the witch hadn't noticed in the tunnel's dim light. "Shit, shit, shit," he muttered, as he loosened the strings. He dropped something into the bag with a metallic jangle. Pulled something else out.

The witch's eyes darted up to Sathach, whose Skyn trembled with his effort to move. She tried to speak but only succeeded in voicing a pathetic, stuttering groan. Then a flood of entropine entered her system, and sparks shot from her fingertips. She forced her stiff fingers to shape the sacred K.

The man's right hand moved in a rhythmic circle, producing a series of ratcheting clicks.

She raised her arms and took aim at the shadowy item in his hands. ,

"Witch, no!" Sathach shouted.

Just as she fired, he blinked out of existence. The entropic strike vaporized a chunk of stone wall, but their erstwhile captor was already gone.

"Gods dammit!"

The witch tried to rise, but she'd been cut off from the master contract when time stopped and it hadn't yet replenished her stores. The Dread Lord slid an arm under her shoulder and helped her stand on trembling legs.

"Why did you fire, Witch?" he asked. "The cigarette-smoking man was clearly trying to help with our investigation!"

"Bullshit!" She disentangled herself from Sathach, weaving slightly as her entropine levels returned to baseline. "First, he wasn't a smoking man. He was a vaping douche. Second, if he wanted to help, he'd say something like, 'Hello, immensely powerful and superhot witch. I hear you're looking into some weird-ass murders. FYI, the butler did it.' Then he'd drop a bag of evidence, testify in court, and clean my freaking apartment."

Sathach's rubbery brow furrowed in a frown. "Why would he clean your apartment?"

The witch blew out a frustrated sigh. "*That*"—she jabbed a finger at the pile of loose stone where the man had stood—"was not our friendly neighborhood informant. He was a shady asshole with a hidden agenda."

"He said we weren't ready—"

"Can a human neutralize both a witch and an Archon?"

"No, but—"

"Did you sense Archonic magic?" she asked. "Or see even the faintest flash of netherlight?"

"Well, *no*, but—"

"And did he feel like a natural-born badass to you?"

"What do you mean?"

"Everyone knows you eldritch horrors can smell witches like a hog sniffs out truffles. Did you pick up any"—she waggled her fingers jazz hands–style—"big witch energy?"

"He was male!"

Wisps of acrid smoke curled over his head as her eyes burned two small holes in the forehead of his Skyn. "You know godsdamned well what I mean."

"All right, fine!" Sathach threw up his hands. "No, he wasn't a witch."

"What does that leave? What else could've given him that kind of power?"

The witch saw the precise instant he understood. His eyes widened and met hers.

"That's right," she said. "Magical . . . fucking . . . artifacts."

* * *

The Mindless Mother's profane temple beneath the Catachthonic River was redolent with the aroma of waffles and bacon. The witch couldn't *see* the full spread, as it was laid out atop a seven-foot-tall table—Za'gathoth flatly refused to adjust either her form or her furnishings to human scale—but she could smell it. The old Archon, a kaiju-esque stag beetle with four human hands protruding from her midsection, sat hunched in a massive ladderback chair. She tugged a crocheted shawl over the . . . shoulders? . . . of her liver-spotted carapace, flexing her serrated mandibles in irritation.

The Dread Lord stared up at her and forced a queasy grin. "Hello, Mother."

The witch, who didn't particularly enjoy being on the short end of a power imbalance, levitated herself to Za'gathoth's eye level. She nearly swooned at the smorgasbord of culinary delights on display. Maybe brunch wouldn't be so bad.

"You're late," Za'gathoth barked. "The eggs have gone cold." She whispered a word in Ouranian-Barbaric and the entire spread, from bacon to bagels, vanished in a blaze of octarine light. "Nothing worse than cold eggs."

The witch's stomach gave a dejected gurgle.

"I'm sorry, Mother," Sathach said. "I stopped to pick up a gift for you."

He raised the paper bag as though presenting an offering. A withered tentacle smacked it out of his hand.

"I'm in no mood for your nonsense!" Her faceted eyes watched from their drooping stalks as the Dread Lord knelt and retrieved the bag. "I'm still grieving my poor Yi'danag—"

If that was the case, she was stuck firmly in the *anger* phase.

"—and how many of you have stopped by to check on me? Why, not a damned—"

Her voice record-scratched to silence as the Dread Lord stood, holding the magazine in front of his face with both hands. The witch burned a little entropine to triple its size.

"Is that the summer solstice special issue of *WWE Magazine*?" Za'gathoth snatched the periodical and eyeballed the cover. "I'll tell you what, I wouldn't kick Seth Freakin' Rollins out of bed for eating crackers." She gave a phlegmy chuckle and waved a tentacle toward the table. "You're down here, so I s'pose you may as well sit a spell." She looked Sathach up and down. "And take off that ridiculous rubber suit, dummy."

"It's not ridiculous," the Dread Lord muttered.

But he complied. A barbed tentacle pierced the Skyn at its Adam's apple and sliced it open from neck to crotch. His natural form—a cavernous maw lined with jagged fangs and ringed by thrashing tentacles—slithered free and expanded to proper Archonic dimensions. The witch repressed a reflexive dry heave and floated to an empty chair.

Za'gathoth looked him up and down as he arranged himself in a seat. "You're too skinny."

Bring back the food, bring back the food . . .

"That woman doesn't know how to feed you, that's what it is."

"I've told you, Heather and I are equal partners—"

"It's not an equal relationship when one of you can swallow the other one whole." She snorted. "Not that you'd dare."

"Can we not talk about my wife?"

"It's my house," Za'gathoth said. "I'll talk about whatever I please."

Sathach's tentacles braided into a torso-like trunk, giving the impression of a man squaring his shoulders to face an unpleasant but necessary task. "Well, *I'd* like to talk about my f—"

"About the Unquenchable Flame," the witch said. A pair of tentacles tipped with eyeballs whiplashed in her direction as Sathach glared at her. "Have you seen him since he got back from his trip?"

"Flame?" The Mindless Mother's wilting eyestalks stiffened in surprise. "Haven't seen *him* since the Emergence." She shook her head dolefully. "If it wasn't for me, he'd have been left behind with the Swarm, but do you think he ever once said thank you?"

"I'm gonna go with no." The witch conjured a notepad and pencil. "What can you tell us about him?"

Za'gathoth shrugged. "I found him when we were on the run from the Swarm. His egg had been left behind on a battlefield—a whole settlement, razed to dust. He was the only survivor."

"What do you know about his . . . family history?"

"Do I look like a genealogist?"

She looked like a homicidal beetle with a grandma fetish, but that sort of response would prompt a WWE-style smackdown.

"Any idea why he didn't know his own name?"

"He's not all that bright, if that's what you're hinting at." Za'gathoth's human hands traced a rune in the air. A cup of green Jell-O and a plastic spoon appeared on the table. "Where are my manners?"

Two more Big Gulp–sized containers of Jell-O appeared—one for the witch, one for Sathach. The Dread Lord swallowed his whole, but the witch took a pass. Congealed bone water was low on her list of shit that qualified as food, right below Styrofoam and spinach.

"It takes a while for our young to mature," the Mindless Mother said, "but Flame was way behind the others. He was like a feral hound of Tindalos for the first couple millennia. Didn't talk. No real personality." She scooped a wobbling spoon of Jell-O in her mouth. "And the pickiest eater I've ever seen."

"Fascinating," Sathach said. "But getting back to my—"

"What did he eat?" the witch asked.

"I'll tell you this," Za'gathoth said, "that brat would've eaten every last one of *us* if I hadn't kept an eye on him. I'd packed snacks, of course—plenty of rat-things, Shoggoths, Shantaks . . . you know, all the stuff kids like. But not Flame. Nothing I offered was good enough for *him*." She took another bite of Jell-O and jabbed her spoon in the witch's direction. "I bet he ran away from home a hundred times. I finally figured out he was off skulking around the mini-cosmos of our pocket dimension gobbling up *stars*, if you can imagine." She sniffed. "Damn vegetarians."

The witch scribbled a few notes, missing Magnolia with finger-cramping intensity. "Did he have beef with the Unseen Creeping Horror?"

"I just told you he wouldn't eat meat, moron!"

She bared her teeth in a smile-adjacent expression. "I meant did they ever argue?"

"Argue?" Za'gathoth rolled her eyes. "Flame barely acknowledged his siblings. He never . . ." Her voice trailed off, and she took a pensive bite of Jell-O. "You think *he* had something to do with Yi'danag's death?"

"He's been missing since it happened," the witch said, "and the UCH was burned to death by blue fire."

Za'gathoth waved a human hand in dismissal. "No chance. Flame's always been a coward."

Wow. The Dread Lord's parental angst was suddenly making a hell of a lot more sense.

"Ahem."

The witch scowled a warning at Sathach, but he ignored her.

"Mother, do you have any idea what killed Yi'danag?"

"Or *who*," the witch added.

"I wasn't there, was I?"

"But can you think of anything powerful enough?"

"Oh, any of the Outer Gods could've done it"—Za'gathoth snapped the fingers of all four human hands—"like *that*. So could the Great Old Ones or their servants." Her faceted eyes drooped on their stalks. "But they're all gone now. And so is Yi'danag."

The witch squirmed in discomfort. She was supposed to say something here, wasn't she?

"I'm, uh . . . I'm sorry for your loss."

Za'gathoth slurped another spoonful of Jell-O. "Shit happens."

"Mother!"

But the witch understood this angry, detached brand of grief. Za'gathoth had lost her home world and her parents, partners, siblings, and friends. When people lost too much too fast, they sometimes ran out of give-a-shit.

"All right, out with it," the old beetle said. "I know you didn't come just to chat. What the Gug is going on?"

The witch glanced at Sathach and arched an eyebrow, but he motioned for her to take the lead. She walked through everything that'd happened since she and Chad visited Sibyl's tent Friday night. Za'gathoth sat in uncharacteristically docile silence throughout the far-fetched monologue. Her pensive quiet continued even after the witch concluded her account with the Vaping Douche's question.

"So tell me," the witch said, "what do you—"

A thunderous snore cut her off midsentence. Za'gathoth flailed to wakefulness and dabbed viscous green drool from her mandibles with the fringed edge of her shawl.

The witch tossed her pencil on the table in disgust. "For fuck's sake, were you even listening?"

"I was just resting my eyes."

"Then answer the question."

"I'd say the answer is . . ." Za'gathoth drew out the pause, clearly stalling for time. "It depends?"

"Ahem," Sathach said. "Very . . . astute. But the *other* question is the one posed by the Smoking Man."

"The Vaping—"

"Which *is*"—he raised his voice to drown out the witch—"how did Lovecraft know so much about the Archons?"

"Oh. That." Za'gathoth drummed the fingers of one hand on the clear plastic tablecloth. "He always said he dreamed it, didn't he? There've been a couple of humans over the eons who could visit the Dreamlands in their sleep."

"But even if he could," the witch said, "it still wouldn't explain jack shit. There'd have to be an Archon in the Dreamlands for him to observe, or at least talk to. You said so yourself when I visited last fall. The rest of the Dreamlands is just eldritch flora and fauna, right?"

"More or less," Za'gathoth said. "But I also told you the Morpheus Gate was sealed. Every Archon had come home to fight the Swarm, so there was no one in there. And nobody besides us escaped the Swarm."

"Who sealed the gate?"

"The Swarm, you imbecile! Who else *would* seal it?"

Again with the name-calling. The witch closed her eyes and took a deep, not-so-calming breath.

"Could the other races of the Dreamlands have told Lovecraft about you?" the witch asked.

Za'gathoth scoffed. "Psssh! Most of them aren't even sentient. Besides, have you read the drivel that man wrote about the Dreamlands? He had moon-beasts eating goat people, for Shrike's sake! And half of what he wrote about Archons was pure nonsense."

"But the other half was true?"

"True-*ish*."

"And you've never tried to figure this shit out?" The witch massaged her temples. *The Archonomicon* had really oversold Za'gathoth's whole esoteric knowledge schtick. "It seems pretty freaking important."

"Sometimes, little sister," Za'gathoth said, "you just don't get to know the answers."

"That's some grade-A bullshit."

"We have to open our minds," Sathach said. "The Smoking Man warned us that the answers would fly in the face of everything we think we know." He gripped the edge of the table with his tentacles and aimed a steely gaze at the witch. "I want to believe."

Za'gathoth yawned. "*I* want a nap."

"You already took one," the witch said.

"I was resting my eyes!"

"May I ask one final question, Mother?"

"Hell no. I'm done with questions."

The Dread Lord snaked a tentacle down the table and wound it through her wrinkled hands. *"Please."*

She tugged her fingers free, but her faceted eyes softened. "What is it, Sathach?"

"Will you tell me about my father?"

"Your father . . ." Za'gathoth wheezed a clotted sigh. "You get your mind-flaying from him," she said. "And your shape-shifting."

"You mean my battle form?"

She nodded absently. "Your father thought he was the Ultharian cat's pajamas. Pretty high up in the Archonic hierarchy, too. Matter of fact, that's one reason I've never talked about you children's fathers. I didn't want to drag that stratified craptrap into this universe."

As much as the witch empathized with the Dread Lord's desire to discover his roots, she kind of understood Za'gathoth's decision. Once people had the option to sort themselves into *greater than* and *less than*, the whole thing slid into classist shit-show territory quicker than you could say *landed aristocracy*.

"You know, he fancied himself a scientist," she continued. "Always messing about with electrical whatsits, taking apart metal doodads and building slightly different doodads. Oh, but he was 'too busy' to help with the kids."

Sathach's tentacles drooped. "He wasn't a good father?"

"Well, he didn't eat you."

"I suppose that's something."

"I don't mind telling you, that male drove me mad," Za'gathoth said. "Drove *everyone* mad, truth be told. He was a chameleon—never the same from day to day. Always hatching his next big scheme."

"I wish I could've known him," the Dread Lord said with a wistful sigh.

Za'gathoth pushed herself out of the chair with a symphony of pops and creaks, a clear sign their audience was drawing to an end.

"Thank your lucky stars you never did."

CHAPTER TWELVE

Selective Deduction

From: witch@tophetcounty.gov
To:phærasthewheel@midnightcarnival.net;
dreadlordofhr@tophetcounty.gov
CC: countyclerk@tophetcounty.gov; officeofthemayor@tophetcounty.
gov
Subject: hey losers. sathach and i have new info. wtf meeting this afternoon. 2:00. my office.

The witch pressed send and stared longingly at the corner of her office that'd once housed Magnolia's desk. Those dipshits from Facilities had replaced it with a conference table and a potted tree, which she was doing her level best to neglect to death. Naturally, the freaking thing was thriving.

Gods, how she missed Magnolia's terrifying efficiency, fantastic taste in sandwiches, and deranged love for administrative bullshit . . . and Magnolia herself. But her former assistant now sat at the helm of Boss Babe Enterprises, overseeing Sustainable Skyns, Toys in Us, and the aptly named leggings empire, Giza Athleisure—which left the witch to go it alone in the treacherous wilds of Tophet County's bureaucracy. And she was feeling pretty godsdamned alone at the moment.

She checked her texts for the thousandth time. Chad still hadn't responded to the messages she'd sent him last night, and her wounded pride wouldn't allow her to send another.

The witch heaved a self-pitying sigh and took a sip of her coffee.

Which was cold.

Because she'd had to get it herself.

She stuck her index finger in the cup and nuked it to an acceptable temperature.

Keyser Söze chittered from his perch on the windowsill. She looked up to see what'd caught his interest. Probably a squirrel. (He felt a deep spiritual kinship with squirrels, as he was also perpetually trying to get a nut.) But what she saw outside her window was no furry woodland creature. Jenkin's wrinkly old-man face was pressed against the glass. Keyser grabbed the pull cord and lowered the blinds.

Something weird was going on with that janky murder puppy.

The witch walked to the window and reached for the cord, but Keyser rumbled a growl of caution. She considered looking anyway but decided against it. Over the years, she'd learned that trusting her familiar's instincts usually paid off.

Except when it came to nutrition.

And controlled substances.

And lady raccoons.

Well, it *occasionally* paid off.

A faint rustle drew her gaze to her backpack, which was on the floor in the corner where she'd propped her broom. The canvas twitched.

Sibyl's cards.

The witch stopped by her desk for a searing gulp of coffee, then she grabbed her bag and pulled out the clear plastic evidence bag. Inside, the cards were shuffling themselves with ostentatious acrobatics. The chubby-cheeked little shits clearly had something to say. Vera Vásquez's Apple of Discord bolo tie, which was looped through her key ring, glinted gold from the depths of her backpack.

She narrowed her eyes at the apple. "Is this Your brand of bullshit?"

True to form, Discordia kept her silence. Meanwhile, the cards continued to riffle.

The witch carried the deck back to her desk and slid it free of its bag. It jerked and shuddered in her hands.

"Knock it off!" It sulkily subsided into stillness. "Sibyl said you'll tell me what I need to know, but that's not how this is going down. I'm asking a question, and you're answering it. Otherwise, back in the bag you go."

The cards didn't move. She'd interpret that as *message received.*

"Who killed the Unseen Creeping Horror and Sibyl?"

The deck launched into another sensational shuffle, then assembled itself neatly in front of her. She cut the deck and restacked it. Two cards slid from the top and turned themselves face up.

The first was Stormy frigging Heather; the second, Split Kit.

Present and past from Sibyl's reading-on-repeat, only their order was reversed. Not helpful.

The witch inserted the cards back into the deck. "Let's try this again," she said. "How can I figure out who killed Sibyl and the UCH?"

Another shuffle. Another cut. Another three cards.

On the left was June Moon. To absolutely no one's surprise, the card depicted the Moon—only it had a petulant face and a spaceship jammed in one eye socket. Cute.

But at least the message was clear. She needed to talk to the moon-beasts.

In the center was an artistic masterpiece called Weird Wendy. A warty witch gazed into a crystal ball filled with eyeballs, bats, frogs, and snakes. Seeing as only one witch was still shuffling around this mortal coil, that had to be her . . . unless it was trying to tell her to use Sibyl's baby-pink crystal ball. It wasn't an artifact—she'd tested it at the crime scene.

Huh. She'd put a pin in that one for later.

The last card was Cu-Joe. As expected, it featured a rabid dog with a face grinning up from the bubbling foam on its muzzle. She stared at the last two images. What if the witch wasn't a witch but a fortune teller?

Sibyl was dead, so there was no chatting with her. The dog, on the other hand . . .

"Murder puppy?" The card exuded yes-ness. "You've got to be shitting me."

The trio of cards slid back into the deck and began another round of shuffling.

"I've heard enough from you for now."

The witch swept up the cards, fished a rubber band out of her desk drawer, and bound the little devils into a tight bundle. She stuffed them in their pouch, sealed them in the evidence bag, and returned it to her backpack.

Over Keyser's protests, she opened the blinds and looked out the window. Jenkin was gone, so Cu-Joe was shit out of luck for the moment. And until she mastered necromancy—not likely, given her weak stomach—so was Weird Wendy.

June Moon, on the other hand, was telling her, practically *commanding* her, to talk to Chad and get an update on Tootle Translate.

The witch was but a mere pawn of forces beyond her understanding. She grabbed Keyser, whistled for her broom, and saddled up.

The witch pulled her broom up to a seventh-floor window at the City Hall Annex. She cupped her hands and peered into the office. Chad sat at his desk facing away from her, his attention glued to the rightmost of his three monitors. She rapped her knuckles on the glass. His shoulders twitched, but he didn't get up to let her in. She pounded on the window hard enough to hurt her hand, but he *still* didn't move.

The witch's feelings cycled from hurt, to miffed, to apocalyptically enraged.

If she'd pissed Chad off, he needed to tell her. Whatever *this* was, she didn't deserve it, and it was going to stop. Now. She reversed her broom, got a running go, and shot through the windowpane. Her supersonic entrance stirred up a cyclone of papers that drifted down to cover every available surface in Chad's office, including the top of his head. She dismounted, propped her broom by the door, and crossed her arms as she waited for him to acknowledge her.

Keyser, sensing her mood, scuttled under the desk to hide (and, from the sounds of it, indulged in the dog bowl of trail mix Chad kept tucked away for him).

"Hey there, Witch." He reached up and plucked a Post-it from his hair.

"What the hell, Chad?"

He winced at her tone but said nothing.

"You've barely spoken to me since Saturday night, you won't answer my texts, and now you ignore me when I'm at your window?"

"I'm trying to get this translation app—"

"Look, I get that I'm not good at relationshit." She dropped her bag next to her broom and approached his desk. "It's all . . . it's new for me. And uncomfortable. And I'm probably screwing up right and left. But crap like this"—she waved her hand at the tension-filled space between them—"is a non-fucking-starter. What did I *do*?"

"Do?" His brow furrowed in confusion. "You didn't—"

"I'm sorry I bailed on the freaking brunch," she said. "There. Is that what you wanted to hear?"

"I'm not upset about—"

"Then *what*, Chad?"

They gazed at each other, the strained silence broken only by the sound of Keyser munching his way through a half-pound of almonds and raisins.

"Do you trust me, Witch?"

"That," she said, "is a question people only ask when they're either lying or hiding something." She sat down in the chair across from him and propped her boots on the corner of his desk. "Which is it?"

He ran a hand through his short locs. "I wouldn't lie to you."

"I see."

"I'm dealing with a tricky situation," he said. "I, uh . . . it's best if I don't tell you about it yet, but I swear to God, I will."

"Best for who?" she asked.

Chad offered a pained smile. "Not for us."

"So I didn't do anything wrong?"

"You didn't." This time, his smile was warm—a pale shadow of its usual sunbeam self, but warm enough to begin thawing the cold lump of hurt in her chest. "I'm just . . . I'm trying to keep something bad from happening."

"And you're sure this is the best way to play it?"

"For now," he said. "And hopefully not for long."

The witch stared at her scuffed boots, her mind sifting through the possibilities. His weirdness had begun when he started working on the Lunatic-to-English translation app, which meant it most likely had something to do with the moon-beasts. But why would Chad think he couldn't confide in her? She could keep a secret. Hell, she'd proven that last year to her detriment. Only . . .

Only this time around, she was co-leading the WTF with an Archon who had legendary mind-flaying abilities.

Maybe it wasn't *her* Chad was hiding things from.

There was more than one way to skin a Shantak. He might not be ready to tell her what was going on, but she could godsdamned well try to figure it out for herself.

"Fair enough." She laced her fingers together and rested them on her stomach. "How's Tootle Translate coming?"

The tension eased from his face. He took a deep breath and sighed it out. "I'm close, Witch," he said. "Like *really* close."

"That's great. I'm hoping the moon-beasts can tell us what's happening."

"I think they can, uh . . ."—Chad's eyes darted to his screen, then back to her—"clear up a few things."

Yep, his deep dark secret was 100 percent moon-beast-related. He sucked at covert ops. She'd get to the truth one way or another. In the meantime, she'd keep him in the loop. If somebody was going to tank this operation by keeping secrets, it wouldn't be her.

Not this time.

"Some wild shit went down yesterday," she said. "Want me to fill you in?"

He opened his mouth, clearly about to say yes, but then he closed it and shook his head.

"*No?*" she asked. "Why not?"

"I'd love to hear about it, Witch, but I can't afford to get distracted." His gaze drifted to *The Necronomicon*, which—in defiance of the library's RAYOR-room-only rule—lay open on his desk. "This app has to be my top priority."

The witch shrugged and swallowed her disappointment. "Suit yourself." She stood and held out her hand, and her broom smacked into her palm with a satisfying thwack. "Hey, would you do me a favor?"

"Sure thing," he said. "What do you need?"

"Text the Whovians and ask if anyone's seen or heard from the Unquenchable Flame." She picked up her backpack and put it on. "Sathach told me he eats *stars*, Chad. Taking out the UCH and Sibyl would've been a piece of cake."

"I . . . okay, I'll ask." Chad reached for his personal iPhone, but his eyes were troubled. "But I'm telling you, I know him. Flame wouldn't—"

"I know. He's your buddy, you've known him for years, he would *never*, et cetera," she said. "For what it's worth, I don't think he was working alone."

"What do you mean?"

"Sathach and I had a run-in with some dude who stole a crapload of magical artifacts from Sibyl's tent." She faced the window and straddled her broom. "Za'gathoth said the Flame's not too bright—"

"He's the strongest Whovian on the team!"

"—so maybe that thieving shitweasel was the mastermind behind the murders."

"Or maybe," Chad said, "the human did it alone."

"The artifacts were stolen *after* the UCH was killed. How could a human have torched him like that?"

"I don't know, but you shouldn't jump to conclusions. You're cherry-picking the facts that support your theory and ignoring everything else."

"I'm not the one engaging in selective deduction here, Chad." She clicked her tongue to summon Keyser. "I know it sucks to be wrong about someone, especially after what happened with Heather—"

"Heather has nothing to do with this."

The witch clenched her jaw in a Herculean effort to keep from saying something awful. "Just let me know if anyone's seen him."

Then she pushed enough entropine into her broom to send it into orbit and streaked out of his office, leaving nothing behind but unanswered questions.

And a trail of fire.

She hadn't even reached the end of the block when she felt her BlackBerry vibrate with an incoming call.

Chad.

He'd apologize, she'd apologize, they'd make up, and everything would be fine.

As the witch slowed her speed from bullet train to freight car, Keyser's nimble paw slid the phone from her pocket. He answered the call and pressed the phone to her ear.

"Hey, asshole."

"I'm trying to reach High Lord Innominanda," said a baffled-sounding male voice.

"Shit, sorry," she said. "You've got her. Who's this?"

"Xay Chanthavong, the Tophet County Medical Examiner," he said. "I've completed the preliminary autopsy report for Sibyl Tiburtine."

"Great. What was the cause of death?"

"Um . . ."

She was an idiot. Anyone who took one look at the body could tell what killed her.

"I mean, I know she was burned alive, but *how*?"

"That's actually why I called before I emailed the report," he said. "These are only my preliminary findings, but as of now, I have no choice but to attribute her death to . . ."

"To what?"

She listened with growing impatience as Xay took a deep breath and sighed it out.

"Spontaneous human combustion."

The witch fumbled her BlackBerry and nearly dropped it before recovering enough composure to end the call.

What the Fortean *fuck*?

CHAPTER THIRTEEN

Hard Evidence

The raccoon equivalent of *bow-chicka-BOW-wow* echoed through the witch's mind on repeat. She'd dropped off Keyser Söze at her apartment for an amorous liaison with his lady friend, and he'd wasted no time getting down to business. As much as she tried to keep his shenanigans walled off, her familiar's exploits sometimes got a little *too* familiar, infusing her psyche with persistent low-grade horniness.

Not exactly the ideal mindset for a WTF meeting.

The witch stepped back from her conference table and examined the spread. After delivering Keyser to the Love Shack, she'd swung by Dee's 'Nuts to pick up meeting supplies. A cardboard coffee dispenser sat in the center of the table next to a stack of disposable cups and lids, a selection of sweeteners, and a bowl of creamer pods. She'd also picked up a box of sticky 'nuts and stolen a thick wad of napkins. It might not be Magnolia-level hospitality, but it was pretty godsdamned close.

She grabbed a stack of agendas, still warm from the printer, and placed one at each of the six spots around the table. Then she made the rounds again with a copy of the ME's preliminary autopsy report. Reviewing that piece of shit with Spooky Sathach would be about as much fun as—

"Do I smell sticky 'nuts?" lisped the Dread Lord.

Speak of the tentacled devil . . .

The witch turned to see him standing in the doorway. He'd swapped his blond Ken-doll Skyn for a black-haired, bearded version that reminded her of . . .

Nah, couldn't be.

It was tough to tell with the rubbery face, but Sathach seemed better. Brighter. More like his pre-parental-angst self.

"You're looking chipper."

"I portaled out to visit Heather and the twins after we left Mother's house." Sathach whipped out his phone, cornered her, and flipped through thirty-two pictures of dazed infants doing infanty things. "They've gotten so big, haven't they?"

Sawyer and Skyler looked exactly the same size as they had in the last photos she'd seen, but she knew the drill by now. "Threateningly enormous."

He grabbed a sticky 'nut, sat down, and ate it in one enthusiastic bite. "You know, Witch," he said, dribbling cinnamon syrup into his beard, "I've turned a corner since our conversation with Mother. I'd been so lost, so overwhelmed, but now that we've cleared the air about my sire, I feel free."

"Sweet."

The Dread Lord stood and gazed at her expectantly. "Notice anything?"

She gave him a once-over. "Bitchin' Skyn."

"It's the Keanu," he said, confirming her earlier suspicion. "Heather's latest design. Anything else?"

"Come on, you know I hate guessing games."

"I left my ghost-hunting equipment at home!" He twirled to showcase a belt with only two holsters—one for his personal iPhone, one for his BlackBerry—before taking his seat. "As Mother said, sometimes we simply can't have the answers we want. I think I'm ready to leave my paranormal interests behind, Witch."

As he picked up the handouts and began to read, three words glowed in her memory like a neon casino sign.

SPONTANEOUS! HUMAN! COMBUSTION!

Of frigging course. The moment he was ready to let go of that horseshit, the ME saddled them with a metaphysical mess.

"Listen, about that . . ."

A pinprick of netherlight opened over the conference table and disgorged Phæras's shimmering silver orb. Before the witch could greet him, a larger portal formed near her desk. Ellie Dawson wheeled through the open office door just as the Clerk stepped out of the second portal with Hank in tow.

The witch bit her lip. She hadn't known he'd be joining the Clerk. Gods dammit, she was already overrun with auric raccoon pheromones. The visual treat that was Deputy Eye Candy was the literal last thing she needed right now.

"Good afternoon," Ellie's pale blue eyes swept over the table. "Maggie would be so proud."

The witch smothered a reflexive smile and lifted one shoulder in a faux-nonchalant shrug. "Learned from the best." She sat down at the head of the table. "Well, the gang's all here. Let's do the damn thing."

The Clerk and Hank took the pair of seats across from Sathach, Phæras hovered next to him, and Ellie parked her wheelchair at the far end of the table.

"First things first," the witch said, "the ME sent over the—"

"I knew it!" The Dread Lord waved the autopsy report in triumph. His face rippled and stretched as the tentacles beneath writhed in spasmodic glee. Blessedly, the Keanu held firm. "Spontaneous human combustion!"

Ellie's smooth brow creased in a frown as she scanned the short summary. "This is a . . . startling development."

"It was obvious to the trained eye." Sathach sat up straighter, quivering with excitement. "Trust me, Witch, I derive no pleasure from proving you wrong," he said, visibly deriving great freaking pleasure from proving her wrong. "This just proves there are more things in heaven and Earth, Horatio, than are dreamt of in your philosophy."

"Who in the seven hells is Horatio?"

The Clerk's half-dozen eyes flicked over the report. "The only facts I see here are that Sibyl had no drugs or alcohol in her system, and no traces of accelerant were found on the body," she said. "*This* is all the information Xay can provide?"

Hank raised his hand.

"You don't have to—" The witch took a deep breath and sighed it out. "Just talk."

"Did the crime scene folks recover any lighters or matches at the scene?" he asked. "Or maybe a candle?"

"Nope."

"Did Sibyl smoke?"

"She vaped," Phæras said.

That explained the cloying, fruity smell in Sibyl's tent. It looked like the killer had stolen more than her magical artifacts.

The Dread Lord met the witch's eyes and gasped. "The tunnel!"

"We'll get to it, Sathach."

"Weird," Hank said. "So no hard evidence was found at the crime scene?"

Hard evidence.

Discordia, take the wheel . . .

"Correct," she croaked. The witch swigged a masochistically huge mouthful of nuclear coffee. Her melting taste buds provided a powerful distraction. "Xay is going to check with a few colleagues and get back to me later this week." She cleared her throat. "There's not much else to say—"

"I have *so* much to say," the Dread Lord crooned.

"—so let's move on to item two."

"The Vaping Douche?" Phæras's tinny voice rang with amusement. "Witch, I am waiting on tenterhooks."

"Ahem. I prefer to call him the Smoking Man."

"Except it was a vape pen. And he was vaping."

The Clerk smacked a tentacle on the table. "Explain yourselves!"

The witch opened her mouth, but the Dread Lord had already launched into an accurate, if somewhat melodramatic, account of their encounter with the man in the tunnel.

"How could a mere human overpower the two of you?" the Clerk asked.

"He had Sibyl's magical artifacts, didn't he?" Phæras tilted on his axis, directing his attention to the witch. "Her entire collection was gone when you discovered her body. I'd wager her Morley vape pen wasn't found at the scene either."

"Nope," the witch said. "Do you happen to know what any of the artifacts did?"

Phæras rotated in his version of a head shake. "The only one she talked about with me was the broken umbrella. It creates a perceptual distortion that leaves observers with the impression that items in its vicinity are unworthy of notice."

"That's the thing that made the artifacts look like worthless junk?"

"Yes," Phæras said. "Sibyl kept detailed notes on the collection in her journal, but . . ."

"But the bastard got that too."

The Clerk's eyes exchanged a glance. "Who else knew these items were magical artifacts?"

"As far as I know, she told no one other than me."

An awkward silence fell.

The witch couldn't say what everyone else was thinking, but her own memories drifted to a Swarm-possessed Dr. Carcosa. He'd always been nearby when shit went down, always chimed in with a key bit of information, always offered to *help*.

As if her preexisting trust issues hadn't been bad enough.

"On a purely unrelated note," Sathach said, "Phæras was kind enough to permit me to flay his mind and ensure he had not . . . missed anything when sharing his story."

The Clerk's rigid eyestalks relaxed a bit. "We appreciate your transparency, Phæras."

He bobbed an acknowledgment.

"What happened after your encounter with"—Ellie pursed her lips, clearly unwilling to say *the Vaping Douche*—"the man who stole the artifacts?"

"We can't be certain he stole them," Phæras said. "All we know is that he has them now."

Ellie nodded. "That's an important distinction. Thank you, Phæras."

"After that, we had a little visit with Za'gathoth," the witch said. "She hasn't seen or heard from the Unquenchable Flame, but she told us what she knew about him." She shared the sparse details they'd learned from the Mindless

Mother. "My money says he took off. He jets around eating stars. Why would he stay in the solar system if he knows we're onto him?"

"Onto him?" the Clerk repeated. "You have yet to establish his guilt."

"Even if he's innocent, he's gotta realize he's suspect number one."

"I know the Director of the Mountains of Madness Observatory through my work with Dr. Carcosa," Ellie said. "I'll ask her to keep an eye out for anomalous astronomical events." She jotted down a note on a yellow legal pad. "Did the Mindless Mother have any insight into the, um, vaper's question?"

"She couldn't tell us jack shit." The witch gave her head a rueful shake. "No Archons were in the Dreamlands when the Morpheus Gate was sealed. And even if there were, they would've been assimilated when the Swarm rolled in."

"I'm just glad the moon-beasts made it out okay," Hank said with a dimpled grin.

The Clerk lassoed a sticky 'nut and dragged it under her shroud. "And that presents yet another mystery."

"Can we circle back to the topic of suspects before we move on to"—Ellie glanced at the agenda—"'moon-beast shit'?"

"Knock yourself out."

"Phæras and I had extensive discussions about both the burst of electromagnetic energy he sensed and the unknown Archon." She flipped back through her legal pad to a page filled with equations so arcane they made an Ouranian-Barbaric grimoire look like *See Rat-Things Run*. "We cannot conceive of a method by which an Archon's etheric footprint could be altered. That doesn't mean it's impossible, but based on our research, I believe it's highly unlikely."

"So we really *are* dealing with an unknown Archon?" the Clerk asked.

The witch wouldn't have thought a floating orb of quicksilver could look smug, but Phæras pulled it off.

"When the Unseen Creeping Horror was killed," Ellie said, "Phæras felt the burst of electromagnetic energy first, then he sensed the unknown Archon's portal signature. But when Sibyl died, there was no EM surge, yet he detected the same etheric footprint. Though both victims burned to death, the blaze at Dunwich Park would've consumed the Black Galley if the witch hadn't put it out, while nothing in Sibyl's tent was even singed." She tapped her pen on the notepad. "It seems we may be dealing with two different killers—"

"Exactly!" the Dread Lord exclaimed.

"—one of whom, based on your encounter in the tunnel, is human."

The witch smirked at Sathach. "Exactly."

Hank raised his hand. "Could it be the same perp using different weapons?"

"An intriguing theory, Deputy O'Brien." Two of the Clerk's eyes darted to the Fitbit buckled around one oozing tentacle. "I hate to rush you, but Mayor Dawson and I have a call to update Gomorrah Township's leadership council. Let's move on to moon-beasts."

"Okay. I, um, talked to Chad this morning." The witch cleared her throat, pushing aside her lingering hurt. "He said the app should be ready in a day or two. Once we've got that up and running, we'll interview the moon-beasts and see what they know." She cautiously met Hank's eyes, girding her loins against acts of smoldering. "How are they holding up?"

"Great!" he said with a reassuringly platonic grin. "Mayor Ellie was right about those volcano rocks. Cat U sent a bunch over, and they chowed down. They're much perkier now."

"Has the Sheriff tried to eat any more of them?"

"Quite the opposite," the Clerk said. "I actually think they're growing on him."

Hank frowned. "I thought that was just fungus from the cavern."

"Thank you for the updates, High Lord Innominanda," Ellie said, wheeling back from the table. "When would you like to reconvene?"

"I'll set something up once we've talked to the moon-beasts," the witch said.

"Excellent."

"Deputy," the Clerk said, "I trust you can find your own way back to Dunwich Park?"

"Sure can!" Hank said, though she'd already slurped herself into a portal and vanished.

Sathach's personal phone dinged, and he pulled it out and broke into a teary smile. "Barclay just sent a video of the twins!"

As he cornered a panicked Phæras, the witch fled the conference table for the relative safety of her desk. A wave of round-two raccoon lust brought a flush to her cheeks. She felt Hank watching her as she cracked open a desk drawer, fished out her flask, and added a slug of Chicken Cock to her cup of Dee's finest.

"Whiskey in your coffee, eh?"

She glanced up to see him standing a few feet away, one eyebrow arched in question.

"Do you have any Irish in you?" he asked.

"No clue." She raised the cup to her lips.

He stepped closer and leaned his head toward hers. "Do you want some?"

The witch gasped in a breath of coffee and bourbon, choked, and glared up at him. "All right, that's *enough*!" she snapped. "What the actual fuck, Hank?"

"I don't know!" He shook his head as though trying to clear it. "I feel . . . weird. Hungry. Maybe I need to eat something?"

She gestured toward the table. "Then get a 'nut, for Ghroth's sake."

Hank's eyes glinted blue, and he opened his mouth.

"So help me, if you say a single godsdamned word, I'll—"

Sathach shrieked.

The witch shoved past Hank and stalked to the conference table, where the Dread Lord and Phæras were huddled over his iPhone.

"What's wrong?"

He stared up at her, one eye spinning wildly in its socket. "The ghost is back!"

"Gods, Sathach, I thought you said you were ready to let this shit go."

"What ghost?" Hank leaned past her, craning his neck to see the screen.

"The motion sensors in my basement just triggered an alarm."

The Dread Lord shoved his phone in her face, and she instinctively batted it away.

"You must look, Witch," Phæras said, his resonant voice breathy with awe.

She reluctantly took the iPhone and glanced at the screen. Security cam footage showed a framed photo of Heather and the twins drifting through midair in front of Sathach's basement command center. As she gaped, stunned speechless, a terrifyingly complex intimate accessory sailed into view, trailing at least a dozen buckled restraints.

"What on Earth?" she breathed.

Sathach snatched his phone and pinned her with a steely gaze. "That's exactly what we're going to find out."

A sphere of netherlight bloomed from his chest and sucked all four of them into reality's quantum underbelly.

CHAPTER FOURTEEN

Yohimbe Love Darts

The witch stumbled out of a shrinking portal into the gloom of the Dread Lord's basement. Next to her, Sathach landed in a three-point superhero pose—feet planted wide, one arm raised behind him, and the tented fingers of his left hand resting on the floor. His head snapped up, and his eyes flicked to a wall-mounted pegboard. Hank and the witch—and presumably Phæras, it was tough to tell—watched in silence as he somersaulted across the ten-foot span of floor and popped up like a jack-in-the-box to retrieve his paranormal paraphernalia.

Sathach donned his headlamp, then handed the thermal imager to Hank. He turned on the EMF meter, but it immediately glowed red from Phæras's proximity so he holstered it and grabbed the spirit box. Holding a finger to his lips, he gestured toward the greenish glow emanating from the bank of monitors in the rear of the basement, which was hidden from view by a wall of boxes labeled Yohimbe Love Darts. The Dread Lord pointed in the direction of his command center, then back to himself, followed by a series of complex hand signals.

The witch made a hand signal of her own, pushed past him, and stalked toward the green glow. He huffed and dodged in front of her to take the lead. Hank fell in step beside her, with Phæras trailing behind. As they traversed a maze formed of stacked boxes and mounds of misprinted leggings, the air grew steadily colder. Hank aimed the thermal imager toward Ghostbusters HQ. The screen displayed a blob of dark purple.

He elbowed her and mouthed, *Cold.*

They emerged from the labyrinth facing the wall of screens where Sathach spent his nights watching earnest paranormal investigators scare each other shitless. The photo of Heather and the twins had been returned to his desk, but the mystifying marital aid hung in midair before them, its various tendrils lifting and lowering as though someone were trying to put the godsdamned thing on.

"State your business, Spirit!" Sathach lisped. He turned the knob on the spirit box, producing a rush of static. "Are you my . . ." His voice cracked, and he took a shaky breath. "Are you my father?"

A gusty sigh whooshed from the box. "I mean, *technically*," said a wry male voice.

The witch shook her head. The spirit box was nothing more than a glorified walkie-talkie. Anyone with a radio could be screwing with Sathach (in which case, she'd hunt the shithead down and hex them with hangnails and haunted warts). As for the floating sex pretzel . . .

She walked up to it and passed her hand above the tangled nest of straps, then below it. No strings.

"Stop!" the box said. "That tickles."

Phæras drifted closer to the witch. "I do sense a weak electromagnetic field."

"Yeah, but look at all the freaking electronics!"

"I assure you, I can tell the difference."

The Dread Lord ignored them, as did the asshat on the radio.

"Father, have you passed beyond the veil?"

The static stuttered. "Have I what?"

"Are you dead?" Sathach asked with a trace of irritation.

"Uh . . ." One of the silicone straps twirled idly in a circle. "Yep. Dead. *So* dead."

The rubbery forehead of the Keanu wrinkled in a frown.

"I don't think he's really dead," Hank said in a stage whisper.

"No shit," said the witch. "How are you doing this, you little prick?"

"It's a ghost thing, obviously, and my prick is not—"

"Well, knock it off." She glared at the empty space where a head would be. "Mark my words, I will find your sorry ass. And when I do—"

A maniacal titter echoed from the spirit box. "You'll *what?*" the voice said, dripping with malicious glee. "You have no idea who you're—"

"I feel it!" Hank spun the witch to face him and gripped her shoulders.

"Gods dammit, now is not the time for your horny bullshit!"

Maybe it was partly *her* horny bullshit? She still wasn't quite sure.

"It's coming," he said in a flat monotone. His face, which was normally either lit with a dopey grin or glazed in a film of good-natured confusion, was eerily blank.

"What are you talking about?" The witch wriggled free of his grasp. "What's wrong with you?"

"Don't you feel it?" His eyes flashed. Literally *flashed*. "It's so angry."

"Uh . . . Phæras," she said, glancing at her reflection in his shining orb.

"Something is seriously wrong with Hank. Can you take him to the psychic surgery? He's been acting weird ever since—"

"He's right." Phæras's metallic voice carried the alarmed clang of a warning bell. "Something *is* coming. It feels like—"

"Run!" roared the spirit box.

The bewildering sex toy dropped to the floor in a noodly heap, and a rain of yellow pencils fell from the ceiling like #2 hail.

A blaze of blue light flared at the opposite end of the basement, accompanied by a sizzling *zap*.

"EM burst," Phæras said in a tinny whisper. "That's what I felt at the park!"

Hank's head swiveled mechanically to face the light. "It's here."

A sinuous azure ribbon shone on the ceiling, emanating from whatever had just arrived in the basement. It began to advance through the maze of boxes in a fluid, serpentine motion.

The witch fired up her shields and pulled as much entropine as she could hold from the master contract, sending up a grateful prayer to Discordia that Keyser was safely at home. Keeping her eyes trained on the flickering glow, she curled her fingers into the sacred K.

She was going to light this motherfucker *up*.

Phæras drifted between her and the Dread Lord. "Sathach, I'll take Hank," he said in a voice so low it was more vibration than sound. "You take the witch. We'll meet at—"

Sathach raised his hand, palm out, silencing Phæras midsentence. He pointed toward the advancing glow.

We need to see it first, he mouthed. *Then we can go.*

Phæras wobbled uncertainly, then he bobbed a quick nod.

The Dread Lord gestured for the witch and Phæras to move behind a tower of boxes emblazoned with the legend: It Really, Really Hurts!™ Extra Strength Weight-Loss Wraps. He took Hank's elbow and tugged him into the shadow of a square support column.

The witch watched the cerulean light's progress on the ceiling tiles as the intruder snaked toward them. A tsunami of fury crashed into her, but the emotion wasn't hers. It was alien. Predatory. *Other*. It seeped into her bones and soaked into her psyche, but it didn't kindle rage in her soul.

What she felt was fear.

The witch had been afraid before. She'd known monsters were real since her earliest memory. Hell, she'd been raised by a cosmic horror and worked in close proximity with a dizzying array of eldritch beasties, some of whom could eat people like popcorn. Over the years, she'd watched as the Dread Lord bit off her middle finger, as the Sheriff liquefied and drank a ravening ghast, as her familiar was turned to electrons by an agent of the Swarm.

She'd felt fear in all its forms—fear of pain, fear of loss, even fear of death.

But this was something different. Something far more powerful and much, much worse.

The glow rounded the final bend, and the monster slithered into the open area in front of the monitors. A wyrm made of sapphire flame—the precise blue of a pilot light—lifted its diamond-shaped head. A forked tongue flicked out of its mouth like a firebolt as it scented the air. The hairs on the witch's arms stood on end, and her body tingled with an electric buzz. She wanted to raise her hands, wanted to hit the wyrm with everything she had, but she couldn't move. It wasn't the time-stopped frozenness she'd experienced when the Vaping Douche deployed his magical artifact.

No, she was immobilized by the utter paralysis of mind-numbing, pants-shitting terror.

The witch saw the smooth surface of Phæras's orb ripple from the corner of her eye. She was powerless to turn her head, but she suspected he was in thrall to the same overpowering dread.

Move, she told herself. *Move or die.*

She strained against her fear and raised her arms in a panicked jerk. The serpent's head snapped toward her, and its jaws gaped open to reveal plasma-arc fangs the length of her forearm. Sizzling beads of light dripped from its lightning teeth. It hissed, and sparks flew from gaping jaws. She felt Keyser's presence in her auric field as her alarm roused him from a post-coital nap. He filled her mind's eye with an image of herself blasting Megawhite with the entropic strike. His meaning was clear: *FIRE!*

The witch reached for her magic, but fright made her slow. Clumsy.

The wyrm darted toward her, its jaws stretched wide. Her breath hitched in her chest, and she squeezed her eyes shut.

Burned alive. Such an infuriatingly stereotypical way for a witch to die.

But death did not come.

When she dared to open her eyes and squint into the blinding blue glare, a man stood between her and the monster. A broad-shouldered man in a Spectral Forces uniform.

The serpent hissed again, and sparks showered Hank's arms.

He didn't flinch.

Instead, he leaned toward the wyrm until his blazing blue eyes were mere inches from the tip of its flicking tongue and said, "Mine."

"Phæras!" Sathach shouted. "Get the witch to safety!"

The wyrm whipped toward him almost too quickly for her eyes to follow. She felt the cool kiss of liquid metal as Phæras's orb made contact with her bare arm.

The last thing she saw through the neon haze of netherlight was the serpent's jaws closing on the Dread Lord's neck.

CHAPTER FIFTEEN

Trouble in Paradise

The witch fell out of a chest-high portal and crash-landed in front of her desk. She scrambled to her hands and knees, then used the desk to pull herself to her feet.

"Take me back, Phæras!"

The usually smooth spin of Phæras's orb juddered. "Sathach wanted you safe," he said, his voice ringing with regret. "Going back would be suicide."

"Then don't stay!" She reached for him, but he dodged out of the way. "Phæras, *please*. I might be able to do something. I could . . . I could distract it, give him a chance to get away."

"It's too late."

"No," she said, shaking her head wildly. "We'd know if he was gone. We would have felt it—just like with the Unseen Creeping Horror." She lunged toward him and plunged her hand into his quicksilver core. "Now! Take me now!"

"I—"

His voice cut off abruptly, and the erratic spin of his orb ceased.

"What?" the witch said. "What is it?"

"I think . . ." His mirrored surface rippled. "I think I just felt it leave."

"Then take me—"

She squinted against a blaze of netherlight.

"—back!"

This time, the witch landed on her feet. The wyrm was gone, and the air in the basement no longer held the same buzzing, electrical charge. Hank still stood where he'd been when Phæras portaled her out. He shook himself like a wet dog, and the blue glow faded from his eyes.

"Witch?"

She ignored him and rushed to the Dread Lord, who lay motionless on the floor. The Keanu was blessedly intact. The witch knelt next to him, rested her hand on his shoulder, and gave him a gentle shake.

"Sathach?" His head rolled limply to the side. She glanced up at Phæras through a veil of unshed tears. "He'll be okay, right?"

"I . . . I don't know."

"Sathach!"

The witch smacked him, and he drew a sharp intake of breath and sat up like a vampire rising from a coffin. She wrapped her arms around his stupid shoulders and squeezed. Then she panicked at the close contact and smacked him again.

"Ow!" he said, pressing a hand to his cheek. "I must've fainted . . . and I seem to have soiled my Skyn."

"Yeah, well, I nearly soiled mine, too."

"Let's get you up." Hank offered his hand to the Dread Lord and pulled him to his feet. "I'm not really sure what just happened."

"That makes four of us," Phæras said.

"We need to talk this shit through."

"Agreed." Sathach took an audibly sloshy step. "I might just take a moment to . . . freshen up." He pointed toward the stairs at the far end of the basement. "I'll meet you in the living room." He stepped into a portal and left them in the basement's eerie gloom.

Phæras followed Hank and the witch through the maze. (She took the lead after Hank made three consecutive wrong turns in the leggings labyrinth.) They found their way to a living room decorated in an aggressively #BossBabe aesthetic. An entire wall was dedicated to showcasing Top Seller trophies and merch from Heather's various side hustles. A primary-colored baby mat with dangling toys occupied the center of a patterned rug, and the infant equivalent of an open-topped dog crate sat at the far end of the couch. Family photos cycled through a digital-photo frame on the mantel—a wedding portrait, a few shots from a Caribbean honeymoon, and an endless reel of baby pictures. (The witch's personal favorite was an exhausted Sathach rocking the twins to sleep in a makeshift swing formed by tentacles.)

The witch sat in a glider by the fireplace, where no hot-but-clearly-impaired co-workers could squeeze in next to her. Hank plopped down on a love seat, and Phæras hovered over one end of the couch. Fortunately, no one attempted small talk, which belonged in the eighth circle of hell, as far as she was concerned.

There's nothing like a near-death experience to put people in the mood for quiet reflection.

The Dread Lord strode into the room a few minutes later. The Keanu's hair was damp, and he no longer sloshed when he walked. He took a seat on the couch and propped his elbows on his knees.

Sathach looked up at the witch through a curtain of black hair and said, "Witch, I saw my life flash before my eyes." He clasped his hands in prayer. "Azathoth has spared me for a greater purpose."

"Perhaps." Phæras made a tinny throat-clearing sound. "Sathach, what material is your Skyn made of?"

"Silicone rubber," he said. "Very high-quality stuff. Heather has a great manufacturer in . . ." His voice trailed off, and he frowned. "Why do you ask?"

"When the, uh . . ."

"Fire-snake," Hank said helpfully.

"When the fire-snake arrived," Phæras said, "I felt the same burst of electromagnetic energy as when Yi'danag was murdered at Dunwich Park."

Sathach sat up straighter. "I detected it on my EMF meter!"

Phæras bobbed. "The creature's teeth and tongue looked like lightning, yes?"

"Yeah," the witch said. "And?"

"Lightning is a plasma," Phæras said, "and plasma is ionized gas. The passage of charged particles through the lightning's path creates an electric current."

"Cool." She cocked her head and gazed at him. "Still not sure where you're going with this."

"Silicone rubber does not conduct electricity."

"The Keanu saved my life!" Gloopy tears formed at the corners of the Dread Lord's eyes. "*Heather* saved my life."

"What about your unknown Archon?" the witch asked. "Did you sense that portal signature when the fire-snake turned up?"

"I did not."

Hank raised his hand.

Phæras's orb tilted. "Yes, Deputy?"

"What about me?"

"What *about* you," the witch repeated. "You've been acting"—*hornier than a Valhalla alehouse*—"pretty freaking weird ever since the UCH was killed."

"Would you mind walking us through what happened at the park?" Phæras asked.

Hank shrugged. "Not much to tell," he said. "I saw a flash of lightning and heard a zappy sound, and then the fire-snake attacked. I think I got off a shot with the ball lightning cannon, but I don't remember anything after that."

"The ball lightning cannon . . ." Phæras drifted around the coffee table in a pensive, elliptical orbit. "Lightning is a pathway for the movement of ions. I wonder if some part of the fire-snake's essence traversed that channel and landed—"

"In me," Hank said.

"Precisely."

"But I haven't hurt anyone. I *wouldn't*."

"*You* wouldn't," the witch said. "And you haven't. But you've been a total horndog—"

"Witch!" Sathach said.

"—and your eyes were glowing blue."

"There's also the fact that the creature did not attack you," Phæras said. "You were entirely defenseless. Yet not only did the fire-snake leave you be, it respected your claim on the witch."

Hank turned earnest eyes—*brown* eyes, which she should've known, gods dammit—on her. "I don't know why I said you were mine, Witch. I didn't mean . . . I have no idea what I meant. It just came out!"

"You probably saved my life." She squirmed in discomfort and added, "Asshole."

"Should I . . ." He ran a hand through his hair. "Maybe I should have the Sheriff lock me up until this is all over."

The witch paused, considering. She hated the thought of Hank in a cell, but she remembered very clearly what Carcosa had gotten up to when his pale passenger took the wheel. "I hate to say it, but—"

"No." Sathach shook his head. "If anything, we should keep Hank close. He felt the fire-snake coming even before Phæras did—and he warned us. Then he placed himself between you and the monster." He reached out and patted Hank's knee. "Welcome to the WTF."

"I gotta say, I'm feeling a little hesitant here, Sathach," the witch said. "What if the thing can . . . I don't know, look through his eyes and figure out where we are or listen in when we're making plans?"

"If that's the case, it's had other opportunities to track us down. Why wait until now?"

The witch had no answers. All she had, in fact, were more questions. "Could it have been the Unquenchable Flame? Could he make himself look like that?"

"Flame would *never* attack me!" the Dread Lord said. "He has a deep respect for the field of human resources." His outrage melted into uncertainty. "But . . ."

"But what?" the witch said.

"He formed himself into the shape of a rhinoceros policeman last Halloween, so I suppose he *could*."

"That sounds like a Judoon," Phæras said. Blank stares all around. "It's from *Doctor Who*. Even if he could assume the fire-snake's appearance, I don't think he could broadcast such unbridled rage."

"I'm not trying to be a dick here, but Flame has a very pissy vibe."

"There's a difference between a pissy vibe and fury so profound it induces paralytic terror," Phæras said.

"Yeah, but it's a difference in degree," the witch said, "not in kind. Za'gathoth said she knew next to nothing about him. Maybe this wyrm form is the next phase in his life cycle or something. First he's an egg, then a larva, then a grumpy security guard, and now a fire-snake."

Again, the Dread Lord shook his head. "Witch, I just don't think—"

"You don't *think* it's him," she said. "But do you *know?*"

Sathach's crossed eyes shifted to Phæras, who wobbled a shrug.

"No," he said. "I guess I don't."

Keyser Söze was waiting for the witch on the park bench in front of her apartment building. He waddled toward her at top speed, climbed her like a tree, and grudgingly accepted a brief hug. Then he perched on her shoulder, gripping her braid to steady himself.

"Aw, you were worried about me."

He chittered a grumpy reply, but he also nuzzled his face against her cheek.

The witch hitched her backpack higher and trudged to her apartment, overcome with a wave of bone-deep weariness. She was short on sleep, long on worries, and well overdue for a few hours curled up in her papasan chair with *Chaste Makes Waste*. A cold beer sounded pretty godsdamned good too. She unlocked the front door, bracing herself for the mess she usually returned to after leaving Keyser alone, but her apartment was . . .

Holy Chao. Her battered Roomba whirred by on a mindless circuit across the spotless floor.

No spilled trash. No litter box mishaps. No half-eaten brownies.

She arched an eyebrow and looked down at Keyser. "You really *were* worried. Well, everything's gonna be—"

A muffled thud sounded from her bedroom.

Oh, gods. His lady friend was back. If that little she-devil had pissed the bed again, the witch would lose her freaking mind. Keyser growled and tore down the hall.

Trouble in paradise?

She sighed, propped her broom against the wall, and followed him. Keyser crouched in front of her closet door, emitting an angry rumble. She felt a prickle of unease. Whatever was in there, he didn't like it one bit. Her mind inevitably pulled her back to the Dread Lord's basement, but she felt no fear, sensed no apocalyptic furnace of rage.

This was something else.

"Who's there?" she asked.

A furtive rustle was the only reply.

"Listen, do you have any idea who you're screwing with?"

Thunk.

Her fingertips tingled with magic, but she set her proverbial phasers to *stun* rather than *disintegrate*. Always a chance it was some shit-eating teenager on the wrong end of a double-dog dare. She gripped the doorknob, twisted it, and yanked it open.

Nothing.

Well, not *nothing* nothing. A pile of dirty clothes on the floor. A sparsely populated rack of smart-ass T-shirts. But no—

Something catapulted up out of her laundry and hit her in the chest like a fleshy bowling ball. Scrabbling claws plucked at her clothes as the thing clambered toward her face. She instinctively squeezed her eyes shut.

"Get off, get off, *get off!*"

She felt Keyser tugging on her jeans, then two warm, dry paws gripped her cheeks.

"It's high time we had a little chat," said a woman's caustic voice.

The witch opened her eyes and found herself face-to-gruesome-visage with a miniature old man.

Godsdamned Jenkin.

CHAPTER SIXTEEN

The Book of Azathoth

Keziah Mason," the witch repeated. "Nope. Doesn't ring a bell."

Jenkin glowered at her. "You're telling me you've never heard of the most famous witch ever to walk the Earth?"

"'Fraid not."

But the name *did* have a beguiling ring of familiarity. The witch dispatched her auric self to root around in her palace of memory.

"Well, I'm her." Keziah gave a haughty sniff. "And I'll have you know, I was an absolute *legend* in my day."

"Looking like that?" The witch eyeballed the pubic-furred, old-man-faced dog-rat. "I'm not buying it."

"Jenkin is my familiar." The creature settled onto his haunches on the witch's kitchen table and glared at her with baleful red eyes. "That's why your maimed raccoon hates him. Familiars are fiercely territorial."

Keyser was, in point of fact, currently pouting under her bed, but loyalty compelled her to defend his honor. "My maimed raccoon would mop the frigging floor with whatever *that* is," she said, waving a hand at the pitiful beast.

"Ha! Witches are fiercely territorial, too." Jenkin smirked at her. "Oh, we'd band together in times of crisis, join forces to hex our enemies, that sort of thing. But other than that, we always kept to ourselves. Covens were just for—"

"Dancing naked and getting shitfaced?" The witch raised a coffee mug of Chicken Cock in an ironic toast.

"So you do know *some* witch lore." Jenkin's pale tongue flicked over his lips. "Could I, um . . ." One hairless, rodent-like paw gestured at the bottle.

"Why the hell not?"

The witch grabbed a cleanish bowl from the counter and sloshed a slug of bourbon into it. Jenkin crouched and lapped up the liquor, then pointed at the empty vessel in an obvious *hit me again* request. She grudgingly complied.

"Ah, that hits the spot," Keziah said. "Listen, we're about to be in a world of hurt here. I tried to warn Sibyl, but only another witch can understand Jenkin, and you wouldn't even give me the time of day."

"How in gods' names was I supposed to know you were in there?"

"I made it as obvious as I could," she said. "Weird Wendy. Ring any bells?"

So Weird Wendy *was* a witch . . .

Just not *the* witch.

"Those dumbass cards are the opposite of obvious."

"I hate that deck." Jenkin's face dipped into the bowl of liquor again. He raised his head and gave it a disgusted shake. "What a humiliating place to spend my afterlife."

Keziah's soul must be linked to the cards, just as Lovecraft dwelt in *The Necronomicon*. That *would* be a shitty end to an allegedly storied magical career.

"I didn't start out in here, I'll have you know," Keziah said. "I used to live in a very nice Marseilles deck. Quite dignified. My many-times-great-grandniece spilled grape Kool-Aid on it back in the eighties, and those cursed trash can cards were the only thing around." Jenkin's bony shoulders lifted in a shrug. "I've done the best I could with them."

"But why bind your soul to anything?" the witch asked. "You just weren't ready to die?"

Keziah snorted. "I was born ready. But I had a sacred duty to future witches." Jenkin's whisker-sprinkled chin lifted in an expression of noble determination. "A duty to all mankind."

The witch regarded Keziah . . . Jenkin? . . . *both* of them with a skeptical eye. "I'm not trying to shit on your vocation here, but doing love readings and selling lotto picks at the Midnight Carnival hardly sounds like a sacred duty."

"It's not, you spectacular idiot!" Keziah snapped. "I had a vision foretelling the Emergence. I kicked up a huge fuss about it and warned every witch who'd listen, but I got the date wrong by a couple decades. Never been much for math. When the fateful day came and went with no chthonic catastrophe, I lost all credibility." Jenkin stared off into the distance. "I am the Cassandra of the witches."

"The who?"

"The one nobody believes," Keziah said. "A laughingstock." Jenkin lapped up the rest of the bourbon and belched. "When the Archons burst forth from their lair, I had to watch as my descendants charged into an unwinnable battle." She shook her head. "They left me behind—just like they left *you* behind."

"I was a newborn," the witch said. "Pretty sure I'd be much less alive if they'd taken me along. Besides, it's not like I'd have tipped the balance in their favor."

"Maybe not, but we wouldn't have wound up alone, would we?"

The witch thought of Chad.

Of Sathach, Magnolia, and Hank.

Even the godsdamned County Clerk.

"I didn't wind up alone."

They sat in contemplative silence, each lost in her own thoughts, until a sulfurous *puff* from Jenkin's hindquarters nearly made the witch lose her lunch. She gagged and fanned the air in front of her face.

"So, um . . . gods, that's foul . . . what did you do after the Emergence?"

"As far as I knew, the world was fresh out of witches," Keziah said. "That meant I couldn't talk to anyone, so I went to sleep for a while. The cards still drew on my power to do basic fortune-telling, but I paid it no mind. Didn't much care what happened, if you want the truth. Until . . ."

"Until what?"

"Until *you*." Jenkin flopped down on the table and rested his chin on disturbingly pink paws. "When you walked into Sibyl's tent, you dumped a bucket of psychic ice water over my head. And as soon as I woke up, another vision hit me like a sledgehammer. With Sibyl there, all I could do was use the cards."

"Tell me more about the . . ."

The witch's voice trailed off as a memory-induced knowledge bomb detonated in her mind.

"About the what?" Keziah asked.

"Holy hell. I remember who you are."

The witch had read as little Lovecraft as possible, but thanks to Mother Mayhem, she'd been compelled to skim his greatest hits. Keziah Mason was the name of a character in at least one of his tales, a charming specimen called "The Dreams in the Witch House." In the story, a college student took an attic room in an old house and had a series of increasingly unhinged run-ins with Keziah, an evil witch, and her human-faced familiar, Brown Jenkin. Good ol' HPL had rolled out all the usual witch stereotypes. Keziah had a hunched spine, a hooked nose, a guttural voice, and . . .

Oh, Howie, you weapons-grade asshole.

"I'm gonna go out on a limb here and assume you didn't actually sacrifice a baby to Azathoth?"

Jenkin leaped to his feet and broke into a fit of barks that brought Keyser Söze charging into the kitchen at a dead run. Keyser's fur was so puffed up he was almost spherical. He launched himself at the bedraggled dog-rat like a cannonball. The witch barely managed to snatch him out of midair and clasp him to her chest.

"Base slander!" Keziah growled. "That chicken-hearted, evil-tongued liar utterly *ruined* my good name." Jenkin stood on trembling legs, panting with rage.

"Good gods, calm down!" Keyser snarled and lunged toward the creature, but the witch held him back. She stared at Keziah's familiar, struggling to repress a shudder of revulsion. "I'm guessing you didn't feed Jenkin your blood either."

"Of course not!" Keziah said between furious yips. "First the bastard steals my book, and then he writes that ridiculous smear piece." With a sigh of canine resignation, Jenkin collapsed on the table in a decrepit heap. "Fucking Lovecraft."

"What do you mean, he stole your book?" the witch asked.

"The Book of—" Jenkin cocked a leg and commenced an intimate personal grooming session. "Knock it off!" Keziah yelled. Her familiar grumbled, but he obediently moved his face away from his crotch. *"The Book of Azathoth."*

The witch eased Keyser to the floor and topped off their drinks. "Start at the beginning, and tell me everything."

Keziah took a deep breath. "I was born in Salem, Massachusetts, the eldest daughter of a—"

"You know what I mean," the witch said. "Don't be a dick."

"I haven't talked to anyone in thirty years!"

"I've got Animal Control on speed dial."

"Fine." Jenkin's tiny rat-like fingers drummed the table. "I've already told you I have precognitive visions, but my true occult passion was astral travel."

The witch lifted a shoulder. "Kinda boring, if you ask me."

"Which I did not," Keziah said. "I had a real gift for it. Unlike most witches, I could travel to other dimensions."

Other dimensions?

Damn. That was actually kinda badass.

"Like a certain pocket dimension in the Fathomless Abyss?"

"What?" Jenkin fixed the witch with a red-eyed scowl. "No, I went to the Dreamlands. And there, I met an Archon."

The witch inhaled a lungful of fine Kentucky bourbon. Jenkin watched with thinly veiled amusement as she coughed and hacked.

"No Archons . . . there . . ." she croaked. "All taken . . . by the Swarm . . ."

"Oh, that's what he wanted everyone to think." Jenkin's face shone with self-satisfaction. "But this was no rank-and-file tentacled nightmare. This was an Outer God."

"Not . . . possible . . . to hide . . ."

"It is for a shape-shifter," Keziah said. "A true cosmic horror, this guy. Myriad manifestations. At first, he wore a different shape every time I talked to him." Jenkin tilted his head as his mistress relived the distant past. "But he's as vain as a peacock. It wasn't long before he showed me his natural form. The sight would've driven me insane if I was physically present."

"What kinda shit did he say to you?"

"He mostly talked about himself, but once he got going, he gossiped like a fishwife." Jenkin locked eyes with the witch. "And I wrote it all down."

"In *The Book of Azathoth*?"

"Yes. I'd had a vision of the Emergence soon after my first visit to the Dreamlands," Keziah said. "So I knew it was important to learn all I could about the Archons. It wasn't long before my fiendish friend tried to drive me to madness and bully me into starting his cult back here on Earth. A day came when I knew it wasn't safe to see him again."

"But you had the book."

"I had the book," Keziah said. "The only problem was I lost it."

The witch gaped at her. "You *lost* it?"

"Back in my day, witches had to move around a lot," Keziah said. "Stay in one place too long, and you wind up on the business end of a noose."

"Or burned at the stake."

Keziah chuckled. "If anyone was fool enough to try it, I'd have pulled an Agnes Nutter, packed my skirts with gunpowder, and blown the bastards into Discordia's loving arms." The smile on Jenkin's face faded. "From Salem, I moved to Boston, then on to Philly. I spent a few years on a farm in Vermont before I finally wound up in Arkham, Massachusetts."

Arkham . . .

The witch had a sneaking suspicion she knew what happened next. That particular town was notoriously the summer home of one Howard Phillips Lovecraft.

"I bought a nice place, fixed it up, started a poison garden," Keziah said. "But I screwed around and cured one too many social diseases. The locals started calling my place 'the Witch House.' It wasn't long before a mob came in the night—pitchforks and torches, the whole nine yards. I grabbed everything I could and ran, but—"

"You left *The Book of Azathoth* behind."

Jenkin's face creased in a frown. "I'd swear on a stack of grimoires that I packed it," Keziah said. "But here's the thing . . . my Dreamlands chats with—" Her voice cut off, and a grimace of fear flashed over Jenkin's features. "With the Outer God weren't just about *me* getting into *his* head. He got into mine too." Jenkin's lips puckered in a moue of concern. "I think he wanted that book to get out. No, he *needed* it to get out. Worship is like food for a god, and he was ravenous. All it takes is speaking his name, and he can get his hooks into you."

The witch drained her mug, rocked back in her chair, and crossed her arms. "Let me guess . . . a struggling young author bought your house."

"Nailed it in one," Keziah said. "He used *The Book of Azathoth* as inspiration—he renamed it *The Necronomicon*—and started pumping out eldritch horror." Jenkin huffed. "*I* write about chthonic monsters, and I'm a crackpot. *He* does it, and it's literature."

"So all of that about HPL dreaming his stories was bullshit?"

"Pure manure."

The witch chewed her lip, shuffling the facts like Garbage Pail Kids cards.

There *had* been an Archon in the Dreamlands—and not just any ol' tentacled beastie, an Outer God. This shape-shifting OG must be Phæras's unknown Archon. Transforming into a serpentine blue blowtorch would be a cakewalk for a being that powerful.

Then again, while Phæras had sensed the same portal signature at the scene of both murders, he had *not* detected it during the attack in Sathach's basement.

Gods, the threads of this case were as tangled as the Flying Spaghetti Monster's noodly appendages.

The witch massaged her aching temples. "Did you see what happened when Sibyl was murdered?"

"Wasn't there. I was riding shotgun with Jenkin," Keziah said. "We were following *you*. By the time we got back . . ."

Her voice trailed off.

The witch remembered Sibyl's adoration of Jenkin, her inexplicable tenderness toward the unsightly little creature. "I'm sorry. That must've been—"

"Yeah," Keziah said. "It was."

"The night before Sibyl's murder, an Archon was killed," the witch said. "Burned to death, just like she was."

"The Unseen Creeping Horror."

"You heard about that?" she asked. "About the fire-snake?"

"Like I said, we've been following you." Jenkin pawed at his oversize old-man ears. "Listening in."

"Do you think your Outer God could've done it?"

"My second sight tells me he's here and he's involved, but the details are murky. He certainly *could* have done it." Jenkin's expression grew pensive. "But he never struck me as the type to get his hands dirty. Before the Archons' war with the Swarm, he never had to risk his own skin. He always had his Million Favored Ones chomping at the bit to please him. If he escaped, maybe one of his pet monsters did, too."

A Million Favored Ones, or just one Unquenchable Flame?

If they were working together, it could explain why neither the electromagnetic burst nor the unknown Archon's portal signature appeared during all three attacks. Maybe the OG was setting his disciple up as a patsy—taking on a similar fiery form so he could blame his doomed devotee later.

But *why?*

"Assuming this god is involved, do you have any idea what his motive might be?" the witch asked.

"To kill another Archon? No clue. But for Sibyl . . ." Jenkin's face drooped, and he seemed to age a decade in an instant. "Well, I'm sure he was furious when I never returned to the Dreamlands. If he sensed my magic in the cards, he could've murdered her as an act of vengeance. In which case, her blood is on my paws."

"Even if that's true," the witch said, "it's not your fault. *You* didn't kill her."

"I didn't save her either."

A cloak of silence weighted with bitter regret descended on the kitchen. The witch had been where Keziah was. In her experience, there were only two cures: time and action. She couldn't help with the first.

The second, on the other hand . . .

"Let's nail this eldritch assclown."

Jenkin perked up. "How?"

"We have to start with *who.*" She propped her elbows on the table and met the creature's gimlet gaze. "Is there anything you can tell me without speaking his name?"

"Nine hundred ninety-nine avatars. Spreads madness like it's going out of style." Jenkin arched a scraggly eyebrow, clearly expecting her to know who the OG was. "Also known as the Crawling Chaos."

A wave of lightheadedness crashed into the witch, and she damn near slid out of her chair.

Because she *did* know who they were dealing with.

The Outer God currently roaming Tophet County in who-knew-what guise was one of the most feared and well-known figures in the entire Mythos.

Nyarlathotep.

CHAPTER SEVENTEEN

Tootle Translate

Keyser waddled toward the moon-beasts with his lopsided three-legged gait. Fluted blasts of greeting echoed in the cavern as a gang of diminutive toad-people surrounded him. The witch felt his flush of pleasure at the warm welcome.

She'd scheduled yet another WTF meeting for immediately after the weekly General Session, which would begin in—she checked the time on her BlackBerry—an hour and a half. The news of Nyarlathotep's survival was far too explosive to share via email, and County leadership needed to know as soon as possible. Keziah (and Jenkin) would join the task force in the Clerk's office to relate Keziah's firsthand account of her Dreamlands encounters with the Crawling Chaos. In the meantime, Keziah had taken Jenkin out to sniff around for any hints of the OG's presence. The witch, with nothing specific to do and a burning desire to do *something*, had opted to swing by Dunwich Park and check in on the Lunatic refugees.

The fluted yowl of moon-beast speech echoed in the cavern. Threading through the discordance was the pleasant lilt of another instrument. Hank sat in the center of a circle of beasts, wooden flute in hand, attempting to teach them "Sweet Caroline." The witch's heart gave a painful twinge at the sight of him patiently positioning knobbly gray fingers on bone flutes. He might be a total doofus, but he was also a good guy. A *great* guy, actually.

Gods, she hoped whatever had happened to him was reversible.

Since her last visit, the space had been transformed into a moon-beast-friendly dormitory. The beasts had carved niches into the stone walls to serve as beds, and three porta-potties now stood in a shadowed corner. A few hotel ice machines sat next to a buffet table laden with chunks of porous black rock. It wasn't exactly homey, but it was a damn sight better than the ruins of the Black Galley.

"Let's give this another try."

The witch spun toward the sound of a familiar voice. A knot of moon-beasts had gathered in front of a round table, blocking her view of the human who sat there, but she didn't need to see the speaker to identify him.

Chad.

She threaded her way through the hopping horde and circled around the table.

"Hey," she said. "What are you—"

Chad slammed his laptop closed like he'd been caught eyeballs-deep in a cam show. "Witch! What are you . . ." He ran a hand through his hair and forced an obviously fake smile. "It's good to see you."

She cocked her head. "Is it?"

"Of course it is." His features softened. "Sorry. I've been awake for about thirty hours trying to get Tootle Translate up and running. I dropped in to test it, but there's so much background noise in here that the app can't—"

The witch clapped her hands, and a cone of silence formed around the table. The moon-beasts exchanged quizzical, eyeless glances at the sudden quiet.

"Fixed it for you." She sat down and gestured toward the laptop. "Fire that thing up. I've got questions."

"Uh . . . okay." His forehead creased in a pained frown. "But I haven't tested it yet. It's probably still buggy."

"Only one way to find out."

Chad rested his hands on the computer, hesitating. It was starting to feel like he'd very much prefer it if she weren't here.

Well, tough shit.

The witch crossed her arms and glared at him. He shook his head, sighed, and opened the laptop.

"This," he said, passing her a black microphone, "is your mic. Hold down the button while you're talking, and the translation will broadcast here." He tapped a Bluetooth speaker in the center of the table.

"Simple enough."

Chad patted the empty seat next to him, and one of the three moon-beasts hopped up and squatted on its haunches. He placed an identical device in front of the beast and said, "I'll operate their mic since they need both hands to talk. Go ahead whenever you're ready."

"Hold up a sec." The witch pulled out her BlackBerry and tapped out a text. "Sathach and Phæras should hear this too."

"Are you sure?" Chad asked. "We don't even know how accurate it is. And it might be better to get an idea of what these guys have to say before we bring in—"

Chad's voice broke off as two pinpricks of netherlight formed in the cone of silence.

Oops. She'd forgotten about Chad's newfound mistrust of the Dread Lord. But it was too late to change her mind now, and she wasn't sure she *should*. The more people who knew what was going on, the better.

At least, she hoped so.

Phæras and Sathach emerged from their portals and took spots on either side of the witch.

"Eyewitness interviews," the Dread Lord said, rubbing his hands together with a chorus of squeaks. "This is *so* exciting, Witch!" His crossed eyes shifted to Chad. "I believe I see an outstanding performance award in your future, Mr. Chadwick."

Chad gave a wan smile. "Let's see if Tootle Translate works first."

"What do you think I should ask?" The witch drummed her fingers on the table. "Should I start with what happened on the Moon? Or skip straight to the Unseen Creeping Horror's murder?"

"Perhaps we should begin with introductions," Phæras said. "These events must have been quite traumatic. It may be wise to ease into the hard questions."

The Dread Lord sat up straighter. "This calls for an icebreaker!" He chewed his rubbery lip. "Two Truths and a Lie might be too complex given the cultural differences. We could always try—"

"Hello," the witch said, pressing the mic's button with a ferocity born of desperation. "I'm the witch of Tophet County. What's your name?"

A blast of music blared from the speaker, startling the seated moon-beast so badly it fell from its chair. The trio of beasts huddled on the cavern floor, fluting softly among themselves. After a brief discussion, the original beast leaped back onto the seat and raised its flute. Chad pressed the button just in time for it to answer.

"Dave."

"Ahem," the Dread Lord said. "Did he say . . . Dave?"

"I'm still working out the kinks." Chad flashed an *I-told-you-so* at the witch. "Let me check the transcription." He raised his eyebrows and nodded. "It's spelled *D*-apostrophe-*A-Y-V*-apostrophe-*Y-E*. D'ayv'ye."

What was it with eldritch creatures and godsdamned apostrophes?

The witch watched the moon-beasts rejoin their fellows around the igneous rock buffet. Hank waved to her enthusiastically, then rounded up his amphibian friends and led them out of the tunnel for a picnic.

"Mr. Chadwick," Phæras said, "would you be so kind as to email us a copy of the transcript?"

"No problem." Chad slid his laptop into the padded sleeve in his messenger bag and stood. "I'm heading to the library to brief the Dread Librarian. I'll send it when I get there." He circled around the table and leaned down to whisper in the witch's ear. "I miss you. Can I see you tomorrow night?"

Chad missed her?

He was the one who'd been avoiding her like a plague of haunted warts, and now he *missed* her?

The witch bit back her knee-jerk retort and shrugged. "Maybe." His face fell, and a pang of guilt pricked her conscience. "Probably." She grabbed a fistful of his polo shirt and pulled him closer. "But I want an explanation for your shady bullshit," she said, "and it'd better be good."

The tiniest of nods was his only acknowledgment. "I'll text you." Chad kissed her forehead, said goodbye to Phæras and Sathach, and left.

"I must confess," Phæras said, breaking the cone-induced silence, "I am not sure what to make of the moon-beasts' tale." He drifted around the table in a lazy circle. "Their hierophant—"

"That's the big bastard who burned to death at Dunwich Park, right?"

Phæras bobbed a nod. "The hierophant sailed the Black Galley from the Dreamlands to our universe three hundred seventy-eight lunar cycles ago, and—"

"What does that mean in regular years?" the witch asked.

"It means they arrived within days of the Emergence." Phæras's quicksilver orb rippled in agitation. "That cannot be a coincidence."

"The Swarm took the Dreamlands not long after they left," Sathach said. "Maybe the hierophant knew they were out of time?"

The witch shook her head. "I don't think so. Dave said their leader told them they'd be safe here, but he didn't say they'd be safe from the Swarm. The hierophant said they'd be safe from—"

"The co*met*," Phæras said. "According to Dave, the co*met* was what the hierophant feared."

"I soiled my Skyn at the very sight of it!"

Dave's hands had trembled violently on his bone flute as he told them how the co*met* lanced down from the stars and massacred dozens of moon-beasts, how it later immolated the Unseen Creeping Horror. Unfortunately, the beasts' attention had been on their hierophant when the UCH was attacked, so they could neither confirm nor deny the witch's theory that the Unquenchable Flame was the culprit. But the moon-beasts were certain both attacks were committed by the same perpetrator.

Whether the co*met* was one of Nyarlathotep's 999 avatars or the Unquenchable Flame acting on ol' Nyarly's orders, the witch had no doubt the OG was in this up to the tips of his tentacles.

Which reminded her . . .

"Flay me, Sathach," she said. "Last night. Five thirty or so."

He frowned. "Why?"

"I know shit."

The Dread Lord was practically vibrating in his Skyn. "Is it a conspiracy?" he asked hopefully. "That goes all the way to the top?"

"See for yourself," she said. "The new info is why I called the WTF meeting, but it's probably better if you find out now."

The Dread Lord beckoned to Phæras, whose silver orb darted over and swallowed his head. Together, they looked like a business-casual chrome lollipop. The witch felt his featherlight psychic touch as he flipped through her memories. A few heartbeats later, he cried out in shock, and Phæras's orb exploded into a fine silver mist.

"The Crawling Chaos has returned!" Sathach cried.

The witch cast a panicked glance around the cavern. Thankfully, the beasts were outside, and they were still protected by the cone of silence. The last thing Tophet County needed was another tantrum of terror.

Phæras gradually coalesced into standard spherical form, but his spin was wobbly and erratic. "The unknown Archon is an Outer God," he said in a tinny whisper. "But Nya—" He caught himself just in time to avoid speaking the name. "But *he* must have been on the master contract. I should still be able to recognize his etheric footprint."

"To me, the bigger issue is that the OG should be *dead*," the witch said. "Swarmified." She waved a hand. "You know what the hell I mean. How did he escape both your home universe *and* the Dreamlands without being transformed?

"All we know of Outer Gods came from Lovecraft and from Mother's stories," Sathach said. "Unreliable narrators, to put it mildly. The Crawling Chaos may very well have arcane powers beyond our comprehension."

"On the topic of incomprehensible shit," the witch said, "what possible reason would the OG have for slaughtering a bunch of moon-beasts and offing the UCH?"

Phæras made a metallic, throat-clearing sound. "Does he *need* a reason?" he asked. "He was known for sowing the seeds of madness."

Sathach gasped. "Do you think he was behind NFTs?"

"Well, they *are* crazy, but—"

The witch froze with her mouth hanging open and her eyes mid-blink. Through slitted lids, she saw an immobilized Dread Lord and a glint of Phæras's quicksilver. Rhythmic ticks and a plume of fruity steam heralded the arrival of the Vaping Douche. As before, he wore a dark business suit. Though the cavern was well lit, his face was cloaked in shadows.

"You've learned the truth of *The Book of Azathoth*," said the Douche. "An Outer God survived in the Dreamlands—the Crawling Chaos, the Masked Messenger, the Thousand-Faced One!" His voice rang with ardent fervor.

Oh, the OG definitely had his hooks in this dude.

"Now you must uncover hidden secrets."

Tick.

Tick.

Tick . . .

The clicks were beginning to slow.

"Believe the unbelievable. Imagine the unimaginable."

Tick . . .

Tick . . .

The witch's hands tingled as entropine began returning to her body.

As before, the man produced another artifact from his bag of tricks and turned a hand crank.

"Seek ye the Circle."

CHAPTER EIGHTEEN

Beyond Human Understanding

Ellie Dawson nodded solemnly to the wheeled aquarium containing Nommaquth's glowing, mutagenic bubbles.

"Thank you for the updates, High Lord." She glanced at her agenda. "Next up, we'll hear from the High Lords of Public Safety and Health and Human Services regarding their joint efforts to aid the lunar refugees."

Achartho and N'eithamiqug both dove for their mics in a *Jeopardy!*-esque race to buzz in. N'eithamiqug beat him to the punch and pushed the button with a grotesque, hairy spider's leg, prompting a shiver of revulsion from the witch.

"As High Lord of Health and Human Services," N'eithamiqug said, "caring for displaced populations is a natural fit for my department. I am pleased to lead the relief effort—"

"Co-lead!" Achartho bellowed.

"—with minor support from my colleague in Public Safety."

The witch snorted. Quite a change in tune since the emergency General Session at Dunwich Park. She watched N'eithamiqug's eight glittering eyes dart to Ellie as she listed the improvements made to the cavern, shouting to be heard over Achartho's periodic interjections.

Anything to win the approval of She Who Won the Gold . . .

The witch's BlackBerry vibrated, and she picked it up to check the notifications.

A text from Chad.

Now that Tootle Translate was up and running, Chad was free to join the task force, but she'd forgotten to mention this morning's WTF meeting when she saw him at the cavern. If she could bring him in, make him part of the investigation, maybe he'd deign to share the nature of the bug that'd recently crawled up his ass. So she'd texted him the details and invited him to attend.

The witch took a deep breath and opened his reply.

NERD-ROMANCER: Thanks for the invite, but I can't make it.

Her heart sank. What the hell happened to *I miss you?*

NERD-ROMANCER: Booked solid with meetings this a.m. Can you fill me in tomorrow night?

She supposed it *had* been short notice. And in Tophet County, missing a meeting could cost an arm and a leg.

Or a head.

WITCH: Sure. When & where?
NERD-ROMANCER: How about Asenath's at seven?

Asenath's Alehouse was the scene of their first kiss. Going back could be kind of . . . romantic.

If she was into that sort of thing.

Which she was not.

Not *really.*

WITCH: Sounds good.
NERD-ROMANCER: My place after. I have something to show you.

Something to show her?

Chad Chadwick, you naughty devil . . .

The witch's finger hovered over the eggplant emoji, but she decided to go for an air of mystery and leave him on read. She turned her attention back to the meeting.

"—remind the community to respect the 'No Wake' signs posted around Tehom Lake," Ellie said. "A pair of jet skis recently woke the Undersea Monstrosity from his decade-long slumber, and he consumed a pontoon boat in retaliation." She directed a stern gaze toward the audience. "Let's be neighborly."

The acting mayor passed the oratorial torch to Y'ggarlos, High Lord of Economic Development, who launched into a sadistically detailed account of the last Zoning Board meeting. Just as the witch was considering melting through the floor to escape, her BlackBerry buzzed again.

Email from Dread Librarian.

Another text from Chad would've been nice, but this was almost as good. The witch had emailed Chlogha to ask for help interpreting the Vaping Douche's latest cryptic clue: *Seek ye the Circle.* Why the asshole wouldn't just come out and say what he meant was beyond her, but if anyone could help, it would be the Dread Librarian.

From: dreadlibrarian@derlethmemoriallibrary.org
To: witch@tophetcounty.gov
Subject: Re:

Dear High Lord Innominanda,

Without knowing the broader context, I can only speculate about what "the Circle" might reference, but here's my best guess.

Over the course of his life, Lovecraft corresponded with a number of friends and protégés who contributed to the Mythos—authors such as August Derleth, Clark Ashton Smith, and Donald Wandrei. These writers came to be known as "the Lovecraft Circle." I have attached a spreadsheet listing the Circle's literary works. Please let me know if I can be of further assistance.

Warmly,
Chlogha

The witch opened the attachment and found hundreds and hundreds of titles. If the answer to the Vaping Douche's asinine riddle was hidden in there, it would take her a year to find it. She sighed, closed the PDF, and turned her attention back to the meeting.

"—granted a business license to Sphinxter's Peep Show, a longtime staple of the Midnight Carnival, to open a burlesque show-bar," Y'ggarlos said.

"We're always happy to welcome a new venture to Tophet County." Ellie looked out at the audience. "The floor is open for community feedback."

Blessedly, the audience remained seated and quiet.

"Thank you for your time and attention," Ellie said. "The General Session is adjourned."

"Tell them, Keziah," the witch said. "Tell them everything."

Jenkin nodded and cleared his throat portentously. "It all began centuries ago when I—"

"Ahem," Sathach said. "Um, Witch, as delighted as I am to meet your colleague, she appears to be speaking . . ." He cocked his head and regarded the dog-rat with a quizzical gaze. "A canine tongue?"

"Gods dammit, I forgot. Only witches can understand a familiar." The witch chewed her lip, searching her mental catalog of spells. She dug a box of lancets from her backpack, pricked the tip of her thumb, and smeared a few drops of her blood on Jenkin's lips. The weird little shit licked it off and grinned. A whisper of Ouranian-Barbaric, a burst of entropine, and voila . . . "Give it a try now."

Keziah said, "It all began centuries ago—"

"It worked!" Phæras said.

The Dread Lord rubbed his hands together in an excited flurry of squeaks. "I have the perfect name for this spell." He indulged in a dramatic pause. "Poodle Translate."

"Over my actual corpse." It actually wasn't bad, but she hadn't come up with it herself. Ergo, *nope.* The witch gestured for Keziah to continue. "Let's get this show on the road."

The ancient witch told the tale of her astral entanglement with Nyarlathotep, ending with two earth-shattering revelations: He was alive, and he was *here.*

"The Crawling Chaos lives?" the Clerk warbled. "I . . . I simply cannot believe it. Are you sure?"

Jenkin's bony body quivered. "We still have a thread of psychic connection," Keziah said. "I can feel him. He's in Tophet County."

A stutter of blinks rippled over the Clerk's half-dozen eyes. "But why would he conceal himself from us? Why would he kill Yi'danag? And why isn't he on the master contract?"

The witch's eyes drifted to a framed poster of the evil grand vizier from *Aladdin,* who glowered at the task force members from the wall above the Clerk's desk.

"There's only one way out of an Archonic contract," the witch said. "I should know."

The Dread Lord shifted uncomfortably and tugged at the collar of his dress shirt. "There are *two* ways," he said. "Death and collusion with the ancient enemy."

Phæras rotated sharply on his axis. "Impossible!" His tinny voice rang with certainty. "Nya— *He* is not dead. And as for cooperating with the Swarm, what possible reason would he have to betray his own kind?"

"He's the only Outer God still standing." The witch shrugged. "Survival is a godsdamned powerful motive."

They sat in silence. She looked from face to face around the table. The Clerk, stunned. Ellie, contemplative. Sathach, worried. Phæras, shiny. Jenkin, older than dirt. And Hank, confused.

Or maybe horny. Tough to say these days.

What she didn't see was determination. Resolve. A desire to act.

"All right, losers," the witch said. "Snap out of it. We need to figure out what we're going to *do*."

Ellie stiffened her spine and sat up straighter in her wheelchair. "Quite so, High Lord Innominanda." She removed the cap from her pen and positioned a yellow legal pad in front of her. "Keziah, what more can you tell us about your Dreamlands interlocutor?"

Jenkin limbered up with a brief downward-facing dog, turned in three circles, and flopped down on the table. "Well, he had a big chip on his shoulder about the other Outer Gods. Before the war, he was their mouthpiece and their messenger. He spent his days serving them and spreading madness on their behalf. To hear him tell it, they took him for granted." Jenkin huffed and rolled his red eyes. "Whatever he's doing, I guarantee at least part of his plan is to position himself at the top of the Archonic hierarchy and rebuild his cult."

"I've got contacts in the cults from last year. I'll reach out, see if his name comes up." The witch scribbled a note on her agenda. "Anything else that might help us figure out what he's up to?"

"Let me think . . ." Jenkin scratched his ribs with a back paw. "He was fascinated by human culture—especially ancient Egypt," Keziah said. "And he asked endless questions about science, technology, and witchly magic. He loved the idea of occult tools. Wands, chalices, athames . . . that sort of thing."

The witch exchanged a glance with Sathach and Phæras. "What about magical artifacts?"

"He wanted to hear all about them," Keziah said. "The old goat was a sucker for gadgets, whether magical or mundane."

"Maybe our OG had the Unquenchable Flame take Sibyl out," the witch said. "Then he gave her collection to the Vaping Douche."

Jenkin's wrinkled face creased in a frown. "Why would he go to all that trouble just to give the artifacts away?"

A godsdamned good question.

"Um . . . motives beyond human understanding?"

"I'm not human," the Clerk said, "and it doesn't make a bit of sense to me."

Hank raised his hand. "What did all that stuff do, anyway?"

"Most of the glassware—the cups and vases—stored entropic energy that could be used to recharge other artifacts," Keziah said. "Sibyl had a broken parasol that diverted attention from items in its vicinity. The thermometer was actually one of my personal creations. I made it before I . . ."

Jenkin pawed the deck of cards on the table before him as unspoken words rang in the air.

Before I died.

"The thermometer's just a cooking tool," Keziah said. "Handy for whipping up hot meals when you're on the run." Jenkin licked his nose and panted, thinking. "There was also an eggbeater that could summon storms. And the Newton's cradle—"

"The what, now?" the witch asked.

"The clicky ball thing. It stops time for a few seconds. What else . . ." Jenkin drummed tiny claws on the table. "Oh! The orrery is a teleporter."

"I don't know what the hell an orrery is—"

"A mechanical model of the solar system," Ellie said. "It shows the movement of moons and planets."

"The Douche must've used that cradle thing to freeze us," the witch said, "and the clockwork teleporter to get in and out."

"I concur." Phæras tilted on his axis in a thoughtful posture. "If the Outer God stole those items, perhaps he did so to enable this human to serve as his spokesman."

"But the Smoking Man has been giving us clues," Sathach said. "Wouldn't that mean the Crawling Chaos is on *our* side?"

"I don't even know what 'our side' is!" The witch threw up her hands. "Why go to the trouble of all this cloak-and-dagger horseshit when he could just roll in here right now and state his business? It drives me freaking crazy!"

Hank raised his hand again. "Maybe *that's* why," he said. "The puppy said he spreads madness."

Jenkin's hackles rose, and he growled menacingly. *"Puppy?"*

"Deputy O'Brien makes an excellent point," the Clerk said. "We cannot ascribe sane motivations to an Outer God who prides himself on embracing insanity." Two of her eyes swiveled on their stalks to meet the witch's. "I suggest another visit with Mother."

"Already on my list." The witch consulted her agenda. Next item: trash can cards. "Let's move on to Keziah's reading."

She shook the deck free of its drawstring bag, removed the rubber band, and deposited it in front of Jenkin. The Garbage Pail Kids shuffled themselves, and three familiar cards turned up. Jenkin rested a hairless pink paw atop Split Kit.

"This card represents the past," Keziah said. "The root cause of the situation. Split Kit usually indicates a traitor or a deceiver."

"Or perhaps a shape-shifter?" Phæras said.

"I know!" Hank's hand shot up. *Again.* "The Crawling Chaos!"

The Clerk patted his head with a tentacle, sizzling off a patch of hair with her acidic slime. "I rather suspect you are correct."

Jenkin pointed at the center card. "Stormy Heather is analogous to the Tower in traditional tarot. Disaster. A sudden downfall. A catastrophe."

"Or, with a more literal interpretation," Ellie said, "a lightning-tongued fire-snake."

"Fryin' Ryan represents the future in this spread," Keziah said, indicating the final card. "It means total destruction."

"That sounds bad," Hank said.

One of Jenkin's rheumy eyes squinched shut in a horrible wink. "It ain't great, handsome."

"Witch, are you confident in the accuracy of this . . . reading?" the Clerk asked.

Confident was a strong word, but Keziah was a powerful witch. She'd been around the tentacled block a few times, and she had a history with Nyarlathotep—which was more than anyone else in the room could say.

"Keziah's the real deal," the witch said. Jenkin puffed up his scrawny chest. "The deck also sent me to the moon-beasts." She turned to Sathach, who'd been uncharacteristically quiet. "Can you walk them through the transcript?"

He perked up and launched into a spirited dramatic reenactment of their conversation. Hank even chimed in with his flute to represent the moon-beasts' speech.

The witch's third eye conjured an image of Dave, trembling in fear as he described the attack on the Moon. Why would the all-powerful Nyarlathotep attack a colony of peaceful little toad-people? Unless . . .

"Hey," she said, cutting Hank off mid-tootle. "What if the OG had beef with the moon-beasts' hierophant?"

The Clerk's eyes widened and waved excitedly on their stalks. "If that were true, the Crawling Chaos may have sought only to settle a score," she said. "Poor Yi'danag could have been collateral damage in his assassination of an enemy."

"And Sibyl?" Phæras said.

Jenkin whimpered piteously.

"I think Sibyl died because of me," Keziah said. "I'm sure *he* was angry when I ended our visits. I . . . I must've drawn him to Sibyl, and he killed her."

"Or he had someone else kill her," the witch said. "The Unquenchable Flame is still missing. Chad checked in with his friends—no one's seen or heard from him. Why the hell would he be in hiding if he wasn't guilty of *something*?"

"Though I still find his involvement improbable," Phæras said, "it is a question worth asking."

"Not to put too fine a point on it, but he's literally made of blue fire."

"I simply refuse to believe it was Flame who attacked me in my basement," Sathach said. "We have always had a warm relationship. He's never missed a single primal-scream circle!"

"But if the OG got his hooks into the Flame..."

Hank's eyebrows drew together. "You can't hook someone who's made of fire. The hook would go right through—"

"Hey, Ellie," the witch said, "did you hear back from your star-nerd friend at the observatory?"

"I did." The acting mayor opened an email on her BlackBerry. "Dr. Sturman's digital sky survey has images of the Unquenchable Flame leaving Sol System the morning of Sunday, June ninth. She saw him return the evening of Friday, June twenty-first, and she has no evidence of him leaving the system since then."

"If he was around Friday night," the witch said, "that means he got back from his stellar foodie tour just in time to attack the moon-beasts."

"Did Dr. Sturman's survey capture photos of the attack on Luna?" Phæras asked.

Ellie shook her head. "I'm afraid not."

And on that unsatisfying note, the meeting was adjourned.

Phæras portaled back to the Midnight Carnival for his afternoon shift, and Ellie stayed behind to review boring budget shit with the Clerk. Then Jenkin disappeared into the sewer tunnels beneath City Hall to organize a surveillance team of rat-things, leaving the witch to trudge through the subterranean maze of hallways with Sathach and Hank. When they reached the elevator, Hank dove for the button and pushed it at least a dozen times.

"If you don't need me tonight, I'd like to visit Heather and the twins." Sathach's eyes brimmed with goopy tears. "I need to tell her what's happening, and we must . . ." He sniffled and took a shaky breath. "We must make arrangements for a prolonged separation."

"A separation?" she repeated. "I thought she was just giving you a few weeks to get settled. Are you two, uh . . ."

"Not that kind of separation." The Dread Lord ran a hand through the Keanu's floppy hair. "I was attacked in our *home*, Witch," he said. "Whether the fire-snake is the Unquenchable Flame, an avatar of the Crawling Chaos, or something else entirely, I cannot expose the twins to such danger."

He was right. Heather needed to keep the infants far, far away from this homicidal shit show, but Sathach adored his family. The witch couldn't deprive him of time with his children for gods knew how long.

"Go," she said. "In fact, you should stay with them. I've got Phæras and Hank to help out. There's no reason for you to—"

The Keanu burst with a tortured, rubbery squeal, filling the alcove with a flailing mass of tentacles. "I am a sworn human resources professional," he roared. "I will not run! I will not hide! I will not rest until—"

Ding.

"Elevator's here," Hank chirped from behind a mass of writhing limbs.

Sathach shrieked and slurped himself into a portal.

"I think he still wants to help out, Witch."

"No shit, Shoggoth."

She sighed, followed Hank into the elevator, and watched him gleefully push the button for the lobby.

"If I could just figure out what that godsdamned Outer God is up to, I'd bet dollars to sticky 'nuts I could make some godsdamned progress."

A wave of entropine-infused adrenaline hit her with the force of a tsunami, a delayed reaction to the Dread Lord's outburst. Sparks spewed from her fingertips, and her limbs filled with liquid fire. "What—"

She kicked the wall.

"—the fuck—"

Kick.

"—does—"

Kick.

"—the OG—"

Kick.

"—want?"

The witch collapsed against the dented wall, chest heaving. Hank rested a hand on her shoulder, and she flinched and glared up at him. If he smoldered at her right now, so help her gods, she'd turn him into a horny toad.

But his eyes were brown, not electric blue, and his smile was gentle and kind.

"It sucks when life doesn't make sense," he said. "Sometimes all you can do is raise your hand and ask a question."

A bolt of inspiration struck the witch like a fire-snake.

"Hank," she said, "you're a godsdamned genius."

CHAPTER NINETEEN

A One-Way Ticket to Crazytown

I'm not so sure this is a good idea."

The witch glanced at Hank, who stood in the doorway of Dr. Carcosa's former underground laboratory. His typically smooth brow was creased with worry lines. Keyser Söze chittered in agreement from his perch on Hank's shoulder.

But it was the only idea she had—and besides, Hank was the one who'd suggested it.

Sometimes all you can do is raise your hand and ask a question.

And that was what she planned to do.

Whether the killer was Nyarlathotep or the Unquenchable Flame, death stalked the streets of Tophet County. An Archon and a human had already been murdered, along with dozens of moon-beasts. Only the Keanu had saved Sathach from the same fate. Hank had been . . . infected by whatever attacked the Unseen Creeping Horror. Chad knew information that was causing him to keep secrets, driving a wedge between them and potentially obstructing her investigation. Sathach was suffering through a sustained separation from his wife and children. And Keziah's reading predicted total destruction. Until the WTF knew what Nyarlathotep wanted and what his plan was, they were powerless to change the course of events.

Someone had to do something, and that someone was her.

"This could be dangerous, Witch," Hank said.

There was no *could be* about it. Her plan *was* dangerous.

Hank would secure Keyser in the heavily shielded viewing room where she'd once tried to break her magical contract, then he'd leave and get to safety. The witch would remain in the lab and meditate her way to the astral plane. Once she was there, she'd summon Nyarlathotep and ask him what he wanted. Based on what Keziah had told her about the OG, she had no doubt he'd show up. It was possible that he'd roll in and devour her body, mind, and soul, but she didn't think so. Throughout the Mythos, Nyarly's personality was the most humanlike of all the Archons. She was banking on the fact that he'd want to deliver his villain speech, and she'd be an eager listener.

The witch's lips curved in a grim smile. "Danger is my middle name," she said. "But, uh . . . if you haven't heard from me in an hour, call the Clerk."

"Keyser and I are staying right here."

"Like hell!" She stalked across the bare concrete floor, which still bore a blinding white starburst where the QT had once punched through to the Swarm's realm. "You're taking Keyser in *there*." She pointed at the six-inch-thick glass of the viewing room's window. "Then you're leaving. End of story." The witch propped a hand on her hip and glared at him. "You said you wanted to help, so—"

"I can't help you if I'm not here." Hank crossed his arms, stretching his uniform shirt over bulging biceps. "If *he* sends the fire-snake after you, I'll feel it coming. And if it comes, I can protect you."

"*Protect* me?" She barked a laugh. "I don't need you to . . ."

The witch's voice trailed off as his words sank in. The fire-snake had respected his claim on her. What if the blue eyes were a sign that Nyarlathotep had adopted Hank as one of his Million Favored Ones? In that case, staying wouldn't endanger him, but she couldn't ask him to take such a risk.

"It listened to you *once*," the witch said. "That doesn't mean—"

"If you want me gone, you'll have to move me yourself."

Last year, she'd hauled Hank's fine ass all over downtown Asphodel while he was drunk as a skunk and bellowing "The Widow and the Devil" at the top of his lungs. She could bundle him up and get him out of here, no problem, but there was also Keyser to consider. If shit started to go sideways, he'd find a way out of the viewing room and rush to her side. She hadn't wanted to bring him at all, but she was twice as strong with him nearby, and she needed every drop of entropine she could get for a one-on-one with an Outer God.

"Go ahead," Hank said. "Kick me out. I'll just wait until you're in your magical trance and come right back."

The witch sighed, feeling a mixture of relief and gnawing guilt. "Fine. It's your funeral."

Discordia, protect him.

Hank held up his hand, palm out, and Keyser high-fived him.

Traitor.

She shrugged out of her backpack and fished around until she located her keys. Looped through the keyring was Vera Vásquez's golden apple bolo tie. She detached it, slid it over her head, and snugged the clasp around her neck.

It was now or never.

The witch closed her eyes and began to chant.

A marble statue of a nude goat-headed woman towered in the great hall of the witch's palace of memory—an astral replica of the one in her childhood bedroom. On her twelfth birthday, that statue had come to life, launching the year-and-a-day–long period of preparation before her initiation as a Discordian. Her palace held everything she'd learned from Nanny, as well as her accumulated witchly knowledge and her mundane memories.

Rather than plundering the recollection-filled rooms as she did on most visits, the witch crossed the hall, unbarred the double doors, and stepped outside into the perpetual twilight of the astral plane. The red-orange glow of the setting sun, which had disappeared behind a range of black mountains, shone in the west. To the east, a handful of stars and planets twinkled in the indigo sky. A cool breeze scented with night-blooming jasmine rippled the tall grass in a susurrant hush.

The witch took a deep breath and followed the overgrown path that circled around behind the palace to her astral temple. She'd constructed it when she was thirteen and borderline obsessed with Stonehenge. A circle of massive standing stones surrounded a stone table piled with an occult shop's worth of astral tools. The table and its implements were coated in a layer of etheric dust. She hadn't visited her temple in years. The witch had always been an April-Fools'-and-Clusterfuck sort of worshiper. Fortunately, Discordia was a low-maintenance deity.

Her fingers strayed to the golden apple at her throat, and the words Vera had spoken when she gave it to her echoed in her mind.

May the golden apple of this unsacred neckwear remind you that Discordia is always with you.

Gods, she hoped the Baroness of Bedlam was paying attention right about now.

The witch hesitated, unsure how to proceed with phase II of her plan. Was this a *Beetlejuice* situation? If she said Nyarly's name three times, would he appear? Or was there some magic word, the occult equivalent of a secret handshake? She hadn't really thought through this part of the plan.

Screw it. Nothing ventured, nothing gained.

She planted her hands on the table and cleared her throat. "Um, hey there, Nyarlathotep," she said. "Got a minute?"

Nothing.

"I've heard all about you from Keziah Mason."

More nothing.

Wait . . .

The back of her neck prickled with a familiar *someone's staring at me* sensation.

"I'm sure you're swamped. Madness doesn't spread itself, am I right?" She forced a painfully awkward chuckle. The only answer was the soft breath of the wind. "Anyway, I was hoping you could squeeze me in for a quick chat."

The witch tried to ignore the increasing weight of the Outer God's regard, which was making her sphincter want to crawl up her spine.

"If you're too busy, I'll just head on back to—"

The flagstones beneath her feet shook, and a mass of clotted gray clouds rolled toward her across the grassy plain. She fell to her knees as the tremors intensified, growing so violent the flat stone on which she knelt cracked in half. The clouds congealed into a pillar that stretched up into the purpling sky, and the night air echoed with eerie whispers.

The Dweller in Darkness draws nigh!
All hail the Stalker among the Stars!
Bow before the Thousand-Faced One!

To hell with that noise.

The witch wasn't bowing before anyone, no matter how many faces he had. She stood on trembling legs.

The wall of roiling mist parted, revealing a golden-furred creature the size of a hippopotamus. It had a row of five heads, each of which sported a fanged mouth rimmed with lashing tentacles.

What in the eldritch hell was *this*?

"Wrong number," the witch said. "I was trying to reach—"

"WHO DARES TO CALL NYARLATHOTEP?"

The roaring voice sounded like a choir of tortured angels. A gust of wind dispersed the cloud bank, and the witch saw that what she'd taken for a creature was, in fact, a *paw*. Looming over her stood a Godzilla-sized Sphinx.

"I'm Magna Innominanda," she said. "The witch of—"

"BEHOLD THE GREAT SPHINX!"

The hurricane blast of its foul breath nearly knocked her on her ass.

"Very fearsome," she shouted, craning her neck to see its human face three stories above her. "I damn near shat myself. But this would be a lot easier if you'd pop into something a little more human-sized."

A blinding flash of light seared her retinas, imprinting them with the afterimage of Nyarlathotep's Sphinx. When she could see again, the behemoth had been replaced by a figure from the annals of history.

A tall, slender man stood before her wearing robes of a shimmering fabric that fractured light into rainbows. The tall double-crown of a pharaoh glowed atop his shaved head. His swarthy face was young and unlined, but the eyes . . .

The eyes were metallic orbs of gold that carried the weight of eons.

"Does this form please you, little witch?" His mocking lips parted in a horrible grin.

The witch swallowed, struggling to moisten her mouth, which was as dry as the Sahara. "It's not bad, I guess." She looked him up and down. "Keziah wasn't kidding about you being an ancient Egypt fanboy, huh?"

"Perhaps you would prefer this."

She blinked, and the pharaoh was replaced with a twelve-foot-tall satyr the color of midnight.

"Or this."

He took the form of a hunched beast with bat's wings and the infamous three-lobed burning eye.

"Whatever floats your—"

"Or I could wear my true form," he said, his voice sliding into a lunatic titter.

Nyarlathotep's true form was said to be so horrific that the human mind could not comprehend it. A one-way ticket to Crazytown. She grasped the golden apple and whispered a prayer to Discordia as the bat-winged monster vanished in a blaze of light. Through the glittery mist of Goddess-given astral contact lenses, she beheld Nyarlathotep in all his sanity-shattering glory. His flesh was bile green and mottled with oozing yellow patches. He had a human-standard pair of thickly muscled arms and legs and, as with most Archons, thrashing appendages sprouted from various points on his body. His head was an eyeless white cone that grew into a thick tentacle the color of arterial blood. A fanged maw at the cone's base dripped black ichor onto the shattered flagstones.

The witch couldn't be sure how the sight would've affected her without Discordia's protection, but honestly, Nyarly was nowhere near as gross as the unshrouded County Clerk.

"Your true form works for me."

The wrinkled flesh of his featureless face shifted in an approximation of surprise. "No mere human can look upon me without—"

"I'm no mere human." She squared her shoulders and straightened her pointy hat. "I'm a godsdamned witch."

"I could also do a Leng spider, a spectral ghast, a corner hound, a moonbeast . . ." He flexed his crimson tentacle-head like a gym bro posing for the 'gram. "Take your pick. I've got nine hundred ninety-nine avatars."

But a witch ain't one.

"This'll do just fine."

The witch pulled entropine and sculpted a pair of overstuffed armchairs from the etheric stuff of the astral plane. She plopped down on the one closest to her and gestured toward the other. Nyarlathotep adjusted his size to fit the furniture and settled into the cushy chair. Though he had no eyes, she felt him gazing at her expectantly.

"So, um . . ." She tensed, preparing to flee the astral plane if he so much as twitched a tentacle in her direction. "What do you want?"

"What do *I* want?" he repeated. "You called me. What do *you* want?"

A cold, oily tendril of awareness brushed her mind. *Oh no, you don't, you cone-headed asshole.* She gritted her teeth and drew on the contract's torrent of power to reinforce her psychic shields.

"Well, I'd love to put a stop to all the immolating."

The color drained from Nyarlathotep's cranial tentacle until only the faintest hint of pink remained. He shivered and rubbed his oddly jointed arms. "The co*met*." His voice was taut with what sounded very much like fear. "Then our purposes are aligned," he said. "I accept your offer of assistance."

Offer of *assistance*?

But that would mean . . .

Holy Chao.

Nyarlathotep wasn't the killer.

CHAPTER TWENTY

Always a Bridesmaid

Let me get this straight," the witch said. "*You*, a godsdamned Outer God, need *my* help."

Nyarlathotep's cone-head bobbed in something like a nod.

"With what exactly?"

"I told you," he said. "Stopping the co*met*."

"How in the seven hells do you expect me to stop it? I don't even know what it is!"

The slender tentacles protruding from his midsection lashed in frustration. "Didn't you understand my clue?"

"Clue?" she repeated.

His nightmarish true form vanished, only to be replaced by a man wearing a dark suit.

"Seek ye the Circle." His eyes—a normal human pair, save for the burnished gold irises and vertical pupils—searched her face. "Ring any bells?"

"Holy shit," she said. "*You* are the Vaping Douche?"

Shadows gathered around Nyarlathotep in a corona of malignant gloom. "I am no douche," he said in a voice sharp enough to flense flesh.

But the witch was too stunned to be scared. She held up her hand. "Give me a minute. I'm trying to wrap my head around this."

She stood and began to pace the circular perimeter of her astral temple. Nyarlathotep's human head swiveled a full 360 degrees to follow her.

"You're not the asshole who torched the Unseen Creeping Horror and the moon-beasts."

"I am not."

"And whoever—*what*ever—did it wasn't acting on your orders."

"On my orders?" he said, incredulous. "The co*met* is trying to kill me!"

The witch stopped and glared at him. "Then why would you waste time with cryptic clues?"

Nyarlathotep shrugged. "I am the Great Sphinx," he said. "Riddles are my stock in trade."

"'Seek ye the Circle' isn't a riddle."

"It's close enough for government work." He propped his elbows on his knees and looked up at the witch. "I've been missing in action since your world was young, Witch. My past is . . . complicated. I couldn't just *show up*."

She sat down, recalling the Vaping Douche's first clue. "You wanted me to talk to Keziah so the Archons could get used to the idea that you'd survived."

"How did they take it?"

Again, she felt an exploratory psychic tentacle probe at her mind's defenses. "Knock that shit off," she said. "They were . . . concerned. Thanks to Lovecraft, you've got quite the reputation."

"Lovecraft?" Nyarlathotep shook his head. "Never talked to the guy. Oh, he made a few attempts to summon me after he got his hands on Keziah's book, but he was too much of a try-hard, if you know what I mean." He leaned back and steepled his fingers. "But the Circle? Derleth, Bloch, Wandrei . . . them, I spoke to in dreams."

The witch almost felt sorry for Lovecraft. Ol' Nyarly had shunned him, only to grant exclusive interviews to all his friends. Always a bridesmaid, never the bride . . .

"If you'd read the Circle's works," he said archly, "you'd know that the only beings in the multiverse who strike fear into the rotting hearts of great Nyarlathotep are the fire elemental Cthugha and his spawn. In Derleth's story, 'The Dweller in Darkness'—"

"Who the hell is Cthugha?"

"That's not important," he said. "What matters is the co*met*." The Douche examined his fingernails in a show of faux nonchalance. "I gave them that name, you know. It's a portmanteau. *Ka* is the ancient Egyptian word for the life-force, the vital essence. Sekh*met* was a war goddess whose bloodthirst was so great, she nearly destroyed the human race." He cocked his head and grinned a self-satisfied grin. "And the creatures resemble comets as they traverse the depths of space. Hence, ka'met."

The witch was gripped by a deep grammatical foreboding. There was an eldritch apostrophe in that godsdamned name or she'd eat her pointy black hat.

"It was the ka'met who killed your foggy friend and slaughtered my moon-beasts," said Nyarlathotep.

My moon-beasts?

"Great Bieber's ghost," she said. "You're their hierophant, aren't you?"

He flashed a razor-toothed smile. "Guilty as charged."

The big moon-beast hadn't burned to death under the UCH's glitter-dome. Nyarlathotep had portaled away from the attack. And that meant Phæras's unknown Archon hadn't been the perpetrator of the crime, but its intended victim.

"I told Donald Wandrei all about the ka'met, but he called them fire vampires in his stories."

Fire vampires . . .

The term was definitely familiar, but she couldn't recall the details of Wandrei's story. And there was something else, some other memory eluding her like a lost word on the tip of her tongue.

"So pedestrian." He shook his head sadly. "Ka'met is more exotic, don't you think?"

"What I think," the witch said, "is that you need to tell me, in plain freaking English, what's really going on."

"Very well." Nyarlathotep cleared his throat in what was clearly the preamble to a pompous mansplanation. "Back in the old country, the ka'met were extensions of their King Regent, Fthaggua—the son of Cthugha. They fed on the life-force of sentient beings, consuming both their vital essence and their memories, which were added to Fthaggua's consciousness."

Gods, if the ka'met was merely a part of a bigger, badder Archon—one that even an Outer God feared—they were all as screwed as a honeymooning bride. "Where is Fthaggua now?'

Nyarlathotep shifted uncomfortably. "He was taken by the Swarm, but a ka'met survived his demise. The how of it is one of life's little mysteries." He broke into a maniacal chuckle, but the witch could tell his heart wasn't in it. "What you must understand is that a ka'met is nearly unstoppable, even for one as great as I."

"If it's unstoppable, what in Discordia's name do you expect me to—"

"*Nearly* unstoppable," he said. "I am an artificer of surpassing skill. Give me instruments of glass and metal, and I can combine them into arcane tools for any occasion. I once crafted an amulet to bind the ka'met, but it was . . . left behind when I fled the Swarm."

"So make another one."

"Well, why didn't I think of that?" Nyarlathotep snorted derisively. "I'm no longer a party to the master contract, Witch. I have only my innate power to work with, and it simply isn't enough."

"There are only two ways out of that contract," she said, "and you don't look dead to me."

"I served the other Outer Gods for ages as their mouthpiece and messenger, and they abandoned me to the Swarm." He heaved a melancholic sigh. "So I faked my own death, fled to the Dreamlands, and hid as a moon-beast. When I felt the Archons awaken, I sailed the Black Galley to this layer of the multiverse and established a colony on the Moon."

"Why would you do that?"

"The moon-beasts are rather low on the sapience scale." Nyarlathotep crossed his legs and rested his clasped hands on his knee. "I suppose I missed the proximity of my own kind. But I didn't know if my betrayers had survived, so I remained in hiding." His golden eyes fixed on her with unnerving intensity. "Just out of curiosity, who came here from the old world?"

"Za'gathoth," the witch said. "And as many of your young as she could carry."

His swarthy cheeks paled. "Does Za'gathoth know of my return?"

"Not as far as I know. She stays holed up in her den under the Catachthonic River. Doesn't really get out much these days."

He exhaled a pent-up breath in obvious relief.

The witch had a keen nose for bullshit, and Nyarly's story reeked to high hell. First, how could he have faked his own death? Fooling an Archon was one thing, but fooling a magical contract? As far as she knew, it couldn't be done. She'd tried. Second, he spoke perfect modern English, which meant he'd clearly been keeping a close eye (and ear) on Earth. So why hadn't he revealed himself after the Swarm was defeated? Third, he'd neglected to share an important detail— why the ka'met wanted him dead in the first place.

Nyarlathotep was hiding something, and she needed to know what it was.

"Look, the Archons want this ka'met dealt with," the witch said. "I'm sure they'll add you to the contract if you ask."

"Unfortunately, power isn't the only problem," he said. "The ka'met was once bound by my amulet, and it knows the scent of my magic. If I use so much as a trickle, it can track me through the ether." The Douche leaned toward her, his face bright and eager. "But I understand witches are quite skilled in the creation of magical items."

There it was.

He wanted *her* to make the amulet. Keziah said he'd grilled her about magical tools. Speaking of which, *instruments of glass and metal* sounded a hell of a lot like Sibyl's collection.

"You stole the artifacts so you could use them for the amulet," the witch said.

Nyarlathotep's face tensed in an anxious grimace. "I can explain."

"Let me guess, you couldn't resist giving it a try, even without the contract, and the ka'met hunted you down." She swallowed rising bile as the remembered stench of the crime scene filled her astral nostrils. "You left Sibyl there to die."

"I did?" He raised his perfectly arched eyebrows. "I *did*. I . . . I fled in a moment of panic, and the ka'met consumed her."

Nyarlathotep must've been using magic on Luna, and again at Dunwich Park. The Clerk had been right when she said Yi'danag was collateral damage. The ka'met had devoured the UCH to get to him.

"After what happened up there," he said, staring up at the gibbous moon, "I knew running was my only chance of survival. I sensed the presence of my old friend Keziah Mason and sailed the Black Galley to Tophet County."

"You flipped me off!"

"You were staring." He sniffed. "It's quite rude."

The witch's irritation melted into growing excitement. The jumbled puzzle pieces of this case were finally coming together. Her visit to Sibyl had awakened Keziah just before the attack on the moon-beasts' colony. In the aftermath, Nyarlathotep—terrified and desperate—hauled ass toward the one person he knew who could help him recreate the amulet.

Keziah Mason.

And he brought the ka'met with him.

"Little did I know Keziah was long dead, a mere shade haunting a grotesque deck of cards." He met her eyes with his reptilian gaze. "But *you* are strong. *You* are powerful. *You* could craft the amulet of binding."

"I'm not exactly fully trained in the magical arts," she said. "Your tentacled buddies wiped out the witches when they woke up, and there was no one to teach me how to—"

"*I* shall teach you," he said. "And in exchange, you will make the amulet and bind the ka'met." He held out his hand, and his lips curled in a horribly warm smile. "Do we have a deal?"

The witch stared at his outstretched hand.

The ka'met wanted Nyarlathotep. It would annihilate anything that stood in its way, but it had only killed when its prey was nearby. The sociopathic solution would be to let them have him.

"I don't need to invade your mind to know what you're thinking." The Douche withdrew his hand, and the warmth in his smile chilled to icy malevolence. "If you refuse to help me, know that I will portal into a daycare center, or a retirement home, or to the midway of the Midnight Carnival. I will surround myself with innocents, and I will use them as a living shield against the—"

"Oh, for fuck's sake," she said. "I get it."

The witch chewed her lip, considering what she knew of Nyarlathotep from the Mythos. Where the motivations of the other Outer Gods tended toward the incomprehensible cosmic horror end of the spectrum, his were more human. More selfish. He was a liar. A manipulator. He craved worship and attention, and he was immensely, unimaginably powerful.

Could she really risk working hand-in-tentacle with a trickster god?

"I am a dangerous enemy but a wonderful friend," he said, in a seductive purr. "Once we've bound the ka'met, I will teach you forbidden magic and raise you up as my High Priestess. You'll be by my side as we usher in the Age of Crawling Chaos." Again, he offered her his hand. "All I ask is one small favor, and I'll make you the most powerful witch in the universe."

"Too late," she said. "I already am."

"Then do it to save those you love." His golden eyes flashed menacingly. "Because if the ka'met doesn't kill them, *I* will."

The witch snapped her fingers. Nyarlathotep's armchair dissolved into the ether, and he crashed onto the flagstones. She wreathed her astral body in flames and levitated above the temple, borne aloft on winds of rage. This fucker needed her alive, and she'd be godsdamned if she'd sit idly by while he threatened her friends.

"Try it," she said, "and I'll give you to the ka'met myself."

Then she raised both middle fingers in the eldritch salute, pulled her awareness back to her physical body, and opened her eyes.

CHAPTER TWENTY-ONE

Like a Moth-Man to a Flame

Hey, Witch! How did it—"

Hank's voice broke off, and his sun-bronzed face paled.

"What's wrong?" The witch unfolded her legs, wincing at the unpleasant tingle of blood returning to her limbs. She struggled to her feet and staggered toward him. "Are you okay?"

Keyser Söze, who was perched on his shoulder, released his grip on the collar of Hank's uniform shirt and pointed a shaking finger behind the witch.

Oh, gods . . .

Nyarlathotep must've somehow infected her with his magical taint. That shithead probably did it on purpose, and his scent had drawn the ka'met like a moth-man to a flame. She turned to face it, pulling entropine and sending up a fervent prayer to Discordia. But what had shocked Hank speechless wasn't the fire-snake.

It was the Vaping Douche. His eyes glowed with golden light, and he cradled a clockwork device—a bronze gadget formed of gears and orbs. Sibyl's orrery. According to Keziah, the artifact was a teleporter, which meant he could sneak around without leaving an etheric trail.

The Douche raised one hand and curled the fingers in a little wave. He bent and gently deposited the orrery on the floor in the corner of the lab. Then he stood and smoothed the wrinkles from his charcoal suit.

His lips curved in a Joker-esque grin. "Long time no see."

Without warning, he exploded into a cone-headed, tentacled nightmare.

Shit.

Nyarlathotep's true form would leave Hank as mad as a hatter. The witch spun and hit him with a sanity-protecting face shield.

"Take Keyser and run!"

The Outer God ignored her outburst and lazily stretched his muscled arms. "The thing is, little witch, your willing cooperation is a nicety," he said. "Not a necessity."

"Is that so?" Her eyes darted to Hank and Keyser, who hadn't moved a godsdamned inch. She shoved them toward the door with a burst of entropine. "Go ahead and use your magic. The ka'met will eat your scaly ass alive."

The fanged maw at the base of his cone-head gaped in a horrible mimicry of the Douche's grin. "Fortunately, I do not need magic to overpower one insignificant mortal."

She fired an entropic strike at the thick tentacle hurtling toward her like a javelin. It dissolved in a sparkling cloud, but before she had time to get her hopes up, *two* tentacles had taken its place.

Son of a Shoggoth. In her panic, the witch had forgotten what she learned last year. Witches produced entropine. Archons *were* entropine. Fighting fire with fire sounded great in theory, but when it came to Archons, it was exactly the wrong strategy. Mistakes like the one she'd just made were how the witches lost the war.

Time for a new tactic.

She launched a concussive spear of air at the wall, and a chunk of concrete broke away with a deafening crack. Her makeshift cannonball rose from the rubble, and she gathered power to throw it at Nyarlathotep. But she was too slow. His blood red cranial tentacle hit her shoulder, wound around her throat, and hauled her into the air. While the witch was busy gasping for breath, Keyser took charge and levitated her body so her neck wouldn't break.

Sadly, that didn't do a godsdamned thing for the throttling.

Nyarlathotep roared, sensing Keyser's interference. "Vermin!"

One of his newly formed tentacles, baby pink rather than the bilious green of his festering hide, lassoed Keyser and yanked him from Hank's shoulder. Hank lunged for the ropy limb, but another tentacle grabbed him and hurled him across the lab. He slammed into the wall and slid bonelessly to the floor, leaving behind a bright streak of blood.

The witch screamed and burst into flame. Though her body didn't burn, her T-shirt and the tail end of her braid went up like dry autumn leaves. Nyarlathotep screeched as his flesh blistered and blackened. He dropped her, but his grip on Keyser tightened convulsively. She felt her familiar's rib crack as if it were her own.

"Submit!" shrieked the enraged Outer God.

"Go to hell!"

Nyarlathotep shook Keyser like a rag doll. His shrill cries of pain sliced her heart open like razored tentacles.

"Okay!" The witch raised her hands in surrender. "I'll do what you want," she said, blinking back tears. "Just stop hurting him."

"Swear it." The scorched ruin of his cranial tentacle snaked toward her, and the tapered tip wound around her wrist.

Her mind filled with Keyser's defiant rejection, his insistence that she not make the oath. But she *had* to. He was already hurt. All it would take was one squeeze and he'd be . . .

"Fine," she said. "I—"

The fluorescent lights overhead flared, and a tube burst in a shower of glass and sparks. The remaining bulbs flashed erratically as the air grew heavy and charged.

"It's hunting you," whispered a throaty voice.

Hank no longer lay unconscious on the floor. He walked toward Nyarlathotep, his movements jerky in the strobing glare. One side of his head dripped blood, and his eyes . . .

His eyes shone icy blue.

Nyarlathotep yanked his tentacle free of the witch's hand and dropped Keyser like a piece of trash. The witch caught him in cupped hands made of compressed air and pulled him into her arms. She poured magic into him, and his broken bone began to heal.

Hank advanced on the trembling Outer God, who scrambled away from him, retreating until his tentacled back was pressed against the wall.

"I can feel it searching for your scent." Hank took a deep breath in through his nose, and a flickering tongue of lightning darted from his parted lips.

Nyarlathotep flinched and shrank away from him. "What . . . what *are* you?"

"Something new, I think," Hank said. He stepped closer, until he was practically nose-to-cone-head with the terrified Archon. "Something *hungry*."

A disc of neon netherlight formed on the wall behind Nyarlathotep, and he stepped backward into his portal. As the opening shrank, a bolt of azure lightning struck the floor. The fire-snake flowed into the lab, following the scent of the Outer God's magic.

Hank pointed at the wall, where the portal had just closed. "He went that way."

The ka'met hissed and vanished in a streak of cerulean fire.

He turned to the witch, who stood cradling Keyser against her bare chest. Hank's gaze darted to her exposed skin, and the blue of his eyes intensified. He squeezed them shut and started unbuttoning his shirt.

"Uh, Hank?" she said, trying not to stare at a torso so sculpted it belonged in the Louvre. "What are you doing?"

He tossed the shirt toward her. It landed on the floor ten feet to her left. "I need to leave."

"What?" She watched his broad back as he stalked, shirtless, toward the door. "You're *bleeding*. At least let me take a look at your head."

Hank gingerly massaged his scalp, his temple, his cheek. "My head's fine," he said. "Not even a scratch."

Then where had all that blood come from?

"But you need—"

"It's not safe for you to be near me when I'm this hungry."

"I've got some trail mix in my bag," she said. "Have all you want."

Hank stopped walking, but he didn't look back.

"You don't understand," he said. "What I'm hungry for is *you*."

Sathach pressed a trembling hand to the parted lips of his brand-new Keanu.

"Oh, Witch," he said. "You should not have taken such a risk without informing us."

"Don't you *should* all over me." The witch snipped the charred end from her braid and dropped her scissors in a desk drawer. She leaned back in her chair, careful not to disturb Keyser as he slept off a food coma in her lap, and propped her boots on the corner of her desk. "What's done is done."

Phæras drifted around her office in a lazy circle. "A fire vampire," he said. "But how could it have survived the demise of Fthaggua? If the ka'met are living limbs of their King Regent, they should've died with him."

"The Unquenchable Flame was just an egg when Za'gathoth escaped." She stroked Keyser's silky fur, and he rumbled in contentment. "Maybe fire vampires didn't become part of Fthaggua until they hatched. That would explain it."

The Dread Lord shook his head. "It still doesn't make sense. If Flame wasn't bound by . . . by *his* amulet, he couldn't have caught the scent of the Crawling Chaos's magic."

"You don't know that," the witch said. "It could be that if one ka'met knows something, they all know it—whether they're eggs or fire-snakes."

"I suppose," Sathach lisped.

"According to the Mythos, fire vampires have only one purpose," Phæras said, "and that is to feed. Tophet County is full of sentient life—"

The witch snorted. "Depends on how you define *sentient*."

"In any case, why has this one been so restrained?"

"Restrained?" Keyser stirred in her lap, and she made an effort to lower her voice. "That blue bastard killed a few dozen moon-beasts. Ask Dave if that's *restrained*. It killed the Unseen Creeping Horror, and Sibyl, and it—"

"But it was simply trying to reach Nya—*him*," Phæras said. "He was disguised as a moon-beast. Perhaps the ka'met couldn't tell which one he was. And it burned through Yi'danag only because *he* was aboard the Black Galley."

"*He* drew the thing to Sibyl, too."

"That was spontaneous human combustion," the Dread Lord muttered.

The witch ignored him. "But it also attacked Sathach. The OG wasn't in that godsdamned basement, so why did the ka'met show up?"

"I have no idea," Phæras said, his tinny voice ringing with frustration. "But my point is that it could've devoured every sentient being in Asphodel by now. Why hasn't it done so?"

"Let's not look a gift star-steed in the mouth." She chewed her lip. "The real question is, what do we do now?"

"Ahem. I don't mean to be insensitive given your recent trauma, Witch," Sathach said delicately. "But if the fire-snake did not catch the Crawling Chaos, I suggest we call a truce with him."

A wave of spikes washed over Phæras's quicksilver orb. "A *truce*? He just tried to kill the witch!"

"He's the only one who knows how to bind the ka'met," the Dread Lord said.

"Look, I hate to admit it, but if he'd wanted to kill me, you'd be talking to a corpse right about now." She replayed the scene, forcing aside her memories of Keyser's agony. "He *needs* me. And gods help us, we need him, too."

Phæras rotated sharply, shifting his focus from the witch to Sathach and back. "I cannot believe what I'm hearing," he said. "How could we possibly trust *him*? What happens once he gets what he wants?"

"The freaking fire-snake will stop torching people!"

"Perhaps the Outer God wouldn't have killed *you*," Phæras said, "but he would've had no compunction about murdering your familiar, or Deputy O'Brien, or anyone else he viewed as disposable. How can you forgive that?"

"How can I *forgive* that?"

"Oh, no," Sathach whispered.

The witch jabbed her finger in the Dread Lord's direction. "He ate my middle finger, and he's one of my closest friends!"

"Do you really mean it?"

"And you squiggly assholes tantrummed around the Earth and annihilated every witch but me." She took a deep breath, struggling to calm her temper. "I've gotten pretty godsdamned good at forgive-and-forget. I didn't exactly have a choice."

"I . . . I'm sorry, Witch." Phæras's orb dipped in an apologetic bow. "I did not mean—"

"I know you didn't," she said, "and you're right about the danger. But the OG will be on his best behavior now that he's seen what Hank can do."

"Then you must keep Hank close," Sathach said. "He's connected to the ka'met. He can feel its presence, and he knew what it wanted even before you told him it was hunting the Outer God."

The witch shivered, gripped by an emotion somewhere between fear and desire.

What I'm hungry for is you.

"I wonder . . ." Phæras resumed his pensive orbit. "We know fire vampires feed on the life force, the vital essence, of sentient creatures. And we suspect part of the ka'met traversed the plasma arc of the ball lightning cannon and took residence in our deputy."

"Yeah?"

"Mh'imbra told me she caught Hank outside the peep show the night you visited my trailer," Phæras said. "She said he could see only the audience from where he stood."

The witch shrugged. "Everybody's got a kink."

"What if he was there not to peep, but to feed?"

"On what?" Sathach asked.

"On lust." Phæras's placid silver surface rippled. "Under the right circumstances, copulation creates new life. Sexual energy, therefore, must be closely related to the vital essence."

"You think Hank eats *horniness?*"

"Based on his behavior," Phæras said, "it certainly seems possible." He tilted on his axis. "You said his head wound seemed to have spontaneously healed. I imagine such an expenditure of energy would've left him quite depleted."

"And hungry," the witch said.

"Which is why he left so abruptly."

"You guys think I should, um, keep him close while I work with the OG?"

"For your own protection," Sathach said.

The witch unscrewed her hip flask and took a slug of Chicken Cock. Despite Hank's nuclear hotness, she'd never had any romantic interest in him. Sure, the man was a tasty snacc, but that wasn't the problem.

The problem was that she—a sexually frustrated horndog with a romance novel habit—was a frigging five-course meal.

CHAPTER TWENTY-TWO

No Strings Attached

Jenkin squatted in the center of the mayor's conference table, his face screwed up in a grimace of distaste.

"An amulet of *binding*?" Keziah repeated. "I don't know how to make one, and I wouldn't help you even if I did."

The Clerk's eyes exchanged a surprised glance. "But why? The ka'met has killed before. Without the amulet, it will most likely kill again."

"This creature is a sentient being, and binding is—"

"The ka'met was just a limb of Fthaggua, like . . . like a leg," the witch said, patting her thigh. "What makes you think it's sentient?"

"I *know* it's sentient because it hates." Jenkin turned a fierce glare on the witch. "Magic like this is a theft of free will. I'm surprised you'd even consider it."

Phæras's silver orb bobbed in agreement. "I agree with Keziah," he said. "The ka'met has—"

"The frigging ka'met has murdered an Archon, a human, and who knows how many moon-beasts!"

"High Lord Innominanda is right." Ellie Dawson propped her elbows on the arms of her wheelchair and scanned the faces around the table. "We have a duty to protect the people of Tophet County. If we can stop the ka'met from harming anyone else, we must act."

Jenkin ignored the acting mayor and kept his crimson eyes fixed on the witch. "Have you ever asked yourself why the gods allow bad things to happen?" Keziah asked. "Or why Discordia would permit the near-total eradication of witchkind?"

Sathach shifted uncomfortably. "Words cannot express how—"

"Little fish eat minnows," the witch said. "Big fish eat little fish. The Undersea Monstrosity eats big fish. And pontoon boats." She shrugged. "It's just the way of the world."

But the truth was, she'd spent many a night as a lonely witchling asking herself that very question. If Discordia had the power to bend reality to Her will, why would She sit on Her divine ass and watch the witch-pocalypse without lifting a freaking finger?

"Here's the hard truth," Keziah said. "Discordia *could* have stopped it. She could've jammed her metaphorical hands into some fanged orifices and worked the Archons like puppets. She could've made them bow and scrape, say please and thank you, play nicely and share their toys." Jenkin cocked his wizened head. "How does that sound?"

"It sounds awful," Sathach said with a squeaky shudder.

"Sounds to me like there'd be a lot more pointy hats walking around." The witch blew out a frustrated breath. "You're the one who keeps prophesying doom if we don't stop this thing, Keziah."

Jenkin stomped his tiny paw. "I told you, seeing the future is not an exact science! For all we know, trying to bind the ka'met could be what *causes* Armageddon."

"In that case, you should keep your godsdamned cards to your godsdamned self."

The tension in the mayor's office was thick enough to hack with a rusty machete . . . until Sathach squirmed in his Skyn, producing a Tupperware-ish toot.

"Apologies," he murmured. "I'm still breaking in the new Keanu."

"Don't you see, Witch?" Keziah's voice was taut with concern. "This is how *he* weasels his way in. Sowing madness and discord, making us doubt each other . . ." Jenkin turned in a circle three times and flopped down. "Maybe we should take our chances with the ka'met."

"You really think we should sit on our thumbs and wait for this thing to devour Tophet County?"

"We can't afford to wait." Ellie bit her lip, then shook her head. "If the Mythos is even remotely accurate, our Outer God is a textbook psychopath. I have no doubt he'll follow through on his threat to sacrifice innocent lives to preserve his own."

Hank raised his hand, and Ellie gestured for him to speak. "Maybe the ka'met already got him," he said. "It left the lab just a second after *he* did."

"Seymour's Florals delivered a bouquet of carnivorous plants to my office this morning." The witch dug a crumpled note card from the back pocket of her jeans and held it up. "This came with it."

She tossed the note to Hank, but the Clerk snatched it from midair with an oozing tentacle.

"'Dearest Witch,'" the Clerk read, "'I apologize for my behavior yesterday. My emotions got the best of me. The offer of assistance still stands, but with no strings attached. You know how to reach me. Warmly, N.'"

"'No strings attached'?" Sathach lisped. "Perhaps he learned a lesson. I've struggled with angry outbursts myself. I credit primal scream therapy with my transformation. It is proof positive that people can change."

"Not *him*," Hank said. "That guy is a jerk. He tried to squish Keyser Söze!"

A surge of remembered rage and fear flared hot in the witch's chest. She smothered it. Drowned it. Buried it.

Therapy, schmerapy. She'd take repression over expression every day of the week.

"Look, I'm not exactly dying to work with the OG, but we're running out of options," she said. "I spent my whole-ass morning in the Read at Your Own Risk room wading through Nomicons and grimoires. Didn't find a thing."

Not strictly true. Sathach had finally returned *The Get-It-On-Onomicon*. The witch had found plenty in there.

She looked up to find Hank staring intently at her. A hint of blue flashed in his eyes.

Oops.

"Some magic is too monstrous to be written down," Keziah said darkly.

The witch cleared her throat and broke eye contact with Hank. "Sathach and I are visiting Za'gathoth tomorrow. We'll ask her about the ka'met, dig for dirt on the OG, and see if she knows anything about this amulet. But if she doesn't . . ." She shook her head, drumming her fingers on the table. "If she doesn't, I vote we move forward with our cone-headed friend."

Phæras bobbed erratically, clearly unhappy with the plan, and Jenkin's face telegraphed Keziah's vehement disapproval. But Sathach nodded, as did Ellie and the Clerk.

Hank raised his hand again. "Um, I was just wondering . . ."

"Yeah?"

"What about me?"

Right. Hank was supposed to stay close to her while she was working this case. Given the combination of her recent reading material, his current nutritional needs, and the fact that she was seeing Chad tonight, that seemed like a spectacularly bad idea.

"The OG will give me at least a day to consider his offer," she said. "And after his near miss, he'll be keeping a low profile."

Phæras rotated sharply in negation. "That is a dangerous assumption, Witch."

Hank waved his hand. "That's not what I—"

"Keyser Söze will stick close to you for tonight, Hank," the witch said. "If shit goes sideways, he'll feel it and let you know."

"Okay, but—"

"I'll send him to you on the broom. If the Clerk's cool with it, you should take the rest of the day off and . . . and grab a, um, snack at the Tunnel of Love." The place was saturated with a miasma of horny vibes so strong even normies felt it. "You can come with me and Sathach tomorrow and—"

"No," he said. "I mean, is there a way to *fix* me?"

The witch's mouth hung open as the choking grip of guilt robbed her of words.

Finding a cure for Hank hadn't even made it onto her agenda.

The witch wrapped up her recap of the unfolding apocalyptic fiasco, drained her beer, and crushed the can on the table.

"Damn. That's a *lot*," Chad said, shaking his head. "You've had one hell of a week, and it's only Wednesday."

"Ain't that the truth." She caught the bulging eyes of their waitress, a Deep One hybrid, and lifted her chin to signal for another round. "I need this to be done, Chad. I just want my life to get back to normal. I want . . ." She took a deep breath to steady her nerves. Relationship talk made her antsy. "I want *us* to get back to normal."

He squeezed her hand. "Me too."

A little more than six months ago, they'd sat in this very booth belting out "Friggin' in the Riggin'" after a night of heavy drinking. And then . . .

Then he'd kissed her.

Chad met her eyes, and she knew he was reliving the memory too. A tipsy butterfly fluttered in her stomach.

"So, um . . ." The witch leaned toward him, drunkenly smooshing her lips on his ear, which ruined her attempt at a seductive whisper. "You said you had something to show me back at your place?" She pulled back and waggled her eyebrows suggestively.

The drowsy warmth drained from his features. It was like she was watching him sober up on fast-forward.

"I do," he said. "But we need to talk first."

Feelings.

It was probably feelings.

But she was a little bit drunk, a lotta bit frisky, and willing to suffer for the cause.

"Shoot."

"Promise you won't get mad?"

Mad?

Shit. Now *she* was sobering up, too.

"That's a vow I can't make." The witch gently tugged her hand free of his in case she needed it for hexing. "But I promise not to cause you grievous bodily harm."

Chad sighed. "I think you're right about Flame being a ka'met. It explains why he's different, why he had no name, but—"

A gilled waitress set two sweating cans of Keystone on the table and cleared away their empties.

When she'd gone, he said, "You said your OG is the moon-beasts' hierophant, right?"

"Yeah."

"And you think Flame is the one who attacked him." She nodded. "So wouldn't the OG have recognized Flame when the Black Galley was moored at Dunwich Park?"

He was right.

Why hadn't Nyarlathotep freaked the fuck out when he saw the Unquenchable Flame standing watch?

"I . . ." The answer struck her like a fire-snake. "Moon-beasts don't have eyes, Chad."

"But they can still *see*."

She groaned. "I don't want to talk about this. Can we please not—"

"And Flame was just an egg when the Archons came here. He'd never even met the OG, so how could he track him?" he asked. "And why would he want to kill him?"

"Chad—"

"He's my *friend*, Witch," he said. "I'm a nerdy introvert with social anxiety. I don't have too many of those."

Her frosty annoyance melted a bit. That, she could empathize with.

"I understand." She patted his forearm awkwardly. "I'm not out to get him. I just want to find him and bind him so no one else gets hurt."

"But Flame didn't hurt anyone." His gaze held hers, radiating earnest belief. "I *know* he didn't, and I—"

His voice broke off as a spark of netherlight formed over their table, grew to man-size, and disgorged the Dread Lord of Human Resources.

"We have a situation!" A tentacle shot from one leg of the Keanu's gym shorts and lassoed her wrist. "The ka'met was sighted near the Bridge of Sighs. We must protect Mother!"

Za'gathoth was their best hope of learning more about the ka'met, about Nyarlathotep, and about the amulet. It couldn't be a coincidence that the fire vampire was sniffing around the bridge over her underwater lair.

"Witch?" Chad said.

She opened her mouth to answer, but Sathach yanked her into the portal.

Chad's concerned face was swept away by a cresting tide of netherlight.

CHAPTER TWENTY-THREE

Orders from Headquarters

T he fire-snake was definitely here."

A faint sheen of blue glazed Hank's eyes as he stared at the arched bridge spanning the Catachthonic River. Keyser Söze, who sat perched on his shoulder clutching a pawful of hair, gazed intently toward the horizon where the jagged cliffs of the Mountains of Madness hulked in ominous, fuligin glory. The moon-lit streets of Asphodel were preternaturally silent, save for the gentle lap of the river against the bridge's support pillars. No rustling rat-things. No shambling ghasts. It felt as though the night itself were holding its breath.

The witch stood with Sathach and Phæras, watching from a distance to avoid contaminating whatever etheric spoor Hank's inner ka'met detected. She opened her third eye and peered at the bridge, but all she saw were flickers of octarine netherlight shining up from Za'gathoth's underwater dwelling.

A forked tongue of lightning slashed from Hank's parted lips as he scented the evening air. "There was something else here," he said. "Some*one* else. But their trail is all mixed up with the fire-snake."

"Did the ka'met . . . consume the other party?" Phæras's metallic voice rang with concern.

"It didn't attack," Hank said. "I'd be able to feel it."

The witch breathed a sigh of relief. "Could this 'someone else' be the OG?"

Nyarlathotep had made a point of asking who came to this universe from the old world, and her dumb ass had told him exactly where Za'gathoth lived. If he'd portaled over here, if he'd reached for even the shadow of his magic, the ka'met would've sensed it and come for him. Thankfully, the Mindless Mother was unharmed and totally oblivious. Sathach had already checked on her, only to be shouted back to the surface with dire threats of disembowelment if he ever dared interrupt the WWE Main Event again.

But if the old beetle knew something Nyarly didn't want them to find out . . .

Hank closed his eyes and inhaled, then shook his head. "It wasn't *him*," he said, closing the distance between them. "I've tasted his scent. I'd recognize it."

The witch met Sathach's crossed eyes. "Walk me through what happened," she said. "Who called to tell you about this?"

"No one *called* me," the Dread Lord said. "I got a text message." He slid his BlackBerry out of its holster, unlocked it, and passed it to the witch. "See for yourself."

She glanced at the small screen.

SECURITY: Fire-snake at the Bridge of Sighs!

The originating number was a string of five digits rather than the typical ten. And the mysterious warning wasn't the only text in the thread. The previous message read *Our records indicate that your security credentials will expire on April 13. Please complete Form 666d in triplicate to prevent revocation of your clearance.*

"Who sent it?" the witch asked, returning the device.

"It had to be someone with access to the security alert system." Sathach reholstered his BlackBerry and sighed. "But that's at least a dozen employees—plus the Clerk, the Sheriff, and the mayor. There's no way to tell specifically who."

"Are you sure?"

"Well, *no*," the Dread Lord said. "But we could ask the Dread Lord of IT to look into it."

"No need," she said. "I've got Tophet County's best technomancer on standby. Besides, Chad's already up to speed on what's been going on." She whipped out her phone, dashed off a quick message, and tapped send. "Okay, so Anonymous Asshole texted you. Then what?"

"I picked you up and flayed a distress call to Phæras."

"I left the Wheel, located Deputy O'Brien, and portaled directly here." Phæras tilted on his axis, regarding Hank with a considering eye. Er, orb. "It is . . . interesting that the message used *your* term for the creature rather than ka'met or fire vampire."

Fire vampire.

Again, the term tugged at a thread of memory. The witch would swear she'd never read Wandrei's story, but—

"*I* didn't send it!" Hank pointed at Keyser, who was draped over his shoulder digging trail mix out of his shirt pocket. "He was with me all night—just ask him."

Keyser Söze looked up, fired off an eldritch salute, and resumed his excavation.

"If the sender wasn't you," Phæras said in his tinny voice, "it had to be someone involved in this investigation. We've made no public safety announcements. The general public would not know to report such a thing."

Hank shrugged. "Yeah, but the Sheriff was there when I talked about what I saw, so . . ."

No need to finish that particular sentence.

Lomelzar wasn't exactly known for his discretion. And even if he hadn't been screeching the details around town, someone else could've blabbed. Besides the four of them, those in the know included the Clerk, Ellie, the Dread Librarian, Chad, and Keziah. But any of *them* would've contacted the WTF directly. Speaking of which, why send the message to Sathach instead of her? After all, she was the one who put the *witch* in Witch's Task Force.

She didn't like this.

Not one bit.

But with no imminent danger and nothing to investigate until they'd tracked down the sender of the text, Phæras went back to his shift at the Midnight Carnival, and Sathach portaled off to visit Heather and the twins.

"My Hummer's at City Hall," Hank said, idly scratching Keyser's ears, "or I'd offer you a ride home."

"I'm actually headed to Chad's," she said. "My broom's parked at the office, too. It's just a few blocks. Come on, you can be my escort." *Escort.* Her cheeks burned. "I mean, let's walk together."

"Sure thing!"

They'd taken only a few steps away from the Bridge of Sighs when Hank stopped in his tracks. Fearing another Vaping Douche visitation, the witch wiggled her fingers experimentally. They were working just fine, thank the gods. Time hadn't frozen, but Hank had.

"You okay?" she asked.

He turned back toward the bridge, moving with serpentine grace. "I feel . . . I feel something. I think it's—"

Hank's voice broke off as an electric blue firebolt slashed down from the clear sky and struck the forested saddle between two craggy peaks at the western end of the Mountains of Madness. The witch squinted against the blinding glare. An afterimage drifted over her closed eyelids, but it wasn't a color-reversed negative of the lightning strike. Her fingers drifted to the slim black cord at her throat, where the same shape formed the slide of a bolo tie.

A godsdamned golden apple.

"Are you sure about this?" Hank asked, as the witch fumbled with the keys to her office.

She dropped them for the third time, lost her temper, and destroyed the lock with a targeted entropic strike.

"No, but we're doing it." She realized what she'd just said and looked up at his earnest, dimpled face. "*I'm* doing it."

The witch stalked toward her desk, where the item she'd just sprinted three blocks to retrieve glinted dully in the moonlight. Sibyl's orrery. She had only the vaguest idea of how the teleportation artifact worked, but the godsdamned thing was made *for* witches *by* witches. If she couldn't figure out how to use it, it was time to hang up her pointy hat.

"Any clue what's in that part of the mountains?" she asked.

"The convention center and the observatory are at the eastern end of the range." Hank walked to the window and peered toward the distant cliffs. "The west is all wilderness."

"Uninhabited?"

"Unless you count the Mi-go. And the Shoggoths."

The witch glared at the Discordian shrine on her desk. *I hope you know what the hell you're doing, Lady.*

"The Sheriff won't even send us in to look for missing hikers," Hank said. "If they're gone overnight, they're . . . well, they're just gone." He looked at her over his shoulder, his forehead creased with worry. "Deputy Woods says there are hounds of Tindalos out there, too."

"Yeah, well, Deputy Woods had his brain lightly scrambled by the Swarm," she said. "Corner hounds are nasty business, but they need straight lines and clean edges to manifest in this plane."

The witch was an avid indoorswoman, but even she knew nature wasn't known for precise geometry.

As for the crab-shaped, fungiform Mi-go, they shunned light and would stick to their subterranean tunnels with the moon nearly full. No problem there.

Shoggoths, on the other hand . . .

Those oozy, homicidal horror slugs were nothing to screw around with. She'd put down a few in her time, but the last thing she wanted to do was to try her luck again.

What she *wanted* to do was go to Chad's house and finish their date—even if it was all Netflix and no chill. But Discordia's sign had been crystal clear, and messages from the Divine were the sort of thing a witch didn't ignore.

Not more than once, anyway.

"Witch, the fire-snake isn't hunting right now," Hank said. "It's . . . I think it's resting. Maybe we don't need to—"

"Like I said, *we* don't need to do anything." She picked up the orrery, which was surprisingly heavy for its size. "I'm teleporting over there to check it out. If I see the ka'met, I'll get out of Dodge."

"But what if your magic planet thing doesn't work?" he asked. "Or what if it runs out of juice?"

The witch's hands glowed as she pumped the orrery full of as much entropine as she and Keyser could hold. She sagged against the desk as the Archonic contract replenished her stores.

"There. Fully charged."

"Do you know how to use it?"

Good question.

She closed her eyes and formed a detailed mental picture of the hall outside her office, then she turned the crank on the orrery. Her skin crawled as she felt a queasy lurch, a slick sliding sensation. When she opened her eyes, she was standing in the doorway.

"Whoa," Hank breathed.

The witch grabbed her backpack from the desk and shouldered it. Sensing her readiness, Keyser wriggled in Hank's arms, and Hank put him down.

"It's go time. Keyser and I are off to check this shit out."

"But *why?*"

"Orders from headquarters," she said as her familiar waddled toward her. "It's a witch thing."

Hank lunged forward, scooped Keyser up, and gripped her shoulder with his free hand.

"If you're going, I'm going too."

The witch felt the hot prick of tears in her eyes and blinked furiously. For the second time in as many days, Hank was putting himself at risk to help her. She wouldn't have asked it of him, but saints below, she was glad he'd offered.

"Hank," she said, squeezing his hand, "I was really hoping you'd say that."

The orrery deposited them in a clearing at the low point between two craggy peaks. A gibbous moon gilded the surrounding forest with silver light. The forbidding mountains towered overhead, casting black pools of shadow, and a summer breeze stirred the trees in an eerie whisper.

The witch tucked the orrery into her backpack, zipped it, and glanced up at Hank. "Which way—"

He covered her mouth with his hand. Branches snapped and cracked as something moved through the dark woods. Something *big*.

She peeked through Keyser's nocturnal eyes and scanned the tree line. The amorphous mass of a Shoggoth slithered over a rotting log a few hundred yards away. Its formless body could take on whatever shape it desired. Based on prior experience, that shape typically consisted of foot-long fangs, stinger-studded tentacles, and a ravenous gullet. The protoplasmic blob flowed into a tunnel under a tree stump, oozing toward a dinner of fungal crabs. She almost felt sorry for the doomed Mi-go—even if they *did* have a nasty habit of stealing human brains.

Once the last of the creature's sticky mass had slurped its way underground,

Hank removed his hand and pointed at the sheer cliff face a quarter-mile to their west. His eyes glimmered with the faintest hint of blue.

"That way," he whispered.

The witch craned her neck, following the vertical rise to a dizzying height. Gods, she hoped they didn't have to climb. She could easily levitate herself and Keyser, or she could levitate Hank. But all three of them at once? She'd burn through entropine as fast as the Archonic contract could replenish it. Gravity was a persistent bastard.

Hank gently detached Keyser's paws from his shirt and passed him to the witch. Then he prowled across the clearing, as silent as a panther on the hunt. Her familiar—who'd usually charge headlong into a natural environment in search of something to eat, beat, or screw—clung to her like a bad habit. His fur stood on end, and his puffy, striped tail lashed back and forth in agitation. As they drew closer to the lightless woods beyond the clearing's edge, she again rerouted her vision through Keyser's night-adapted eyes, and the impenetrable blackness shifted into high-contrast shades of gray.

The witch followed Hank into a dense thicket of trees, listening to the absence of hooting owls, shrieking nightgaunts, and rustling rodents. The ka'met was here, and the forest felt it.

A flash of movement in the dense undergrowth caught her eye. She tugged Hank to a halt and pointed to a plume of smoke jetting from a tangle of brush.

"Look," she said, in the faintest of whispers. "The ka'met passed this way."

Hank shook his head. "No fire."

Weird. How could there be smoke with no fire?

The billowing clouds solidified into an angular muzzle, which gaped open to reveal a mouthful of crystalline fangs and a thin, flexible proboscis in place of a tongue.

"Tindalos," Hank said, in a voice hoarse with terror.

A corner hound? But they needed straight lines to take physical form. Whatever this was, it couldn't possibly be—

Her eyes snagged on a forked tree limb.

Oh, *fuck*. She'd forgotten about branches.

More smoke congealed into canine shoulders studded with sharp, bony protrusions and a sleek, pearlescent body with a ridged spine. Just looking at the thing hurt the witch's eyes—no, it hurt her *mind*. Its oddly jointed legs, which ended in feet tipped with hooked talons, met its body at impossible angles. Bits of the creature shifted in and out of view as though it were an optical illusion, but the subdimensional predator was all too real.

A low snarl rumbled from the monster as it stalked toward them on stiff legs.

The warning growl ceased in a moment of tense silence, and the corner hound attacked.

CHAPTER TWENTY-FOUR

A Raccoonnaissance Mission

As the witch stared into the gaping maw of certain death, she expected time to slow down and her life to flash before her eyes. But Discordia chose not to subject her to a greatest-hits reel of her dumbest mistakes, of which this evening hike through the monster-infested Mountains of Madness was a recent standout. Oh, time slowed, all right. She had time to appreciate the prismatic sheen of the hound's opaline skin. Time to watch its jaws stretch wide enough to swallow a bowling ball. Time to admire the glint of moonlight on teeth that glittered like diamond crescents.

She did *not*, however, have time to run.

Instead, the witch shoved Hank aside with a blast of air and—echoing the trick she'd used on the Sheriff a few days ago—fired an entropic strike at the ground between her boots. She dropped like a stone into a freshly excavated ten-foot-deep shaft. As the hound of Tindalos sailed through the patch of air that had recently hosted one terrified witch and one murderously furious raccoon, it snatched the pointy hat right off her head.

Before the thing could regroup, the witch pulled a shitload of entropine and shot skyward out of the hole. As she rose, she wrapped Keyser Söze in a cushion of compressed air and hurled him into the brushy undergrowth. Below her, the hound dug its talons into the forest floor and skidded to a halt. Its hindquarters pivoted at an inconceivable angle, somehow moving around and *through* its own head and torso so it faced in the opposite direction.

She gagged. Non-Euclidean geometry was godsdamned revolting.

No time for nausea.

The witch had bigger fiends to fry.

The beast was now aimed squarely at Hank. It growled and hunkered down, preparing to launch another attack. She conjured immense entropic hands, ripped a tree up by its roots, and dropped it on the hound.

And fucking *missed*.

Except she didn't.

The creature's body just wasn't where it was supposed to be anymore—or at least bits of it weren't.

Her vision dimmed from overexertion, and she spiraled to the ground. She'd be as useless as decaf coffee until the contract kicked in and replenished her. Sensing weakness, the hound's attention shifted from Hank to the witch. The thing *grinned*, and a tubelike proboscis quested from the dental debacle of its jaws. Unlike the Sheriff, who had the decency to spray his victims with acid before he sucked them down like a kid with a juice box, the hounds of Tindalos consumed their prey whole and alive. The occult geometry of their eldritch mouthparts allowed them to hoover up anything smaller than Hank's Hummer—including, and perhaps especially, a nearly unconscious witch.

Keyser burst out of the brush at a furious waddle. Though she'd used up his stored entropine, he still had teeth, claws, and a violent temperament at his disposal, and he was hell-bent on using all three to protect her.

"No," she moaned, struggling to all fours.

The hound spun toward him, its limbs flexing at angles her mind couldn't bear to behold. The glistening proboscis retracted, but its face still wore that horrible grin. Her breath hitched as the beast lunged toward Keyser, but Hank dove between them and shoved him out of the way. Teeth like shards of glass snapped shut on Hank's forearm with the sharp crack of breaking bone. He screamed, and blue sparks showered from his skin. The monster yipped in pain, folded in on itself like an origami nightmare, and reappeared twenty feet away, glaring at Hank with a near-comical expression of grievous offense.

The witch's body tingled as the entropic floodgates finally opened and a tidal wave of power surged into her bloodstream. She lassoed Hank and Keyser with ribbons of magic and yanked them behind her.

The hound's blank white eyes locked onto her, radiating malevolent rage. Its spiked tail lashed wildly, more feline than canine. The whipping motion drew her eye to a tendril of smoke that trailed from the end of its tail, linking it to the forked branch through which it had manifested.

Angles.

It needed sharp angles and straight lines to materialize on this plane. If she could just—

A vicious snarl sliced through her thoughts like crystal fangs through bare flesh. The hound advanced on her, its pace slow and deliberate.

Ignoring the monster took every ounce of willpower she had, but the witch forced herself to focus on its point of origin. She plunged her right hand into the black loam, and her magic surged through the earth, into the roots of the bushy shrub, and up through its branches. The slender limbs curved toward each other as she tried to convince them they'd much rather be a circle than a vee. The corner hound flickered. Its empty eyes darted toward the bending branches, then it abandoned its methodical approach and leaped.

Grow, gods dammit!

With a dizzying burst of entropine, the ends of the branches met, melded, and rounded into a lopsided circle.

The hound vanished.

"It doesn't even hurt," Hank said.

But his eyes burned blue, and sweat beaded on his forehead despite the cool evening air.

The witch swallowed a surge of bile as she knelt next to Hank and examined his forearm. His inner ka'met had closed dozens of lacerations and stopped the bleeding, but she could see an unnatural bulge just below the knob of his wrist bone. She glanced down at Keyser Söze and nodded. He climbed into Hank's lap and rested his front paw on the misshapen arm.

"Light him up," the witch said.

Hank's eyebrows drew together in confusion. "Light me—"

Keyser hit him with a dose of magical morphine. Hank's eyes grew dreamy and unfocused, though they didn't lose their cerulean hue. The witch gritted her teeth, gripped his wrist, and realigned the bone. Her hands glowed as the broken ends of his ulna knitted together. Shiny pink lines marked the aftermath of the hound's hooked teeth, but otherwise, the arm looked as good as new. She let Hank drift in dreamland as she stood and scanned the surrounding woods with both her third eye and Keyser's night vision. Their battle with the corner hound had scared off most of the wildlife. If they were going to push on, now was the time.

The witch touched Hank's brow with the tip of her index finger and jolted him into sobriety. He shook his head as if to clear it and gazed up at her. Was it her imagination, or was the blue even brighter?

"Are you okay?"

"I think so." Hank pushed to his feet and stood, but he staggered and leaned against the trunk of a broad sycamore. "Maybe a little woozy."

When Nyarlathotep had thrown him into the wall, the ka'met had healed his head, but the expenditure of energy had left him . . . hungry. Being alone in the woods with a hungry Hank was asking for trouble of the libidinous variety.

The witch shrugged out of her backpack and unzipped it to grab the orrery. "Let's get you back to Asphodel."

"Not yet." He pointed a trembling finger at the cliff face they'd seen from the clearing, which was now just a hundred yards away. "It's right there. I can feel it."

"You can barely stand, Hank," she said. "There's no way you can climb, and I don't have the juice to—"

"I don't think we have to climb."

"Then where the hell is the ka'met?"

"Let's find out." Hank pulled away from the tree. He stood, swaying slightly, then took an unsteady step. "See? I'm fine."

"Gods dammit," the witch muttered. She zipped her backpack, put it on, and tucked her shoulder under his arm. "You're lucky I'm tall."

Keyser Söze trundled out in front so she could borrow his eyes, and they followed him through the dark forest. Hank leaned heavily on her as they walked. His skin burned as though he had a fever. The woods were silent save for the sounds of their passage. The whisper of leaves as they brushed against branches. The snap of dry twigs. Hank's ragged inhalations.

And she could feel his hunger growing with every step.

The witch ducked under a low-hanging bough, and they emerged into a half-moon-shaped glade at the cliff's base. She scanned the shadowed clearing and saw no sign of the ka'met. But then Keyser waddled toward what she'd taken for a depression in the jagged rock. Through his eyes, she saw that it was, in fact, the mouth of a cave. The opening was shaped like a rough triangle that rose from the ground to knee-height. Even if Hank weren't on the verge of collapse, he couldn't fit inside. She might be able to squeeze through, but she'd have to slither on her belly while white-knuckling it through claustrophobic panic.

Keyser moved to enter the cave, but the witch used their bond to hold him back.

"No," she whispered. "Too dangerous."

"The fire-snake won't bother Keyser." Hank's voice was thin. Weak. "It won't even see him."

Nyarlathotep had told her the ka'met consumed the vital essence of sentient beings. Thanks to their magical bond, Keyser was much more than a mere raccoon, but his body still belonged to a nonsentient species.

"Are you sure?"

Hank nodded. Then, as though the effort of even that small motion had been too much, he rested his cheek on the top of her head. She sagged under his weight. They really needed to wrap this up and get him out of here.

At her psychic nudge, Keyser darted into the cave on a raccoonnaissance mission.

The witch had been worried that even Keyser's superb night vision would be stymied by the cave's lightless interior. But as she looked through his eyes, she saw a faint aura of blue glimmering up ahead in the twisting passage. He crept through the tunnel on silent paws, squeezed around a sharp bend, and peered into an open chamber.

The ka'met lay coiled around a mound of smooth, silvery stones like a dragon protecting its hoard. Its serpentine head lifted, and it looked around the cavern. The witch's heart stuttered in a staccato drumbeat, but the creature's gaze passed over Keyser like he wasn't even there. Emboldened, he inched closer for a better view. She counted seven stones—bottom-heavy ovals shaped almost like . . .

Like *eggs*.

The ka'met was nesting.

The sight dredged a recollection from the mucky riverbed of the witch's memory, and she realized why the term *fire vampire* had been so maddeningly familiar. She hadn't encountered it in a Lovecraft Circle story. She'd found it in the godsdamned *Archonomicon*.

She tugged Keyser's psychic tether, and he inched backward through the tunnel. Once he was safely around the bend, she dipped into her palace of memory.

The witch sat in the Read at Your Own Risk room in Derleth Memorial Library. She'd visited Za'gathoth's lair the previous evening—the night of the Yellow King's play. A slim Nomicon lay open on the table before her as she searched for information about the invading Swarm. She skimmed an account of the Archons' eons-long war with their mortal enemy. In an early skirmish, a colony of Archonic fire vampires had stormed a settlement of little white men in retaliation for the destruction of their nesting grounds—and their eggs. But instead of being consumed like other sentient life, the extreme heat of the fire vampires' attack transformed little white bodies into syntropium crystals. And the Swarm had weaponized those crystals in their anti-entropic spheres and used them to defeat the Archons.

The witch blinked, returning to the here and now.

A single ka'met had killed a boatload of moon-beasts, an Archon, and a human as easily as she'd swat an insect from Shaggai. What would happen when Mama Fire-Snake had seven little mouths to feed?

Keyser bustled out of the cave mouth, rushed to the witch, and tugged on the leg of her jeans. He pointed at Hank, who lolled against her, limp and heavy. Gods, she had to get him out of here.

"Hank," she whispered. "Can you stand up? I need to get the orrery."

No response.

"Hank?"

She used her free hand to ease his weight away from her so she could reach the backpack. But instead of standing on his own, he collapsed bonelessly to the ground.

The witch dropped to her knees and patted his cheek. "Hank!"

Her panicked shout echoed against the cliff face. Keyser's head whipped toward the tunnel that led to the ka'met's lair.

Shit, shit, *shit!*

She patted Hank's cheek again—more of a slap, to be honest—and he finally roused. His eyes snapped open, filmed with the faintest haze of blue.

"It's awake," he said. "It's *angry*." He gripped her wrist. "You need to leave. I'm too weak to—"

"Kiss me!"

His eyes widened. "What?"

Through Keyser's eyes, the witch saw a flicker of blue light shine from the tunnel. Her third eye filled with a vision of a snarling raccoon being dragged from her den. Keyser's mother had lost that battle, but the witch knew what he was trying to tell her. No animal was more dangerous than a parent defending their young.

"Kiss me!" she shouted. "Kiss me now!"

So he did.

CHAPTER TWENTY-FIVE

Another Way to Lie

The witch flew in a circle over Chad's house, staring down at the unassuming duplex he'd once shared with Heather. She was bone-weary—damn near ready to fall off her broom from sheer exhaustion—but she knew she'd never be able to sleep until she told Chad about the kiss.

It wasn't that she felt guilty. Not *really*.

Her bottomless reservoir of untapped horniness had possibly saved Hank's life, and it had definitely saved hers. The kiss had restored him enough to hold off the ka'met while she cranked up the orrery and got them the hell out of there. Given the limited options available at the time—either jump-start Hank's motor, or get fried like an egg by an enraged fire-snake—it had been the right thing to do.

But keeping what had happened a secret?

That would be wrong.

It would break something between her and Chad. Something fragile. Something precious. Something she very much wanted to protect.

And oddly enough, despite the fact that Hank was now an eldritch lust vampire, kissing him had only confirmed what she already knew: Chad was the one she wanted.

It wasn't that the kiss had been bad—quite the opposite, in fact. Between the witch's adventures in the Tinderverse and her die-hard romance novel habit, she'd encountered kisses that curled toes, induced swoons, and dropped pants. Hank's had been hot enough to liquefy loins.

But there'd been no *there* there. It was like . . .

Every couple of months, the witch scraped together the cash for a massage from a Swedish-trained therapist. She spent way too much time hunched over either a computer or a broomstick, and periodic untying of the knots in her back was the only thing that kept her from twisting up like a pretzel. Lorna knew exactly what to do to release her tension, exactly where to press and how much pressure to use. On the other hand, when she hung out at Chad's house, he'd often have her sit on the floor between his feet while he sat behind her on the couch. Then he'd rub her shoulders while she bitched about her dumbass day. Lorna was far more skilled, but Chad's enthusiastic amateur efforts filled up that hollow place in her chest where other people stored their . . .

Ugh. Feelings.

Better didn't always mean *better*.

Hank's kiss had triggered a tsunami of lust, but it had left her feeling empty. Probably because his vampiric ass had sucked the *wanna bone?* right out of her, but that was beside the point.

The point was, she needed to stop procrastinating and talk to Chad.

The witch spiraled down to the yard, parked her broom by a Weeping Angel statue, and knocked on the door.

The summer night was silent save for the creak of Chad's porch swing. The witch chewed a hangnail on her thumb, caught herself doing it, and slid her hands under her thighs. She'd rushed through her explanation, the words spilling out in a near-incoherent flood, but she'd told him everything.

Everything everything.

Chad cleared his throat. "So, you're saying that . . ."

"Yeah?"

"Even though Hank is, and I quote, hot enough to make Satan sweat—"

That might not have been the best turn of phrase.

"—and this kiss unleashed a horny tidal wave—"

She'd actually said *tsunami*, but now was probably not the time for corrections.

"—the only reason you told him to kiss you was that his life was in danger—"

"Both of our lives."

"Your *lives* were in danger. But I shouldn't be worried, because at the end of the day, my amateur back rubs, which are nowhere near as good as Lorna's, fill your empty torso with"—Chad hooked his fingers in air quotes—"feelings or some shit?" He cocked his head and looked at her, his face an expressionless mask. "Does that about cover it?"

The Switch's heart sank. It had sounded way better in her head.

"Yeah. That, um . . . that covers it." She gave her head a rueful shake and stood. "I'll see myself out."

Chad burst out laughing, grabbed her hand, and tugged her back onto the swing. She stared at him in confusion as he wiped tears from the corners of his eyes.

"You're not pissed?"

"Pissed?" he repeated. "Because you kissed a living Adonis with a lust-inducing superpower, then hopped on your broom and flew to my place to tell me I'm the one you really want? It's a little awkward, I'm not gonna lie." He cupped her face in one hand. "But no, I'm not pissed."

"Oh. Good. I was afraid—"

Chad kissed her.

It was a toe-curler. A swooner. A liquefier of loins. Unlike Hank's kiss, which could only *take*, this one *gave*. Warmth spread along the length of her body, from the crown of her head to the soles of her feet.

Sometimes better *was* better.

He rested his forehead against hers and said, "I'm glad you told me what happened."

"Well, I've learned the hard way that keeping secrets is just another way to lie."

Chad flinched and pulled away from her. The porch light cast pools of shadow under his eyes.

He looked tired. Haunted.

"Witch, I . . ."

His voice trailed off, and he shook his head.

"What's wrong?"

"I need to show you something."

She examined his face, which was strained and serious. "I take it that what you want to show me isn't in your pants."

"I'm afraid not." His lips curved in a sad smile as he stood and offered her his hand. "Come on."

The witch took it, though she didn't want to, and let him pull her to her feet. "I'm not gonna like this, am I?"

"Just do me a favor," he said, squeezing her hand.

"What's that?"

"Remember I tried my best to do the right thing."

Chad led the witch along a path of round stepping stones imprinted with intricate geometric patterns. (On a previous visit, he'd told her the stones spelled out *There's no such thing as an ordinary human* in the Gallifreyan language of the Time Lords. Peak nerd. She kinda loved it.) The path circled around behind the duplex to his backyard, where crisscrossing strands of string lights lit the patio with a warm glow. She followed him past an outdoor kitchen and dining table to a semicircle of TARDIS-blue Adirondack chairs. The seating area faced a terracotta chiminea with a foil-lined black metal grate in its bulbous belly. He gestured for her to sit as he picked up a pair of oven mitts from a side table and slid them on.

"By the way," he said, "I, uh . . . I found out who sent that security alert."

After her ordeal in the Mountains of Madness, the witch had all but forgotten that someone texted the Dread Lord of Human Resources about the ka'met seen near the Bridge of Sighs.

"Oh yeah?" she said, leaning forward to prop her elbows on her knees. "Who sent it?"

He gripped a handle on the metal grate and lifted it free. Blue light shone from the firebox.

"I think it's best if I let him speak for himself."

Chad propped the grate against the chiminea's stand and stepped aside. An azure blaze leaped up with a *whoomph* and a burst of warm air, and the witch found herself face-to-flame with her missing suspect.

Monsieur Flambé.

The truth thudded home like a crossbow bolt, piercing her newly filled heart.

For four days, for *four frigging days*, Chad had let her run around Tophet County like a rat-thing with its head cut off, searching for the Archon he was hiding in his godsdamned backyard.

First, he'd shut her out. Then, he'd been terse to the point of rudeness. And finally, he'd listened as she shared every shred of information she had. And—

And, oh gods . . . he'd fed that information to the Unquenchable Flame. He must have, because the text Flame sent to Sathach used Hank's term. *Fire-snake.*

Last year, the witch had placed her trust in the wrong person with nearly world-ending consequences. She'd tried so hard to do things differently this time—to be open, to be honest, to *trust*. And look what it had gotten her.

So much for making new and different mistakes.

Chad took a halting step toward her. "Witch, let me explain. I—"

"Don't," she said. Her voice was so icy that frost formed on her lips. "Don't you say a single. Fucking. Word."

Without looking at him, she used entropic hands to pick him up and plunk him down in the chair furthest from hers. Her heart, which had felt so full just a few minutes ago, ached with emptiness.

It *hurt.*

It hurt so badly that Keyser stirred in his sleep back at her apartment.

The witch's treacherous freaking face crumpled in a pained grimace, but she forced her features into smooth placidity. She didn't trust herself to speak, so she crossed her arms and glared at Flame with her best *Get on with it* expression.

An earnest face formed in the crackling fire. "I didn't kill Yi'danag."

She could feel the pressure of Chad's eyes on her. Her mouth opened to ask a question, but the words wouldn't come. She waved her hand for him to go on.

"I . . . I saw it happen, and I ran," Flame said. "I'm not proud of it, but what would *you* do if you saw a mirror image of yourself murder someone in broad daylight, and you knew no one would believe you, and the Sheriff was right there, and he has a tendency to . . . to get out in front of the facts, and—"

"Back up and—" The witch's voice broke. She cleared her throat and tried again. "Start with your vacation."

Two red spots appeared on the blue face, right where the cheeks should be. "My personal life has nothing to do with this," he snapped, a hint of his familiar assholery entering his voice.

"Well, you're *personally* Suspect Number One in a string of murders."

Agitated tongues of blue flame licked from the firebox, leaving smudges of soot around the opening's mouth. "I didn't murder anyone!"

"If you don't want to talk to me," the witch said, digging her BlackBerry out of her pocket, "you can tell your story to Lomelzar."

"Witch," Chad said, "this is why I didn't—"

She snapped her fingers and muted him. "The Sheriff's just a phone call away."

"I'll talk!" A tentacle made of cerulean fire snaked out of the firebox. "I'll even swear to tell the truth."

This was going to hurt, but she had to do it. She gritted her teeth and offered her hand, fully expecting Flame's appendage to wind around her wrist and give it a sadistic, skin-searing squeeze. But the burning limb brushed against her open hand, making only enough contact to seal the magical oath.

A single blister formed on the witch's palm. The contract tried to heal her, but she left the burn as it was. She needed the distraction.

"Out with it."

"I'm not like the other Archons," Flame said. "I don't eat—"

"You eat newborn stars. Za'gathoth told me."

Sparks of annoyance spewed from the fire. "Then what exactly do you want to know?"

"Did you see anything weird while you were out there?" the witch asked. "Or maybe run into your little blue friend?"

Flame shook his fiery head. "Everything was normal until I got home Friday night. I crashed for a few hours, then Lomelzar summoned me to stand guard at the field."

She cocked her head. "Was this nap before or after you slaughtered the moon-beasts?"

"I had nothing to do with that," he said. "I didn't even know there *were* moon-beasts!"

If the Unquenchable Flame had been behind the attack, the magical oath would've choked him to death on his own lie. But it hadn't.

Could it be a Jekyll-and-Hyde situation? Maybe Flame didn't *know* he was a killer.

Only one way to find out.

"So you were standing guard?" she prompted.

"You won't understand. It's so hard to—" Flame's piercing blue eyes locked on the witch, blazing with fierce intensity. "I think . . . Witch, you actually might be the only person in the cosmos who *can* understand."

"Understand what, for fuck's sake?"

"When I was at the park, lightning struck the dome, and I saw . . . I saw *me,*" Flame said. "But not me as I am—me as I could have been."

Chad made a muffled sound, trying to draw the witch's attention. She ignored him.

"What do you mean?"

"I'm not like the other Archons," he said. "I've always been different. I couldn't eat what they ate. I had to teach myself how to portal. I had no name." The flames died down until his face was half the size it had been. "And I was dangerous. I grew up totally—"

"Alone," she said, her third eye filling with a vision of a lonely witchling in an entropically sealed cellar.

Perfect.

A bonding moment.

"Alone," he repeated. "There was no one to teach me, no one to guide me. I just had to figure things out as I went. But then I saw the fire-snake. It wasn't me, but it was *like* me." The pupils of Flame's eyes flickered in a wistful dance. "Then it killed Yi'danag, and I felt it . . . I felt it *see* me, so I ran. Once I calmed down, I realized how it would look." He flashed a pained smile. "I'm not exactly well liked—even by Mother. I knew no one would believe me, so I texted Chad and came here."

Texted Chad?

Of course. The night Sibyl was murdered, Chad had gotten a message that rattled him. After he read it, he'd pleaded exhaustion and gone home instead of going with her and Sathach to meet Phæras.

She'd been such a fool.

"Why would you hide here?" she asked.

"I may look like a fire," he said, "but I have an electrical signature. Clay is a terrible conductor, so I knew the Other wouldn't be able to find me if I stayed inside the chiminea."

"No." The witch pointed at the patio beneath her boots. "I mean, why *here*?"

"Well, you know Chad." Flame's features softened as he looked at his human friend. "He's the only person I've ever met who wanted to get to know the real me. It's like . . . it's like he sees past my attitude, past the thousand-degree fire, past the risk of severe burns, to who I truly *am.* I knew he'd listen." He turned back to the witch. "I knew he'd help me."

"So you didn't attack the moon-beasts, you didn't murder Yi'danag, and you didn't kill Sibyl?"

"I didn't," he said. "I swear it."

The witch's magic assured her he spoke the truth—or at least what he believed to be true.

"But it *was* me at the bridge," Flame said. "After Chad told me about the fire vampires, I wanted to know more. I thought I might be able to sneak down and see Mother while Chad was out with you, but the Other felt me. It showed up at the bridge, and I ran. Chad told me I was your top suspect, so I texted Sathach instead of you."

"Chad told you that, huh?" The witch turned and looked at Chad. "Sounds like he told you pretty much everything."

"He did," Flame said eagerly. "And he's been trying all along to help me prove my innocence. He even talked to the moon-beasts to see if—"

"So *that's* why you were in the cavern," she said, glaring at Chad. "And here I thought you were working out the bugs in your software."

Chad waved his arms frantically, and she unmuted him.

"I *was* working out the bugs," he said. "And I was going to tell you everything I learned—"

"Just like *I* told *you* everything?"

"Witch, you told me multiple times that if—no, *when*—you found Flame, you'd turn him over to the Sheriff."

"Yeah, Chad," she said. "Because he's accused of murder."

"But he didn't do it." Chad's eyes searched her face. "You *know* that now, right? So you have to understand why I couldn't—"

"Oh, I understand," the witch said. "I understand perfectly." She stood and stalked toward the path of round stones, then stopped and spun to face him. "I understand that you let me spill my guts to you. I understand that you hid a fugitive. I understand that you barely spoke to me—"

"I didn't want to lie!"

"Then try telling the godsdamned truth!"

CHAPTER TWENTY-SIX

Something the Ghast Dragged In

Text from Nerd-romancer

The witch dismissed the notification with extreme prejudice, slid her BlackBerry into her pocket, and levitated her way onto Za'gathoth's monstrous floral couch. Chad had sent twelve texts since she left his house last night, and she hadn't read any of them. The whole thing was still too raw, too painful.

Her BlackBerry vibrated again.

She ground her teeth and fished it out, handling the thrice-cursed device like unexploded ordnance. If it was him again, she'd drown the godsdamned thing in the Catachthonic River.

But it wasn't. Her latest message was a reply from the County Clerk.

Though the witch was apocalyptically pissed at Chad—and, for reasons she couldn't quite articulate, at Monsieur Flambé—she'd sent an email letting the WTF know that the Unquenchable Flame was no longer a suspect. She'd feel awful if the Sheriff stumbled on his hiding place and exacted his permanent brand of justice.

Maybe not awful, but bad.

Mildly regretful, anyway.

She'd expected the news to earn a smug *I-told-you-so* from Sathach, but his primary emotion had been relief that his primal-scream circle wasn't losing its angriest member. The Clerk offered to call off Lomelzar and his Spectral Forces goons, and this text confirmed the deed was done. So the witch's relationship was in the shitter, she had no idea where the surplus ka'met had come from, and a narcissistic Outer God was on the loose, but at least Flame would not be extinguished unjustly.

Fan-frigging-tastic.

"Brought the whole gang this time, did you?"

Za'gathoth's truculent glare passed from Phæras, to Hank, to the witch, and finally settled on the Dread Lord of Human Resources. In deference to her disdain for his human-positive progressivism, he'd left the Keanu safely on the bridge, where Keyser Söze and his lady friend were currently using it as an air mattress.

"Sathach," she said, "if you think you can bully me into blathering on about the worthless male who fathered you—"

"I respect your boundaries, Mother," he lisped. But his tentacles drooped with the dejection of dashed hopes.

"And you . . ." Za'gathoth's withered eyestalks wobbled as she gave the witch a rheumy once-over. "You look like something the ghast dragged in. I'd bet my last cup of Jell-O you haven't slept a wink."

Sathach's tangle of limbs writhed in concern. "She's right," he said. "Your eyes are very puffy, almost like you've been—"

"If I was feeling any better, I'd have to take something for it," the witch said. "It's just . . . allergies."

She was, as it turned out, highly allergic to heartbreak. Symptoms included fits of rage, copious consumption of Chicken Cock, and watery ocular discharge. Those dumbasses who booked love spells suddenly seemed slightly less dumb. Out of habit, she reached up to tug the brim of her pointy hat down over her pathetically puffy eyes, forgetting that said hat was currently located inside a corner hound, bound for subdimensional parts unknown.

The Mindless Mother watched her with a knowing expression. "Allergies, eh?"

"We've got more important shit to discuss than my face. We need to—"

"Is it my imagination," Za'gathoth said, shifting her focus to Hank, "or do you look tastier than ever?" She winked horribly and sucked her false teeth. "I've half a mind to eat you again." Hank blanched, and the ancient Archon chuckled. "Oh, settle down, handsome. I can't eat until I take my hearts pill."

But the old beetle had a point. In stark contrast to the witch, Hank looked well-rested and fully restored. After their adventure in the Mountains of Madness, she'd taken him to the Midnight Carnival, where he'd presumably loitered around the Tunnel of Love and Sphinxter's Peep Show until his randy reserves had been replenished. He'd seemed a little hesitant around her when they met at the bridge that morning to visit Za'gathoth. But once she reassured him for the twenty-third time that neither she nor Chad were mad at him, he'd settled into his usual hyper-cheerful demeanor.

"It must be the ka'met," Hank said. "Ever since it turned me into an honorary fire vampire—"

"A what, now?"

The witch exchanged a glance with one of Sathach's roving eyeballs. Za'gathoth couldn't have heard Nyarlathotep's oh-so-clever sobriquet for the creatures. And since her preferred reading material had half-naked wrestlers on the cover, she probably hadn't delved into the collected works of the Lovecraft Circle to encounter Wandrei's term.

Phæras produced a stuttering series of metallic clangs equivalent to the clearing of a throat. "It seems Yi'danag was murdered by one of Fthaggua's living limbs."

"Ha!" Za'gathoth barked. "The Swarm got Fthaggua just like they got everyone else. The only parts of him that survived were . . ." She hesitated, then tossed her insectile head. "Doesn't matter. They're all gone now, and that's a fact."

"But we know one of them still lives, Mother."

"Two, actually," Sathach said. "The killer and the Unquenchable Flame."

Za'gathoth's mandibles flexed in agitation. "You think Flame is a Fthagguan? That'd be like one of *his* elbows," she said, pointing a gnarled human finger in Hank's direction, "living on after the rest of him died." She huffed. "I don't know where you came up with that damn fool notion, but—"

"The Crawling Chaos told us!" Hank grinned and belatedly raised his hand. "Sorry to interrupt."

The Mindless Mother's head swiveled toward him in slow-motion, horror movie style. "What did you say?"

"We're not supposed to speak his name, but it starts with *Nya* and ends with *tep*." Hank waggled his eyebrows. "*You* know. Anyway, he told the witch a ka'met is after him."

The vertical fanged maw in Za'gathoth's thorax gaped open. Her liver-spotted carapace pulsated, and a high-pitched squeal not unlike the whistle of a tea kettle shrilled into the momentary silence.

"Oh, no," Phæras said. "She's going to—"

"Hold your nose, Witch!" the Dread Lord shouted.

She frowned. "Hold my—"

The whistle escalated into a deafening shriek, and Za'gathoth exploded into a seething swarm of stag beetles. An iridescent river of insects flowed over the arms of her glider and streamed toward the gargantuan chintz sofa where the witch sat between Sathach and Hank. The cavernous room echoed with the buzz of wings and the click of serrated mouthparts. The rustling din settled at the base of the witch's spine and unleashed a wave of primitive lizard-brain terror. She scrambled away from the edge of the sofa and pressed herself against the back cushion as the surging tide reached the hideous dust ruffle. Her vision narrowed to a constricted tunnel, and her breath came in panicked gasps.

A cold, clammy pressure in the witch's ears silenced the insectile cacophony. It took her a moment to realize Sathach had jammed a tentacle in each of her ears to block out the noise—and, it seemed, the fear.

HOLD YOUR NOSE!

His psychic shout was so powerful it made her wince, but she was still half convinced she'd heard him wrong.

Sensing her confusion, Sathach flayed an image of a thumb-sized beetle excavating its way into her brain pan. The witch urgently clamped her nose shut. She yearned to fire up her shields, but that would fry the Dread Lord, and his eldritch earplugs were the only thing standing between her and mindless terror.

Mindless. Za'gathoth's nickname suddenly made a hell of a lot more sense.

Though Hank had been the one to trigger this entomological detonation, the ravening beetles cut a wide swath around him. He sat unmolested on a chintz island while the horde swarmed up the witch's legs. She swatted at them frantically, caught in a mental spiral of *get them off get them off GET THEM OFF*, but the only tangible result of her efforts was a smattering of pinches vicious enough to leave blood blisters.

Well, she'd be godsdamned if she'd sit here and be mandibled to death. It was shields-up time, and Sathach would just have to forgive her for shocking the shit out of him. But just as the witch started shunting entropine to her defenses, Phæras's orb rippled like a puddle in the wake of a T-rex, and the hairs on her arms stood on end. She heard the *bzzzzzzzt* of a bug zapper, and the beetles were jolted into stillness.

"That was a warning, Mother," Phæras said, in a voice like an angry cowbell. "Now, pull yourself together!"

Za'gathoth cradled a teacup large enough to hold a soccer ball in four trembling hands. Steaming liquid sloshed over the edges as she raised it to her maw and took a generous slug. The slightly astringent, piney smell of Beefeater gin cut through the floral bouquet of chamomile with a pleasant bite. The Mindless Mother called it a *Calm Your Ass Down Special.*

"I should've known that cockroach would find a way to survive." Za'gathoth set her cup in its saucer with a ceramic clatter. She looked somehow smaller than she had when they'd arrived. Older. And sadder. "The Crawling Chaos is the architect of every evil that has befallen the Archonic races since the Swarm's first attack."

Hank patted her wrinkled carapace with the absent-minded fondness people reserved for the elderly. "He did seem like kind of a jerk."

Za'gathoth gave him a considering glance. "You might just be smarter than you look."

"Thanks!"

"That douche's assholery isn't what we came to discuss," the witch said. "We need to know if the binding amulet is for real."

"Oh, it's real, all right." The Mindless Mother adjusted the tattered remains of her crocheted shawl, which was somewhat the worse for wear after her outburst. "He's used it before. Tell me, what do you know about the Fthagguans?"

"You mean the fire-snakes?" Hank asked.

"I s'pose that's as good a name as any."

"They consume the vital essence of sentient organisms," Phæras said. "And they are powerful enough that even an Outer God like *him* is afraid of them."

"And with good reason," Za'gathoth said. "Fthaggua was born of Cthugha, a fire elemental back in the old country. Cthugha and his line were the only entities the Crawling Chaos feared—and he hated them for it. They were on the contract, so they didn't run around gobbling up Archons willy-nilly, but they could scorch the scales off a Shantak without breaking a sweat." She waved a pair of hands in a *get-on-with-it* gesture. "What else?"

"After our little chat last fall," the witch said, "I hit up *The Archonomicon* and found out that the Swarm used fire-snakes to make their secret weapon. They baited the ka'met into attacking, and the flames turned little white men into syntropium crystals."

"That's horrible!" Hank said. "The Swarm sacrificed their own people just to make weapons?"

"It's not really a sacrifice for a hive mind to lose a few bees," Za'gathoth said. "Azathoth Himself wept when the Swarm figured out how to make those crystals. They turned the tide of our war." She stirred her tea with a spoon the size of a garden spade and took an oddly dainty sip. "At first, the Outer Gods didn't know how they were doing it. But then they sent CC—"

"Who is CC?" Phæras asked.

"The Crawling Chaos, dummy!" She sucked her teeth and shook her head. "Try to keep up. CC was sort of a servant to the other Outer Gods. They ran him all over creation—starting cults here, spreading madness there. And when this new weapon popped up, they asked him to use his shape-shifting skills to spy on the Swarm."

"Let me guess," the witch said. "Shit went sideways."

"Nailed it in one." Za'gathoth's gaze unfocused, shifting to the distant past. "He got cocky. Then he got caught. Oh, CC was just *sure* the rest of the Outer Gods would trip over their tentacles to break him out, but he was dead wrong."

"They abandoned him?" the Dread Lord asked.

"More like they figured he was toast, and they didn't see the sense in haring off on a fool's errand." The Mindless Mother rocked in her glider, lost in memory until a phlegmy cough drew her back to the present moment. "By then, CC knew the secret of the crystals. The Swarm was running out of them, and they were desperate to make more. So he cut a deal."

"Holy hell," the witch breathed. "He made that amulet for the Swarm, didn't he?"

Za'gathoth opened her mouth, but no words came. She squeezed her eyes shut and nodded. After another sip of *Calm Your Ass Down* and a few deep breaths, she said, "That traitor sold the survival of our race for the price of his own freedom."

"Collusion with the ancient enemy!" Sathach's nest of tentacles writhed with the anguished excitement of a bitter discovery. "*That's* why he's not on the contract."

"He was booted the second he gave them the amulet," Za'gathoth said. "We all knew what he'd done. Fthaggua tried to save his . . . his fire-snakes, but it was a suicide mission. The Swarm took him out. I figured they got CC too, but it sounds like he hauled ass for the Dreamlands and locked the Morpheus Gate behind him." She sniffed. "Left the rest of us to die—even his own . . ."

Hank raised his hand. "His own what?"

"He left everyone, didn't he?" she said. "That cursed amulet kept the fire-snakes alive even after Fthaggua was gone. I thought they must've died off eons ago."

"Well, one of the blue bastards is back," the witch said, "and it's out for ichor."

"What I'd like to know is how it got here from the old country and why it didn't show up until now." Za'gathoth fixed her gaze on the witch. "Did you see any sign of it when you were over there with the Great White?"

She replayed the scene in her mind. The Great White's obligatory villain speech. The moment she'd gripped his hand and flooded his realm with chaos. The heavy pull of unconsciousness as she succumbed to entropic depletion. And . . .

And, just before she passed out, a streak of blue flame that lanced up from the horizon like reverse lightning.

"Gods dammit, I *did* see something," the witch said. "I just didn't know what it was." She chewed her lip. "Shit. You're not gonna like this."

Phæras tilted on his axis. "We aren't going to like what?"

"I think the frigging thing came through when they brought me back."

"I'll tell you one more thing you're not gonna like," Za'gathoth said. "You said the Fthagguan is nesting in the Mountains of Madness?"

The witch nodded. "Keyser saw seven eggs."

"You'd better sort this out before they hatch," she said. "The parent might be focused on vengeance for now, but that'll change when it has mouths to feed." Za'gathoth tutted, clicking her mandibles. "If there's one thing I know about babies, it's this: The little devils are always hungry."

CHAPTER TWENTY-SEVEN

Scream It Out

Keyser Söze waddled through the maze of City Hall with an exhausted witch trailing along behind him. The combination of shitty sleep, emotional fatigue, and a hard-core adrenaline crash after Za'gathoth's freak-show freakout had left her about as peppy as a day-old corpse. She needed coffee. She needed food. She needed a godsdamned nap and a long vacation. But before she could indulge, she had an unpleasant task to attend to—inflicting what she'd learned upon the Unquenchable Flame.

To the witch's tremendous annoyance, the parallels between Flame and herself were distressingly strong. Both of them were orphans. Both had begun their lives nameless. Both were abrasive dickheads with anger issues and more baggage than a transatlantic flight. She knew firsthand how it felt to be the last one to learn the truth, and it was about as pleasant as an acid bath from the Sheriff. So like it or not—and she did not—she was in for an awkward visit with Flame, who was still holed up in Chad's chiminea to evade detection by the rogue ka'met.

After a spirited internal debate, the witch had also decided to lend him the orrery. The fire-snake had turned up like a bad penny when Flame portaled to the Bridge of Sighs. Fortunately, no one else had been around, but they might not be so lucky next time. He could travel faster than light under his own steam, but so could the killer ka'met. The orrery would give him the ability to slip away without leaving a trail. Or sparking an innocent bystander barbecue.

She'd expected to feel good about what she was doing. After all, she was protecting the community and helping someone in need. But the *helping* part was much less satisfying when the *someone in need* was a flaming asshole.

Speaking of assholes, the witch rounded a corner to find that some inconsiderate jerk had blocked her office door with what looked like a TV tray. A Dee's coffee cup sat on the small table next to a flat, white box. *FOR THE WITCH OF TOPHET COUNTY* was neatly printed on a neon sticky note on the lid. She'd know Chad's tiny all-caps font anywhere. She opened the box and saw a half-dozen gloriously gooey sticky 'nuts. On the inside of the lid, in black Sharpie, he'd written *I'M SORRY, WITCH. CAN WE PLEASE TALK?*

Talk? What was there to say?

Chad didn't trust her. He'd made that abundantly clear.

A small, mean part of her wanted to make him suffer for hurting her. That part didn't just want him to be sorry. It wanted him to feel as bad as she did. No, *worse*. A bigger part of her—the better part—wanted to forgive him and move on. She knew his intentions had been good.

Just remember I tried to do the right thing.

What the witch was remembering at the moment was how she'd felt last fall as she apologized to Chad for getting Heather elected Mayor. She'd expected him to twist the knife, but as soon as she said she was sorry, he'd forgiven her. And then he'd never mentioned it again.

That's how it works, Witch, he'd said. *You mess up. You apologize. You move on.*

But they'd just been coworkers then—not even close friends, not really. Now they were so much more. She'd thought he knew her, thought he trusted her, and she'd been wrong.

What if an apology wasn't enough to fix that?

What if she *couldn't* forgive him?

Keyser broke the reverie of her romantic Ragnarok by tugging persistently on the leg of her jeans and making puppy-dog eyes at the pastries. She broke off a piece of sticky 'nut and handed it to him. It would be a crying shame to let fresh 'nuts go to waste.

The witch unlocked her office, picked up the box and the coffee cup, and kicked the tray down the hall. She bumped the door open with her hip, but Keyser rumbled a growl of alarm and surged through ahead of her. Psychic senses on high alert, she followed him inside.

A dingy gray return air grille lay on the floor beneath a square tunnel of open HVAC ductwork. Keyser Söze stuffed his sticky 'nut in his mouth, bustled over to the trash can, and tipped it over, spilling out crumpled paper, a few Diet Dr Pepper dead soldiers . . . and Jenkin. Keyser hissed at the old-man-faced dog-thing, raised his tail, and rubbed his butt vigorously on the trash can. (Prior internet searches had revealed that this raccoonian habit was a form of territory marking involving the words *anal* and *glands*.)

Jenkin lifted his jowly chin and hopped up onto her desk with an air of bruised dignity.

"Thank the gods you're here," Keziah said. "You won't believe what—"

"Oh, I'm up to my eyeballs in unbelievable shit." The witch set the pastry box down, plopped into her chair, and drained her coffee dry. She waved a hand, setting the trash can to rights, and dropped the empty Dee's cup inside. "I've got a lot to catch you up on."

Jenkin opened his mouth to interject, but the witch charged into a recap of everything she'd learned since the WTF meeting yesterday afternoon.

Almost everything.

She glossed over the whole *apparently, Chad doesn't trust me as far as he can throw me, and he's a nerdy mathlete, so that was never very far to begin with* thing.

Jenkin arched his eyebrows, furrowing an already copiously wrinkled brow. "So the Unquenchable Flame is a ka'met, and the killer is a ka'met, but Flame is not the killer?"

"He's not," the witch said. "I questioned him under magical oath." She propped her boots on the corner of her desk and sighed. "And since the killer ka'met can track Flame's movements, I'm going to loan him the orrery until we sort out this mess."

On that note, where the hell *was* the orrery? She'd left it on her desk, she was sure of it—right where Jenkin's happy ass was currently sitting.

The scraggly creature watched as the witch registered the orrery's absence. "That's what I was trying to tell you," Keziah said. "*He* took it."

"He who?"

But even as she asked the question, the answer grabbed her by the throat like a throttling tentacle.

"The Crawling Chaos," she said, confirming the witch's suspicion. "I was in the air duct, just about to open the vent and come in, when I felt his spectral ghost avatar enter your office. See for yourself."

Colored light shone from Jenkin's eyes and projected a movie clip on the witch's bare white wall. On the makeshift screen, the orrery shot upward as though lifted by unseen hands. The handle turned as the invisible intruder cranked it, then the device vanished into thin air.

Nyarlathotep had mentioned his spectral ghost avatar when the witch met him on the astral plane, but that detail had gotten lost in the aftermath of his attempt to choke her into submission. With the orrery in hand, that traitorous cone-head could be ghosting around Tophet County, getting up to all sorts of . . .

Hold the freaking phone. *Ghosting.*

What the witch had just witnessed was eerily similar to the security footage from the Dread Lord's basement—only on that particular occasion, she'd been confronted with a levitating multispecies sex swing instead of a floating orrery. A so-called "paranormal phenomenon" had communicated with Sathach through his spirit box and claimed to be his father. Unfortunately, their little chat had been cut short by the murderous fire-snake's arrival.

Snippets of Za'gathoth's comments about the Dread Lord's sire floated to the surface of the witch's mind like turds in the paternal punch bowl.

You get your mind-flaying from him . . . and your shape-shifting.

Pretty high up in the Archonic hierarchy.

Drove me mad—drove everyone mad, truth be told.

The fact that Za'gathoth had exploded into a swarm of stag beetles upon hearing of Nyarlathotep's return suddenly made a lot more sense. Her ex was back in town.

And that meant Nyarlathotep was the Dread Lord's fucking *father.*

"The orrery could take him anywhere." Sathach stared dolefully at the front door of the home he shared with Heather and the twins. "What makes you think he'd come *here?*"

The witch shrugged. "Call it a hunch."

The bastard was here. She *knew* it.

Nyarlathotep would want to stay close to the investigation. And based on the fact that Sathach had been experiencing paranormal visitations for weeks, the old cosmic horror had taken quite an interest in his son and grandkids. Hiding out in the Dread Lord's weird-ass basement ticked all the boxes.

"The Crawling Chaos is nearby," Keziah said, scenting the air through Jenkin's bulbous nose. "I can sense it."

A faint sheen of blue briefly glazed Hank's eyes. "I think I feel him, too."

"And you're *sure* he's my father?" Sathach asked. "Don't you think Mother would've told me when she was relating his history?"

At least he could say the word *father* without scream-crying now. It was a marked improvement over the past hour.

After she'd put the facts together, the witch had stormed into the Dread Lord's office and had him flay the ugly truth from her mind. Once she'd waited out a fit of sobbing hysterics, he'd reluctantly agreed to pick up Hank and take them to follow up on her theory about Nyarly's current whereabouts.

"Told you?" the witch repeated. "Told you what exactly? 'Hey, son, know how you've always wanted to find out who your father was? Well, as it turns out, he's the psychopathic Outer God who was single-handedly responsible for the decimation of our race and the destruction of our home universe. But he didn't eat you when you were a baby, so he's got that going for him.'"

"Way harsh, Witch," Hank said.

She gave the Dread Lord's shoulder her best attempt at a comforting pat. "No, I don't think she would've told you."

"But . . . but I don't *want* it to be him."

"Come on, Sathach," the witch said. "You can scream it out in your therapy circle later. But for now, we need every bit of leverage we can get with this asshat.

He's obviously curious about you. You said you mind-flayed the universe itself calling out to your father. Well, he came. He may be a coward and a traitor, but that's gotta count for something. Now, let's just—"

"Open the godsdamned door," Keziah snapped.

Sathach took a deep, shaky breath and unlocked three deadbolts and the doorknob. Jenkin and Keyser both tried to squeeze through the door first, and a brief tussle ensued. Keyser's relative youth and superlative girth won the day, and he sealed his victory by stamping Jenkin's forehead with a glandular kiss. He waltzed over his fallen foe and waited for the witch in the foyer. She couldn't help feeling a surge of pride.

Jenkin picked himself up, scrubbed irritably at this head with a rat-like paw, and stepped daintily across the threshold. Then he froze, his skinny body quivering in anticipation.

"He's definitely here," Keziah whispered. Jenkin started down the darkened hallway at a trot. "Follow me."

Jenkin led them along the now-familiar route to the basement stairway. Keyser seemed to consider cutting in front of him, then thought better of it and let the bedraggled beastling retain the lead. The witch charged up her shields and preemptively pulled entropine. She knew better than to hit Nyarlathotep with an entropic strike, but given his terror of the ka'met, a flamethrower that spewed blue fire might be just the ticket. That brand of magic would have catastrophic consequences for Heather's decor, but she'd burn that bridge when she came to it.

They crept through the silent basement, which was lit only by the glow of the Dread Lord's command center. Boxes of acidic weight-loss wraps and eldritch intimate aids towered overhead as they wound through the chthonic gloom. Jenkin padded confidently toward the far corner of the basement, which was occupied by a waist-high heap of rubbery noodles in a variety of skin tones.

Hank pointed at the bizarre tangle. "What's that?"

"Discarded prototypes for Heather's signature romantic restraint system," Sathach said. "But they've been disturbed."

The witch eyeballed the snarl of straps, tethers, and buckles. "They're disturbed, all right."

Jenkin stood up on his hind legs and peered into the tangled knot. "Nyarlathotep, show yourself!"

Keziah's voice echoed in the basement, but nothing happened.

"Oh, this is ri-godsdamned-diculous."

With a snap of the witch's fingers, the silicone love nest lofted into the air. She saw no sign of the Crawling Chaos, but a hidden hoard of junk had been tucked under the pile of discarded prototypes. A broken umbrella. A clacky-ball desk toy. A bunch of random metal and glass stuff.

Huh. Heather had always seemed like a neat freak until the witch poked around in her basement.

"Aha!" Jenkin picked up the umbrella in his teeth, dragged it away from the pile of trash, and hurled it onto a mound of moldering leggings.

Once the umbrella was gone, the witch saw the collection for what it truly was: the missing artifacts. She deposited the pile of prototypes next to Sibyl's collection, propped her hands on her hips, and looked around the basement.

"Come out, come out, wherever you are!" she called.

"Dad?" the Dread Lord said in a quavering voice. "Are you here?"

The romantic restraints twitched and writhed, then the Vaping Douche's head appeared atop the pile like a meatball on a mound of occult spaghetti. Rubbery appendages thrashed wildly as he wriggled his way free. Nyarlathotep stood, brushed the wrinkles from his black suit, and turned to face Sathach. He opened his arms wide in an invitation to embrace.

"My son!"

CHAPTER TWENTY-EIGHT

Playing with Fire

You called to me through the black void of space," Nyarlathotep said. "Your hearts reached out to mine, like calling to like, and I—"

"Like calling to like?" Sathach's voice, so quavery just moments ago, was as acidic as the Clerk's corrosive ooze. He spat a sunflower seed shell at the Douche's feet. "I am *nothing* like you."

After the Dread Lord's weepy outburst upon hearing the bad news, the witch would've expected an eruption of viscous tears, perhaps a hallelujah chorus of tortured wails. But his eyes were bone-dry. The Keanu's rubbery face was expressionless, save for a hint of disgust evident in the purse of the lips. She hadn't known cold fury was in Sathach's emotional repertoire.

Nyarlathotep let his arms fall limply to his sides. "Ah," he said. "I suppose you've spoken with your mother."

The ensuing stillness was shattered by the liquid patter of urine soaking fine merino wool as Keyser Söze exacted excretory retribution for his broken rib. He lowered his leg and strutted toward the witch. Nyarlathotep stared down at his soaked trousers. His golden eyes lit with incandescent rage, and he lunged toward Keyser, but before the witch could so much as raise her hands to hex him, Hank had inserted himself in the Douche's path.

"I really wouldn't do that if I were you."

Hank's broad back was facing the witch, but based on Nyarly's flinch of alarm, the witch would bet her entire collection of Amish romance novels that his pupils glowed luminous blue.

"I knew you were a treacherous bastard," Keziah said, "but collaborating with the Swarm?" Jenkin's jowls wobbled as he shook his old man's head. "That's low—even for *you*."

Shadows slithered from the corners of the basement and wreathed Nyarlathotep in an aura of malice. "Keziah Mason," he said in incongruously dulcet tones. "Why, it's been ages since we last spoke." He fixed Jenkin's pitiable form with a disdainful gaze. "It pains me to see you reduced to such a state as this. If we were still friends, I'd be tempted to restore you, but alas . . ." The shadows billowed and stretched to form a pair of arced goat's horns. "You abandoned me."

Jenkin stomped a rat-like paw. "You were trying to drive me mad!"

Sathach clapped his hands and the overhead lights blazed into brilliance, dispelling Nyarlathotep's ominous sheath of shadows. "It doesn't feel good to be abandoned, does it, *Dad*?"

"Let me explain." Nyarlathotep's features shifted into a mask of piteous remorse. "Your mother only told you one side of the story. Shouldn't I have the chance to share mine?"

"Whatever." Sathach dug a pinch of sunflower seeds from his pocket and stuffed them in his mouth. "Follow me."

The Dread Lord led them to his command center. He picked up a remote and turned the monitors off, then Hank helped him set up a few folding chairs in the circle of open floor space. Sathach sat down in his ergonomic desk chair and gestured toward the vacant seats. When Nyarlathotep moved to sit next to him, Sathach blocked him with an outstretched arm.

"This seat's taken," he said in a sullen lisp.

Keyser Söze squeezed between the Outer God's legs and hopped into the chair. The witch could practically hear Nyarly grinding his teeth as she and Jenkin took the other empty spots. He was left to stand in the center of a loose semicircle of chairs with Hank positioned behind him, alert and ready to summon blue vengeance should the need arise.

Sathach slouched in his chair, serving up a heaping helping of pissy teenager. "Well?"

For an immensely powerful cosmic horror with a thousand faces and eons of life experience, Nyarlathotep was shockingly bad at concealing his feelings. The witch watched his face cycle from outrage to wounded pride to cold calculation. She only hoped the Dread Lord was seeing him as clearly as she was.

"I'm sure your mother cast me as the betrayer in this tale of woe," he said. "But I assure you, my son—"

"Don't call me that."

Nyarlathotep recovered without missing a beat. "I assure you, I am not the betrayer, but the betrayed." He clasped his hands behind his back and began to pace. Hank walked in step with him, moving with serpentine grace. "I was always a loyal *servant*"—a flicker of anger flashed in his eyes—"of the other Outer Gods.

When they asked me to use my gifts as a shape-shifter to investigate the Swarm's new weapon, I was eager to aid the Archonic cause. Heedless of the danger to my own person, and knowing I had a newborn child who needed me, I nevertheless assumed an appropriate avatar and ventured behind enemy lines."

Nyarlathotep paused to gauge his son's reaction to his heroism, but the Dread Lord simply shrugged.

"The witch went alone into enemy territory, too," he said. "Only *she* won."

Oh, *shit.*

Absolutely savage.

She watched Nyarly fight down a wave of fury so hot it scorched his suit.

"How . . . irrelevant," he said. "*My* mission was one of information-gathering. Being an experienced operator, I discovered the Swarm's secret in no time. Unfortunately, my daring act of bravery resulted in capture. I used the mutual aid clause of our shared contract to notify my fellow Outer Gods, but they did not come."

Nyarlathotep stopped pacing and stared off into the distance as though tormented by the demons of the past. His eyes darted to Sathach to ensure he was appreciating the performance.

"I tried to escape. I tried to fight my way free. My people needed to know how the Swarm was making its crystals. But my efforts were in vain. I watched helplessly as other high-ranking prisoners were . . ." He covered his mouth with one hand and indulged in a theatrical pause. "Taken. I knew my day was coming soon, and I would not go gentle into that white night."

Nyarlathotep fell to his knees and raised his outstretched arms to the heavens— or, more accurately, to the ceiling. The single remaining #2 pencil quivered in its ceiling tile, then fell to the floor.

"I beseeched Azathoth for aid," he cried in the ardent voice of a televangelist. "I prayed for deliverance! And when it did not come, I did what I had to do to deliver myself." Nyarlathotep lowered his hands. "I would've done anything, Sathach, *anything* to protect my only child."

"If you wanted to protect me, why did you leave me behind?" he asked. "Mother told me what you did. You ran off to the Dreamlands and locked the Morpheus Gate behind you."

"Lies!"

Sathach sat up straighter and jutted out his chin. "Mother wouldn't . . ." But his voice trailed off into contemplative silence.

The witch suspected he was replaying scenes from his childhood. She'd never had a mother, but she'd seen enough of them to know that a healthy one-third of parenting seemed to involve strategic manipulations of the truth. Babies delivered by giant aquatic birds. Larcenous fairies with a hard-core dental fetish. Annual home invasions by a bearded saint.

Yeah, Mother probably *would* lie.

"She wouldn't make up stories about something this serious," the Dread Lord said.

"Wouldn't she?" The Outer God stood and brushed the creases from his suit, conspicuously skipping the soaked left leg. "Your mother and I did not have the best relationship."

Sathach snorted. "Surely, you jest."

The witch gaped at him. She hadn't even known he could *do* sarcasm.

"I freely admit I was a bit of an eldritch whore in my youth," Nyarlathotep said. "But Za'gathoth was no picnic either. I tried to contact her after the Swarm released me, but she would not respond."

"Well, in her defense," the witch said, "you'd just given your enemy the ability to harness fire vampires and mass-produce anti-entropic super weapons." She lifted a shoulder. "It's the kind of thing that tends to piss people off."

Sathach pointed at her. "What she said."

"Let us leave the past in the past." Nyarlathotep adjusted the flawless knot of his necktie. "What's done is done, and it cannot be undone. The important thing is that you cried out to me, and I came. I want to be part of your life, part of your children's lives. I want to make peace with your mother and restore my position in Archonic society."

The witch felt Jenkin's gimlet gaze fix on her, and she met the creature's eyes. She didn't need magic to know what Keziah was thinking.

Restore my position in Archonic society.

Ol' Nyarly had plans, no doubt about it.

"I used my magic to look in on you, Sathach," he continued, speaking in a hypnotic drone, "to communicate with you. And in so doing, I drew the attention of the vengeful ka'met." Nyarlathotep took a step toward the Dread Lord. "Had you not called me, had you not spurred me to use my magic, well . . ." He spread his arms, holding his hands palms-up. "We've all made mistakes, haven't we?"

"It's my fault," the Dread Lord said in a hoarse whisper. "The moon-beasts, the human woman, Yi'danag . . . they all died because—"

"They died," Keziah said, "because Nyarlathotep betrayed his people to save his own skin."

"Silence, foul witch!" The Outer God instinctively reached for Jenkin, but Hank cleared his throat significantly and he lowered his hand. "I merely meant to point out that this situation is the result of—"

"You." The witch crossed her arms and regarded him. "*You* bound the fire vampires. *You* handed them over to the Swarm. *You* abandoned your people."

Again, she caught a fleeting glimpse of Nyarlathotep's true feelings as they flitted over his face. He'd once been a god, but in the past few minutes, he'd been pissed on by a raccoon, lectured by a talking dog-rat, and threatened by a sex vampire. And to top it all off, he couldn't survive without their help.

His features smoothed, and the hint of rage vanished as though it had never been.

"You are correct, Witch," he said, bowing his head. "The blame is mine alone. Sathach, can you forgive me?"

The Dread Lord pressed his lips together and squeezed his eyes shut.

Nyarlathotep's lips curled in a sad smile. "In the old world, we Archons had a saying," he said. "Forgiveness is the ichor which a pulsating sac sprays upon the tentacle that crushes it."

The witch scoffed. "What's that supposed to mean?"

"It, um . . . ahem," Sathach said. "It means that even when someone has been grievously wronged, they can choose to respond with forgiveness, bringing beauty forth from pain."

"Sounds like a load of horseshit to me." The witch propped her elbows on her knees and met the Dread Lord's crossed eyes. "Let's put a pin in the family feud for now and talk through what we're doing next."

"You're right, Witch. It's been *thousands of years.*" He glared at his faux-repentant father. "It will keep."

"A wise decision, Sathach," Nyarlathotep said. "I stand ready to assist the witch in crafting the amulet of binding. We can use the magical artifacts as our raw materials, and—"

"What if we could get the Unquenchable Flame to broker a deal?" the witch asked.

"A *deal?*" Nyarlathotep's voice rang with skepticism. "The ka'met are mindless beasts. You cannot bargain with them."

"Flame isn't mindless," Sathach said. "And he's not a beast." He rubbed his bearded chin thoughtfully. "I *am* a certified mediator. Mediation should always be the first step in resolving interpersonal conflict."

"It's worth a try." Jenkin scratched an oversize ear with one hairless paw. "Binding is an atrocity. That traitorous devil's amulet is what started this mess in the first place."

"Then it's settled," the witch said. "Keziah, you and Hank stay here and babysit His Doucheness—"

"Hey!"

"—and Sathach and I will pick up Phæras and talk to Flame." She stood and stretched. "We'll take the orrery and the clicky ball thing with us, but you can inventory the rest of the artifacts and make sure they're charged in case things go pear-shaped."

Nyarlathotep shook his head. "This is a fool's errand."

"Oh yeah?" the witch asked. "I don't think I'm the fool in this equation."

His eyes glowed gold, the pupils mere slits of black.

"I warn you, Witch," he said. "You are playing with fire."

CHAPTER TWENTY-NINE

Bigger on the Inside

The witch lowered her backpack to the ground, careful not to jostle Keyser out of his fifteenth nap of the day. She slid her hands into a pair of silicone oven mitts and removed the metal grate on Chad's terra cotta chiminea. It was two o'clock on a Thursday afternoon, so Chad was still at the office—a fact that inspired both relief and disappointment. Part of her longed to see him, but she still wasn't sure how she felt. Gods knew now wasn't the time to figure it out.

Sathach leaned forward eagerly in his Adirondack chair as she gestured toward the open chiminea like a magician's assistant. As if on cue, a cerulean blaze leaped up with a *whoosh*, and a familiar face formed in the fire. The Unquenchable Flame locked eyes with Sathach, and they issued twin screams of rage. A jet of azure fire roared from the belly of the firebox, narrowly missing the cardboard box that contained the orrery and ball sculpture.

"Hey!" the witch snapped. "Knock that shit off!"

"Apologies," Sathach lisped, wiping tears from his eyes. "It's the sacred greeting of our primal scream therapy circle." He pressed a hand to his chest and sighed. "Oh, Flame . . . I'm so relieved you aren't a mass murderer!"

Flame's broad grin dimmed a few lumens. "You actually thought I was capable of—"

"I mean, congratulations!" the Dread Lord cried with forced cheer.

"For not being a killer?"

"On your impending parenthood."

Flame's mouth gaped open in shock, leaving an empty spot in the roaring fire. "My *what?*"

Sathach glanced at Phæras, who tilted on his axis, telegraphing his confusion.

"The eggs?" the witch guessed, taking the seat next to the Dread Lord.

"Well, procreation requires a combination of at least two individuals, and—"

"*At least* two?" the witch asked at the same moment Flame said, "Procreation?"

"It must have been a rapid courtship," Sathach said. "Not that there's anything wrong with that." He clasped his hands with a soft squeak. "Was it love at first sight?"

"But I've never even, you know . . ." Flame's voice trailed off into a painfully awkward silence.

"*Never?*" Phæras asked.

The witch shook her head, resisting the impulse to wonder how in the seven hells a sphere of liquid metal engaged in gland-to-gland combat.

"The other ka'met got here less than a week ago," she said. "Flame can't possibly be responsible for those eggs."

Flame's eyes darted from Sathach to Phæras to the witch. "*What* eggs?"

The Dread Lord waved a dismissive hand. "According to Lovecraft's bestiary, some Archonic offspring are born before they are even conceived."

"Would someone *please* tell me what in Azathoth's name you're talking about?"

Phæras cleared his nonexistent throat with a tin can rattle. "Perhaps we should pause and share all we've learned before we proceed."

The Dread Lord flinched. Flame, whom he considered a good friend, was about to learn that his father had bound his ancestors, delivered them to the Swarm, and pretty much single-handedly lost the war for the Archons.

The witch rested a hand on Sathach's knee. "Do you want me to—"

"No." He lifted his chin and met Flame's gaze. "This burden is mine to bear."

He squeezed his eyes shut and started talking.

The Unquenchable Flame's robust blaze had diminished with every word of Sathach's bleak recitation. By the time he finished, Flame's face had vanished entirely, and he was barely the size of a pilot light. The witch welcomed the brief respite from his searing heat. The afternoon sun was bad enough without a bonfire of cosmic rage raising the temperature to triple digits. But the strained silence countered any relief she felt.

"I'm so sorry," Sathach whispered in a subdued lisp. "I wish I could—"

"Well, you can't."

A blue inferno billowed from the firebox and wreathed the chiminea in flame. The witch and Sathach recoiled, and Phæras shot a few feet skyward.

"Let the ka'met have that traitor! Let it take vengeance for Fthaggua," Flame roared. "Vengeance for *all* of us!"

"If we do that," Phæras said, "we are no better than the Crawling Chaos. He delivered your forebears to the enemy, and we would be—"

"Evening the score. Balancing the scales." The leaping flames died back to a more moderate size. "Making things *right*."

"What my father did was monstrous," Sathach said, "but his death wouldn't undo anything, Flame. And handing him over to die would forever change who you are."

"Who I am?" Flame's voice was as quiet as the crackle of a campfire. "Who *am* I, exactly? A remnant. A fragment. A limb of a long-dead king."

Sathach shook his head. "You're so much more than that. You may have begun your life as a *part*, but you grew into a whole."

"I shouldn't have had to."

The witch cleared her throat. "As the only other sole survivor here," she said, "I get it. I mean, for fuck's sake, Flame . . . I'm living in a world run by the monsters who killed every witch but me."

Sathach winced and Phæras gave an awkward wobble, but Flame?

He was *listening*.

"I was bound against my will to work for you assholes, and the anger ate me alive for decades. Then I learned the truth about what happened, about why the Archons came here, about how it all went down." She shrugged. "It was ugly. It was vicious. It was *war*. And who I would've been died in combat with the other witches." She propped her elbows on her knees and met the glowing embers of his eyes. "Stay pissed if you want. I did. But it's like climbing into a bath filled with acid and expecting your enemy to melt."

"So we'll bind the ka'met *again* to save the Crawling Chaos?" Flame spat, spewing sparks.

"It's not just about him," the witch said. "Even if we deliver His Doucheness on a silver platter, there are seven little fire-snakes on the way, and they'll need to eat."

"But binding—"

"Binding is what dear old dad wants us to do, but with your help, we might not have to." She stood and gazed at the distant peaks of the Mountains of Madness. "Are you up for a little field trip?"

Flame couldn't see the mountains from inside the chiminea, but by the look on his face, he knew what she meant. "You can't be serious," he said. "Look, I feel for the fire vampire, I really do, but I was there when it attacked Yi'danag. I saw what it can do."

"Nya—" Phæras cut himself short before speaking the Outer God's name, for all that it mattered at this point. "The Outer God was its true target," he said. "The ka'met could have attacked indiscriminately since its arrival, but it hasn't. It is *not* a mindless beast."

"But if fire vampires consume the life force of sentient creatures," Flame said, "approaching it puts all of us at risk—including me."

The witch picked up the cardboard box on the ground in front of Sathach's chair. "Allow me to introduce you to our backup plan," she said. "I've got magical artifacts that can pause time and get us the hell out of there."

Flame shook his fiery head. "Are you faster than lightning, Witch?" he asked. "Because that's how it strikes, and there's no way to protect yourself from—"

"Actually," Sathach said, "there is."

The witch frowned at him. "What are you talking about?"

"I'll be right back."

"Where are you—"

But the Dread Lord had already vanished in a flare of netherlight.

"No." The witch crossed her arms and glared at the object Sathach was offering her. "Hell no. Fuck no. *All* the no."

Phæras bobbled uncertainly above what the Dread Lord had brought for him. "I am inclined to agree with the witch," he said in a voice that rang with tinny displeasure. "This is . . . undignified."

Flame strutted across the patio in his asbestos-lined Skyn, which looked a hell of a lot like Chad. Sathach insisted this model was based on Donald Glover, the hotter-than-Hades actor best known for playing Amos in the Netflix adaptation of *The Thrill of the Chaste*. But given that Heather—Chad's freaking *ex*, for Ghroth's sake—had developed the design, the witch wasn't buying it. It didn't help matters that Flame had used Chad's spare key to raid his closet for cargo pants and a polo shirt.

"I don't know, guys." The Unquenchable Flame vogued like an Instagram model. "I think it's a great idea." He flashed a horribly familiar grin (except for the blue glow between the teeth). "And that Skyn might just save *your* skin."

The witch snatched the limp, silicone shell from the Dread Lord and thrust it at Flame. "Then *you* take the Kim Kardashian," she said. "And I'll wear the Chad."

"I told you, it's the Glover." Sathach grabbed the Skyn from Flame and tossed it to her. It struck her chest with a rubbery smack and slithered to the ground. "He can't wear Kim. She's not fireproof."

Muttering curses so vile they curdled the air itself, the witch picked up the black-haired silicone sheath between thumb and forefinger and glowered at it. It was eight inches shorter than she was, but the Dread Lord insisted the extra room in the butt-and-boobs department would give it enough stretch to fit. She stared at the Kim's artificially plumped pout in horrified fascination and shivered.

"Nope. Can't do it." The witch wadded it up and hurled it at Sathach. "I'd rather burn."

He sighed. "Then I shall wear the Kim, and you can take my Keanu."

"Didn't you piss yourself in there?"

"I cleaned it!"

Keyser poked his head out of the witch's backpack and fixed her with a pleading gaze.

"Gods, *fine*," she snapped.

The patio fell silent, save for the squeak of silicone rubber and a furious stream of increasingly ardent profanity. Getting into the godsdamned thing was worse than putting on a strappy sports bra. It probably didn't help matters that the witch was wearing the Keanu over her clothes. But after a long, sweaty battle, she defeated the Skyn, jammed her feet into her boots, and sullenly slid into the boxer briefs Sathach insisted she wear for decency's sake.

Flame looked at her and laughed so hard tiny jets of flame shot from the Chad's nostrils. She opened her mouth to tear him a new one, but then Phæras drifted into view. His quicksilver orb was now wrapped in the rubbery tendrils of Heather's romantic restraint system. The witch tried valiantly to keep her shit together, but she choked, sputtered, and broke into helpless gales of laughter.

"You look," she wheezed, "like a ball of rubber bands!"

"I hate everything about this," Phæras said with metallic vehemence. *"Everything."*

The patio door slid open, and a reality TV queen emerged wearing plaid rain boots, a pair of Chad's basketball shorts and a T-shirt emblazoned with an iconic blue phone booth. *Bigger on the inside.*

The Kim's slightly crossed eyes met the witch's.

"Let's do this," Sathach lisped.

CHAPTER THIRTY

An Easy Win

Sweat stung the witch's eyes as she paced the perimeter of the half-moon-shaped clearing. Even in the shadow of a towering cliff, the temperature in the Mountains of Madness had to be in the low nineties, and she was wearing a T-shirt, jeans, and the thrice-cursed Keanu. Its floppy hair kept falling over her face and obscuring her vision. When this was over, she was going to set it on fire and dance on the ashes. Her initial plan had been to identify and destroy any corner-hound-friendly forked branches around the glade, but as it turned out, that would involve reducing the entire forest to splinters. They'd just have to hope the nocturnal devils slept through this little adventure.

The witch cast an anxious glance at the cave mouth. Keyser Söze had darted inside to confirm that the ka'met was in residence while Sathach and Phæras delivered a whispered pep talk to the Unquenchable Flame. He hadn't been all that confident to begin with, and he'd begun having serious second thoughts the moment they'd orreried into the glade. To her relief, Keyser darted out of the cave, whole and unharmed. He met the witch's eyes and nodded.

She opened her mouth to call out to her silicone-ensconced teammates, but a violent thrashing of branches deeper in the woods inspired a recommitment to stealth. She was halfway across the clearing when she heard the *bzzzt bzzzt* of her BlackBerry in her backpack. With Hank and Keziah back at Sathach's babysitting a narcissistic, sociopath deity, she couldn't afford to ignore incoming messages.

The witch dug her BlackBerry free and checked the screen.

Text from Deputy Eye Candy

She ignored the oily churn of fear in her belly and opened the Messenger app.

DEPUTY EYE CANDY: Hi, Witch! Keziah wants me to tell you that some of the artifacts are missing—a thermometer and a vase. Mr. N also sucked all the entropine out of the storage artifacts we have, but he won't say why.

Her phone buzzed again.

DEPUTY EYE CANDY: And Keziah also says he's a mouthy whoreson (sorry to be rude!!!!) and she hates him.

The witch sighed and started typing a reply but before she could finish, another text from Hank arrived.

DEPUTY EYE CANDY: She asked me to scorch him just a little bit, but I really don't think I should.

Oh, for the love of Lovecraft. Had they forgotten she was about to get up close and personal with a life-force-devouring fire-snake?

WITCH: We'll deal w/ it when I get back.

After a moment's consideration, she sent another message.

WITCH: And don't scorch him.
Unless he's being a real dick.

The witch reflexively tried to slide her BlackBerry into her back pocket, but the Keanu was only wearing boxer briefs.

Phæras was right. This shit was undignified.

She sighed and returned the phone to her backpack, located Keyser (curled up in the hollow at the base of a tree), and walked over to join Sathach, Phæras, and Flame.

"—but what if the Crawling Chaos is right?" Flame was saying. "What if the ka'met *is* just a mindless beast?"

The witch nudged the cardboard box at Sathach's feet with a booted toe, jostling the artifacts in a metallic clank. "Then I'll stop time, and we'll pull an Irish goodbye and get the hell out of here." She bent and picked up the orrery in one hand and the clicky ball thing in the other. "Let's do the damn thing before I drown in my own sweat."

Flame looked at her from eyes hauntingly similar to Chad's, except for the pilot light pupils. "It's not that simple," he said. "How would *you* feel if it was a rogue witch we were up against?"

She bit back her knee-jerk smart-ass retort and tried to imagine the cocktail of contradictory emotions.

Hope and fear.

Joy and pain.

Relief and dread.

"I'd be a fucking mess," she said. "But I'd see it through. I wouldn't want to watch history repeat itself."

Flame held her gaze for a long moment, then he gave a brisk nod. "Okay."

Sathach shoved the Kim's long black hair over one shoulder and propped his fisted hands on the rampageous curves of his hips. "Now, how do we konvince it to kome out?"

The witch stared at him. He was pronouncing his *C*s with a breathy gargle. "How do we *what?*"

"Konvince it to kome out." The Dread Lord's hands flew to his mouth. "I kan't say it properly." His eyes widened. "It must be the Kim!"

"Give me some room." Flame stepped around the witch and faced the cave mouth. He clenched his fists, opened his mouth, and roared a jet of blue flame. He looked over his shoulder and grinned Chad's crooked grin.

"That should do the trick."

A blue firebolt lanced from the cave mouth, riding on a searing wave of fury. It struck Flame's Skyn squarely in the chest. He staggered at the impact, but the Glover remained intact. As it had in Sathach's basement, the fire-snake's arrival smote the witch with paralyzing fear so primal it skated right past her lizard brain and took her straight to single-celled organism status. She stared helplessly at the ball sculpture dangling from her hand, but her rigid fingers would not so much as twitch.

Unable to penetrate the silicone sheath, the lightning zapped toward Phæras. His rubber-wrapped orb wobbled alarmingly, but he did not burst into flames. The ka'met flowed into fire-snake form and darted toward Sathach. Its plasma-arc tongue flicked out with an audible sizzle as though scenting the air, and its serpentine body wound around the supple curves of the Kim. It paused, hovering in midair with its face inches from Sathach's. Again, the forked tongue flickered from fanged jaws.

Zzzt, zzzt.

The witch's breath caught in a painful hitch. Sathach was Nyarlathotep's *son.*

What if his etheric signature was close enough to his father's to tempt the ka'met? She strained to move her frozen muscles. The hand holding the clicky ball toy jerked, but the metal balls all swayed in unison rather than clacking into each other.

Time marched on.

The fire-snake made one more sinuous circuit around the Kim, then it slithered toward the witch. She squeezed her eyes shut and pressed her lips together, trying to minimize the available avenues to breach the protective Skyn. The Keanu's shaggy hair concealed her ears, but there wasn't a godsdamned thing she could do about the nostrils.

If she died by nasal immolation, she'd be *so* frigging pissed.

Based on the lack of bug zapper sizzles, the ka'met didn't even flicker its tongue at her. When the witch dared to crack open her eyes, it had returned to the opening of its den. A length of wyrm-like tail flowed back into the cavern, but its front half stood as tall as a cobra facing a snake charmer. It swayed slightly in the muggy air, its gaze firmly fixed on Flame. It cracked its jaws and hissed, and the paralysis lifted.

She raised the kinetic sculpture and reached for the leftmost ball. The fire-snake hissed again, spewing a shower of sparks. The display eerily echoed Flame's fiery reaction to the prospect of binding the creature when they'd talked back at the chiminea.

"Wait," the Dread Lord said urgently. "I think it's trying to—"

"It's talking." Flame's voice, usually acidic to the point of a chemical burn, was soft with wonder. "No, not talking. It's more like it already talked to me, and I'm remembering."

"Memories." The crisp metallic tone of Phæras's voice was somewhat muted by the tangle of silicone rubber, but the word was as clear as a bell. "Witch, didn't the Outer God tell you that ka'met consume memories along with the vital essence of their prey?"

The creature's jaws stretched wide. Another hiss. Another spray of sparks.

"It wants to know . . ." Flame's voice grew thick and broke off. "It wants to know what's wrong with me."

Sathach crossed his arms over the Kim's ample chest. "Absolutely nothing!"

"What does it want from us?" Phæras asked.

"Based on the multiple attempts on our cone-headed friend's life," the witch said, "I'm pretty sure it wants him dead."

The fire vampire rasped another hiss that carried the melancholy of a weary sigh.

The Glover's Chad-ish features creased in a frown. "I don't understand."

It tried again, producing another rain of shimmering sparks.

"It says this isn't about the Crawling Chaos."

"Of course it is," the witch said. "It tried to kill the bastard three times!"

"But it's not out for vengeance." Flame took a step closer to the dancing fire-snake. "I don't think it even understands the concept."

"Bullshit," the witch said. "I can *feel* how furious the godsdamned thing is."

"I think . . ." Flame's voice trailed off as the ka'met hissed again.

"What?"

"I think it's sort of an existential resting bitch face."

The witch could relate. "If it doesn't want revenge," she said, "what *does* it want?"

"Memories!" This time, when Phæras uttered that word, it carried a note of dawning realization. "It wants memories of Fthaggua, doesn't it?"

"It wants to be whole," Flame said.

Hissssssssss.

"It says, 'The Betrayer remembers.'" Flame looked at the witch over his shoulder. "*He* knew Fthaggua in the old country. The ka'met thinks consuming him is the only way to resurrect its fallen lord. No one else in this universe ever knew him. No one would remember."

"I mean, there's Za'gathoth," the witch said. "She'd remember. But—"

Hissssssssss.

"It says it needs the Betrayer's memories so it can join with its other selves." He turned back to the ka'met. "What do you mean? What other selves?"

The fire-snake spoke in a series of sibilant bursts that rained sparks like a tiny meteor shower.

"The eggs aren't its children," Flame breathed. "They're its siblings." He shook his head. "No, that's not it. They're the other limbs of Fthaggua. When the ka'met were bound in the Swarm's realm, they had no source of food so . . ." He shuddered. "They fed on each other."

Hissssssssss.

"It was the only way," Flame said. "The only way to preserve the memories. After it took the moon-beasts and . . . and Yi'danag, it had enough energy to bring back the others."

"Well, as a parent, I kan konfirm that Mother was right about infants," Sathach said. "They're always hungry. When will its other selves hatch? What will it feed them?"

Sparks arced from the ka'met's gaping jaws.

"They'll hatch soon, and it will feed them the Betrayer."

Hissssssssss.

"It says the Betrayer will not be lost." Flame gazed at the swaying fire-snake. "His memories, his essence, will live on forever, and when Fthaggua is restored, they will leave this place, and . . ."

Hissssssssss.

"I don't know." Flame swayed, mirroring the creature's movements. "I have to think about it."

"You have to think about it?" Sathach gave a little cry of dismay. "He may be an unholy terror, but he is my father—the twins' grandfather. We kan't just stand by and let them eat him!"

Flame flinched as if he'd been struck and whirled to face the Dread Lord. "That's not what I . . ." He closed his eyes and took a deep breath, sighing out a flicker of blue flame. "Listen," he said, turning back to the ka'met, "the Betrayer corrupts everything he touches. He is a liar. A deceiver. Would you really want him to be part of you?" The ka'met cocked its diamond-shaped head as though considering his words. "You remember Fthaggua. You already have the memories you need. The only missing piece is the energy."

Flame hooked his fingers under the upper lip of his Skyn and slid it over his head. The silicone shell fell to the ground in a limp pile.

"There's another way to feed," he said. "And I can show you how. We can go right now. We can—"

The fire-snake surged toward him . . . and into him. A geyser of blue flame shot thirty feet into the air. The witch stumbled away from the blistering heat. There'd been no bolt of lightning, and she heard no psychic screams of pain. It wasn't killing him—or at least she didn't think so.

"Newborn stars!" The voice belonged to the Unquenchable Flame, but it was overlaid with the sparking sibilant hiss of the ka'met. "We could taste the very fires of creation," it cried. "We could drink the memories of the universe itself!"

The memories of the universe? That was what Flame ate?

No wonder he was the MVP of Chad's trivia team.

Phæras drifted closer to the pillar of fire. "Leave the Betrayer here to live out his days as an outcast, while you roam the stars." His tinny voice almost seemed to carry a hint of longing. "Whole and free."

The ka'met flowed out of Flame, who now took the form of a man made of azure fire. Sathach rushed to his side, but the witch strode past him to face down the fire vampire. She felt Keyser rouse from his nap, alarmed by her proximity to an apex predator.

"What's it gonna be?" she asked. "The Betrayer, or the stars?"

Don't say both. Don't say both. Don't say both . . .

Sparks sprayed from the hissing ka'met's jaws, burning pinprick holes in the Keanu's exposed chest and arms.

"The stars." Flame's voice was clear and confident. "It chooses the stars."

The witch's fingers strayed to the Keanu's navel, where a hidden zipper would let her strip off the Skyn like a banana peel. "Will it swear a magical oath?"

Keyser growled and left his hiding place, waddling toward her at a dead run. He knew she'd need physical contact to seal such a vow, and he was—to put it mildly—not enthused.

Sathach's fingers clamped around her arm. "Witch, you kan't touch the ka'met!"

She swallowed a surge of fear. Sometimes, scary shit just had to be done. "It touched Flame without eating him," she said. "And I've touched Flame without being eaten. It'll be . . ." To tell the truth, she wasn't at all sure how it would be. " . . . fine?"

"He's right," Flame said. "You can't do it. Even if you could, those eggs will hatch soon, and the oath wouldn't cover them." He stared at the fire-snake, watching as it coiled protectively before the entrance to its lair. "I believe what it says, Witch. All it wants is to be whole, and now that there's another path—"

"I believe it, too," Phæras said. "It will not risk sullying Fthaggua's memory."

The witch turned to Sathach. "What about you?"

"I . . . I'm afraid of the ka'met." He offered her a hesitant smile. "But sometimes the things I'm afraid of turn out all right."

Their eyes met, sharing the memory of facing Megawhite together. Sathach had taken his battle form for that fight, the thing he feared the most: a certain sharp-tongued witch.

"That's it, then?" The witch looked from Sathach, to Flame, to Phæras. "Problem solved?"

"We still have my sire to kontend with," the Dread Lord said, "but . . . yes, I think so."

Well, praise Discordia and all the angels of Chaos.

For once, an easy win.

CHAPTER THIRTY-ONE

Double or Nothing

Hank's eyes flared blue in indignation.

"You're cheating!"

The Vaping Douche recoiled from his luminous gaze but quickly recovered his composure. "Which one of us, precisely?"

He and Hank were seated cross-legged on the floor, along with a yellow-green mound that looked like a sinus-infection sneeze but was apparently another of Nyarlathotep's 999 avatars. The Douche and the Ooze each held only one Uno card, but Hank had a fistful. The witch averted her eyes from the snotty simulacrum, fought back a surge of nausea, and flopped into the chair in front of Sathach's command center. She should be relieved now that the immediate threat of fiery destruction had passed, but she felt troubled. Restless.

"They keep trading cards and skipping me so I never get a turn." Hank threw his hand down in disgust. "I quit."

"Don't be like that, Deputy," the Douche said with a sly smile. "One more round. Double or nothing."

"I already owe you twelve hundred dollars!"

Jenkin hopped up onto the Dread Lord's desk with a grunt of effort. "Idiots," Keziah muttered. The scraggly dog-rat cocked its head and met the witch's eyes. "What happened out there?"

"Yes, I have been waiting with bated breath, Witch," Nyarlathotep said, scooching closer.

His mucilaginous avatar collapsed into a puddle of ooze and flowed into his open mouth. The witch gagged and vomited on his shiny black dress shoes. He pursed his lips and scowled at the mess.

"Better out than in." She snapped her fingers and summoned a roll of paper towels and a Christmas tree air freshener. "You're welcome."

Flame, ensconced once more in the asbestos-lined Chad Skyn, shook his head. "I don't think we should talk in front of him."

"I agree." Sathach leaned against a stack of boxes sporting a fresh Keanu, a *Trust No One* T-shirt, and a grimace of worry. "Cone of silence?"

She sighed and nodded. "Coming right up."

The Dread Lord glared at his father and jabbed a finger toward a stack of boxed Yohimbe Love Darts. "Go stand over there," he said. "And don't mess with anything. I know you've been poking through my inventory. You opened at least one box of weight-loss wraps, and I just saw that you've chewed a hole in a carton of edible undergarments."

As if on cue, Keyser Söze trundled by dragging what looked like a section of chain-link fence made from fruit leather.

Nyarlathotep flashed a smug smile. "You were saying?"

"Just go," Sathach snapped. "Flame and Hank will be keeping their eyes on you."

The Douche shrugged, stood, and made his way to the wall of boxes, ostentatiously turning his back on the rest of them. Sathach herded everyone else into the open area in front of his signature Wall o' Monitors, and the witch pulled entropine and formed a double-strength cone over the group.

The Unquenchable Flame positioned himself so Nyarlathotep was in his line of sight. "You really think this is strong enough to keep him from eavesdropping?"

"What I think is that we should cut his cone-head off and deliver his tentacled corpse to the ka'met at dawn," the witch said, watching Nyarly for any sign of reaction.

He didn't so much as flinch.

By contrast, Phæras's quicksilver orb dropped two feet, and he made an alarmed sound reminiscent of two saucepans banging together.

"Witch!" the Dread Lord said. "How could you—"

"Simmer down, sweetheart." She lifted her chin in the Outer God's direction. "Just testing the spell."

"So what happened?" Keziah looked expectantly from face to face. "Do we have a truce?"

"I think Flame should do the honors," the witch said.

The Unquenchable Flame gave a brisk nod of agreement. He kept his eyes glued to Nyarlathotep throughout his rapid recitation of the facts.

Jenkin's body, which was perpetually vibrating with tension in the way of all tiny dogs, sagged in relief. "No binding," she said. "Thank the gods."

Phæras bobbed his agreement. "Indeed. The ka'met threat has been mitigated, but we must still determine the future of our . . . guest."

"Ahem," Sathach said. "My— The Crawling Chaos must face judgment for his crimes: a fair trial and a fair punishment."

"That's a good thought," the witch said, "but the only thing keeping him from using his magic is the threat of the fire vampire. If he thought he was facing death either way, he'd have no reason not to defend himself. And he's a *god.*"

Flame smiled Chad's familiar crooked grin. "Even gods are afraid of something," he said. "I can keep him in line."

Hank raised his hand. "On that note, I'm getting pretty hungry." He blushed adorably. "Flame, could you keep an eye on him while I stop by the carnival for a, um . . . snack? I also wanted to pop in and see the moon-beasts. I miss those little guys!"

"Oh, it would be my pleasure," Flame said, his eyes fixed on Nyarlathotep.

"I can take you to the carnival, Deputy," Phæras said. "If no one needs me this evening, I'll work my shift at the Wheel. The Phæries become despondent if I'm absent too long."

The witch nodded. "Fine by me."

Phæras immersed Hank's head in his sphere of silver, and they blinked out the basement with a flash of netherlight.

She caught Sathach's eye. "You should go see Heather and the kiddos for at least an hour or two."

The Keanu's face lit with joy. "I . . . Yes, I think I will," he said. "But I am only a heartbeat away if you need me." He stepped into a portal and vanished.

"I'll hang out with our traitorous friend." Flame patted the back pocket of Chad's cargo pants. "I have my BlackBerry if you need anything. You should get some rest." He wrinkled his rubbery nose. "And maybe a shower."

The witch flipped him off, but she smiled to take the sting out of it.

Besides, he was right. A few ninety-degree hours in a silicone skin had nearly drowned her in her own sweat. The aroma in her general vicinity was a cross between hot rubber and dirty laundry.

She knelt so she was closer to Keziah's eye level. "What's *your* plan?"

Jenkin's red eyes glowed with a pulse of canine anxiety. "I'm going out to look for the missing artifacts."

"Why are you so freaked out about them?"

"The thermometer doesn't really concern me, but that vase holds enough entropine to power Tophet County for a week. I'll retrace Nyarlathotep's steps through Asphodel. Hopefully, they'll turn up." Jenkin looked over his bony shoulder at Nyarly. "I don't trust him, Witch, and I have a bad feeling, a . . . a foreboding," Keziah said. "Do you have my cards with you?"

"They're in my backpack."

She shrugged free of the straps, fished them out, and placed the deck on the floor in front of Jenkin. The creature rested one hairless, rat-like paw on it and closed his eyes. The cards flew in a dazzling waterfall shuffle and re-stacked themselves. Jenkin tapped the deck, and four cards slid off the top and arranged themselves in a row. The now-familiar trio of Split Kit, Stormy Heather, and Fryin' Ryan were joined by a fourth card—a new one. Beth Death. It depicted the Grim Reaper, scythe in hand, positioned in front of an hourglass whose time had run out.

"Uh . . . I don't suppose that card is like Death in the Tarot," the witch said uneasily. "More of a metaphorical thing? An ending and a new beginning?"

Jenkin arched a caterpillar eyebrow. "These cards aren't exactly nuanced, Witch," Keziah said. "No, something is wrong here. *Very* wrong."

"Can't you use your . . ."—the witch tapped her third eye—"to figure out what it is?"

"Doesn't work that way." Jenkin tapped the deck. The cards reassembled themselves, and he pushed them toward her. "Stay alert, and keep these close."

"But—"

"I'm going to hunt down the missing artifacts," Keziah said. "We should keep the rest of the collection together." Jenkin jabbed a paw toward a laundry basket filled with metal and glass. "Leave the orrery and the kinetic sculpture with the others, and move the basket out of Tall-Dark-and-Scaly's sight."

"Will do."

She watched Jenkin trot off into the labyrinthine passageways of Sathach's basement. Keziah wasn't the only one who felt unsettled. Something was nagging at the witch like a pebble in her shoe, but it slipped through her fingers every time she tried to grasp it. She shook her head and lowered the cone of silence. Once she'd transferred the artifacts from her backpack to the laundry basket, she concealed it behind a heap of unused electoral swag. Then the witch returned to the command center to speak to the Unquenchable Flame.

"I'm heading out," she said. "I have my broom. I can be back here in less than a minute if you need me."

"We'll be just fine," Flame said. He cocked his head and regarded Nyarlathotep. "Won't we?"

"Shall we pass the time with a game of cards?" asked the grinning Douche.

"I have a game we can play." Flame grabbed a Sharpie from the desk and drew a circle on the concrete floor around Nyarlathotep's vomit-scented shoes. "Set one foot outside that line and I'll eat you."

The witch crossed her arms and regarded the sleeping man propped against the front door of her apartment.

"Fancy meeting you here."

Chad woke with a start and scrambled to his feet holding a bottle of Chicken Cock and a smokable bouquet of hallucinogenic herbs and dried cannabis leaves from Seymour's Florals. The bags under his eyes put Samsonite's finest to shame. He looked, to quote the Mindless Mother, like something the ghast dragged in.

"I know you're pissed," he said, "and I get it, I really do, but could we please talk?"

"I don't—"

"You don't even have to say anything." Chad met her eyes, practically vibrating with miserable earnestness. "Just listen. Please."

"Gods, *fine*," she said. "But I'm showering first."

"Great!"

She arched an eyebrow at him.

"Not great about the shower," he said, failing to conceal a surge of panic. "Although, um . . . Anyway, I meant it's great that we're talking. Or that *I'm* talking. And you're listening. You know what, why don't I make you a drink while you shower? Or . . . or I could cook dinner?" He shuddered and shook his head. "No, I can't take another Hot Pocket. Not that there's anything wrong with Hot Pockets. They're just . . . well, they're not exactly *food*, are they? I'll order something. Thai, maybe? Or—"

The witch muted him, unlocked the door, and went inside. Keyser Söze bit the hem of Chad's cargo pants and dragged him in after her. She dropped her backpack on the papasan chair and turned to face Chad, hands propped on her hips.

"I'm unmuting you, but don't say a godsdamned word until I've had a drink." She thought better of it and said, "Make that *two* drinks."

He gave an energetic nod, and the witch snapped her fingers, spun on her heel, and stalked to her bathroom. She took her time with the shower—even did the whole *wash, rinse, repeat* thing. It was a good forty-five minutes before she emerged in her finest pajama pants and an oversize *Witch, Please* T-shirt. The kitchen smelled of garlic and onions, lemongrass and basil. A ridiculously large collection of Styrofoam clamshells cluttered the table.

The witch cast an incredulous glance at Chad, who mouthed, *I wanted you to have leftovers* and handed her what looked like an old-fashioned.

"A Chicken Cocktail?" she asked. "Don't mind if I do."

He hovered anxiously as she sipped it and flashed him a thumbs-up. A pang of conscience slightly dimmed her enjoyment of what was otherwise a fantastic drink.

"You can talk." She waved her hand, restoring his voice. "But for gods' sakes, take it slow."

Chad pointed at the food. "Eat first," he said. "Knowing you, you haven't had a real meal in days."

He filled a plate and passed it to her, then he picked at a spring roll as she demolished the best drunken noodles in the state.

The witch was partway through her second drink when she decided to put him out of his misery. "All right, let's hear it."

"Okay," he said. "Okay, so it's like . . . Okay. Um—"

"Take a breath, Chad."

He closed his eyes and inhaled through his nose, then sighed it out.

"I know you, Witch." He opened his eyes and met hers. "I know who you are underneath all the prickly shit. And I'd trust you with my deepest, darkest secret—with my *life*, if it came to it. But this wasn't about me. It was about Flame, and he—"

"He didn't trust me."

"No, he didn't," Chad said. "Flame knew what *I* knew—that innocent people were murdered, that you'd do your damnedest to bring the killer to justice, and that you truly believed *he* was that killer."

The witch drained her glass and set it on the table. "For days, you knew where my primary suspect was, *and* that he was innocent. You could've told me at any time, but you didn't trust me enough to—"

"If you were planning a surprise party for me, would you tell Sathach?"

"Would I . . ." She sloshed more bourbon into her glass and took a drink. "What's that got to do with the price of souls in R'lyeh?"

"*Would* you?"

"Not a chance," the witch said. "He'd never be able to keep his shit together long enough to pull off a surprise. Sathach is constitutionally incapable of stealth."

"But do you think he's a good person?" Chad propped his elbows on the table and leaned toward her. "Do you trust him?"

"I see what you're trying to do here, Chad, and I'm calling bullshit." She took another sip of her drink and shook her head. "It's not the same. No one burns to death at a surprise party." After a moment's consideration, she added, "Well, not usually."

"The stakes are different, but there's a common thread of truth." He reached across the table and took her hand. "You don't care about rules, but when it comes to the big things, you do what you believe is right. I knew that telling you about Flame would put you in a shitty position. I wanted to find a way to prove his innocence, and then I planned to tell you everything." Chad squeezed her hand. "And when I couldn't come up with proof, I decided to tell you anyway. I wanted you to come to my place after we went to Asenath's, remember?"

His terse text floated to the surface of her mind: *My place after. I have something to show you.*

"I want to be very clear," he said. "I was wrong. I screwed up. I should've told you. But I just wanted a chance to explain. I didn't want you to think I don't trust you, because I do. I thought I was protecting you from an impossible situation, but, well . . . we both know you don't need *me* to protect you." He chewed his lip and shook his head. "I'm sorry. Can you forgive me?"

The witch didn't trust herself to speak, so she nodded.

Chad released her hand and tentatively traced a finger along her jawline. "The past few days have been awful. I hated feeling this distance between us."

She cleared her throat against a sudden and mysterious tightness. "Me too."

"I've really missed you."

"Me too."

"And, Witch? I, uh . . . I think I—"

She pressed a finger to his lips and smiled. "Me too."

Chad stood and offered her his hand. The witch took it, and he pulled her to her feet and into a kiss. His hands wound in her still-damp hair, and for a breathless moment, the whole world was greedy lips and murmured sighs and roving hands. He pulled away, just far enough to rest his forehead against hers.

"I have something to show you," he said.

The witch's heart beat a little faster. "Is it in your pants?"

"As a matter of fact, it is."

CHAPTER THIRTY-TWO

If Only

The witch slapped frantically at her arms, legs, and torso, but her efforts were futile. The fire was inside her, and she was melting from the inside out. Her nostrils filled with the choking stench of scorched meat. She screamed in agony, but the pain was gone almost as soon as it had begun, and the smell vanished with it. A wave of emotion crashed into her, dragging her down with a riptide of fear, fury, and heartbreak. When the wave subsided, it left a gaping hole in the etheric bond that tied her to the Archons of Nether Realms.

That hole had a shape.

It had a name.

Za'gathoth.

"Witch?" Chad's voice broke through the stifling haze of fear and confusion. "What's wrong? Are you okay?"

"It's Za'gathoth," she said. "She's . . . she's . . ."

The word she couldn't make herself say was *dead*.

The witch buried her face against Chad's bare chest. She hadn't known the Mindless Mother all that well, but the Archons' matriarch had been kind to her. Well, maybe not *kind*, but Za'gathoth had never tried to eat her—not even once.

"She's what?" Chad asked. "What happened?"

"I don't know, but—"

The witch's voice broke off as a starburst of netherlight appeared, illuminating her bedroom with a purple-green glow. A flailing tentacle whipped through the opening, accompanied by a soundtrack of grief-stricken wails. It lassoed her around the waist and yanked her into a quantum rectum before she could even blink. She reformed in Za'gathoth's home under the Catachthonic River, as naked as the day she was born. The air was thick with a pungent, acrid scent—a nauseating blend of burnt chitin and charred flesh.

Sathach released her and dissolved into a mass of weeping, writhing tentacles. The witch pulled entropine to summon her BlackBerry and her pajamas. She quickly dressed and sent a message to Chad, then she glanced around the room. She and Sathach were alone save for the Clerk, whose unshrouded tentacles trailed streamers of netherlight as they wove a complex pattern. An octarine sphere formed in midair, then grew to encompass the entirety of the chamber in a shimmering forcefield. Through the Archonic contract, she knew the Clerk had just blocked portal activity—probably a good idea, as every Archon would've felt Za'gathoth's death, just as she had.

Two of the Clerk's bloodshot eyes flicked to the witch. "Mother is gone," she said. "Murdered by the ka'met."

The searing heat.

The burst of rage.

"I'm so sorry. I—"

"Sathach," the Clerk said, her voice hoarse and trembling, "please convey a message to the Sheriff. Tell him I've sealed Mother's rooms. I need him to disperse the Archons arriving at the river."

He moaned a piteous affirmative. "Should we ask him to evacuate Tophet County?"

"The ka'met can travel faster than light," the witch said. "There's no outrunning it. We should keep people home, keep them off the streets until—"

"This is *your* fault, Witch." The Clerk's voice carried a promise of imminent annihilation that drove her fight-or-flight system to DEFCON 1. Micana'gos glided toward her soundlessly, growing to full kaiju proportions as she approached. "Had you done your job, Mother would still be alive."

"We tried," the witch said, craning her neck to meet the towering monster's half-dozen eyes. "I thought we had an agreement with—"

"An agreement?" The Clerk's limbs whipped wildly, upending two dining chairs. "You *bargained* with the entity that immolated Yi'danag?"

The witch retreated a step toward the Dread Lord. She felt a sharp jab of pain in the ball of her left foot, but she didn't dare take her eyes off the Clerk. "We uncovered a bunch of shit over the past few days," she said. "And we didn't want to make the same mistake as—"

"Not forty-eight hours ago, we discussed crafting the amulet of binding so we could contain this creature, did we not?"

"We did, but—"

"In fact, I clearly recall stating that, without the amulet, the ka'met would kill again." One of the Clerk's eyes swiveled toward the back of Za'gathoth's glider. "Yet here we are, and Mother is *dead*."

"Oh, Micana'gos, I can't believe she's really gone!" Sathach hurled himself at the Clerk, who was left with no choice but to embrace him.

The witch took advantage of the momentarily decreased likelihood of death and/or dismemberment and knelt to examine her foot. She winced as she pulled out a shard of glass. The contract dispersed a gush of entropine to seal her sliced flesh. With Sathach and the Clerk distracted by their shared grief, she steeled her nerves (and her stomach) and walked toward Za'gathoth's glider. The stench increased the closer she got, and she pulled her T-shirt up to cover her mouth and nose.

When the fire vampire had attacked the Unseen Creeping Horror, he'd burned away to glittery dust in an inferno so hot it partially consumed the Black Galley. But the Mindless Mother's glider was in perfect condition, cushions and all, as was the bear-trap-semicircle of her false teeth. Her body was blackened but intact. Maybe that was due to the fact that, as a flesh-devouring fog monster, the UCH hadn't had a body to begin with.

As the witch stared at Za'gathoth's remains, Sathach related to the Clerk— between bouts of hitching sobs—their justification for seeking a truce. They'd learned the ka'met's primary motivation was not vengeance. It wanted to restore its fallen King, and for that it needed memories—memories belonging to only two beings in the multiverse: a certain cone-headed Outer God and the Mindless Mother.

Oh, *balls*.

Nyarlathotep.

The Unquenchable Flame was guarding him back at Sathach's place. She'd know through the contract if Flame had been attacked, but Nyarlathotep's traitorous ass wasn't on it.

The witch opened her BlackBerry to find that a shit-ton of texts and emails had arrived in the minutes since Za'gathoth's death. She scrolled past messages from Chad, the Dread Librarian, and at least fifteen other County officials until her eye snagged on a text she'd received an hour ago.

DEPUTY EYE CANDY: Hi, Witch! The little fire vampires just hatched—I can feel them! Can we go visit tomorrow?

Seven hatchlings . . .

Whether they were its children or its siblings, the ka'met now had hungry newborns to feed.

WITCH: U ok, Hank?
Za'gathoth is dead.

DEPUTY EYE CANDY: That's awful!
She was so nice, except for the time she swallowed me whole . . .
What happened?
WITCH: The ka'met killed her.
DEPUTY EYE CANDY: But the fire-snake is with its babies!

The witch started typing a reply, but an incoming phone call hijacked the screen.

Call from That Shithead in Security

Oh, thank the gods. The Unquenchable Flame.

She accepted the call. "Hey, are you—"

"What's going on?" Flame yelled, shouting to be heard over the background caterwaul of a she-cat in heat. "Is Mother really—" Flame roared in frustration. "Would you knock it off?"

But the wailing soundtrack only intensified.

"What in gods' names is that noise?" the witch asked.

"The sadistic jerk put on his giant moon-beast avatar. He's been playing that infernal bone flute for thirty minutes straight."

"But he's alive? The ka'met didn't try to come for him?"

"The ka'met? No, it . . ." His voice trailed off as he parsed the subtext of her question. "It killed Mother?"

"I'm sorry, Flame." She cleared her throat against a growing lump. "Did you sense it on the move tonight?"

"I'm wearing the Skyn," he said. "I can't feel it at all. Are you sure it was the ka'met?"

"I'm pretty godsdamned sure. So much for mediation."

"We—" His voice caught in a sharp intake of breath, a whoosh of roaring flame. "Witch, we didn't include Mother in our agreement."

Shit. He was right.

"But how did it know to go after her memories?" Flame asked.

The ka'met had once followed Flame to the Bridge of Sighs, but it couldn't have understood why he was there. So how . . .

A snippet of their conversation in the Mountains of Madness resurfaced in the witch's mind. Flame had explained that Nyarlathotep was the fire-snake's only hope of reclaiming memories of Fthaggua, and her dumb ass had offered a helpful—and fatal—clarification: *There's Za'gathoth. She'd remember.*

Her BlackBerry dropped from numb fingers and fell to the cavern floor.

Before she could think better of it, before she could penis out and run for her life, the witch crossed the room on wooden legs. She found the

Clerk, human-sized once more, awkwardly patting Sathach's tangled nest of appendages.

"You were right."

The Clerk looked up at the sound of her voice, and the witch forced herself to meet two of her six tear-stained eyes.

"It *is* my fault."

"It isn't your fault, you know."

The witch, who sat cross-legged on Za'gathoth's massive chintz couch, looked down and met Ellie Dawson's ice-blue eyes. "Where the hell did *you* come from?"

"The Clerk opened her portal shield long enough for Sathach to bring me in," Ellie said. "Phæras is here, too."

"And you, uh . . . you're up to speed?"

Ellie nodded. Despite the hour, which had to be somewhere around two in the morning, she was perfectly composed. Her platinum hair hung in a flawless, shining curtain, and she wore a pristine blouse and slacks—and the ever-present Girl Scout vest.

"Did you miss the part where I told the fire-snake exactly who it should eat next?" The witch propped her elbows on her knees and cradled her head in her hands. "Or the part where I had a chance to bind it, a chance to stop it, and I didn't?" Ellie opened her mouth, but the witch held up a hand. "Look, I know I didn't *make* this happen, and I godsdamn well didn't want it to happen, but I made it possible. I just . . . I tried, Ellie. I tried so hard to do better this time, but I—"

"Did *you* kill Za'gathoth?"

"Oh, fuck off with that."

Ellie regarded the witch coolly until sheer discomfort forced her to amend her statement.

"*Fine.* No, I didn't," she said. "But the Clerk would beg to differ."

"I've spoken with her. She was distraught, Witch. She knows the blame doesn't lie with you."

"Well, that makes one of us."

"Do you know why I wear this vest?"

The witch blinked in confusion. "What?"

Ellie merely arched a pale eyebrow.

"So everyone knows you're a badass super-genius, I guess." She shrugged. "It's your version of a pointy hat."

Which she no longer had because a corner hound had eaten it.

"That's not it at all." Ellie took a deep breath, as though steeling herself against a blow. "That day out at Tehom Lake, the day the Deep Ones dragged the rest of my troop down to their underwater city . . ." She pressed her lips together and shook her head. "We weren't supposed to be there. A storm was rolling in. The rest of the girls wanted to go to Larry's Lazertag, but I insisted on kayaking."

"You were just a kid," the witch said. "That's not the same at—"

"You're right." Ellie wheeled her chair closer to the giant sofa. "It's worse. *I* made the decision to go to the lake that day. *I* was the catalyst for what came next." She crossed her arms and gazed at the witch. "So was it my fault?"

"I see where you're going with this, but—"

"I wear this vest to remember my friends," Ellie said. "No, they were more than just friends—they were my sisters. They still are, gills and all. I would've died before I hurt them, but it happened anyway." She blinked back tears and took a trembling breath. "I was so angry, Witch."

"At the Deep Ones?"

"At myself," Ellie said. "That sort of anger is like being stuck in quicksand. The more you rage, the more you punish yourself, the more it drags you down. It's the worst kind of trap."

The witch closed her eyes. She'd been in this place before, with Vera's . . . dis-incarnation. And she'd thought if she did everything right, if she trusted her team, if she didn't keep secrets, she'd never have to be here again.

But here she was.

"So how do you make peace with it?"

"Magic," Ellie said. "The oldest kind there is, and one of the most powerful."

A terrible foreboding filled the most jaded reaches of the witch's heart. "You're about to hit me with some Hallmark-card bullshit, aren't you?"

"I'm afraid so." Ellie smiled and lifted her chin. "Forgiveness, Witch. You have to forgive yourself and place the blame where it belongs." Her smile faded, and her gaze grew fierce. "With the murderer."

The Vaping Douche fell to his knees, raised his outstretched arms to a ceiling pocked with pencil holes, and cried, "NooooOOOOOooo!"

The witch encased him in a cone of silence. After a moment's consideration, she waggled her fingers and pea-sized hail pattered down inside the cone, cutting Nyarlathotep off mid-wail.

They didn't have time for his performative mourning spectacle. They had a killer ka'met to catch.

Ellie and the Clerk were back at City Hall, scrambling to develop a communications plan for dealing with a planet's worth of grief-stricken chthonic horrors. After the witch texted Chad to let him know she wouldn't be coming home, she and Sathach portaled back to his place. Phæras offered to swing by the moon-beasts' cavern and pick up Hank, and they'd gathered in the Dread Lord's basement command center to regroup and plan their next steps. Keziah was there by the time they arrived, but her search for the missing artifacts had been a bust.

They'd just have to hope that the jumble of magically infused glass and metal they had on hand would be enough to craft the amulet.

Nyarlathotep stepped out of the cone (and the hailstorm), pursing his lips in disapproval. "Am I not allowed to grieve the love of my life?"

Sathach crossed the arms of his trusty Keanu and glared at him. "Oh yeah? What color were her eyes?"

His vertical pupils dilated to wide circles as he presumably searched his memory. "Are you sure Za'gathoth *had* eyes?"

"Just as I suspected," the Dread Lord lisped, shaking his head.

"Her ocular system is not a pressing concern." The Douche's features shifted into a self-righteous smirk. "I *did* warn you about the ka'met. If only you'd listened, if only you'd bound it, my eternal beloved would still be—"

"Silence!" Phæras clanged in a metallic voice that bonged like a clock tower's bell.

The witch waited for her fillings to stop vibrating in her teeth. "Flame, you said you were wearing the Skyn the whole time, so you didn't clock the fire vampire on the move, right?" He nodded. "What about you, Hank? Did you sense anything?"

His brow furrowed, and he shook his head. "I felt the eggs hatch," he said. "The fire-snake was really happy—*all* of them were. But then Dave and the moon-beasts wanted me to teach them 'Seven Drunken Nights,' and I guess I got distracted."

"Alas," the Douche sighed. "If only you'd been paying attention—"

His voice cut off in a choked gurgle when a tentacle burst from the chest of Sathach's Keanu and wound around his throat.

"Don't." The Dread Lord gave him a shake and withdrew his tentacle. "*If only* is the foulest phrase in the English language."

"A hair-trigger temper, eh?" Nyarlathotep pointedly massaged his throat and flashed a sly grin. "Like father, like son."

Sathach's face crumpled.

"Za'gathoth's death was a great tragedy," the Outer God said, "but rehashing it will not mitigate the threat we face. My offer of assistance still stands."

His golden eyes fixed on the witch, pinning her with a cold and calculating stare.

"Are you ready to try it my way?"

CHAPTER THIRTY-THREE

Power and Pain

The witch hesitated, reluctant to answer Nyarlathotep's mocking question. Creating an amulet of binding under the direction of a sociopathic eldritch deity was only slightly less appealing than a spirited round of the Dread Lord's icebreakers, but she just couldn't see another path forward.

"What do you think, Sathach?" she asked. "Should we—"

"I think *someone* opened one of my boxes!"

Sathach pushed past the witch and stormed to a wall of the basement's cardboard maze. He pointed an accusing finger at a box of Yohimbe Love Darts on the top row. Jenkin trotted over to join him and gazed up at the opened box. The tape had been torn away, the contents had shifted such that the flaps would no longer lay flat, and a dark spot stained the cardboard near the bottom. Based on the label, the witch assumed a tentacled horror's worth of herbal aphrodisiac had been discharged inside.

"You've been going through my stuff, haven't you?" Sathach snapped, practically spitting the words at Nyarlathotep.

The Vaping Douche shrugged, but the lines of tension in his face belied his pretense of indifference. "Can't blame me for being curious."

"Oh, I can blame you for *lots* of things." The Keanu squeaked alarmingly, rippling under the strain of Sathach's agitated tentacles. "Betraying your people, abandoning your child, getting Mother killed—"

"Me?" Nyarlathotep barked a cruel, bitter laugh. "If you'd listened to me and bound the ka'met, Za'gathoth would still be with us."

"The ka'met wouldn't even *be* here if it weren't for you!"

"Neither would you, my son."

"Don't you dare call me—"

A warning siren straight out of Star Trek cut the Dread Lord off midsentence.

"What is it?" Phæras asked.

"Someone's at the front door." Sathach pushed past his father and rushed to the command center.

The color drained from the Vaping Douche's cheeks. "The ka'met has come for me!"

"I hardly think it would ring the doorbell," Sathach said, flicking through camera feeds. "Aha!" He enlarged the image with a few clicks of his mouse. "Witch, it's—"

"Chad," she said.

Despite her exhaustion, despite her fear and guilt and regret and sadness, a tiny butterfly fluttered in her stomach. The witch jogged through Sathach's labyrinthine basement, thundered up the stairs, and lunged for the door. She had to undo three dead bolts, a security chain, and the twist-lock on the doorknob to get the godsdamned thing open, but she finally managed it. Chad stood in the doorway with Keyser Söze perched on one shoulder. Keyser clambered down Chad's front, nipped the witch's bare toes by way of greeting, and waddled off toward the basement. She yanked Chad inside and wrapped him in an embrace only slightly less crushing than a boa constrictor.

"Gods, I'm glad to see you," she murmured into his neck, "but . . ."

The witch knew what she should say, but the words didn't want to be spoken.

"But what?"

"You should go home."

"Why's that?"

"The Vaping Douche is downstairs, there are homicidal lightning monsters on the loose, and Flame's running around in a Chad suit."

He gently pulled free of her so he could meet her eyes. "I'm not going anywhere, Witch."

"You have to." She took his hands and squeezed them. "It's too—"

"Wait a minute," he said, furrowing his brow. "Did you say a *Chad suit*?"

Nyarlathotep stood inside the circle Flame had taped off for him on Sathach's floor. His golden eyes followed the witch as she formed a double-strength cone of silence around the members of the expanded WTF. He raised one hand and waggled the fingers in a little wave, and the hairs on the back of her neck stiffened. Sometimes being in the same room with him felt like being trapped in a tiger's cage. It wasn't so much a question of *whether* the tiger would eat you; it was a matter of *when*. She forced down her discomfort, turned her back on him, and faced the group.

"Are we doing this binding thing?"

Sathach blinked back viscous yellow tears. "We have to," he whispered. "The ka'met has killed yet again. We can't take any more chances."

"As much as I hate the idea," the witch said, "I'm with you."

"I vote no." A ripple of spikes washed over the smooth surface of Phæras's orb. "While I grieve Mother's death, committing another atrocity will not undo it. There must be another way."

"There's *always* another way," Keziah said. "I also say no. We can't do evil and expect good to come from it—and mark my words, this magic is evil."

"Maybe it is." Flame shifted awkwardly to avoid the gaze of his gobsmacked doppelgänger. Chad hadn't stopped staring since he laid eyes on the Glover. "But it's also reversible. Otherwise, the first ka'met would still be bound."

Hank raised his hand. "I don't want anyone else to get hurt," he said, "but now that the eggs have hatched, won't the amulet get the little guys too?"

The witch frowned. "Isn't that a good thing?"

"They haven't attacked anyone!"

Phæras's spin grew erratic as he tilted on his axis. "Are we to punish crimes that have yet to be committed?"

"We're not punishing," Sathach said. "We're preventing."

Chad tore his eyes away from his silicone twin and turned to the witch. "If the new fire vampires will be bound, what does that mean for Hank and Flame?"

"Shit. I don't know." She chewed her lip, considering the magical implications. "Hank, could you sense the new fire-snakes before they'd hatched?"

He shook his head. "Nope. I didn't even know they were there until Keyser saw them."

"And Flame wasn't caught by the original binding spell when he was inside his egg." Phæras's spin slowed to a pensive pace. "Ka'met are essentially electrical discharges. The eggshells must not be conductive."

"So if Hank and Flame wear Skyns," the witch said, "they should be safe."

"They *might* be safe," Keziah said. "Given the danger, that's not a decision anyone should make for them." Jenkin craned his neck to catch Flame's eye. "Are you willing to risk your free will?"

Flame sighed, producing a gust of superheated air. "I think we should do it"—he winced as Jenkin stomped a hairless paw in outrage—"but on one condition."

"What's that?" the witch asked.

"Once they're bound, I want to take them to the stars and release them." Flame crossed his arms, noticed that Chad had *his* arms crossed, and braced his hands on his hips instead. "They have Za'gathoth's memories of Fthaggua. Once I show them another way to feed, they'll have no reason to attack us."

Jenkin's crimson glare shifted to Hank. "And you?"

"I just want to keep people safe."

Hank's biceps bulged as he reached up to stroke the patch on his sleeve, which bore the motto of the Sheriff's Spectral Forces Division: *Servite. Tuere. Liquefacere.*

Serve. Protect. Liquefy.

"If we do it Flame's way, I'm in," he said.

Phæras made a clanging, throat-clearing sound. "I still find the concept of binding . . . distasteful, but if we pledge to release the fire vampires once the immediate danger has passed, I will support the plan."

The witch knelt next to Jenkin. The bedraggled dog-rat huffed and scooched away from her. "Are you with us, Keziah?"

Jenkin sniffed. "I'd like a private word."

Everyone cleared out of the cone, save for Jenkin and the witch.

"What's up?"

"I'll have no part of this," Keziah said. "It's malefic magic to begin with, and that monster corrupts everything he touches."

"Then give me another godsdamned option!" The witch took a deep breath to rein in her fatigue-frayed temper. "I don't like it any more than you do, but we can't just sit here and let people die—and people *will* die, Keziah. Your own cards said so." She leaned down so she was at eye level with the bony creature. "Are you sure this is the wrong decision?"

Jenkin looked away. His jowls wobbled as he shook his head.

"If you're not sure—"

"Do what you feel you must," Keziah said. "And I'll do the same."

The witch threw up her hands. "You've been immensely helpful. Any other words of wisdom?"

Jenkin's gaze flicked to Nyarlathotep.

"Whatever you do, don't let *him* get his hands on the amulet."

Hank carried the laundry basket of artifacts to an open span of floor space, and the witch crouched next to it to conduct an inventory. Jenkin watched in stony silence as she removed the artifacts one by one.

Keziah might've refused to help, but she'd graciously stuck around to sit in evil-eyed judgment.

"Okay, we've got one clicky-ball toy, one naked umbrella, three glass cups, a magnifying glass, the orrery, an eggbeater, a glass bowl, and . . ." The witch pulled out the final item and held it up for Jenkin's inspection. "I thought you said the vase was missing."

Jenkin trotted to her side and stared at the intricately etched crystal vase. "It wasn't there before," Keziah said. "I *know* it wasn't." Jenkin rested his front paws on the glass and closed his eyes. "It's drained dry!"

Hank raised his hand. "Maybe all the magic spilled out in the laundry basket."

"It doesn't work that way." Jenkin whirled to face Nyarlathotep. "There was a power plant worth of magical energy in there. What did you do with it?"

"Me?" The Vaping Douche raised his eyebrows in an expression of near-comical bafflement. "I freely admit I borrowed a few of your precious relics, but I assure you—"

"It's called stealing when you don't ask first," Hank said.

The witch carefully returned the artifacts to the basket and stood. "We've wasted enough time talking. It's time to rip off the Band-Aid and get this shit done." She met the Douche's golden eyes. "How many of these things do we need to make the amulet?"

"Why, all of them." Nyarlathotep spread his hands wide. "With magic like this, it isn't so much about quantity as it is—"

"Quality?" the witch guessed.

"Sacrifice." He brushed imaginary lint from the lapels of his suit jacket to prolong the dramatic pause. "To craft an amulet strong enough to bind the ka'met, one must give all that one has—metal and glass, power and pain, will and intention."

Power and pain?

She very much did not like the sound of that.

"Well, these are all the artifacts we've got," the witch said. "Let's get to it."

"It would be safer if we performed the work in a magically sealed environment."

"Safer for who?"

Nyarlathotep grinned. "You. Me. The residents of Tophet County." He quirked an eyebrow. "Did I not mention that this particular working is quite . . . hazardous?"

"No the fuck you did not."

"Hold up," Chad said, raising both hands palms-out. "How hazardous?"

The witch stood and pushed the laundry basket toward the Douche with her foot. "*You* do it, then."

"Alas, without access to the pooled power of the Archonic contract, I cannot." He sidled closer to her, still grinning. "But if I were to sign on . . ."

Sathach brushed the Keanu's floppy hair out of his eyes and glowered at Nyarlathotep. "Not happening."

"The Clerk is quite powerful," Phæras said. "Perhaps *she* could—"

"I'm afraid not." Nyarlathotep shook his head sadly. "When it comes to entropic magic, common Archons function as containers. An Outer God such as myself, on the other hand, is a conduit—a trait shared by our friends of the witchly persuasion."

"So it has to be me," the witch said.

"It has to be you."

"It shouldn't be *anyone*." Jenkin backed away from the artifacts, pausing to gaze up at the witch. "I wash my paws of this."

And after a brief tussle with Keyser Söze, Keziah's familiar fled like a rat-thing deserting a sinking ship.

The Douche rubbed his hands together eagerly. "All we need now is a safe space."

"The twins' nursery has anti-entropic shielding," Sathach said. "Would that work?"

Nyarlathotep's sadistic grin returned. "You tell me, Witch."

Shadows flowed from the dark corners of the basement. They slithered up the length of his slim body and gathered in his eye sockets and the hollows of his cheeks, transforming his face into a grinning death's-head.

"Does that space call forth soul-deep rage and despair?" His golden eyes glowed like candle flames in pools of midnight black. "Does it evoke your darkest memories? Does it—"

Hank aimed his Spectral Forces–issue Maglite at Nyarlathotep's face, dispersing the shadows.

"Hey!" the Douche snapped. "I was working up to a big finish!"

The witch ignored Hank's cheerful retort.

An entropically sealed space that summoned her worst memories and filled her heart with pain and fury?

Sadly, she knew just the place.

CHAPTER THIRTY-FOUR

The Wicked Witchery

B ut the Witchery is such a wicked place," the Dread Lord said.

The witch tossed back an offensively tiny mug of espresso and gingerly returned the cup to its saucer on Sathach's dining room table. "Places aren't wicked. People are."

"*We* were wicked!"

"Sathach, we've been through this—"

"We isolated you, Witch." He stared up at the portrait mounted over a white buffet table, a soft-focus masterpiece of Heather cradling their newborn twins. "We traumatized you. We stole your childhood. The Witchery is—"

"Perfect." Nyarlathotep's voice was the smooth purr of a contented cat. "When shall we go?"

Phæras's orb tilted toward the Douche. "Perhaps we should develop our plan further before we proceed."

"Make the amulet," Nyarlathotep said. "Bind the ka'met." He brushed his hands together. "Plan complete."

"There are eight of them now, right?" Chad glanced at his rubbery twin for confirmation. At Flame's nod, he said, "How will you get them all in one place?"

The Douche's lips spread in a too-wide grin. "We don't need to," he said. "The ka'met are all connected, so we only need one."

Hank frowned and raised his hand. "I don't think the original fire-snake will want to leave its hatchlings."

"Then collecting the full set is not an issue, is it?"

"This binding . . ." Chad drummed his fingers on the table, his face troubled. "Is the effect pretty much instant?"

Nyarlathotep's smile dimmed a few shades. "It's not *instant*, but—"

"Then what will keep the ka'met from attacking while the witch binds it?"

She released a long-suffering sigh. "I'll wear a godsdamned Skyn. Anything but the Kim."

Nyarlathotep delicately cleared his throat. "I'm not certain the spell will work if you wear a Skyn. To bind the ka'met, you must be able to sense and manipulate its essence."

"Ah, I see," Phæras said. "Because it is an electricity-based life-form, the Skyn would interfere."

The witch glared at Nyarly. "How the hell did you pull it off the first time?"

"The little white men formed an inhuman shield to protect me as I performed the working. We will need . . . Ah, yes!" He raised his eyebrows and his slitted pupils dilated to round circles. "I will command my moon-beasts to perform this task."

"You want to let the fire-snake *eat* them?" Hank's voice was low and dangerous, and his eyes flashed blue.

"Not all of them," the Douche said. "Just enough to keep the ka'met busy while the witch binds it." His grinning face melted into a domed head with slick, gray skin and a face full of wriggling pink tentacles. "I am their hierophant, after all. Their god. It is fitting they should give their lives to save me."

The witch snorted. "And here I thought gods were the ones who did the saving."

Nyarlathotep assumed his Douche face once more and sniffed. "I've never been that sort of deity."

"Well, we're not doing that," Hank said.

"You're godsdamned right we're not. We'll find another way."

"Me." Hank pressed his hand flat against his broad chest. "*I'm* the other way. I'll protect you while you hold it off."

"But you can't protect me if you're wearing a Skyn," the witch said.

"Then I won't wear one."

Sathach gasped. "Wouldn't you be bound along with the ka'met?"

Hank looked at the Unquenchable Flame, who gave him a grim nod. "The witch will unbind me once Flame takes them to the stars."

"What if I can't? What if something goes wrong?" She shook her head. "Hank, I won't let you—"

"It's not up to you." His luminous blue eyes held hers until she looked away.

"The binding spell will establish the conditions for release," Nyarlathotep said into the strained silence. "The original amulet was designed such that the ka'met would be freed once they could make no more syntropium crystals."

The witch's memory pulled her back to her final moments in the Swarm's realm. She'd flooded the Great White with entropine, putting an end to the little white men. With no LWM to convert into crystals, the conditions of release had been met. She'd seen the last remaining fire vampire escape in a ribbon of blue flame.

"So the witch could set a distance condition," Chad said. "They ka'met are released once they're ten light years from Earth—something like that?"

Nyarlathotep lifted a shoulder in a careless shrug. "Sure," he said. "Why not?"

Why not?

That was an oddly indifferent reaction to a pretty freaking critical element of the plan. What she'd seen last year confirmed Nyarlathotep's claims about the conditions for release, but he was holding something back. She'd bet her life on it.

Which was, in fact, exactly what she was preparing to do.

"What will keep the ka'met from fleeing the second it sees the amulet?" Sathach asked. "It can travel faster than light. It could be out of our solar system in the blink of an eye."

"Then we let it go," the witch said. "Problem solved."

"I rather suspect its fellows would take offense to our attempt to bind it." Nyarlathotep's mouth curled in a wry smile. "*Mortal* offense."

"I have an idea," Chad said. "But it's a little out there, and I'm not sure we could pull it off."

The witch hooked a thumb at Nyarly. "His bright idea involved Lunatic sacrifice. I'm pretty sure you can top that." She gestured for Chad to speak. "Let's hear it."

"What about a Faraday cage?"

"A what?"

An excited tremor rippled over Phæras's quicksilver orb. "A Faraday cage is an enclosure that blocks external electromagnetic fields without disturbing the electrical activity within it. If the witch only needs one ka'met to perform the spell, we can contain the rest of the creatures in the cage."

"Exactly!" Chad ran a hand through his locs. "My only question is whether it would shield the fire vampires inside from the binding. I mean, if the Skyn will protect Flame—"

"The Skyn is different," Phæras said. "It is made of nonconductive material, but the cage is not. The spell should disperse over the entire structure, binding all ka'met within it. As long as one of them remains outside to anchor the magic, I am quite certain it will work."

"Then our challenge would be creating a large enough cage."

"I can help with that," Phæras said. "But how would we get them inside?"

"Ahem." Sathach darted a quick glance at his father, then averted his eyes. "They've always appeared when Nyarlathotep used his magic."

"Do you think they'd still show, even after our agreement took eating him off the table?" The witch's eyes darted to the Douche. "For now, at least."

Flame met Hank's eyes and gave a slow nod. "I think so," he said. "Given their history with him, they'll want to know what he's up to."

Nyarlathotep blanched. "You want to use me as *bait*?"

"Calm your ass down," the witch said. "We'll stuff you in a Skyn."

Sathach cocked his head and smiled sweetly.

"I can spare a Kim."

Nyarlathotep stood in the center of the Witchery's basement. He gazed intently at the cinder block walls, the concrete floor, the bare light bulbs. The witch watched as he walked to the mahogany cradle where she'd slept as an infant. He trailed a slender finger along the arched headboard and brushed the back of his hand against the dangling nest of glass shards that served as a mobile.

Mother Mayhem had tried, but she never quite got the hang of human child-rearing's best practices.

The Vaping Douche took off his suit jacket and draped it over one end of the cradle. "You grew up here?"

She felt Sathach's eyes on her, sensed the weight of sadness this place evoked in him—even greater than their last visit, now that he was a parent himself.

"Yep," she said, wishing with every cell of her body that Chad was here instead of back in Asphodel, working on a science project with Phæras and Flame.

"No human caretakers?" Nyarlathotep walked a slow circuit of the room, stopping to examine the chalk lines that'd tracked her growth over the years. "No playmates?" He ambled to the edge of the industrial-strength containment circle chiseled into the floor and leaned down to peer at the Ouranian-Barbaric runes. He jerked upright with a hiss of displeasure. "No friends?"

"Nope." Keyser Söze poked his head out of her backpack and nipped her left earlobe. "Not until I was older, I mean."

Nyarlathotep closed his eyes, tipped his chin back, and took a deep breath through his nose. "Oh, Witch . . . The Witchery is precisely what we need." His eyes glowed lambent gold in the dim light. "I smell despair. Impotent rage. Melancholy." His nostrils flared as he took another deep breath. "And just the faintest soupçon of burgeoning madness." He smiled. "Delicious."

The word hung in the air like a fat spider.

"Dude," Hank said. "That's so messed up."

"You know, it really is a wonder you're a functional adult." Nyarlathotep unbuttoned his left sleeve and rolled the fabric into a neat cuff. "I've kept a close eye on Earth since the Emergence," he said, starting on the other sleeve. "Radio. Television. Dreams, of course. *I* could've done a better job of raising you, and I was hiding out on the Moon." He breathed a rueful sigh. "But I supposed your so-called guardians couldn't be bothered to educate themselves."

Sathach gave a sharp cry, followed by a wet sniffle. "Witch, I—"

"I know what you're trying to do, asshole," she said. "But I'm past all that now. So if you think you can . . . I don't know, drive a wedge between us, you're sorely—"

"You misunderstand me." Nyarly pursed his lips in a pained pout. "I am merely trying to help you achieve the right mindset for the work which lies ahead."

Hank frowned and raised his hand. "You want to make the witch mad and sad?"

"We *need* her mad and sad, my muscle-bound friend."

"But that's awful!"

"Needs must when the devil drives," the witch said absently.

It wasn't until she'd spoken that she realized where she'd last heard that phrase. The Great White had said those very words to her just before he tried to turn her universe into a syntropic wasteland. Doubt spread through her mind like frost crystallizing on a windowpane. Echoing the words of a megalomaniacal supervillain wasn't exactly a ringing endorsement of the plan.

Nyarlathotep flashed a delighted grin. "Why, I couldn't have said it better myself." He pointed at Hank, then gestured toward the laundry basket of artifacts. "You," he snapped in a voice that rang with imperious command. "Carry the raw materials into the circle."

Hank crossed his arms and shook his head. "You do it."

"I *would*," Nyarly said through gritted teeth, "but there are protective runes around the perimeter. It would be . . . unpleasant."

Hank cupped one hand around his lips and leaned closer to the witch. "I think that means he can't," he stage-whispered.

"Can so." Nyarly picked imaginary lint from his sleeve. "I just . . . I would prefer not to. And it will be safer for everyone if this work is performed inside the circle."

Sathach picked up the basket and carried it over the etched perimeter. "Now what?"

Nyarlathotep licked his lips.

"Now the fun begins."

CHAPTER THIRTY-FIVE

Two Truths and a Lie

"Melt them?" the witch repeated.

Nyarlathotep nodded. "Melt them. The materials must be malleable to forge the amulet."

She paced the inner circumference of her unsacred circle. Keyser Söze followed in her footsteps, hissing every time he passed in front of the Vaping Douche. She paused to eye the collection of glass and metal artifacts, which a certain piece-of-shit umbrella insisted were nothing but worthless junk.

"Sathach, can you flay a message to Flame to portal out here? I'm sure he can—"

"*You* must do it," Nyarlathotep said, "with magic."

"What, like . . . like a magical blowtorch? *Indoors?*" The witch braced her hands on her hips and skewered him with a skeptical glare. "You can't seriously expect me to maintain a jet of thousand-degree flame long enough to melt all this crap without burning the place down—all while I chant my way through that monstrosity of an incantation."

She'd spent the past half hour practicing the godsdamned thing under Nyarlathotep's infuriatingly patient tutelage. She had the Ouranian-Barbaric phrasing down cold, but it was a nasty spell. Literally. The words tasted like rotten fish marinated in gasoline. She'd broken out in canker sores after her third recitation, and Hank's ears had just now stopped bleeding.

"Twenty-six hundred degrees," the Dread Lord said, glancing up from his BlackBerry.

"What?"

"I googled it. The melting point of glass is around twenty-six hundred degrees Fahrenheit."

Hank leaned in and looked over his shoulder. "What's the melting point of witches?"

Apparently sensing the rumbling volcano that was her mood, Sathach took Hank's arm and gently pulled him away from the circle. "Why don't we give the witch some space to sort through the details of the spell?"

"But I'm supposed to keep an eye on *him*." He pointed forked fingers from his own eyes to the Douche in a cartoonish *I'm-watching-you* gesture.

"We can observe from afar," the Dread Lord said, leading him back toward the stairs. "Come on, we'll play Two Truths and a Lie."

The witch watched them walk away, then turned back to her maddening magical mentor. "Well?"

"As I said, you must melt the artifacts with magic." Nyarlathotep raised a professorial finger. "Not with fire, but with pure magic."

She answered with a raised finger of her own, which he ignored.

"You have access to the Archons' reservoir of power." His eyes glittered with greed. "These artifacts are containers. If you flood them with entropine, if you force them to hold exponentially more than they were designed to contain, the excess energy is converted to heat. The energy must be channeled slowly, lest the artifacts shatter instead of melt, but it *can* be done."

"What do I melt them in? A cauldron? A kiln?"

"A crucible." His lips spread in a wide grin. "A crucible made of rage. This portion of the spell requires—"

"Let me guess," she said. "Metaphorical magic."

The Douche nodded. "Just so."

"I *hate* metaphorical magic." The witch squeezed her eyes shut and massaged her temples. "Okay, let me see if I've got the order of operations straight. First I make the crucible. Then I—"

"No, my dear Witch," Nyarlathotep said. "The crucible forms *as* you melt the artifacts. That's why this magic is so hazardous." He winked. "Well, it's *one* of the reasons. It's also why no one else can do it for you. The magical processes feed each other. They must occur in tandem."

Good gods. Pulling off either element of the spell would test her limits, but both at the same time?

"Piece of cake," she said archly. "What happens next?"

"Once the artifacts are in a molten state, you'll recite the incantation as you shape the amulet." Nyarlathotep's pupils dilated, leaving only a thin ring of gold around each bottomless pool of black. "But we'll run that gauntlet when we come to it. Any other questions before we begin?"

"I guess not."

He clapped his hands. "Then let's get cooking, shall we?"

Cooking.

The word stuck in her mind like a burr in Keyser's tail.

"Whenever you're ready, Witch," Nyarlathotep said.

Cooking?

Cooking.

There was something there—a connection, an insight . . . but what the hell was it?

"Yeah," she said absently, staring at the pile of artifacts. "Just give me a freaking—"

The witch's voice caught as her third eye filled in what was *not* there: a tall glass cylinder filled with fluid and brightly colored orbs—a Galileo thermometer, according to Chad. Keziah had told her it was a cooking tool. She'd crafted it for use while on the run from the pitchfork-and-torch brigade, a way to have hot food without burning down whatever barn she happened to be hiding in.

Nyarlathotep's eyes narrowed and lost their merry twinkle. "Is everything all right?"

When the ka'met had attacked the Unseen Creeping Horror, the blaze reduced him to glittery ash and damn near burned the deck off the Black Galley. But Sibyl's pink velvet chair hadn't even been singed.

If that thermometer could cook a steak, could it cook something much larger—say, as an entirely random example, a whole-ass fortune teller?

"You're as pale as a maggot." The Douche reached for her, but the circle's protective runes blazed violet. He yanked his hand back, shaking it as though he'd been shocked. "Are you ill?"

The witch shook her head, struggling to follow the table tennis trajectory of her thoughts, which caromed to the mysteriously emptied vase. *Enough entropine to power Tophet County for a week.* If all that magical energy were pushed through the thermometer, would it generate sufficient heat to immolate an ancient Archon?

Oh, gods . . .

She'd stepped on a piece of broken glass at the scene of Za'gathoth's murder. A small shard—just a sliver, really.

But where had it come from?

The energy must be channeled slowly, lest the artifacts shatter rather than melt.

Keyser tugged on the leg of her pants, flooding her aura with his worry. The witch picked him up and held him close, then she met Nyarlathotep's gaze. His face glowed with pleasure when he saw the truth in her eyes.

The witch sucked in a breath to scream for Hank, but he spoke before she cried out.

"I wouldn't if I were you," he said in a confidential whisper. "My spectral ghast is with your special friend." He cocked his head and arched a sardonic eyebrow. "Chad, is it?"

If she yelled for Hank, could he reach them before Nyarlathotep's avatar had time to act?

How long did it take to snap a neck? To slice open an artery?

Not long enough.

"Witch, it's high time you and I had a little chat."

Nyarlathotep watched with thinly veiled amusement as the witch raised a cone of silence around the two of them. He'd commanded her to leave the rune-warded circle, but he'd taken no notice when Keyser stayed safely inside. Thank Discordia for small favors . . .

Very freaking small.

Nyarly told Hank and the Dread Lord that she needed to practice the incantation, and the cone would protect Hank's ears from further magical assault. Despite the fact that Sathach was currently dominating at Two Truths and a Lie, he didn't clock the Douche's deceit.

Which left the witch—outflanked and outgunned—to deal with the Mythos's last remaining Big Bad completely on her own.

"Did you really think," Nyarlathotep said, tracing a finger along the invisible wall of the cone, "that this inane party trick could shut out the mind of an Outer God?" He smiled and shook his head. "It is right and proper to take pride in one's power, but I fear your arrogance has been your undoing."

The witch swallowed in a vain attempt to moisten a mouth parched by creeping dread. "So you, uh . . . you heard everything we said inside the cone?"

"*What I think is that we should cut his cone-head off and deliver his tentacled corpse to the ka'met at dawn,*" Nyarlathotep said in the witch's voice. "Oh, how I would've *loved* to see you try." A low, silky chuckle burbled from his lips. "Perhaps we'll step into the ring once the ka'met are safely bound."

"But we don't need to bind them," she said. "They already agreed to leave you alone. We were only doing this because—"

"You were only doing this because *I* wanted it done." Shadows flowed from the corners of the basement and pooled at Nyarlathotep's feet. "And you *will* craft the amulet. If not, I'm afraid I have no further use for you."

"If you need a witch to make the godsdamned thing, you'll just have to keep me around," she said, falling back on her old, familiar *last witch standing* safety net. "Pretty sure I'm the only one on the continent."

"Are you?" he asked. "Are you the *only* witch?"

"I mean, there's Keziah, but she's a disembodied soul bound to a deck of cards," she said. "She couldn't pull off magic like this." The witch snorted. "And she wouldn't do it even if she could."

"Have you forgotten my granddaughter?"

Horror froze her in place, immobilizing her as thoroughly as Keziah's time-stopping trinket.

Nyarlathotep had been sniffing around Sathach's house for weeks before the ka'met attacked the moon-beasts. He wouldn't have missed the fact that one of the twins was a witchling.

"But . . . but she's just a baby."

He adopted an expression of exaggerated pensiveness. "Indeed," he said. "I could force my way into her mind and attempt the spell, but who knows if Skyler's infant body could withstand the—"

"Hold up a minute," the witch said. "I thought Sawyer was the witchling."

"Are you sure?"

"Not even a little. Those godsdamned names are—"

"Irrelevant," he snapped. "The salient point is that *I* have options." The Douche bared his teeth in a predator's promise of violence. "*You* do not."

"Do you really think Sathach would let you hurt his kid?"

"*Let* me?" He cast a scornful glance at his son. "Look at him, Witch. He allows inferior Archons to lead when he could grind them beneath his tentacles. He wears that ridiculous rubber sheath when he could easily create his own human avatar—or any other form, for that matter." Nyarlathotep shook his head mournfully. "Sathach is *my* son, the offspring of an Outer God, and yet he makes himself so very small. Za'gathoth's coddling has utterly ruined him. "

"Oh yeah?" The witch smothered her escalating worry under a blanket of bravado. If there was one thing the past few decades had taught her about butting heads with tentacled horrors, it was that showing weakness was always a bad idea. "If only he'd had a male role model around . . ."

The Douche pressed a hand to his chest and heaved an aggrieved sigh. "You wound me."

"Is that why you killed Za'gathoth?" the witch asked. "Crappy parenting?"

Nyarlathotep burst into delighted laughter. "Witch, you are a source of endless amusement. I may just keep you around after my ascension. Every court needs a fool."

Whatever he was planning, it was bigger than binding a few fire vampires. Much bigger.

He wiped tears of mirth from his eyes. "Alas, you are wrong yet again, I fear."

Fear. That was the crux of it.

Since the moment Nyarly had fled the Moon like his ass was on fire (which was very nearly the case), his every action had been driven by fear. He'd said as much when he first told her about Fthaggua and his ka'met.

The only beings in the multiverse who strike fear into the rotting hearts of great Nyarlathotep . . .

"You killed Za'gathoth to get rid of her memories," the witch said. "With the Swarm long gone and the ka'met under your thumb, you'll be at the top of the cosmic food chain, won't you?"

"Will I?" Nyarlathotep adjusted his tie and flashed a self-satisfied smile. "Why, come to think of it, I suppose I will."

The Vaping Douche had played her like a moon-beast's bone flute. He'd used her ignorance—and yes, her arrogance—to manipulate her into protecting him. Now she was the only one who knew the truth and, unless she did what he wanted and made that thrice-cursed amulet, his ghostly ghast would kill Chad.

Nyarlathotep had her by the short and curlies.

If she could get Sathach to flay the truth out of her mind, if she could send word to the others, maybe they could come up with a plan B.

Holy hell, her BlackBerry . . .

But it was in her freaking backpack, which she'd dropped at the foot of the stairs.

The witch ground her teeth in frustration. For the moment, all she could do was humor him until she thought of something better—and if there was one thing the Vaping Douche loved, it was the sound of his own voice.

"How did you pull off killing Za'gathoth?" she asked. "Flame was on your ass the whole time."

"Ah, yes, but you underestimated my abilities. I can inhabit two avatars simultaneously."

The witch widened her eyes in her best attempt at respectful awe. "So you swapped the Vaping Douche out for the big-ass moon-beast," she said. "And you used the flute to drown out your spectral ghast rummaging through the artifacts. Then you teleported to Za'gathoth's and shoved an assload of entropine into that thermometer, and—"

Her voice broke off as Sathach's grief-stricken wails echoed in her mind.

Nyarlathotep, self-absorbed to a fault, took no notice. "As I warned you, the artifacts will shatter if you push the energy in too quickly. The top of the cylinder cracked like an egg," he said. "I suspect it didn't help matters that the thermometer was already filled with liquid."

He was too clever by half to leave the murder weapon at the crime scene, so he must've taken it back to Sathach's. The opened box of Yohimbe Love Darts had been stained with a dark spot. The witch would bet her calamari cookbook collection he'd hidden the shattered thermometer inside.

If she'd just opened the freaking box, if she'd just asked the right godsdamned questions . . .

"It was much easier with the human," Nyarlathotep said. "The thermometer held more than enough energy to deal with *her*."

The witch shuddered, and her nostrils filled with the remembered scent of charred flesh. She swallowed against a surge of bile.

"Sibyl didn't know shit about the ka'met," she said. "She didn't even know about Keziah. Why kill her?"

"Why not? Humans are naught but mayflies—here one moment, gone the next." He grinned a horrible grin. "I sensed Keziah's etheric signature and followed it to the tent in hopes that she'd be of some use to me. But instead of my old friend, I found a treasure trove of the precise materials required to recreate my amulet." He clasped his hands and gazed upward. "It was as though Azathoth Himself reached out from the heart of the multiverse to deliver me in my hour of need."

"Lucky break," the witch said, not bothering to conceal the bitterness in her voice. A leg up from Discordia would sure as hell be nice right about now.

"Oh, don't be too hard on yourself." Nyarlathotep lifted his hands and shrugged. "After all, I *am* an Outer God."

His aquiline features shifted into a knowing smirk.

"Actually, Witch, I'm *the* Outer God."

CHAPTER THIRTY-SIX

The Crucible

What's to stop you from killing me once I make this godsdamned thing?"

Nyarlathotep grinned and raised an eyebrow. "Now, why would I do that?"

"Oh, I don't know . . . maybe because you're an amoral cosmic horror?" The witch crossed her arms and glared at him. "Look, I'm going to need some assurances here. If I don't make the amulet, you'll kill Chad. If I *still* won't do it, you'll kill me and try it with your grandkid, right?" He nodded. "So let's say I do what you want."

"A judicious choice on your part."

"Oh yeah? Why wouldn't you just rip my head off and take the amulet?"

"We've already discussed it." He pursed his lips in a moue of displeasure. "The binding is not instantaneous. If I murdered you, I highly doubt your friends would be willing to protect me from the ka'met while I completed the spell."

Fair enough . . .

Except he'd proven himself to be a liar of surpassing skill—perhaps even as good as a human politician. Nyarly was about as trustworthy as an Election Day Eve campaign promise.

If the witch couldn't trust him, what knowledge could she rely on?

Point the first: Crafting the amulet required more entropine than even Keziah's vase could hold, and the only way to access that kind of power was through the Archons' contract. Nyarlathotep couldn't do that, but she could.

Point the second: If he could've plowed his way into her mind and used her like a puppet, he would've done it. But she'd been shielding her thoughts for decades, and her shields now drew on the Archonic power pool. He'd tried twice to invade her psyche when they first met on the astral plane. The fact that he hadn't made another attempt almost certainly meant he knew it wouldn't work.

Point the third: Sathach was apparently far more powerful than he knew—probably second only to his father in terms of sheer might. If his child were endangered, he'd go full beast mode. Eating the UPS guy would be nothing compared to what he'd do if anyone, even an Outer God, messed with Sawyer.

Skyler?

Either of them.

Which led her to a relatively hopeful conclusion . . .

Nyarlathotep really *did* need the witch to craft this amulet. If she balked, he'd kill Chad. And he'd keep killing until she did what he wanted. But he had to know he wouldn't survive his infant-centric plan B. If Sathach didn't kill him, one of the ka'met would.

And that meant all was not lost—not yet, anyway. But she was going to need help.

She sent a psychic nudge to Keyser Söze, and he stirred and trundled out of the warded circle. Nyarlathotep's golden eyes darted toward the movement, but the witch began pacing the circumference of the cone of silence like a caged animal, which didn't feel all that far from the truth. The Douche pivoted to track her. She stopped when his back was facing the stairs, where Sathach and Hank sat—deep in animated conversation—with her backpack at their feet.

"What's the matter, Witch?" Nyarlathotep asked. "Ultharian cat got your tongue?"

"Don't mind me," she said. "Just trying to outthink your scaly ass."

Keyser rummaged in her backpack, found a baggie of trail mix, and opened it. *It's all yours, buddy. But not yet . . .*

Nyarlathotep put his head on one side, birdlike, and regarded her curiously. "How's that going for you?"

"About as well as you'd expect."

Keyser dug through her bag until his sole front paw closed on her BlackBerry. He dragged it out and hunched over the small screen. The witch peered through his eyes, which left her flying blind with Nyarly, and piloted an outstretched claw to type in her password. As Keyser pecked the keys, she heard the faint whisper of the Vaping Douche rubbing his hands together in eagerness.

"In that case," he said, "let's return to the circle and begin."

The witch directed Keyser's paw to the Messages app, tapped it, and opened the text thread labeled *Nerd-romancer.*

"I've got another question first." She dipped back into her own mind to glance at Nyarlathotep's face. So far, so good. "When do I target the amulet and set the binding's release condition?"

She switched back to Keyser's view, guided his paw back to the tiny keyboard, and started typing her message.

Nyarlathotep's burst of laughter startled her into pressing an *E* instead of a *D*, but she soldiered on.

"And you call yourself a witch?"

She clenched her jaw and ignored him, carefully directing Keyser to the next key.

"There are two parts to this process," he said. "First, there's the crafting, which is what we're doing now. Then, there's the binding, which we'll do later. Two steps. Two spells."

"How the hell was I supposed to know that?" the witch asked, maneuvering Keyser's digits through the rest of the text. "I've never done this shit before."

She examined the message.

n is bae. dont answer. look in box.

"Dont answer" was clear enough, and "look in box" would hopefully spur Chad to open the stained carton of Yohimbe Love Darts.

But "n is bae"?

Gods dammit.

The witch prodded Keyser's paw to the touch screen so she could correct the error.

"What is your creature doing?"

She jabbed her familiar's claw down on the send button and withdrew to her own mind.

Nyarlathotep now stood facing Keyser with both hands braced on his hips. "I've already warned you, Witch," he said. "If you try anything . . ."

Keyser turned toward them and sat up on his hind legs. His muzzle was buried up to the eyeballs in a Ziploc bag filled with nuts and raisins.

"I suggest you let him eat." She could barely hear her own voice over the terror-fueled thunder of her heartbeat. "Trust me, you don't want to see him hangry."

"I don't want him—"

The witch clapped her hands, startling a satisfying flinch from the Douche.

"I don't know about you, but I'm done with talk," she said. "Let's make magic."

Hank crossed his arms and flashed a blue-tinted glower.

"No."

"What do you mean, *no?*" the witch asked.

Nyarlathotep smirked. "I suspect he is unwilling to wait outside with Sathach while you attempt this spell in the company of an unsavory character such as myself."

If the next phase of her plan (which consisted *only* of the next phase at this point) had any hope of succeeding, she needed to keep Sathach out of his father's sight. Even in a silicone skin, the poor bastard had absolutely no poker face.

Hank pointed at the Vaping Douche. "What he said."

"Nyarlathotep needs me to make the amulet, and he needs everyone else to hold off the ka'met while the binding takes effect. If he hurts me, he doesn't get what he wants." The witch angled her body so Hank could see Keyser Söze poking his head out of her backpack. (Sadly, the godsdamned Douche had pocketed her BlackBerry, which Keyser hadn't returned to her bag.) "Besides, I've got backup."

Hank shook his head and jutted out his chin. "I said I'd protect you, and that's exactly what I'm going to do."

"This magic is nasty. Just hearing the spell made your ears bleed. I need to focus, and I can't do that if half my mind is worrying about you and Sathach." She stepped closer and rested a hand on his shoulder. "Please, Hank. It'll be safer for me this way. Do you trust me?"

Chad's voice echoed in her mind. He'd asked her the same question just a few days ago.

One order of crow, please. Hold the feathers.

"I do," Hank said. "*Him*, on the other hand . . ."

Sathach's crossed eyes were troubled. "Are you certain you don't want us to stay?"

"I know my own *mind*." The witch tapped her temple in what she hoped was a clear signal.

Come on, Sathach. Fire up your flayer.

But the Keanu's poreless forehead merely wrinkled in a confused frown. "Ahem. I suppose if you're sure . . ."

"I'm as sure as I was when I told you this guy came back from the dead," she said, hooking a thumb at Nyarlathotep.

The Dread Lord's eyes momentarily uncrossed and met hers, but if he understood the subtext of her message—namely, *I didn't TELL you, you pulled that shit right out of my head, remember??*—he gave no sign.

"Let's go, Hank," Sathach said. "I think the best way we can protect the witch right now is to do as she asks."

"But—"

"Shall we play Would You Rather while we wait?" He grabbed Hank's elbow and towed him toward the stairs.

Hank sighed heavily, but he didn't protest.

"I'd really rather not."

A jumbled mass of glass and metal hovered at hip-height in front of the witch. Nyarlathotep stood outside the circle's rune-inscribed perimeter, practically vibrating with excitement.

"Now, begin channeling entropine into the artifacts," he said. "As long as each piece is touching at least one other, the energy will distribute itself evenly among them."

The witch cupped one of the clicky-ball toy's metal spheres in her hands and opened a channel to the Archonic power pool. Magic gushed through her in a torrent that filled her veins with a heady rush of power. She throttled it back, but not before the ball shattered in a shower of metal shards.

"Too fast," barked the Vaping Douche.

Keyser gave a whimper of sympathy as the contract healed her skin, pushing out bits of shrapnel and knitting the lacerations on her palms.

"Got it."

Asshole.

The witch grasped a second ball and prepared to try again. But as she reached for power, she felt the gentle psychic touch of another mind.

Oh, thank Discordia . . .

Sathach.

Look! she thought desperately. *See!*

If the Dread Lord replayed her conversation with his homicidal father, if he learned the truth, he could reach out to the others and make a plan. That was why she'd needed him to go outside. Learning the identity of his mother's murderer would no doubt push him into hysterics.

But she couldn't afford to focus on what he was doing—not with the gods-damned Douche watching her like a thirsty nightgaunt.

A trickle of magic coursed through the witch's fingertips into the cool metal. She peered through her third eye, watching as the energy dispersed through the hovering collection of artifacts. As each item reached its natural capacity, the flow shifted to another and another. She trembled with the strain of maintaining a steady stream while keeping the artifacts connected and suspended. The minutes dragged on until, at long last, every piece was filled to the brim with power.

"They're full," the witch said. "Now what?"

"Keep going!"

The metal grew warm under her skin. Then hot, and hotter still. Keyser growled as blisters formed on the pads of her fingers. The contract healed her, but the shitty thing about healing was that she had to be injured first.

"For the love of Yog, that burns!" She risked a quick glance at Nyarlathotep. "What do I do?"

"You suffer, Witch," he said in a sensual purr. "Did I not warn you? Power and pain."

Pain was too small a word.

The silvery metal shifted to glowing yellow, then orangey-red, and the witch's flesh burned and healed, burned and healed, burned and healed. Agony prowled her psyche like a great crimson beast, slashing and rending with talons of fire.

She didn't want to give Nyarlathotep the satisfaction of hearing her cry out, but she was powerless to stop it. Jagged screams tore from her throat as the last of the glass pieces finally began to soften.

"Build the crucible!" he shouted. "Do it now!"

"How?" The word was almost a sob. "How do I build it?"

A snarl of tentacles burst from the Douche's chest as he exploded into his true form. He raised his muscled arms, and the artifacts' golden light shone on bilious green skin. The fat, scarlet tentacle crowning his coned head lashed in exultation, and his gaping maw stretched wide to reveal fangs stained black by clotted ichor.

"Summon your rage! Let fury be your clay!"

Molten metal clung to the witch's fingertips. Keyser wailed and thrashed in her backpack, suffering along with her. She couldn't bear it, couldn't go on.

Then a familiar voice pierced the red haze of agony.

FEEL NO PAIN!

And because she'd invited him in, because she'd trusted him to enter her mind, the witch's psyche bowed to Sathach's command. The tide of pain receded.

Nyarlathotep paced around the circle, his tentacles whipping the air in an agitated frenzy. "We're running out of time!"

She stepped into her palace of memory and sprinted down an endless hallway until she reached an iron-barred door. Behind it was her rage against the Archons, a fury she'd clung to like a security blanket since she was old enough to understand her place in the world. She lifted the bar, threw open the door, and there it was—ugly and misshapen, as vicious and merciless as a corner hound. But with the Dread Lord protecting her, with the cool balm of his command soothing her pain, embracing it felt . . .

It felt *wrong.*

"The metal is melting, Witch—you must do it now!"

This was metaphorical magic. The volcanic strength of anger, a boiling pressure that spewed destruction out into the world, was what would give the binding its power.

But there was another kind of anger, wasn't there?

A ghostly image of Ellie Dawson shimmered into view.

It's the worst kind of trap.

The distant roar of Nyarlathotep's voice echoed in the halls. "Build the crucible!"

The witch pushed past her old, snarling fury and ran to another door at the back of the room—a door with a knob made of broken glass. She grabbed it. Turned it. Opened the door.

Memories flooded her mind, each borne on a cresting wave of acid rage.

Hank sinking beneath the surface of the Catachthonic River.

Vera Vásquez vanishing in a blaze of light.

Sathach wailing as he saw his mother's charred corpse.

The rush of images continued. Magnolia's tears. Chad's wounded eyes. The witch gathered the memories of her failures, of all the times she'd fallen short and hurt those who mattered most. She formed them into a toxic clay and sculpted the crucible.

"Yes!" Nyarlathotep cried. "That's it!"

Her consciousness returned to her body. Where the jumbled artifacts had hovered only moments before, there was now a vase-like ceramic vessel filled to the brim with molten metal and glass.

Nyarlathotep's shouted instructions faded into the background.

She already knew what to do.

The witch plunged her hands into the crucible and began to chant the incantation. She pulled the mixture of cooling metal and glass like taffy—folding it, compressing it, shaping it into what she knew it must be. The contract couldn't keep up with the damage to her flesh. She saw flashes of white bone through the orange glow. Her hands moved not by muscle and sinew, but by will and magic alone.

Though she felt no pain, the shock and trauma of her injuries made the witch's breath come in panicked gasps, and her vision narrowed to a long, dark tunnel. She staggered against a wave of weakness, but Keyser pushed all his strength into her. The dead weight of his limp body tugged at her shoulders, nearly bringing her to her knees. She summoned water from Tehom Lake, the place where Ellie had lost her friends, and filled the crucible. Liquid flashed to steam, and the skin of her forearms turned beet red, but she poured more and more until it overflowed.

The witch gripped the amulet and released the crucible. The vessel dissolved into sparkling dust before it even hit the floor. She opened her ruined hands and stared at what she'd created—cruel and shining and beautiful.

The dark tunnel closed in.

CHAPTER THIRTY-SEVEN

A Clinical Case of Bad Vibes

"Are you sure she's going to be okay?"

The witch's eyelids fluttered at the sound of Chad's voice. She squinted into the blinding glare of overhead lights.

"The magic was nearly too much for her," Nyarlathotep said. "But she will recover."

Chad and the Douche in the same room?

Oh, *hell* no.

She sat bolt upright, only to swoon like a romance novel heroine and collapse onto the soft surface upon which she'd reclined. Keyser Söze muttered irritably at her sudden motion and repositioned himself on her lap.

"Don't try to get up, Witch." The blurry shape of the Keanu's rubbery face gradually swam into focus. "We're at my house," Sathach said. "You've been unconscious for almost an hour while the contract healed your hands. Your injuries were—" His voice broke off in a choked gurgle. "Ahem. I'm afraid the spell took quite a toll."

Her hands.

She raised her arms and stared at her mottled skin. Her forearms, which had only been burned by steam, were their normal tawny olive, but her hands were a patchwork of varying shades of pink. The skin looked as soft and new as a baby's, but all ten fingers were present and accounted for.

Minus the fingernails, which were still growing back with an annoyingly itchy tingle.

A visceral image—a flash of white bone immersed in glowing, molten metal—floated to the surface of her mind, prompting a phantom spike of remembered agony that momentarily robbed her of breath. But the Dread Lord had shielded her from that pain. He'd protected her so she could finish the monstrous spell.

"Sathach . . ." The witch's voice was hoarse and gravelly. Chad helped her sit up and pressed a bottle of water into her hands. She took a sip and tried again. "Thank you. If you hadn't—"

"It is *we* who must thank *you*." The Dread Lord's eyes darted to the Vaping Douche, and he gave a tiny, almost-imperceptible shake of his head.

Shit. Right. Things could get very ugly, very fast if Nyarly suspected Sathach had been poking around in her mind.

What she wouldn't give to know how much the Dread Lord had seen while he was in there . . .

"I'm just glad you're okay," Chad said. "We were so worried when we didn't hear from you."

The witch met his eyes, searching for a hidden message. Surely, he'd received her text. Surely, he'd opened the stained box, realized the ugly truth, and made a godsdamned plan.

She saw concern in the taut lines of his face. Plenty of worry. Empathy for her suffering. But beyond that, she just couldn't be sure.

"Could the witch and I have a moment alone?" Chad glanced from the Douche to the Dread Lord. "I . . . well, you know, we're sort of—"

"I suggest we save the romantic reunion until after the danger has passed," Nyarlathotep said in a voice as smooth as satin. "What do *you* think, Witch? Is the risk worth the reward?"

Though she'd just taken a drink of water, her mouth was suddenly drier than desert sand. She knew what he meant by *risk*, and it had nothing to do with the ka'met.

"Let's just get this shit done."

"I enthusiastically concur." Nyarlathotep smoothed the lapels of his immaculate suit and fixed her with an eager gaze. "And I would very much like to see the amulet."

The witch glanced at her empty hands, then scanned the mound of taco-print leggings that had served as her fainting couch.

Nothing.

"Where the hell is it?"

Nyarly's smile shifted into a grimace of distaste. "Your . . . creature took custody of it."

She stared down at Keyser, who was curled on her lap like a sleeping cat. The witch wriggled a hand under his warm, heavy body. He grumbled and stretched, unfurling his bushy tail to reveal the amulet. She slid her finger through its silver chain and held it aloft.

"It looks like a caged pearl pendant," Sathach said. "Heather has one."

Chad cleared his throat. "Yeah, I, um . . . I gave that to her."

But the witch was too busy staring at the abomination she'd created to enjoy the deliciously awkward moment. The amulet was roughly the size of a vending machine gumball, and it radiated cold menace like a Hyperborean ice-demon. Its exterior was an ornate spherical cage adorned with wickedly sharp thorns, within which floated a shimmering, octarine orb. She peeked at the thing through her third eye. Other than a clinical case of bad vibes, it was magically inert—just a vaguely sadistic piece of jewelry.

At least for now.

But metaphorical magic was tricky. Unpredictable. She wouldn't know if her gambit had worked until it was time to use the godsdamned thing—and by then, it would be too late to change course.

"It looks quite different from the amulet I crafted back in the old world," Nyarlathotep said, "but I can sense its power. It feels . . . hungry."

He clapped his hands, slowly and deliberately.

"Well done, Witch." Shadows pooled in his eye sockets, highlighting the golden glow of his gaze. "Well done."

Chad slid his BlackBerry into his back pocket.

"Flame says they're ready whenever we are."

The witch eyed the tray Sathach had just carried down to the basement, grabbed a shot of espresso, and tossed it back.

Then another.

And one more for good luck.

Within seconds, the caffeine hit her so hard that Keyser Söze vibrated in her arms from the contact buzz.

"What's the plan?" she asked.

"While you were . . ."—Chad waggled his fingers, which she interpreted as *doing a flesh-melting spell in the company of a murderous Outer God*—"Phæras and I were working on the Faraday cage. Flame helped us test a simple enclosure made of metal mesh. Our theory was sound, but the experiment failed."

"I don't get it," she said. "If your theory worked, how did it fail?"

Chad ran a hand through his locs and shrugged. "Well, Flame couldn't pass through the barrier, but he was able to generate enough heat to melt a hole in the mesh."

"Then how, pray tell," Nyarlathotep said, "do you intend to contain the ka'met?"

"A Faraday cage."

The Douche furrowed his brow. "But you just told us that won't work."

Chad grinned, and the witch was stricken by a terrible linguistic foreboding.

"A *Phæraday* cage," he said. "With a *P-H*." His face lit with excitement.

"Phæras's . . . body is made of quicksilver, which is an excellent conductor. It took a little practice, but he was able to shape himself into a flexible metal mesh. The only problem is that mercury vaporizes at high temperatures, and the vapor is super toxic."

"Toxic fog . . ." The Dread Lord sniffled and wiped viscous ooze from his eyes. "It reminds me of Yi'danag."

Chad patted his shoulder. "I'm sorry, man."

"Is there a point in this tale at which you solve the problem?" Nyarlathotep asked with thinly veiled impatience.

"Yeah, but—"

"Skip to that part."

"Jeez, okay," Chad said. "But *I* didn't solve the problem. Keziah actually came up with—"

"Keziah's back?" The witch felt a faint flutter of hope. With Za'gathoth dead, the old witch knew Nyarly better than anyone on Earth. If anyone could out-think him, it would be her. "I thought she'd washed her paws of this."

"She, um . . ." Chad cast an apologetic glance at her. "Keziah said we were liable to get ourselves killed without a properly trained witch on hand."

Nyarlathotep chuckled. "Ah, the arrogance of witches is a source of endless delight."

But Keziah had been against binding the fire-snakes from the beginning. She wouldn't set aside her moral objections just to prove her own magical superiority. Her return had to be a sign that the team had a plan.

The witch's flutter of hope turned into a full-on flap. "She came up with a way to keep the ka'met from vaporizing Phæras?"

Chad nodded. "Being stuck inside a . . . whatever Jenkin is—well, it limits her options. But she says she has enough juice to shunt the ambient heat out of the cage."

"And where's this shit show going down?"

"The sacrificial softball field at Dunwich Park," Chad said. "It gives Phæras plenty of room to maneuver, and the field's been off-limits to the public since the Black Galley landed. Everyone's already there waiting for us."

"Excellent." Nyarlathotep locked eyes with the witch, and his slitted pupils dilated to wide black circles. "The hour is at hand."

"We need to suit up in our Skyns first," Chad said. "I call dibs on a Glover!"

The Dread Lord, who'd been uncharacteristically quiet throughout the discussion, escorted them to his stock of remaining Skyns: a box of Kims, three Glovers, and a single Keanu.

Nyarlathotep cocked his head and examined the offerings with a considering eye. "Do any of them come in a Magnum?"

* * *

The witch staggered out of Sathach's portal onto the sun-browned grass of the Dunwich Park softball field. A faint glow on the eastern horizon heralded the coming sunrise and limned the charred ruin of the Black Galley in golden light. She closed her eyes and took a deep breath, taking comfort in Keyser's warm weight against her back.

"Ahem."

The witch turned toward Sathach's voice and opened her eyes to find two Keanus standing before her. Behind them, she saw two Glovers—Chad and the Unquenchable Flame—converging on a shimmering dome of quicksilver mesh. Hank, who stood at attention next to the Phæraday cage, spotted her and gave an enthusiastic wave.

"I must speak with you privately," the Dread Lord said. His crossed eyes darted from his Keanu-clad father to the witch.

Nyarlathotep slowly shook his head. As head shakes went, it was pretty gods-damned eloquent.

If you think I'm letting you out of earshot for as much as a second, you're violently mistaken.

Or something like that.

"We'll talk after the binding's done," the witch said. An odd expression flashed over Sathach's rubbery face. "What's wrong?"

"I'm leaving."

His words hit the witch in the gut like a pair of sucker punches.

"What do you mean, you're *leaving*?"

He wrung his hands, producing a symphony of tortured squeaks. "I'm a spouse now. A parent. Heather and the twins need me. I can't risk . . ." He blinked back oozy tears and shook his head. "I just can't."

"But—"

"I'm sorry, Witch!"

And just like that, Sathach vanished in a blaze of netherlight.

CHAPTER THIRTY-EIGHT

A Method to the Madness

I told you," Nyarlathotep said. "Sathach's mother has ruined him." He shook his head. "*My* son . . . a coward."

The witch scrambled to reassemble the mind-blown shreds of her composure. The Dread Lord had bailed on her like a bad date. Abandoning a friend in need went against everything she knew about him—or *thought* she knew.

But to be fair, what exactly had she expected him to do? Primal-scream his father into submission?

The situation was too emotionally charged for Sathach to be an unbiased member of the team. His passionate longing for a father was what had lured Nyarlathotep out of hiding in the first place. A yearning powerful enough to make the Dread Lord—as he'd once put it—*mind-flay the universe itself* could well be strong enough to make him hesitate at a critical moment. And apparently, he hadn't picked up on the real deal with dear ol' Dad when he'd entered her mind. Her excruciating agony must have drowned out everything else.

Besides, what he'd said was true.

Sathach had a wife. Two children who needed him. He had no business being here.

It was for the best, and she hated it.

"Never fear, Witch," said the Vaping Douche, "a new day dawns." He looked toward the sunrise. "After my ascension, I shall have ample time to . . . reeducate my son."

Well, *that* didn't sound ominous.

"Are you guys ready?" Hank called.

The Vaping Douche grinned, baring far too many teeth. "Oh, yes." His voice carried across the field, despite the fact that he spoke in a voice so soft it was nearly a whisper. "I am more than ready."

The witch followed Nyarlathotep to Phæras's ginormous mesh hemisphere. Two Glovers turned toward them in eerie unison.

That shit was unsettling. If it weren't for the fact that Flame's eyes looked like a pair of pilot lights, she'd have struggled to tell them apart.

The brown-eyed Chad stepped forward and said, "Mr., um . . . Crawling Chaos, we need to walk you through how we'll trap the fire vampires. You need to know—"

"—where Phæras wants us to lure them," Flame said. "We'll have to move quickly once they're here. The Skyn will protect you, but—"

"—if we give them time to coordinate a joint attack," Chad said, "the heat might damage it enough that they could break through."

"We don't want *that*, do we?" Nyarlathotep licked the Keanu's rubbery lips and nodded. "Come along, Witch."

A section of the mesh wall lifted like a stage curtain, and they trooped inside. Keyser wriggled in her backpack until the witch shrugged out of the straps and released him. At first, he tiptoed gingerly across the shimmering silver net that covered the ground. But when it didn't stick to his fur or otherwise offend his raccoonly sensibilities, he threw caution to the wind and made a beeline for the center of the circular space. Jenkin sat at Hank's feet, skewering Nyarlathotep with a crimson-eyed glare. To her shock, Keyser posted himself shoulder to shoulder with Jenkin, curling his fluffy tail over the bedraggled creature's pink paws.

"Ah, my old friend . . ." The Douche stopped in front of Jenkin. A foaming surf of shadows frothed in his wake. "I am so gratified that you've decided to lend your much diminished powers to my defense."

Hank shoved his hands in his pockets and frowned. "Keziah's doing you a solid," he said. "You shouldn't—"

"I'm sure this metaphysical concept is beyond your comprehension," Keziah said, as Jenkin lifted his whiskery chin, "but it's not about *you*."

Nyarlathotep chuckled and leaned down toward the quivering dog-rat. "My dear, it is *always* about me."

"I hate to interrupt, but Phæras said this shape is tough to maintain." Chad took a few steps toward the eastern section of the silver mesh and beckoned to the Douche. "Come on, man."

"I am no *man*, mortal." Nyarlathotep straightened and flashed a chilling grin at Chad. "But I shall come." His golden eyes flicked to the witch. "Shall we?"

"I need to speak with her," Keziah said. "Given my *diminished powers*, she might have to channel power to me during the binding."

The witch's jaw dropped. "You're shitting me, right? I don't even know the actual binding spell. That asshole's planning to feed it to me line by line as we go. There's no way I can—"

"Yes, there is." Jenkin stamped a paw irritably. "And I need to tell you how. If I run out of juice and Phæras flashes to vapor, all of us mortals will drop dead of mercury poisoning, and the fire vampires will escape."

A ripple of unease washed over the Keanu's rubbery features. "That would be . . . unfortunate," the Douche said.

Jenkin locked eyes with the witch. Keziah had something to tell her—something important. She could feel unspoken words hiding behind Jenkin's baleful scowl. And if she could have even a few moments of private conversation with Keziah . . .

"Never fear, Witch. I shall keep an ear open," Nyarlathotep said. "Just in case I can be of some aid to you or Keziah during the binding."

Translation: *I'll be listening to every godsdamned word.*

Jenkin's elderly face drooped, and he seemed to age a century before her eyes. Keziah had caught Nyarly's meaning, too. Chad and Hank walked the Douche to the shining silver net, and the witch heard Phæras's resonant voice as he explained how he planned to trap the ravening ka'met.

"So, this, um . . . this channeling-power thing," the witch said. "How does that work?"

"It's all about thaumic resonance."

She snorted. "That sounds made-up."

Jenkin winked, and Keziah launched into a batshit recitation of magical-sounding words that held absolutely no meaning. But the witch had to admit, the explanation should sound legit to a self-absorbed Outer God who was only interested in plots against his august personage. As Keziah spoke, Jenkin's eyes grew wider. Rounder. In each pool of murky red, a tiny shape formed.

A golden apple.

The images vanished in a scarlet swirl almost as soon as they'd appeared.

" . . . and that's that," Keziah said.

"That's *that?*" the witch repeated. "Uh . . . I'm not sure I got the, um, the underlying theory."

What the fuck am I supposed to do, *Keziah?*

"Oh, you know how magic is." Jenkin's knobbly spine hunched in a shrug. "You don't need to understand what's going on in order for it to work. It's just helpful to know there's a method to the madness."

A method to the madness . . .

Did that mean there was a plan to stop the Douche? She needed a hint. A clue.

"But, Keziah, I—"

"You've done your part, Witch," Keziah said. "Now trust your team to take care of the rest."

Jenkin shifted his gaze from her to Keyser Söze, who grumbled and nuzzled—actually *nuzzled*—the creature's wrinkled cheek. Keyser clearly sensed something in the other familiar, but whatever it was, he was keeping it to himself. Walling it off in a private part of his psyche.

"Just one more thing." Jenkin gave Keyser a nudge. "A little help, friend—one familiar to another?"

A pulse of octarine light passed between them, and Keziah muttered a spell under her breath.

"What are you—"

The witch's voice broke off as a light band of pressure met her forehead, familiar and comforting, and a shadow fell over her eyes. She reached up, already knowing what she'd find. Her fingers traced the felt fabric of the hat's wide brim. She lifted it from her head, examining the coned top that tapered to a traditional witchly point.

It was kind of funny, when she thought about it.

Witch vs. Nyarlathotep! Clash of the cone-heads! Who will survive the terror-dome?

Or maybe not so funny.

"Much better," Keziah said. "You're not a proper witch without a pointy hat, are you?"

The witch opened her mouth to reply, but the words stuck in her throat.

"It's time."

She turned at the sound of Nyarlathotep's voice. He stood a few feet away, grinning his ever-present grin and flanked by a pair of Glovers.

Jenkin sat up on his haunches and stroked Keyser's masked face with a rat-like paw. "No matter what happens, you take good care of your witch."

Keyser nodded and trundled to her side.

Jenkin looked up at the witch and smiled. For an instant, his ancient face was almost . . . beautiful.

"Good luck," Keziah said.

But to the witch's ear, it sounded a hell of a lot like *goodbye*.

The witch stood a few yards in front of the arched opening leading into the Phæraday cage. Keyser Söze crouched between her feet, his teeth bared as though he were defending his den from a coyote. She fished in her bag for a Tupperware container, opened it, and lifted the amulet out by its silver chain. The horrible thing weighed much more than it had a right to. She cupped it loosely in her sweating hands, careful not to let its thorned frame prick her newly healed skin.

Her eyes darted to the bleachers at the field's edge, where a pair of Glovers sat side by side. Frantic questions bubbled in her mind. Had Chad understood her text message? Were he and the Unquenchable Flame preparing an eleventh hour *coup de grâce*? When Keziah had said "trust your team," had she been referring to the Tasty Twins?

Flame fixed the witch with a burning azure gaze. Her heart raced as she watched him intently, alert for a hidden message.

He flashed a thumbs-up and yelled, "You've got this!"

A nice frigging sentiment, but not particularly helpful.

Chad waved to get her attention, then he blew her a kiss and pressed his hand to his heart. She risked a quick glance at Nyarlathotep, who was staring at her intently with his snakelike eyes. He pointedly looked at Chad, then back at her. She peeked through her third eye and saw, as she'd feared, the faint outline of Nyarly's spectral ghast sitting next to the brown-eyed Glover. The thing raised one taloned hand in an ironic eldritch salute.

A pulse of anxiety thrummed in her chest.

Discordia, keep Chad safe.

"Should I summon the fire-snakes?" Hank asked.

The witch tore her attention away from Chad and tried to settle her roiling mind.

Focus.

She needed to focus.

"I thought our scaly friend here"—she jerked her chin toward Nyarlathotep, who stood a few yards to her left—"was going to use his magic and lure them in."

Hank closed his eyes and took a deep breath. When he opened them, they glowed luminous blue. "I feel them, Witch," he said. "They'll show up if I ask. He doesn't have to—"

"Oh, but I *want* to."

Nyarlathotep rubbed his hands together, grimacing at the symphony of silicone squeaks. He raised his arms and began to chant in a profane tongue that raked at the witch's mind like a blood-crazed nightgaunt. Hank flinched and hissed in pain. An agonized scream echoed from the stands, and Chad hunched forward and clamped his palms over his ears. She drew a trickle of entropine and sheathed Chad, Hank, and herself in a protective layer of sensory shielding. Her legs trembled as the spell took effect, and she nearly fell to her knees.

What in the godsdamned hell?

The witch was fully topped off and connected to the Archons' nearly boundless magical reservoir. The amount of power she'd just pulled was the equivalent of scooping a tablespoon of water out of Tehom Lake. She couldn't be running low already.

As if in answer, the ground shook beneath the witch's boots. The tremble hadn't been in her legs. It'd come from the earth itself. Keyser climbed her like a tree and wriggled back into her backpack as a deafening rumble thundered through the early-morning air. A cleft formed in the turf at the edge of the soft-ball field, and Nyarlathotep threw his head back and laughed. Each note rang with sadistic joy—reminding her of who and what he truly was.

An Outer God.

The Crawling Chaos.

An engine of madness and ruin.

The cleft grew into a ravine that spread along the field's perimeter, encircling the Phæraday cage like a noose and trapping Chad and Flame on the other side. Nyarlathotep shrieked a word so vile it would've done irreparable damage to mortal flesh in the absence of her protective magic. A geyser of orange-red lava spewed from the trench on the far side of the cage. Steam hissed and billowed as the freshly carved ravine filled with molten rock.

The witch caught a faint but recognizable glimmer in the air above her and peered at it with her third eye. She saw a portal shield, just like the one Sathach used to protect his home.

But why would Nyarlathotep want a shield in place?

Fire vampires had no need for portals. They'd streak in on bolts of lightning and go where they godsdamned well pleased. Portals would still work within the shielded area, but no one would be able to teleport in or out until . . .

Oh.

Fuck.

She charged up her personal defenses, a futile but somehow comforting ges-ture, and whirled to face Nyarlathotep. "What are you playing at?"

He let his arms fall to his sides and winked at her. "We wouldn't want any innocent bystanders to stumble into harm's way, would we?"

Her handy Nyarly-to-witch translator chimed in.

No help is coming. No Clerk. No Sheriff. No Sathach.

Unlike the witch, this traitorous bastard had a plan, and he didn't want any Archons popping in on a rescue mission. With the portal shield in place, any dumbass with a burning desire to die a hero's death would have to ford a river of lava.

Whatever happened from here on out, they were on their own.

The air grew thick and heavy, and the hairs on the witch's arms stood on end. Keyser thrashed violently in her backpack. She slid free of the straps and lowered it gently to the ground. His worried face poked out of the open bag, and he growled at the sky.

Zzzzzzzzap!

A firebolt struck the ground a few paces in front of her, sending up a spray of soil and grass. A serpent formed of cerulean flame emerged from the after-glow and raised its spade-shaped head. Its fanged jaws stretched impossibly wide, and a lightning tongue flickered from its mouth. Nyarlathotep whimpered and darted behind the witch. He gripped her shoulders and turned her body to keep her between himself and the ka'met.

Zzzzzzzzap! Zzzzzzzzap!

Two more arrived, followed by a rapid barrage of strikes that left the turf pocked with raw divots. Hank circled around behind Nyarlathotep, sandwiching the Douche between them. The fire vampires swirled around them, and an icy ribbon of fear coiled at the base of the witch's spine. She wore no Skyn, and she stood between these beings and the shithead who'd traded their freedom for his life. Flame had said they didn't crave vengeance, but if he was wrong and one of them attacked, Hank wouldn't be able to protect her.

As if on cue, a fire-snake darted toward her. Nyarlathotep yelped and thrust the witch forward like an offering. It hovered inches from her face, beads of light dripping from its plasma arc teeth. In a humiliating repeat of the ka'met's visit to Sathach's basement, she froze like a deer in the proverbial headlights. But the creature merely hissed and showered her with stinging sparks. The indigo hollows of its eyes bored into her own. In its savage, alien face, she saw a flash of something almost familiar.

"Lead them inside!"

The tolling bell of Phæras's resonant voice cut through the witch's paralysis. Nyarlathotep clung to her as they shuffled backward into the Phæraday cage. Terror rolled off him in palpable psychic waves. The writhing mass of fire vampires followed, but the one who'd approached her hung back. Hank broke away from Nyarlathotep and the witch to advance on the outlier. It hissed again, spewing a rain of glowing embers. Hank said something to the fire-snake in a low whisper—something she couldn't hear over Nyarly's ragged gasps—then he herded it away from the cage. They'd need one ka'met outside to anchor the binding spell.

"Close it, Phæras!" Hank shouted.

Liquid metal mesh flowed down to seal the opening, trapping the fire vampires inside. Nyarlathotep convulsively squeezed her shoulders. They vanished from the cage in a stomach-turning burst of netherlight and reappeared on the field just outside the shining silver mesh. The witch braced herself for the remaining fire-snake to attack—to charge the cage in an attempt to free its siblings. But it merely cocked its head and gazed at Hank as though waiting to see what would happen next.

The witch frowned. Imprisoning the ka'met had been far too easy. Even if they didn't understand vengeance, surely they understood captivity—yet the free fire-snake made no attempt to liberate the others.

"Is that all of them?" The Douche's golden eyes were glued to the cage, flicking from serpent to serpent as he counted. "I count eight."

One parent.

Seven hatchlings.

"They're all there," the witch said.

A bolt of lightning lanced from a captive ka'met and struck the interior of the metal mesh, lingering like a finger of light in a plasma ball.

Another firebolt hit the cage.

Then another.

"Start the spell!" Keziah cried. "We can't hold them for long!"

CHAPTER THIRTY-NINE

Until the End of Time

The witch stared helplessly at the thorned amulet cupped in her hands.

"Tell me what to do!"

The lips of Nyarlathotep's borrowed Keanu spread in a slow, sultry smile. He backed away from her and raised both hands, palms up, in an almost apologetic shrug. Then a tentacle burst through the chest of his Skyn and looped around her neck. A razor-sharp barb dug into the delicate flesh of her neck as he lifted her until her booted toes barely touched the ground.

Keyser Söze's snarling face popped out of her backpack, which lay on the ground a few feet away. Through a red haze of panic, the witch hammered him with a psychic command.

RUN!

Her familiar tore out of the bag like a raccoon possessed and waddled to the dubious shelter of an overturned bench, apocalyptically furious at being sidelined.

"Tell you what to do?" Nyarlathotep repeated. Another tentacle snaked out of the torn Skyn, slid through the amulet's loop of chain, and took it from the witch. He met her eyes and flashed a mocking grin. "Why, I'd hold very still if I were you."

Hank lunged toward Nyarlathotep with murder shining in his blue eyes, but the Outer God yanked her closer. The barb caught in her skin, slicing a shallow cut in her neck. A flood of entropine rushed to heal her, but not before sticky dribbles of blood coursed from the wound.

Hank froze.

"I'm sure you're fast, Deputy," Nyarlathotep said in a breathy croon. The witch nearly gagged from the charnel house stench wafting from his lips. "But ask yourself this . . . are you faster than a god?"

Behind Hank, the remaining free fire vampire reared and hissed.

Nyarlathotep's golden eyes flicked to the creature, and a grimace of fear distorted his features. He pulled the witch even closer. "Do you remember what befell the Black Galley when Yi'danag was killed?" he asked. "If the ka'met strikes with your friend practically in my arms . . ." Nyarlathotep tutted and shook his head sadly. "Well, wouldn't that be a shame?"

A spike of fear lanced up the length of her spine, but its impact was muted by a question.

Why in the seven hells hadn't the fire-snake attacked?

It *was* faster than a god.

It was faster than the speed of light.

Hank set his jaw in grim fury, but he angled himself toward the fire vampire and raised his hands like a cop stopping traffic.

The witch blinked in mute surprise. Either she was in the grips of a terror-induced hallucination or Hank was wearing a full set of acrylic nails.

He glanced at Nyarlathotep over one muscled shoulder. "What do you want?"

"What I've always wanted," he said. "Respect. Dominion. Absolute power. And I *will* assume my rightful place in this godsforsaken—"

"Something's wrong!"

Keziah's alarmed shout drew the witch's gaze to the cage, where the captive ka'met hovered in a writhing mass. Dozens of blue plasma filaments extended from their entangled bodies and danced over the metal mesh. Phæras emitted a continuous chime of strain, and Jenkin's red face dripped with sweat.

"Alas, it seems we've run out of time," the Douche said. "It's too bad, really. I had a whole speech planned. You know, 'Bend the knee or lose the head.' Great line, isn't it? Or how about 'Tremble before the eldritch glory of your new god!' I was going to pair that one with a tornado." He gave a sigh of regret. "Oh, well. To quote the witch, needs must when the devil drives."

The Keanu shredded into rubbery confetti as Nyarlathotep erupted into his true form. He cradled the amulet in his clawed hands and began to chant in harsh, ugly Ouranian-Barbaric. Even through the protection of her sensory shield, hearing those words *hurt*. Black ichor drooled from the Outer God's fanged mouth as the corrosive litany droned on. Just when the spell's vicious words breached her defenses and began to burrow into her mind like saw-toothed parasites, the amulet's cage opened like a seashell. The pearl inside shone with a prismatic rainbow of awful, beautiful light.

Nyarlathotep threw back his coned head and laughed.

If there was a plan to stop him, it had to happen *now*.

Keziah had told her to trust her team, but who was left to act?

Sathach had bailed.

Phæras was seconds away from puffing into toxic vapor.

Jenkin's ancient body was surely on the verge of collapse.

And Chad . . .

The witch squinted against the cage's brilliant blue glow and peered at the bleachers where Chad and Flame sat side by side, stuck on the far side of a river of lava. The only atom of good news was that her third eye caught no sign of Nyarly's spectral ghast.

Hank still stood facing the ka'met, but while the witch's attention was on the stands, his aggressively handsome face had been transformed. A pouty-lipped beauty with a freshly chopped pixie cut met her eyes and winked—or tried to. He'd never quite mastered that particular skill.

A godsdamned Kim.

He must've worn it under his uniform and pulled the head up to shield himself from the binding spell.

A spark of hope kindled in the witch's soul. Maybe there *was* a plan.

"I bind the limbs of Fthaggua!" Nyarlathotep's voice rang with exultation. "In chains of hate and fetters of rage, I bind all beings born of elemental fire to do my bidding!"

Ba'al's bearded balls.

Nyarlathotep wasn't binding the fire vampires to protect himself from vengeful enemies.

"I bind the ka'met to burn and kill at my command!"

He was binding them to be his *weapons*.

Without access to the master contract's power pool, Nyarlathotep was vulnerable—Outer God or not. The other Archons could band together and take him down. But with the fire vampires under his control, he'd be . . .

Gods help them all, he'd be unstoppable.

"Bound they shall remain until the stars burn out—"

Her thoughts raced like rabid rat-things.

Keziah had told the witch she'd *done her part*, but what had she actually done?

"Bound until this wretched universe is devoid of all life—"

She'd made the amulet . . . but she'd given the old metaphorical magic a nasty little twist.

Sathach had to know what she'd been trying to pull off—he'd been in her head when she did it. Had he told the others before he fled?

"Bound until the end of time!"

The ringing echo of Nyarlathotep's words faded, leaving the field cloaked in unearthly silence. Phæras's labored chime had ceased, but the interior of the cage now shone with luminous blue so bright the rising sun paled in comparison. The whole structure emitted an infrasonic vibration the witch felt in her clenched teeth. In the charged hush, she sensed the magic in the amulet's rotten heart awakening.

Nyarlathotep had been right. It was *hungry.*

Through the astral vision of her third eye, she watched as slender vines of poisonous purple light unfurled from the caged pearl, each bristling with wicked thorns. They drifted toward her, drawn by the lingering etheric residue of the crucible she'd forged.

Her muscles went rigid, and her breath came in quick, shallow gasps. Metaphorical magic had a tendency to go feral. If she'd miscalculated, if she'd screwed up the spell . . .

But the tendrils turned away from her and quested like blind earthworms toward Hank and the fire-snake, both of whom were as still as marble statues. She watched in impotent horror as they slithered over Hank's silicone-sheathed forearms.

No . . .

Had they been wrong about the Skyn?

Had the binding spell worked?

Nyarlathotep's tentacle tightened around her neck, slicing yet another shallow gash in her skin. He hurled her to the ground at Hank's feet and withdrew the throttling appendage.

"I have no further use for this pathetic creature." The Outer God grinned, exposing shark-like rows of fangs under the eyeless white cone of his head. "Dispose of her for me, Deputy."

Hank's blank blue eyes locked onto the witch, and a panic-fueled gush of entropine roared into her bloodstream. Maybe she could stun him. Or knock him out. She didn't want to hurt him, but if Nyarly had him bound, he'd have no choice but to obey.

"Yes, Master," Hank groaned.

He stuck his arms straight out in front of him like a Romero zombie and shuffled awkwardly in place. The hideous vines fell away, unable to breach the Kim.

A wave of relief washed over the witch, leaving her eyes filled with tears.

That big, beautiful dork . . .

Nyarlathotep shifted into his Vaping Douche avatar and fixed his golden gaze on Hank. The briefest flicker of fear showed on his face when he registered the Skyn's presence, but then he schooled his expression into a sneer.

"And here I thought you weren't clever, Deputy."

The Douche flicked his fingers in a shooing motion, and Hank flew backward like he'd been shot out of a cannon. The witch threw up a wall of compressed air at the ravine's edge just in time to keep him from landing in the lava-filled Lazy River of Doom. He slammed into the barrier and fell to the earth.

The rainbow light of the pearl flickered, and the vines began to retract without so much as acknowledging the fire vampire. But the creature was immobilized, which meant Nyarlathotep's binding must have worked. So why weren't the vines latching onto it?

The witch tensed, waiting for the Douche to notice, to *act*, but he didn't even glance at the sinister tendrils of magic. It was almost like he couldn't see them.

Hell's bells . . .

Maybe he couldn't. It was *her* magic, not his, and it was born of an emotion he lacked the capacity to experience: Anger directed inward rather than out.

Ellie's words in the aftermath of Za'gathoth's murder had been the witch's inspiration.

That sort of anger is like being stuck in quicksand. The more you rage, the more you punish yourself, the more it drags you down. It's the worst kind of trap.

The hairs on her arms stiffened as the vibration emanating from the Phæraday cage escalated to an audible electric hum. Merciful gods, Jenkin and Keziah were trapped inside that thing, siphoning off the heat of eight fire vampires.

The number struck her like a backhanded slap.

Eight.

If there were eight ka'met in the cage, and Flame was in the stands with Chad . . .

Nyarlathotep faced down the fire vampire, raising the amulet like a talisman. "Kill the witch! I command you to—"

His voice cut off as the pearl's thorny vines snaked under the cuffs of his immaculately tailored shirt. The bastard might not be able to see them, but he could sure as hell *feel* them. His hands opened in a convulsive spasm, and he dropped the amulet.

"What have you done?"

The Douche raised his forearms and crossed them in an X in front of his chest. His muscles trembled as he strained against the taut purple tendrils that pulled him toward the pearl. A plume of smoke jetted from the intersection of his arms, flowing to form gaping jaws lined with crystalline fangs. One of his 999 avatars was a godsdamned corner hound.

The witch tugged her pointy hat firmly in place and pushed herself up to stand.

Not today, you geometrically challenged shitbird.

But before the hound of Tindalos could coalesce into physical form, before she could even pull entropine to launch an attack, the ka'met surged forward, opened its mouth impossibly wide, and inhaled the billowing smoke. The cerulean creature recoiled, wracked by a violent fit of coughing. Sparks sprayed as it tried to clear its throat.

A psychic *AHEM* flitted through her mind.

She goggled at the fire vampire. No freaking way.

Nyarlathotep staggered, and the vines dragged his arms down to his sides. He bellowed in outrage and transformed into a glossy indigo arachnid the size of a Shetland pony. A Leng spider.

The witch shuddered and stumbled back from the monstrous thing. She'd rather deal with a corner hound than a spider.

She *hated* spiders.

Thorned creepers encircled every last one of Nyarly's eight limbs. The spider's chitinous mouthparts flexed, dripping venom, and it surged toward her. Hooked thorns pierced its thrashing legs, dragging it toward the pearl, but it fought its way toward her inch by bitter inch. If the vines so much as touched her skin, she knew in her bones she'd be spending eternity locked in a gilded cage with the multiverse's shittiest roommate.

The witch reached for her magic, but Nyarlathotep pummeled her mind with a battering ram of madness and terror. A scream tore from her throat as the spider closed the distance between them. Blue light flared, and the fire vampire morphed into a twenty-foot-long centipede. It scuttled between her and the spider, shaking the ground beneath it with each step. The spider's front legs reared up in alarm, and the vines tightened. Its limbs flailed wildly as it was hauled inexorably toward the pearl. Nyarlathotep flashed from avatar to avatar. Giant moon-beast. Crowned pharaoh. Demon satyr. Sinus infection sneeze. But it made no difference. No matter what he did, no matter which form he took, the tendrils only grew tighter. The rainbow glow of the pearl brightened to blinding brilliance, and Nyarlathotep disappeared behind a thicket of purple vines.

The last thing the witch saw before the amulet's cage slammed shut was the haunted gaze of a three-lobed burning eye.

An octarine shimmer rippled over the centipede, and it swirled into a new shape.

A Keanu.

A *flesh-and-blood* Keanu.

And he wore a pair of cargo shorts and a T-shirt that said *Don't make me use my HR voice.*

"Sathach!" The witch threw her arms around him and squeezed for all she was worth. "I didn't know you could do that, you devious asshole!"

He grinned and held her at arm's length. "Neither did I—not until my . . . until Nyarlathotep told you I could create an avatar in any form I wanted. I found it in your memories." His eyebrows drew together in HR-ish concern. "I hope that's okay."

"Shit, yeah, it's okay. If you hadn't, we'd have been well and truly—"

A sharp tug on the leg of her pants heralded Keyser Söze's arrival. The witch picked him up and buried her face in his fur, then she lifted her chin and met the Dread Lord's eyes—which were still crossed, even in Keanu form.

"You didn't leave us," she said in a hoarse whisper. "You didn't leave *me*. I . . ."

Something caught in her throat.

Dust. Maybe pollen.

"We're a team, Witch," he said. "I would *never*—"

A sharp crack of thunder cut him off midsentence. Behind Sathach, the Phæraday cage rose into the air accompanied by a symphony of electric zaps and sizzles. As it ascended, its shape shifted from a hemisphere into a globe, and it shone with the blue-white brilliance of a neutron star.

Dear gods . . .

Phæras.

Keziah.

"It's over!" the witch yelled. "You can let the fire vampires go!" She shoved Keyser into Sathach's arms and turned to sprint toward the cage, but she ran smack into an outstretched hand.

A hand with perfectly shaped, French manicured nails.

A dribble of blood oozed from the Kim's perfect nose, but thank Discordia, Hank was alive and in one piece.

"He kan't," Hank said. "He *kan't* let them go."

"Why the hell not?"

"I thought you and Flame already told the ka'met that we'll release them once they're far from Earth." Sathach wrung his hands in anxious distress. "They won't be angry, will they?"

"We did," the witch said, "and they won't, but—"

Netherlight flared, and a pair of Glovers stepped out of a doublewide portal. The witch frowned and scanned the sky with her third eye. Nyarlathotep's portal shield was gone.

Nyarlathotep was gone.

The blue-eyed Glover gripped Hank's arm. "Do you feel it?" Flame asked.

Hank nodded.

"Would one of you please tell me what the fuck is happening?" The witch pointed at the hovering sphere. "We've got to get Jenkin out of there before it's—"

Keyser Söze whimpered and reached for her. She took him and cradled him in her arms. The awful truth shone in his black eyes.

Too late.

Keziah had known. She'd known how her role in all this would end, but she'd done it anyway.

Chad slipped his arm around her waist and rested his temple against hers. "I'm so sorry, Witch."

"So am I."

Her voice quavered, but she didn't cry. Somehow the witch knew Keziah wouldn't have approved. But the absence of tears wasn't the same as an absence of feeling. For a few precious days, she'd had something she always dreamed of—another witch to talk to. Someone who understood her in a way no one else could.

That was gone.

Keziah was gone.

"All the fire-snakes wanted," Hank said, gazing up at the massive blue orb, "was to be whole again. Now they are."

The Dread Lord's hand flew to his open mouth. Tears—real human tears, not his usual yellow ooze—pooled in the corners of his eyes. "Is Phæras . . ."

"No," Flame said. "He's alive. He's just . . . something more now. Some*one* more. He's—"

"Phthæggua," Sathach breathed, pronouncing the *ph* with startling eldritch clarity.

Sparks showered from the sphere like luminous rain. The electrical charge in the air built until the witch could feel the buzz of it in her molars, then the orb streaked toward the sun like a comet, leaving nothing behind but lightly burned retinas.

And a river of lava.

"Hey, Witch!"

She glanced at Hank to see him struggling to grasp the amulet's chain, unaccustomed to having inch-long nails.

"What should we do with *this*?"

Oh yeah . . . and an eternally bound Outer God.

The Time Has Come

Two weeks later

The haunting wail of moon-beast bone flutes filled the morning air with vaguely feline strains of lamentation. Hank's fine baritone voice carried over the caterwauling din in a heartfelt rendition of "The Parting Glass," a traditional Irish song of farewell. Weeping, he led the moon-beasts in a solemn procession across the hastily constructed bridge over Nyarlathotep's river of lava. D'ay'vvv'e—

Da'y've'e—

Dave lurched along behind him carrying a black velvet pillow, upon which rested a Tupperware container containing the amulet.

The horde of moon-beasts made their hopping way past a row of Tophet County officials positioned a few dozen feet in front of the newly rebuilt Black Galley. The witch, who stood sandwiched between Sathach and the Clerk, averted her eyes when Dave passed by. She still couldn't look at the amulet without remembering the excruciating agony of forging it. But her pain was offset somewhat by the knowledge that a certain eldritch asshat was crammed inside the pearl like ten pounds of shit in a five-pound sack.

Until the end of time, she thought.

"Citizens of Tophet County," said Mayor Heather Chadwick, her voice magically enhanced to reach the packed stands. "We have gathered here to bid farewell to—"

The twin Heather was holding sneezed, and the mayor's nose turned into a rubber nipple.

"Looks like Sawyer's hungry," the Dread Lord lisped.

Aha! So the *witchling* was named Sawyer.

Sathach elbowed the witch. "It's Barclay's day off. Would you mind terribly to . . ." He shifted the baby on his own hip and waggled his fingers.

Biting the insides of her cheeks to keep from laughing, the witch nodded and restored Heather's nose. Discordian duty compelled her to add a robust septum piercing reminiscent of the one from Sathach's former middle-aged hypebeast human skin. In a perfectly executed act of vengeance, Heather—unflappable as ever—grinned sweetly, stepped out of the line, and shoved the squirming infant into the witch's arms.

Being the twins' sweary godsmother was one thing, but holding one of them was another story.

The baby looked at the witch.

The witch looked at the baby.

Sawyer's cheeks dimpled as she flashed a toothless smile and gripped the witch's finger.

Well, maybe it wasn't *that* bad.

Her little eyebrows drew together, and her face reddened. An ominous rumble sounded from the vicinity of her diaper, followed shortly thereafter by a smell that sent Keyser Söze scampering for the shelter of the Sheriff's tentacles. The witch gagged and rerouted her olfactory system to Sathach, who flinched and fixed her with a glare worthy of John Wick (except for the crossed eyes).

"We have gathered here," Heather said, "to say bon voyage to the moon-beasts—our neighbors and, we're pleased to say, our friends. It is the sincere hope of my administration that this is only the beginning of a mutually beneficial relationship."

The speech meandered on for several interminable minutes, during which the fecal aroma killed what little grass remained on the field.

The Clerk staggered under the onslaught of the relentless stench. "Wrap it up, if you please, Mayor," she trilled.

Heather smoothed the blond mushroom of her hair. "Without further ado, I invite High Lord Magna Innominanda, the witch of Tophet County, to christen the Black Galley."

She held her arms out for the baby. Sawyer reached for her in turn, her bare feet kicking like an Irish Riverdancer. The witch handed her godsdaughter over, shrugged out of her backpack, and retrieved a bottle of Chicken Cock Kentucky bourbon. The moon-beasts hopped aboard in a flurry of toadlike leaps, with the exception of Dave, who followed her to the prow of the ship.

With a magician's flourish, Hank removed the swath of indigo silk draping the figurehead. The witch found herself face-to-tentacled-snout with a startlingly lifelike rendering of Nyarlathotep's *hierophant of the moon-beasts* avatar.

She hefted the bottle eagerly. This was going to be downright therapeutic.

"I ask the sailors of old and the gods of the void to guard this ship and her crew," the witch intoned. "And by the powers vested in me by the Clerk of Tophet County, I christen this vessel the . . ." She looked up at Hank. "What are they calling it?"

Hank whipped out his wooden flute and relayed her question to Dave. As if in answer, the moon-beast cracked open the Tupperware container and, with an assist from Hank, fastened the amulet's chain around the hierophant's neck. The witch used a burst of entropine to fuse the metal to the figurehead. Wouldn't want ol' Nyarly to go drifting off into space.

The beast jammed his flute into a nest of pink tentacles and tootled a reply.

"*The Pearl Necklace*," Hank translated.

"The, uh . . ." She barked a laugh and nearly choked to death on her own tongue. "Is he, um . . . Is he sure?"

Dave gave an emphatic nod.

Sometimes the universe felt like a cold and empty place, devoid of any beneficent divine force.

But other times, like now, she could almost *see* the guiding hand of Discordia.

"I hereby christen this vessel *The Pearl Necklace*."

The witch smashed the bottle of Chicken Cock against the hierophant's blind face.

It didn't shatter.

She indulged in a barrage of cathartic whacks that destroyed the bottle and soaked the figurehead in fragrant liquor. Then, arms outstretched, she levitated over the ship to offer a final blessing.

"May portals to the nether realms open for you," she said. "May the winds of the Forbidden Lands scour your bones. May the sun shine its indifferent light upon your sightless face, the icy sleet of the Cold Waste freeze your flesh, and until we meet again, may Azathoth clutch you in the coils of his tentacles."

Chad nuzzled his face into the witch's neck.

"Are you *sure* you don't want me to sleep over?"

Her day had begun with a ship named *The Pearl Necklace* and ended with a naughty drinking song contest at Sphinxter's Cabaret, where Hank had a new gig as a bouncer. (Ellie and Dr. Carcosa were conducting research to determine whether his condition could be reversed. The prospects weren't great, but at least he wouldn't be going hungry in the meantime.) A witch could only belt out so many rounds of "A Wizard's Staff Has a Knob on the End" before awakening her inner succubus. At this point, her carnal appetites were nearly as voracious as Keyser Söze's, who was—at this very moment—dancing the devil's tango in a back alley somewhere downtown.

But there was tomorrow to think of . . .

"Of course I *want* you to," she said, arching her body into his, "but we both know sleeping's not on the menu. And if you want me bright-eyed and bushy-tailed at nine o'clock in the morning . . ."

"I want you any way I can have you"—Chad pulled her even closer—"but you're probably right." He kissed her forehead and eased out of the embrace. "So you'll meet us at Quiche and Tell?"

Brunch.

With his *parents*.

In terms of smothering the fires of lust, it was better than a cold shower.

"Yep." She bared her teeth in a terrified grimace trying unsuccessfully to be a smile.

Chad gripped the witch's shoulders and locked eyes with her. "They're going to *love* you."

After a kiss passionate enough to make her second-guess nixing the sleepover, the witch pulled on a giant ratty T-shirt (*Hexy and I Know It*) and got ready for bed. She was teetering on the verge of blissful unconsciousness when a rustling sound dragged her from Hypnos's seductive embrace. Adrenaline surged into her bloodstream, followed by a defensive burst of entropine. She snapped her fingers, and the overhead light blazed to life.

No intruder.

No sex-drunk raccoon.

She was alone.

The rustle came again, and she slipped out of bed and followed the sound to her backpack. She picked it up and dumped the contents on the bed. The Garbage Pail Kids cards, still sealed inside a clear plastic evidence bag, twitched and shifted in their pink drawstring pouch.

The witch's heart beat faster. She opened the bag and spilled the deck onto her bedspread. It shuffled itself with showy panache, and three cards slid off the top and turned face up.

The first, Weird Wendy, showed the familiar image of a witch gazing into a crystal ball. Kent Wake Up, the second card, featured a male figure stuck in a dream of showing up naked to school. Classic. And last but not least, Alarm Clark showed a sentient alarm clock about to be smashed by a fist.

A witch . . .

Stuck in a dream . . .

Who needed to wake up . . .

Oh, holy hell, Keziah wasn't dead!

Maybe her soul was stuck in the cards, or maybe it was intact but trapped inside the reborn Phthæggua. Either way, she was still *here*.

The witch dug through her bag for her BlackBerry and fired off a text. A bolt of blue lightning streaked into her bedroom a millisecond after she pressed send.

That whole faster-than-light thing was godsdamned handy.

"What's wrong?" Phthæggua asked, his tinny voice clanging with alarm. "You said you needed my—"

"Keziah's alive!"

His quicksilver orb, now veined with writhing streaks of blue, quivered with a tremor of confusion. "What?"

"Her deck woke up all by itself and gave me a reading. Look," she said, pointing at the cards. "What else could this possibly mean?"

The gleaming sphere contracted down to a more manageable foot-wide diameter and hovered over the grotesque triptych. Then he rotated sharply—a firm negation.

"I'm sorry, Witch."

"Sorry?"

"When I merged with the ka'met, we . . . we consumed her memories." Phthæggua tilted toward the Garbage Pail Kids. "Traces of her live on in me, and her power persists in the cards, which remain a powerful magical artifact. But Keziah's soul—Keziah *herself*—has moved on."

"But this reading couldn't be more clear. A witch"—she jabbed Weird Wendy—"who needs to wake up." She leaned toward him, staring at her own distorted reflection in his mirrored surface. "There are only two other witches in this universe—me and Sawyer. I'm sure as hell not sleeping, and Heather will eat me if I bother that baby."

Phthæggua spun in contemplative silence, then he said, "I shall consult Keziah's memories."

His shining orb grew very still, and the blue veins pulsed with luminous brightness. When he finally spoke, his voice carried a hint of Keziah's dry, sardonic tone.

"The time has come to wake the witches."

About the Author

J. H. Schiller writes satirical stories about tentacled eldritch monsters and the horrors of bureaucracy. In an earlier incarnation, she earned a graduate degree in international affairs and spent more than a decade working for the federal government in Washington, DC. Schiller has since escaped to Ohio, where she writes full-time. Subscribe to her newsletter at horriblyfunny.substack.com.

DISCOVER
STORIES UNBOUND

PodiumAudio.com